O MAGIC AND REINDEER

MAYA NICOLE

CHAPTER 1
ICE DEMON

I'd always thought people who said they felt *actual* electricity in the air were being dramatic. That was before the shimmering string lights on the outdoor patio flickered ominously with timing so perfect it had to be cosmic mockery.

My date hadn't noticed. He was too busy recounting his collection of nutcrackers with all the enthusiasm of a toddler eating sugar cookies.

I hated cookies.

"And you know what's fascinating about Steinbach nutcrackers versus Erzgebirge? The lacquer quality. World of difference." Mike paused to take a sip of his gingerbread espresso martini from the flight of Christmas cocktails he'd ordered himself. "I'm taking you on quite the holiday journey tonight, aren't I?"

A journey directly into the ninth circle of hell, maybe.

This was what I got for not trusting my instincts. I'd nearly canceled this date a dozen times today, especially after Mom's call. Mom and Dad's biannual visits from their research facility in the Arctic were the only family time I had, and I'd found out they wouldn't make it this month because of some solar flare monitoring emergency. Typical. Some people's parents worked regular jobs like accounting or teaching; mine tracked magnetic storms like it was an everyday career choice.

"So when did your love affair with Christmas begin?" Mike leaned forward, elbows on the table as a white flake drifted onto the dark tablecloth between us.

I fought the urge to brush it away. Instead, I took a long, fortifying sip of my mercifully un-festive vodka soda. "I don't celebrate Christmas."

His expression shifted as if I'd confessed to burning nutcrackers in my spare time. "You don't... celebrate Christmas?"

"Not really my thing." I shrugged, watching as another flake landed on his shoulder.

"But... everyone celebrates Christmas!" He reached up to scratch his head, unleashing a blizzard. "It's the most magical time of the year!"

I bit the inside of my cheek hard enough to taste metal. "I prefer temperatures above freezing and not being bombarded by relentless cheer for two straight months."

His face fell, and the instrumental holiday music playing over the patio speakers seemed to grow louder in response. Was there not a single place on earth where Christmas didn't somehow try to inundate my life?

Around us, Palm Springs had the perfect November evening temperature, yet the bistro had already transformed into Santa's fucking workshop. Garlands draped from every possible surface, the nearby palm trees were strangled with twinkle lights, and the sound system played a jazz rendition of "Let It Snow" that made me want to commit arson.

"You know, my family always says I have Christmas in my blood." Mike grinned, sending another flurry from his scalp as he ran his fingers through his hair. "I decorate the day after Halloween. This year I put up three trees."

"Three trees," I echoed flatly. The mental image of three murdered pines shedding needles all over his nutcracker-filled home made my eye twitch.

"You should see my place! I go all out with the lights and

synchronize them to music. The neighbors call me Mr. Christmas." He beamed with pride while I internally contemplated how many ways I could exit this date. Fake emergency call? Spontaneous combustion? Actual death?

"Fascinating." I glanced at his dandruff-dusted shoulders. At this rate, he'd have his own personal snow globe effect by dessert.

A prickling sensation crawled up the back of my neck with the distinct feeling of being watched. I casually turned my head, scanning the patio until my gaze landed on a table in the corner.

Holy shit.

Nine men. Nine impossibly large, handsome men, all staring directly at me with an intensity that made my skin heat despite the increasing chill from the air conditioner wafting out through the patio door. I quickly turned away, focusing back on Mike, who was now detailing his upcoming European Christmas market cruise.

"...and the market in Nuremberg is supposed to be incredible. Seven days of pure Christmas magic!" He scratched his scalp again, this time dislodging what looked like a small avalanche. "Hey, you know, I just had the most amazing thought... why don't you come with me?"

I nearly choked on my drink. "Come with you? We've been on exactly half a date."

"I know it sounds crazy, but we click so well!" He reached for my hand across the table, and I pulled mine back to adjust my hair. "Think about it: mulled wine, handcrafted ornaments, the snow gently falling on cobblestone streets..."

The mere thought of voluntarily subjecting myself to snow, cold, and round-the-clock Christmas cheer made me want to hurl myself into the nearest cactus. To think I'd swiped right because his profile mentioned enjoying quiet nights and documentaries. The man was a Christmas terrorist.

"I can't get the time off work." I hated lying, but sometimes it was absolutely necessary.

The prickling across my skin returned. Against my better judgment, I looked back at the table of nine.

Still staring. If anything, they seemed even more focused now, like I was the last pancake at a lumberjack buffet. One of them, a dark-haired mountain with shoulders that could block out the sun, raised his glass slightly in my direction.

I turned away, my heart inexplicably racing.

"You're missing out," Mike continued, oblivious to both my discomfort and the dandruff situation that was rapidly approaching biohazard levels. It was like he didn't even realize it was happening, even though it was falling right in front of him. "Last year, I stayed in a hotel shaped like a giant gingerbread house. They wake you up with carol singers every morning."

My parents would absolutely love him. They were equally insane about the holiday, their research station probably already dripping with tinsel and those little wooden elves they collected. I'd spent my childhood gagging on the scent of cinnamon pine cones and peppermint everything.

"Sounds like literal torture," I muttered.

"What was that?"

"Sounds like a real adventure." I smiled tightly. The lights flickered again, and I couldn't help but glance at the table of nine overbuilt men, who were still watching me with unwavering attention.

One of them now had the audacity to smirk, like we shared some private joke.

"Please consider my offer. Imagine how magical it will be to go on a sleigh ride. There is so much to do and see." Mike clearly did not get the hint that Christmas was not my jam.

My water glass frosted over beneath my fingers.

Wait. What?

I yanked my hand back, staring at the delicate crystalline patterns forming at the rim. The water inside was turning to slush before my eyes.

"I've actually hand-carved ornaments with a master artisan in Rothenburg ob der Tauber." Mike's voice seemed to come from underwater now. "It's all about the proper whittling technique."

The temperature around our table plummeted. I could see my breath now, forming tiny clouds between us. Mike remained completely oblivious, his cheeks flushing red from the alcohol, white flakes now covering his shoulders.

That's when I realized it wasn't dandruff.

It was *snow*.

Panic rose in my throat. This wasn't normal. None of this was normal.

"Are you cold?" I interrupted, my voice laced with panic. "Do you feel how cold it is right now?"

Mike's expression shifted from confusion to something like alarm. "Your eyes!" He recoiled slightly. "They're... glowing? Like, actually glowing blue?"

"What? No, they're not." I grabbed my phone, switching to the front-facing camera.

Oh shit. My blue eyes were luminous, literally emitting a faint cerulean light. I dropped my phone with a clatter.

The lights above us made an ominous cracking sound.

"Mike, I think we should—"

Too late. The light right above Mike exploded in a perfect cloud of powdery snow that rained down specifically onto our table, coating him like he was some kind of deranged snowman.

The tables around us carried on like nothing was happening.

Mike sat frozen, mouth agape, flakes clinging to his eyelashes. Then he scrambled backward so quickly his chair tipped over with a crash.

"You're some kind of... of wi-witch!" he sputtered, brushing snow frantically from his clothes. "Your eyes! The snow! What the hell is this?"

"I don't know what's happening." I was horrified and confused. My hands were shaking, not from cold, but from a strange humming energy coursing through me like an electric current. "I swear I'm not doing this on purpose."

I watched in stunned horror as Mike knocked over another

empty chair in his clumsy retreat. His eyes were wide with panic, pupils dilated with primal fear normally reserved for people facing apex predators or tax audits.

"Stay away from me, you... you... ice demon!"

"Mike, wait." I reached out, only to watch frost patterns bloom across the tablecloth from my fingertips.

That was apparently all the motivation he needed. Mike bolted through the patio, accidentally clotheslining himself on a strand of garland before breaking free. He disappeared into the restaurant, no doubt leaving a trail of melting snow in his wake.

Movement from the corner caught my eye. Two of the men from the mystery table stood up in eerie synchronization. The larger one, a wall of a human with a presence that made the air feel thicker, nodded almost imperceptibly to his companion before they both followed Mike's escape route.

What the actual hell was happening? First, my body decided to do some weird Elsa-level shit, and now strange men were... what? Going after my date? Warning bells clanged in my head like a five-alarm fire.

I was having some kind of medical emergency. Yes, that was it. Christmas was causing a trauma response that made my core body temperature drop.

Closing my eyes, I tried to calm the electricity still dancing beneath my skin. When I opened my eyes again, the frost had retreated, and the surrounding temperature had normalized. Small victories. Now I just had to pay the bill, slink home in humiliation, and have a good cry in the privacy of my home, where I conveniently kept a bottle of tequila specifically for emergencies.

As I was fishing my wallet from my purse, the two men reappeared, looking suspiciously casual as they returned to their table. The larger one caught my eye for a split second, and I could have sworn I saw the ghost of a smile cross his face.

I broke eye contact first, focusing instead on paying the bill that Mike had so graciously abandoned in his mad dash to escape the ice witch. Of course he'd ordered the most expensive cocktails on the menu. Dickhead.

I signaled for the server, who headed to the table like nothing was out of the ordinary. "Miss? Is everything okay?"

Nice.

The voice in my head made me jump. The server was nowhere near my type and appeared to be college-aged with a Santa hat perched on top of his head.

Maybe instead of going home, I should head to the hospital.

"Yes, I'll need our food boxed up and the bill, please."

He tilted his head, confusion flitting across his features. "Oh, no need. Your bill was paid."

My brain stuttered to a halt. "What? By who?" Maybe Mike had stopped at the hostess stand to pay?

"The men over there." He gestured toward the corner.

I turned to look at the table of nine, only to find it completely empty. It looked as if it had never been occupied at all. No glasses, no plates, not even a chair out of place. They had literally been eating and drinking the last time I'd looked a few minutes before.

I twisted back to the server, who now looked as confused as I felt.

"Huh." He scratched his head, dislodging the Santa hat. "That's weird. I could have sworn... Well, anyway, someone paid for you." He shrugged, clearly already mentally moving on to his next table.

"Right, thanks." I gathered my purse with trembling hands, suddenly desperate to leave this Christmas hellscape.

The server hesitated, looking at me with renewed interest. "You look a little pale. And what happened to all this water?" He gestured to the puddles around our table, the only evidence remaining of the snow.

"Spilled drinks. Clumsy date." I stood up, my legs shaking. "Have a good night."

I walked a little too quickly through the restaurant, past couples enjoying their evenings, past the hostess who gave me a concerned look, and into the blessed anonymity of the Palm Springs night.

I couldn't shake the persistent chill that had settled deep in my bones. I rubbed my arms, looking up and down the street. No sign of Mike. No signs of the mysterious men.

Just me, standing alone under the artificial glow of palm trees wrapped in Christmas lights.

CHAPTER 2
LUMPS OF COAL

I dragged my body through the glass doors of Bartlett & Moore twenty-four minutes later than my regular arrival time. The only thing more aggressive than my hangover was the lobby's ceiling-to-floor Christmas decorations that had materialized overnight like a festive fungal infection.

I mean, it was barely the first week of November.

The lobby's twelve-foot tree—because apparently, a regular-sized one wouldn't sufficiently announce the firm's dedication to overcompensation—twinkled with hundreds of silver and blue ornaments branded with the firm's logo. Corporate Christmas spirit: where the holiday's soul went to die in exchange for tax-deductible cheer.

"Good morning, Neve! Don't you look..." Trinity from reception paused, scanning my appearance with the practiced diplomacy of someone who had mastered the art of lying professionally. "...professional today!"

I'd spent forty-five minutes this morning trying to look like I hadn't demolished half a bottle of tequila while frantically searching for information on "spontaneous ice powers" and "glowing blue eyes medical condition" until three in the morning. The bags under my eyes had bags. My usual sleek black bun had a few rebellious strands escaping, and I hadn't realized until now that my blouse was buttoned incorrectly.

"Thanks." I clutched my to-go coffee closer, the heat of it a welcome contrast to the chill that had clung to me since last night's date from hell. "Did Bartlett send the elves in early this year, or am I hallucinating?"

Trinity beamed. "We're doing a winter wonderland theme. Isn't it magical?"

Magical was not the word I would have chosen. More like migraine-inducing, or pathologically cheerful.

"Nothing says 'we'll ruthlessly defend your freedom from your cheating ex' like tinsel and candy canes." I forced a smile before shuffling toward the elevator, Trinity's tinkling laugh following me like Christmas bells.

Why was my brain comparing everything to Christmas now? I needed a detox already, and it wasn't even December.

My office was a mercifully decoration-free zone and immediately calmed me with its gray-scale aesthetic that matched my personality perfectly. Everyone joked it looked like a prison cell with better furniture, but to me, it was a sanctuary of control in a world determined to sprinkle unwanted sparkle on everything it touched.

I slumped into my ergonomic chair and pulled up the day's calendar while downing half my coffee in one desperate swallow. Two client meetings, document prep, and a front-row seat to one of the longest divorces I'd ever seen.

I'd just choked down two aspirin when a message popped up on my computer screen. Bartlett had moved the Weston divorce meeting to nine instead of eleven. In exactly twenty minutes.

I frantically pulled up the case files and printed out the most recent correspondence. The Weston divorce was not what I wanted to deal with today. They were two obscenely wealthy people determined to punish each other through their children and belongings. They'd been fighting over a taxidermy elk's head for three months. Mrs. Weston's grandfather had shot the elk, but Mr. Weston claimed it was his emotional support animal.

The whole thing was ridiculous, not to mention it made me

sick to my stomach. Like vomit-in-the-nearest-potted-plant level of sick, which would've been a shame because the ficus in the corner was the closest thing I had to office decor.

By some miracle, I made it to the conference room with one minute to spare, legal pad in hand and a fresh coat of nude lipstick applied to at least give the illusion of having my life together.

"Ah, Ms. North." Mr. Bartlett didn't look up from his phone as I entered. "No coffee for the clients today?"

I pasted on my best professional smile as Mrs. Weston swept into the room in a full-length fur coat. In Palm Springs. In November.

"I'll get that right away." I pivoted and nearly collided with Mr. Weston, who wore a camel hair blazer with actual shoulder pads. Like we were still in the eighties.

Five minutes later, I'd arranged an elaborate coffee service, complete with the special raw sugar cubes Mrs. Weston insisted on, and taken my seat at the corner of the table. My role was clear: take notes, look engaged but not too engaged, and never, under any circumstances, offer an opinion.

"Now, regarding the summer home in Aspen." Bartlett shuffled through some papers. "Mrs. Weston, you've requested full ownership despite Mr. Weston having inherited the property from his family."

Mrs. Weston's acrylic nails tapped rhythmically against the conference table. "I've spent twenty years making that house a home. The Christmas traditions alone are worth the value of the entire property."

"Oh, please." Mr. Weston's eye roll was better than any hormonal teenager's. "You hate Christmas. You complained about the tree shedding every single year."

"I most certainly did not."

"You made the staff vacuum three times a day!"

"Because you tracked pine needles everywhere like some kind of forest animal!"

"The children always enjoyed opening their presents with me on Christmas morning."

"Only because you bribed them with those ridiculous electronic gifts!"

"They were educational!" Mr. Weston slammed his hand on the table, jostling the delicate coffee service I'd so carefully arranged.

Mrs. Weston's laugh could've cut glass. "A four-thousand-dollar drone is educational? The neighbors called the police when it crashed through their skylight during Christmas brunch!"

"At least I didn't force them into those hideous matching sweaters for your Instagram holiday card." Mr. Weston loosened his tie with aggressive yanks. "They looked like hostages."

"They were adorable, and you know it." Mrs. Weston's nostrils flared as she turned to her lawyer. "He's bitter because the children prefer Christmas with me."

"Is that why Madison cried when you wouldn't let her spend Christmas Eve at my place last year?"

My pen snapped between my fingers, blue ink spreading like blood across my immaculate notes. "The only thing those children ever wanted was parents who gave a damn about their happiness instead of using them as pawns in your petty games."

The room went silent. Surprised faces turned to stare at me.

I wasn't finished. Something was unraveling inside me, spilling out without permission. "People like you used to get lumps of coal, you know. And frankly, that was being generous."

My voice didn't even sound like mine; it carried a strange, hollow resonance that seemed to echo even with the conference room's acoustic panels. Had the lights dimmed? Was that frost forming on the windows?

Mrs. Weston's mouth opened and closed like a disoriented fish.

Mr. Weston's face had gone an alarming shade of purple. "Who exactly do you think—"

"Ms. North." Bartlett's eyebrows arched so high they nearly disappeared into his hairline as he stood and nodded to the door. "A word."

I blinked, the spell suddenly broken. Holy shit. Holy actual shit. Had I just said that out loud? To clients?

I forced out a laugh that sounded like I was being strangled. "Sorry, I didn't get much sleep last night."

Following Bartlett out of the room felt like following the executioner to the guillotine. The door shut behind us with an ominous click.

"Ms. North." His voice was the carefully neutral tone of someone deciding whether to fire me on the spot or wait until after the holiday bonus payouts. "While I appreciate your... passionate advocacy, perhaps save it for your own future clients once you pass the bar."

Ouch. Did he really need to throw my inability to pass that damned test right in my face?

"I'm so sorry, Mr. Bartlett. I don't know what came over me. Sleep deprivation and..." I flailed my hands uselessly in the air, searching for any explanation that wouldn't sound completely unhinged. "Maybe low blood sugar? Or a temporary psychotic break? I've never... I would never..." My voice cracked embarrassingly as I watched his face remain perfectly impassive, like he was examining a disappointing legal brief. "I can go apologize right now. Or draft a formal letter? Or do you want me to clean out my desk immediately?"

"Take the rest of the day. You look unwell." He didn't wait for my response before striding back into the conference room.

I closed my door behind me and pressed my back to it, keys slipping from my fingers. My chest heaved like I'd outrun something, but the only thing chasing me was my own damn reaction.

Smart move, heart. I'd run from me too right now.

Every memory from the conference room replayed in my mind with excruciating, high-definition clarity. The look of shock on Mrs. Weston's face. How my voice had shifted into something that didn't even sound like me. The way the windows had frosted over in eighty-degree Palm Springs weather.

I peeled myself off the door and stumbled into my bedroom, ripping off my pencil skirt and blouse like they were burning my skin. After rummaging through my drawers, I pulled on black shorts and an oversized T-shirt.

My house felt wrong somehow. The walls seemed to pulse inward, like they were slowly constricting around me. The air felt thick and unbreathable.

I needed to get out. Now.

Grabbing my phone from my purse and my keys from the floor where I'd dropped them, I bolted outside.

The sun hit my face, a physical sensation I could latch onto. The sun was real. The sun was hot. The sun made sense. Unlike whatever the hell was happening to me.

My feet carried me down the sidewalk, past the manicured desert landscaping of my neighborhood. Each step on solid ground should have helped, but the buzzing under my skin only intensified as I moved. The sun that had initially felt grounding now seemed to press down, heavy and oppressive.

The entrance to Rosewood Park appeared ahead. It was a small oasis of shade trees in the desert landscape. I veered inside, grateful for my neighborhood's astronomical HOA fees and absurd rules. They kept families away, which meant the park was usually empty during working hours. No families. No children's laughter. No happiness cluttering up the carefully designed paths.

The familiar thought made me feel uncomfortable. How many times had I been relieved at the absence of families? At the lack of children? Why did that suddenly feel like such a strange thing to appreciate?

I sank onto a bench beneath a sprawling mesquite tree, its shade offering minor relief from the heat. Closing my eyes, I tried to focus on my breathing, but each exhale felt like it carried frost. What was happening to me? First the date last night, then the meltdown at work.

The silence of the park pressed against my eardrums. There

was no distant traffic noise, no birds chirping, and no leaves rustling despite the perpetual desert breeze. Just a thick silence that felt almost watchful.

I bent forward, elbows on my knees and face in my hands, trying to snap myself out of the spiral. This was ridiculous. I was tired. Stressed. Maybe having some kind of quarter-life crisis that manifested as temporary hallucinations and bizarre weather phenomena.

A deep breath steadied me enough to sit up straight again. The solid bench beneath me was real. The warm air was real. This weird thing happening with my body temperature was probably a hormone imbalance or something equally mundane. I needed to get a grip, call my doctor, maybe actually use some of those vacation days I'd been stockpiling.

A soft scraping sound, like something large shifting its weight, broke through the unnatural silence.

I looked up.

Standing in front of me, not ten feet away, was a reindeer. Not a decoration. Not a massive dog dressed up by its owner. An actual, massive, breathing reindeer with an impressive rack of antlers that spanned wider than outstretched arms. Its dark slate eyes fixed on mine with an intelligence that made the hair on the back of my neck stand up.

In Palm Springs.

In November.

The reindeer and I stared at each other in what might have been the most surreal staring contest in the history of staring contests.

My brain cycled through rational explanations with the desperation of someone trying to justify why their ex's belongings were still in their apartment six months post-breakup. Escaped zoo animal? Desert mirage? Elaborate Christmas promotional stunt? The consequences of skipping breakfast while hungover?

I didn't move. Neither did the reindeer.

Its coat was rich brown, glossy, and well-groomed. This wasn't some scruffy wild animal that had wandered in from...

wherever the hell wild reindeer lived. Certainly not in the California desert. The creature's antlers curved majestically overhead, branching out in patterns that seemed almost mathematical in their precision. The reindeer took a step forward, hooves silent against the gravel. Then another. The distance between us shrank. He was close enough that I could see the way his nostrils flared slightly with each breath, the intelligent focus in his eyes.

"You're not ready yet."

I jerked upright, nearly falling off the bench. The voice hadn't come from outside me. It had resonated *inside* my skull, deep and quiet and utterly impossible.

"What the fuck?" My voice sounded weak compared to the rich timbre that had just occupied my thoughts. "What does that even mean? Not ready for what?"

The reindeer blinked but offered no explanation.

"Great. I'm having a one-sided conversation with a hallucinated reindeer in a public park." I tried to rake my fingers through my hair, forgetting it was still in its tight bun from work. "Do you know why I'm suddenly freezing things? Why my eyes did that weird glowy thing? Why Christmas seems to be haunting me?"

Nothing. Just that steady, unnerving stare.

"Is this some kind of karmic retribution for all those years I've spent hating tinsel and threatening to strangle carolers?" I laughed, the sound edging toward hysteria. Why was I talking to a reindeer? "Or am I just sad my parents aren't visiting? They've missed every important moment of my life since I was fifteen because, apparently, magnetic fields are more interesting than their only child."

I guess my parents canceling their visit was bothering me more than I thought.

The reindeer tilted its head, antlers shifting gracefully with the movement. For a moment, I thought I saw something like sadness flicker in his eyes.

"This is absurd," I whispered, more to myself than my antlered audience. "I should be calling my doctor, not confessing my childhood abandonment issues to Donner or Blitzen or whoever the hell you're supposed to be."

Something that sounded eerily like a growl came from the beast. He turned away from me, taking several steps toward the path that led to the hiking trail outside my community.

"Wait!" I called out, jumping to my feet, suddenly desperate. "What's happening to me?"

It stopped and looked back over one shoulder.

"Soon."

I stumbled backward, the bench catching me behind the knees. My heart felt like his silent hooves had stomped on it and altered it in an indescribable way.

Squeezing my eyes shut, I counted to three, trying to regulate my breathing. When I opened them, the reindeer was gone.

I blinked, scanning the park. Nothing. No massive antlered creature, no hoofprints, not even a single reindeer dropping to prove I hadn't completely lost it.

All that remained was the echo of that voice and the overwhelming certainty that something in my life had changed forever.

And just as the voice had said, I wasn't ready.

CHAPTER 3
POSSESSED COOKIES

I spent the next hour searching for "reindeer sightings Palm Springs" and "hallucinogenic desert plants" while sitting rigidly on my living room couch. Each search result offered less help than the previous one, unless I needed to know about the Christmas light display at the botanical gardens featuring wire reindeer sculptures.

Spoiler alert: I very much did not.

My browser history now looked like a conspiracy theorist having a Christmas-themed breakdown. I scrolled through local social media groups and even checked a Palm Springs forum, hoping to find anyone else who'd seen Rudolph's over-sized cousin wandering around. Nothing. Not a single "OMG I saw a reindeer in Rosewood Park!" post to validate my rapidly deteriorating mental state.

Pushing my laptop away, I rubbed my temples where a headache pulsed with vindictive regularity. Maybe the tequila from last night had been laced with something. Or I was having some kind of psychotic break triggered by excessive workplace Christmas decorations. Neither explanation accounted for the weird shit happening with my body temperature or the voice in my head, but it beat accepting that I was telepathically communicating with North Pole wildlife.

My phone vibrated against the coffee table, Mom's smiling

face lighting up the screen for a video call. I swiped to accept, arranging my face into what I hoped wasn't the wide-eyed panic of someone who'd conversed with a magical forest creature. "Neve!" Dad's face filled the screen, much closer to the camera than necessary. His usual exuberant smile seemed dimmed, the corners of his mouth fighting to maintain their upward curve. His silver beard, usually trimmed to perfection, looked unkempt and dull. Dark circles carved half-moons beneath his eyes.

I frowned. "Dad, you look..."

"Fantastic!" He pulled back, revealing Mom beside him. Both wore matching thermal shirts with the Joint International Nordic Glacial Logistics and Ecology snowflake logo. "Just a bit under the weather. Nothing serious!"

Mom adjusted the camera. "How are you, sweetie? Work going well?"

My fingers tightened around my phone. "I had a bit of an incident at work today. I kind of told off some clients and got sent home."

"Oh! That doesn't sound like you." Mom's eyebrows lifted, but her expression remained oddly indifferent.

"It wasn't like me. There was this weird moment where I felt so cold, and my voice sounded different. I told them that people like them used to get coal." I stopped, noting the quick glance my parents exchanged. "What? Why are you looking at each other like that?"

Dad's laugh boomed through the speaker. "Well, it's not like this is the first time you've had a little flare-up."

Mom's elbow shot into his side. "Christopher."

He winced. "What? I meant a tantrum. You know, when she was a kid."

My skin prickled, and I swallowed hard. "What kind of flare-up are we talking about? Did anything unusual happen when I was little? Medical conditions or, I don't know, weird abilities?"

Mom's smile suddenly stretched across her face, completely

fake. "You were just like every other child! Always building snow people and—"

This time, Dad's elbow shot out.

"We never lived anywhere with snow. I grew up in California, and we decided boarding school was the best option for me since the research facility couldn't have kids there." It came out automatically, almost as if I were reading a script to people who weren't my parents.

Dad coughed violently, the camera shaking. "Signal's breaking up! Arctic storms interfering with—"

"Dad, I can see and hear you perfectly fine."

"...call you next week... love you!" The screen froze conveniently on his panicked expression before cutting to black.

I stared at my dark phone screen, my reflection looking back with suspicious eyes. They were hiding something. Parents were supposed to lie about birthday presents and Easter bunnies, not have cryptic reactions to their adult daughter possibly developing ice powers.

The walls of my house closed in again, with the same suffocating pressure from earlier returning. I needed air and food that wasn't questionable takeout leftovers. Grabbing my purse, I headed for the door. Grocery shopping might be mundane, but right now, mundane was exactly what I needed.

Twenty minutes later, I stalked the aisles of Ralph's with the determination of someone barely holding it together, one grocery item at a time. My cart contained the building blocks of responsible adulthood: kale I'd probably throw out in a week, protein bars with ridiculously long shelf lives, and oat milk that tasted nothing like actual milk.

See? Totally not having a crisis.

A woman with a screaming toddler passed, and I reflexively gripped the handle of my cart tighter. The metal frosted over beneath my fingers.

I jerked away, and the frost disappeared almost instantly in the warm store air. It was condensation. Heat meeting cold metal. Science.

I turned down the main aisle, and my feet moved in the

direction of the overwhelming scents of vanilla and cinnamon. My carefully curated grocery route never included the bakery section because I hated baked goods as much as I hated going to the dentist or getting a Pap smear. Maybe even more.

Before I knew it, I was standing in front of a display of holiday cookies with gingerbread men and their stupid smiling faces, snowflake-shaped sugar cookies drowning in blue sprinkles, and an entire army of those weird butter cookies that typically came in the blue tin that everyone's grandmother repurposed for sewing supplies.

My hand reached out against my will, hovering over a package of chocolate chip cookies still warm from the store oven.

"They taste even better if you dunk them in milk."

The deep voice came from so far above me that I nearly got a crick in my neck looking up. And up. And up.

Holy crap, he had to be at least six and a half feet tall. His skin was medium brown, and his golden-brown eyes held a gentleness that didn't quite match his massive frame.

Recognition hit me like a tidal wave. He was one of the nine men who'd been watching me at the restaurant.

"You." I took a step back, nearly colliding with an endcap of fruitcakes. "You were at Sinclair's with your friends last night."

He nodded, one dark curl falling out of place across his forehead. The slight movement was careful, as though he was afraid of startling me.

"With eight friends. At the table that vanished." I narrowed my eyes. "The table that literally disappeared after my date called me an ice demon. You paid the bill."

His expression remained impassive, but something flickered in his eyes. "We left through the back." His voice rumbled like distant thunder, low enough that I had to lean in to hear. "We figured you had enough to deal with."

That was the understatement of the century. I gripped my shopping cart to steady myself, careful to keep my hands on the plastic. "So you just happened to be grocery shopping at the same store as me?" I gestured at his empty hands. "Without a cart or basket."

His massive shoulders lifted in a shrug. "Time is getting short. The signs are becoming more obvious."

Was that supposed to make sense? "What signs?"

"The cold following you. The frost at your fingertips." He glanced meaningfully at the cookies I'd been drawn to. "The way you're pulled toward things you tell yourself you don't like."

Ice slid down my spine. "Excuse me?"

"His magic is fading." He leaned closer, his voice dropping even lower. "The clock's already ticking. Soon it will be gone, and everything will be ruined."

The fluorescent lights overhead flickered, sending harsh shadows skittering across the bakery display. A cold sweat broke out across my skin, icy pinpricks that didn't feel like normal perspiration at all, more like frost forming.

My body was betraying me in ways I couldn't explain, couldn't control, couldn't rationalize with my carefully constructed worldview. I wiped my palms against my jeans, leaving damp smears that glinted with something that looked like tiny crystals before they melted away.

"Who are you talking about? What magic?" My voice came out higher and slightly panicked. Did this guy know what was happening to me?

He looked pained for a moment and swallowed hard. His eyes held mine, urgent and intense. "Jingle all the way."

I backed away. "I don't know what kind of Christmas cult you're part of, but I'm not interested."

Spinning my cart around, I fled so fast I nearly flattened an older man examining an angel food cake. I didn't stop until I reached the self-checkout, abandoning half my groceries and only scanning the essentials.

The bakery section cookies had somehow made it into my cart, and I tried not to hyperventilate. My mouth watered, and my fingers itched to rip into them right then and there.

Maybe being twenty-seven came with its own secret

hormone glitch no one talked about. Was there a quarter-life perimenopause crisis where hormones went haywire? There had to be. Instead of hot flashes, I was getting cold flashes. I grabbed my bags and power-walked to the parking lot without looking back. The giant with the cryptic warnings could keep his cult recruitment speech and his cookie recommendations to himself.

I nearly had a heart attack as I opened the back door of my car and found the package of cookies sitting on the seat.

What. The. Actual. Fuck.

Setting my bags on the floorboard, I used my foot to move the possessed cookies out of my car. There was no way I was touching them with my bare hands.

For good measure, I kicked them behind the rear wheel before sliding into the driver's seat. I cranked the engine and backed up, cringing as I ran over the cookies. I hated wasting perfectly good food, but I was pretty certain something nefarious was going on.

I peeled out of the parking lot like a getaway driver, tires squealing in protest as I pressed the accelerator harder than necessary. My knuckles whitened against the steering wheel, and I kept checking the rearview mirror, half-expecting to see the man running after my car with his cryptic warnings and magical cookies.

The shopping center shrank behind me, and I let out a breath, a visible puff that crystallized in the air.

Something was happening to me. Something I couldn't explain away with WebMD symptom searches or rational thinking, and that terrified me more than any stranger with golden-brown eyes ever could.

I skated through another workday, moving carefully, speaking minimally, and avoiding eye contact with Bartlett. Thankfully, today had been blissfully free of inexplicable frost patterns and reindeer visitations. I even managed to get through a client consultation without suggesting that anyone should receive lumps of coal. Progress.

Friday afternoon freedom beckoned as I put away files and shut down my computer. The weekend stretched ahead like a promise with forty-eight uninterrupted hours where I could lock myself in my house and avoid Christmas decorations, mysterious men, and any form of supernatural wildlife.

As I stepped onto the elevator and caught my reflection in the mirrored walls, I frowned at the noticeable unevenness creeping across my spray tan. The warm glow I'd gotten on Monday was already fading in patches.

Perfect. Just what I needed to complete my week of bizarre bodily betrayals.

I briefly considered letting the tan fade completely. It would certainly save me money, but the last time I'd gone au naturel for longer than a week, a guy at the grocery store had asked if I was filming a vampire movie. My natural complexion wasn't just pale, it was practically translucent. Without the protective layer of artificial bronze, I reflected sunlight with enough intensity to potentially cause traffic accidents.

Decision made, I texted Serena at Glow Goddess to see if she could squeeze me in. Her immediate "come right over" response was the only good thing that had happened all week.

Thirty minutes later, I stood in a paper-thin disposable thong, arms extended like a starfish while Serena circled me with her spray gun. The small booth smelled of coconut and chemicals, a combination that had once been comforting, but now it made my nose itch.

"Hmm." Serena paused, her brow furrowing as she examined my stomach.

I dropped my arms. "What's wrong?"

"It's..." She tilted her head. "It's not taking right. See this?" She pointed to a patch on my ribcage where the color looked almost watered down. "And here." Another spot on my forearm showed the same uneven absorption.

"Maybe the nozzle is clogged?" I offered, trying not to sound as desperate as I felt. If even my spray tans were going haywire, what hope did I have for maintaining any semblance of normal? Serena shook her head. "Let me try the darker formula. Maybe your skin is being stubborn today."

"Whatever works." I resumed my starfish pose, closing my eyes when she began spraying again.

The cool mist hit my skin in even sweeps. I counted my breaths, trying not to think about ice powers or telepathic reindeer or cookies that magically appeared in my car.

"What the hell?" Serena's voice snapped my eyes open.

The new formula wasn't doing much better. In some places it had taken fine, but on my chest and hands it refused to absorb, leaving a mottled, sickly effect.

"Is something wrong with the machine?" I stared down at my blotchy arms in horror. I looked like I was molting.

Serena ran a finger experimentally across my shoulder. "Your skin feels normal. The temperature's fine, no excess oils." She frowned harder. "It's like the pigment is being... rejected."

"Rejected? By my skin?" I squeaked. "That's not a thing. That can't be a thing."

She pressed her lips together. "Well, it's definitely a thing happening right now. I've been doing this for eight years, and I've never seen anything like it."

Of course, she hadn't. Because normal people's bodies didn't suddenly decide to repel spray tans. Normal people didn't frost over windows or talk to Christmas fauna.

After a third failed attempt with yet another formula, I gave up. I looked like I'd been tanning with stickers all over my body. I paid Serena extra for her trouble, mumbled something about seeing a dermatologist, and fled to my car.

By the time I got home, I'd convinced myself this was just one more thing to add to my growing list of "weird shit happening to Neve that she's going to aggressively ignore until it goes away." Right below ice powers and the box of cookies that was waiting for me on my doorstep.

CHAPTER 4
TOTAL HACK JOB

I jolted awake to sunlight streaming through the blinds I'd forgotten to close. Typical. The universe couldn't even grant me the small mercy of sleeping in on Saturday. I groaned and rolled over, my hand sliding across the silky sheets. Something felt different. Wrong.

I lifted my arm into a shaft of sunlight and froze.

Where yesterday there had been a patchy, leopard-print disaster of bronze and alabaster, my skin now gleamed with uniform paleness. Not just my normal paleness. No, this was full-on Snow White territory. As if I'd never applied a spray tan or been in the sun in my entire life.

I scrambled out of bed, tripping over my duvet in my haste to reach the bathroom. The mirror confirmed that every trace of artificial color had vanished. My skin looked like fresh snow. It was absolutely terrifying.

"This is fine. Totally normal." I leaned closer, inspecting my pores, which had always been small but were now nearly nonexistent. "Spray tans fade. Everyone knows that."

They didn't fade overnight. And they certainly didn't fade evenly, leaving behind skin that looked photoshopped.

I ran my hands down my arms and over my stomach, feeling for any residue or explanation. Nothing. Just smooth skin that practically glowed in the morning light.

What in the sparkly vampire was happening? I was actually glowing. A faint, pearlescent shimmer danced across my body when I turned.

Coffee. I needed coffee before I could process whatever fresh hell this was. I stumbled out of the bathroom, avoiding any more reflective surfaces as I made my way to the kitchen, one hand braced against the wall for support.

The kitchen was flooded with morning light, making the white cabinets even brighter. I squinted, heading for the coffee maker, and froze.

On my kitchen counter sat a steaming mug. Not my usual matte black ceramic one with the chip on the handle, but a deep red mug decorated with reindeer. Next to it stood a tall glass of milk and a plate piled high with chocolate chip cookies that looked like they'd been plucked straight from a magazine photoshoot.

I didn't own a mug with reindeer on it.

I didn't make cookies last night.

I certainly didn't set out milk like I was waiting for Santa Claus.

My hands shook as I approached the counter, half-expecting the items to vanish like a mirage. The mug even steamed, sending up lazy curls that smelled like... I leaned closer, inhaling.

Hot chocolate. Rich and dark with hints of cinnamon and vanilla.

I picked up a cookie. It was still warm, as if it had just come out of an oven I definitely hadn't used. The chocolate chips were melty, glistening invitingly.

"Okay, Neve, think." I set the cookie down and backed away. "Someone broke into your house to... bake cookies and make hot chocolate."

The absurdity hit me all at once. I spun around, scanning for signs of forced entry. The doors were locked. Windows secure. My alarm hadn't gone off. Nothing was out of place except for the bizarre breakfast spread.

I grabbed my phone from where I'd left it charging and

pulled up the security app. The footage showed no midnight visitors or movement beyond the occasional shadow cast by passing headlights.

Yet here sat fresh cookies and hot chocolate.

I cautiously dipped a finger into the mug. The liquid was the perfect temperature, hot enough to comfort but not burn. Exactly how I'd like it if I drank it.

The cookies smelled like childhood. Like a memory I couldn't quite grasp.

I picked one up again, turning it over in my hand. The rational part of my brain screamed not to eat mysterious food that had appeared in my locked house. The rest of me, the part that had spent a week talking to reindeer and growing ice powers, was curiously calm.

One bite wouldn't kill me. Probably.

I raised the cookie to my lips and took a bite.

The taste hit me like a freight train of memories. Something familiar and safe, buried so deep I hadn't known it existed until this moment. It tasted like... like...

"Home." The word escaped as a whisper.

Which made no sense. Home for me had been boarding schools and dorms. Not this specific flavor that triggered a long-dormant synapse in my brain.

I dropped the cookie as if it had burned me, watching it break apart on the counter.

The hot chocolate called to me next. I resisted for approximately four seconds before grabbing the mug and taking a sip. Warmth flooded through me, but not the normal kind from a hot beverage. This warmth felt like it started somewhere deep inside my soul and radiated outward.

I set the mug down with a sharp clink and backed away.

The reindeer in the park. The ice powers. The men who disappeared from Sinclair's. The skin that glowed. And now, magically appearing baked goods that tasted like memories I didn't have.

I needed to get out of this house, out of Palm Springs, away from whatever curse was plaguing me. There was no way I could call the police. What would I say? The cookie bandits had left me cookies and drinks?

I paced the length of my kitchen, running through my options. Hospital? They'd think I was on drugs or that it was anxiety. Parents? They would worry. Therapist? I'd fired my last one for suggesting I find my joy.

Mia, my college roommate, was always down for a visit from me. She never questioned my hatred of Christmas, always thought my cynicism was refreshing, and lived in a sleek downtown loft that probably had zero holiday decorations.

Perfect.

I snatched my phone off the charger and fired off a text.

> Me: Hey, is your couch available this weekend? It's been a crazy week, and I need to escape. I can bring wine and zero Christmas cheer.

> Mia: I have a gallery exhibition opening tonight, but yes, please come immediately! Couch is yours. The door code is 2425.

The tension in my chest eased. I pressed my palm against the cool kitchen counter to steady myself, watching as the faintest shimmer of frost appeared beneath my fingertips before quickly fading away. I pulled my hand back, pretending I hadn't seen it. One problem at a time.

I turned back toward the counter and almost dropped my phone. The cookies, hot chocolate, and milk were gone like they had never existed. The counter was clean, empty except for my usual coffee setup waiting to be used.

I reached out, running my fingers across the cool marble surface. Not a crumb, not a drop, not a trace of evidence that anything had been there.

I didn't want to analyze what was happening. I didn't want to process the fact that my reality was unraveling faster than a cheap sweater. I especially didn't want to acknowledge how much I'd enjoyed that single bite of a cookie that technically never existed.

What I wanted was normality. Distance. Perspective.

I practically sprinted to my bedroom, yanking out my overnight bag and throwing in clothes for two days.

Los Angeles was calling, where my friend would roll her eyes at my stories and convince me I was working too hard, was stressed, and needed a girls' weekend of good food and over-priced cocktails.

I just needed to get away. Just for a weekend. Just long enough to forget.

I'D TOLD Mia everything over a bottle of Cabernet and a platter of overpriced cheese. She'd nodded in all the right places, asked reasonable questions, and then systematically dismantled each supernatural element with frustratingly rational explanations.

The reindeer was obviously someone's escaped exotic pet, and the disappearing men at Sinclair's were normal guys who'd left while I wasn't looking. My glowing skin was probably some kind of allergic reaction to Serena's spray tan chemicals. And the cookies that appear and vanish? Classic sleep deprivation.

It all made perfect sense, except for the odd looks she gave me when she thought I wasn't paying attention. They were the kind of sideways glances you give someone who you're worried might be one cheese cube away from a spiral.

"Ready to spend the evening projecting all your unpro-cessed emotions onto other people's creative work?" Mia adjusted her chunky statement necklace as we approached the glass doors of Prismatic, the gallery where she worked as a curator.

I smoothed down the front of my black dress. "Lead the way to the free therapy and alcohol."

Mia pushed open the door, and my stomach immediately dropped to my knees. The gallery had been transformed into a winter wonderland. Not the tacky mall Santa variety. This was high-end Martha Stewart on steroids winter perfection.

Delicate crystal snowflakes hung from nearly invisible

threads, catching the light and sending rainbow reflections dancing across the white walls. Silver birch branches stretched toward the ceiling, dripping with thousands of fairy lights that mimicked falling snow.

"Isn't it horrendous?" Mia whispered, sweeping her arm dramatically. "The artists insisted on an immersive winter experience, like we're not in Los Angeles where it's sixty-five degrees outside. I think it's too much and detracts from the actual art, but what do I know?"

I couldn't respond because my lungs felt like they were filling with actual snow.

"The theme is Winter's Memory," Mia murmured as we moved deeper into the gallery. "The three artists had absolutely zero restraint. I love Christmas, but even I started turning into you after the third snow-drenched installation. They went absolutely wild with the concept, but the pieces will sell for thousands. Nostalgia plus a frosty color palette? Rich people eat that up."

We drifted past photographs of snow-covered landscapes so crisp I could practically feel my face getting frostbite. Sculptures of pine trees made with glass, metal, and resin glinted under the gallery lights. And the paintings? Every shade of sad, snowy blue you could think of.

My fingertips tingled, and I shoved them into my pockets, grateful that dress pockets were a thing.

Mia snagged two flutes of champagne from a passing server and pressed one into my hand. "You look like you need this. Already channeling your Christmas hatred?"

I took a deep swallow, barely tasting the expensive bubbles. "It's beautiful. That's the problem."

"Beautiful?" Mia's eyes widened. "Who are you, and what have you done with my holiday-hating friend?"

A memory flickered at the edge of my consciousness. Something about a night sky filled with dancing lights, my small hands reaching upward, trying to catch the colors...

"Earth to Neve." Mia waved her hand in front of my face. "You're doing that weird zoning-out thing."

I blinked. "Sorry."

"Maybe the wine from earlier hasn't worn off." Mia's tone was light, but her eyes were concerned. "Let's check out the main showpiece and make fun of it before I have to go schmooze the potential buyers."

She led me through a doorway draped with silver organza. The room beyond was circular, painted midnight blue, with a single spotlight illuminating an enormous canvas that dominated the entire back wall.

I froze mid-step.

The painting showed a man in a red suit, but not the jolly, cartoonish Santa from greeting cards. This version was tall and imposing, with broad shoulders and a silver beard. His eyes were painted with startling detail, glowing just like mine had. He stood atop a snowy mountain while the Northern Lights swirled through a sky full of stars.

This wasn't a character or myth, but someone real.

It was my dad.

My champagne flute slipped from my fingers.

Mia grabbed it before it could shatter. "Whoa! You okay? You look like you've seen a ghost."

I couldn't tear my eyes from the painting. The longer I stared, the more details emerged. The subtle pattern of intricate snowflakes on his suit seemed to swirl and move if I looked at them at the right angle.

The snowflake pendant around his neck was identical to the snowflake logo for Joint International Nordic Glacial Logistics and Ecology.

My legs felt rooted to the spot, the world tilting slightly as I tried to make sense of what I was seeing.

Mia gestured toward the painting with her glass. "Another romanticized Santa. They've turned him into a sexy Norse god. Like, pick a lane. Is he bringing presents to children or starring in a Viking calendar featuring silver foxes?"

I wanted to defend the painting. Defend my father. Which was ridiculous since my dad wasn't Santa. He was a researcher who studied... something about magnetic fields. And ice cores. Important, boring science stuff.

"And those eyes. So over-the-top dramatic." Mia snickered behind her hand. "Like he's some kind of zombie ice king."

My cheeks burned hot while my fingertips went numb with cold. The contradiction of sensations made me dizzy, my emotions swinging between confusion and an irrational urge to place myself between Mia and the painting.

"Total hack job." I forced the words out, each one tasting like pennies on my tongue. "Probably commissioned by the Christmas industrial complex to make everyone buy more crap."

The lie felt like a betrayal, though I couldn't articulate why. I'd spent my entire life avoiding Christmas, mocking the commercialism, rolling my eyes at sentimentality. This shouldn't be different.

So why did I feel like buying the painting?

"Right?" Mia laughed, then shrugged. "He said it's about strength wearing thin and how magic can still look powerful even when it's burning out underneath. It hits harder than I expected."

Burning out underneath? My heart stopped, then restarted at double speed.

A throat cleared behind us, the sound like ice cracking on a frozen lake.

I turned and found myself staring up at a man with wind-tousled brown hair and a grin that suggested he'd just outrun a natural disaster and was already looking for the next one. His fair skin had the faintest pink undertone, like someone who'd spent too long in the cold.

One of the men from the restaurant.

I stepped backward, bumping into Mia, who steadied me with a hand on my elbow.

"Sorry if I interrupted your art critique." The man's eyes practically twinkled with amusement. "Though I wouldn't call the artist a hack to his face."

Of course he was the artist. Because my life wasn't weird enough already.

CHAPTER 5
DISTRIBUTION LOGISTICS AND INTERNATIONAL SHIPMENTS

I tried to appear unshaken while internally cataloging every exit point in the gallery. There were four: the main entrance, the emergency door by the bathrooms, the staff entrance, and, if desperate enough, the skylight twelve feet above us. My money was on the emergency door. Less crowded.

I forced my face into a mask of polite disinterest, even as my pulse hammered in the hollow of my throat. This wasn't happening. This man shouldn't be here, in this gallery, in front of a canvas he'd painted that looked disturbingly like my dad.

"I'm Blitz." He extended his hand toward me. "The hack artist responsible for making people want to buy more shit."

"Neve North." I stuck out my hand, matching his confident posture despite the storm of questions battering my mind.

His palm met mine, and the world tilted sideways.

Heat. Not a gentle kind, but a blazing shock of it racing up my arm, chasing away the perpetual chill in my fingertips. My skin tingled where our hands connected, the sensation almost electrical but impossibly pleasant.

Blitz's eyes widened a fraction, his gaze dropping to our joined hands, then back to my face. Did he feel it too?

I yanked my hand back, curling my fingers into a fist to trap the lingering warmth.

"North." He repeated my last name like it meant something beyond a cardinal direction. "Where are you from?" The question felt loaded, like a test I hadn't studied for. "Los Angeles."

"Before that."

My brain short-circuited. Why would he care? Why was I suddenly struggling to remember my standard answer? "I've always lived here." Why did my mouth suddenly feel so dry?

Blitz's stare was unnerving, like he was trying to read something written on my soul.

"And your parents? Where are they from?"

"The Arctic Circle," Mia interjected with a laugh, completely misreading the room. "Her dad studies polar ice caps or glaciers or something equally frigid. The apple couldn't have fallen farther from the frozen tree."

I shot her a look that could have crystallized the champagne in her glass.

Blitz tilted his head, his gaze flickering from my face to the painting, then back again. "Your parents work in the Arctic? That's... interesting."

The word 'interesting' sounded dangerous in his mouth, like a match striking against sandpaper.

I was about to deflect when a shadow shifted at the edge of my vision, and the room's temperature seemed to drop another ten degrees.

A second man materialized beside Blitz. He was tall, solid, built like someone who could bench press a small car without breaking a sweat. He had deep brown skin, short hair, and steel-blue eyes that took in everything without revealing a damn thing. I hadn't heard him approach, which was unsettling given his size.

He was from that night too. One of the men who'd followed Mike when he'd fled the patio.

He didn't speak, just stood there like a wall of granite beside Blitz, studying me with the quiet focus of someone piecing together a puzzle mid-collapse.

"Cole." Blitz acknowledged him with a nod. "This is Neve North."

Cole inclined his head slightly, the gesture almost formal. His eyes never left mine, and something in their depths made my skin prickle with goosebumps.

"Nice to finally meet you." His voice was deep, the words measured like he rationed them by the syllable.

Mia shifted beside me. "Right. Anyway, we should probably circulate. So many art patrons to charm, so little champagne to go around." She hooked her elbow around mine, ready to lead me away.

"Already leaving?" Another voice wove through the crowd, warm and rich like honey.

A third man approached our increasingly uncomfortable gathering, his red curls a shockingly bright contrast to the gallery's stark white walls and the muted tones of everyone's cocktail attire. His smile was radiant and almost out of place among the contemplative expressions of the art crowd.

It felt like I'd inhaled the entire winter scene around us. Did I legit have nine stalkers?

"I'm Kip." The redhead extended his hand toward me, his green eyes filled with a warmth that seemed impossible to fake. Freckles dusted the bridge of his nose and the tops of his pink cheeks, escaping beneath his short beard. His entire demeanor was like a golden retriever who'd learned to walk upright and put on a suit.

I didn't take his hand. My fingers were already tingling again, and I didn't need another electrical shock in front of witnesses.

"Your painting is extraordinary, Blitz." Kip directed his comment to Blitz, but his eyes stayed fixed on me, like I was the real artwork in the room. "The way you've captured the light... it's as if you've been there, isn't it?"

"Been where?"

Three pairs of eyes swiveled to me with perfect synchronicity. None of them answered.

"Neve..." Kip finally broke the silence, my name sitting in his mouth like he was tasting it. "Named after the snow."

My stomach performed a series of gymnastic feats.

"I think it's probably an old family name or something." Mia waved her hand dismissively. "You know how parents are, grabbing random grandparent names off the family tree."

I stared at Mia, not sure whether to be grateful for the lie or offended she'd fabricated my naming story so easily.

"Family names have power." Cole's voice was low, his eyes never leaving my face. "They connect us to who we really are. They're the magic of tradition."

Magic. The word echoed in my head as my cheeks burned and my fingers froze. I shoved them deeper into my dress pockets, feeling the seams strain under the pressure.

"So, you three know each other well?" My question came out more like an accusation.

"We're practically brothers." Kip's smile was so genuine it hurt to look at. "We've known each other forever. You could say we work together."

"On what? Art?" I glanced back at the painting that would surely be part of my nightmares later when I went to sleep.

"That, and we're hoping to get into distribution logistics and international shipments if things go well here." Cole's expression remained perfectly neutral.

Something about the way they spoke with vagueness and the subtle glances they exchanged made my skin crawl.

"Look at the time!" I glanced at my bare wrist, where a watch would have been if I wore one. "We should probably... art... mingle... with people..."

"Absolutely." Mia started to pull me away. "Big potential buyers just arrived."

"I need air." I pulled away from Mia's grip and bolted, not caring how it looked.

The weight of three sets of eyes tracked me, and I forced myself not to run.

What the hell was happening? And why did I suddenly feel

like I was a painting being studied, examined, and completely exposed?

I CHUGGED the overpriced vodka soda like it might wash away the memory of the three men at the gallery staring at me like I was a long-lost artifact they'd finally tracked down. The bass pounded through the floor of Vortex, downtown's newest attempt at exclusivity, vibrating up through my heels and into my chest where it competed with my still-hammering heart.

"You need to relax." Mia pressed another drink into my hand, her voice barely audible over the crush of bodies and synthetic beats. "You practically sprinted out of the gallery."

I accepted the glass, taking a smaller sip this time. "I needed air."

Mia's gallery colleagues clustered around us, discussing art with way too much enthusiasm. I nodded when appropriate, focusing on the burn of alcohol rather than the nonsensical evening I'd survived.

"Want to dance?" Mia was already swaying to the music.

The prospect of voluntarily entering the sweaty mass of bodies seemed about as appealing as a root canal, but remaining stationary made me too accessible for conversation and gave my mind too much room to wander.

"Fine." I downed the rest of my drink, letting the alcohol blur the edges of my anxiety. "One song."

The moment my foot hit the dance floor, goosebumps erupted across my arms. I scanned the room, trying to keep my movements casual even as the hair on my neck stood at attention.

He stood tall and rigid against the far wall, fair-skinned and sharp in a dark button-down, his honey-blond hair neatly trimmed. He didn't even pretend to be interested in anything but me. His gray eyes cut through the dancing bodies between us like they didn't exist.

I knew him. Not his name, but his face. He'd been at Sinclair's that night, one of the nine.

I turned, hoping to slip between the wall of dancers, only to lock eyes with another man at the bar. He lounged casually against the counter, light golden skin catching the glow of the overhead lights, his black hair falling across one eye like it knew exactly what it was doing. His dark brown eyes sparked with amusement and a challenge. He raised his glass in a toast, his smile spreading slowly across his face.

Another one from Sinclair's.

The buzzing under my skin intensified, no longer uncomfortable but... familiar. Like something dormant waking up.

Mia was already dancing with someone, so I pushed through the crowd, desperate to get to the bathroom. My breath came in quick gasps as I navigated the press of bodies. I needed a minute to collect myself.

The air grew thick around me, heavy with something I couldn't name. Other clubgoers seemed to part unconsciously, creating a path I hadn't asked for. Ahead, the bathroom door beckoned to me with safety, privacy, and escape.

I reached for the door only to realize the buzzing had stopped. In its place, a weight settled in my chest, pulling me backward toward the dance floor like an invisible thread connecting me to those men. It was so much worse than the fear I had been feeling. It was as if my body knew them even if my mind didn't.

The music seemed to recede, the crowd's energy dimming against the pounding awareness of two sets of eyes tracking my movements. One pair, precise and calculating, the other wild and challenging.

I yanked open the bathroom door, slipping inside where the bass became a dull thud and the air was mercifully empty of whatever the hell was happening to me. Bracing my hands against the counter, I stared at my reflection. My cheeks were flushed, and my eyes were too bright.

Coincidences didn't exist, not at this frequency. Not when

those men looked at me like that. Not when something inside me recognized them right back.

I splashed cold water on my face, trying to bring myself back to baseline. Just a girl. In a bathroom. Probably just drunk.

I reached for a paper towel and froze. My reflection didn't match me.

She was standing exactly where I was, but her hair was white, her eyes glowed blue, and she wore a deep red coat with white fur trim. A Santa hat sat perfectly tilted on her head.

She smiled.

I screamed.

CHAPTER 6
ROSE THIEF AND SUCCULENT DESTROYER

I stared at my reflection, chest heaving, mascara smudged beneath my eyes. The silver-haired Santa version of me had vanished—if she'd ever been there at all. I'd finally cracked under the pressure of... of what? Having a terrible week? Seeing a reindeer in a park?

The bathroom door crashed open with such force that it bounced off the wall.

A dark-haired man from the bar burst in, eyes wild, scanning every corner of the small space before landing on me. "What happened?"

Before it fully registered that one of my stalkers was in an empty bathroom with me, a second figure appeared behind him. The second one who'd been watching me stepped through the doorway with controlled movements, like he was on some kind of top military mission.

"What the actual fuck?" I reeled backward, colliding with the counter. My hands gripped the edge so hard my knuckles whitened. "What are you doing?"

The door swung shut behind them. No security guard came rushing in. No concerned bartender. No one came to my rescue.

The dark-haired one ran a hand through his already disheveled hair, glancing from me to the mirror and back. "I heard you scream."

"From across a nightclub?" My voice crept higher. "Through walls and over music that could wake the dead?"

He shifted his weight, flashing a concerned smile. "You've got some serious pipes. Pretty sure they heard you on the International Space Station."

The blond one hadn't moved, hadn't smiled, stared at me with those unnerving gray eyes. "We felt it."

"Felt what?" I straightened my spine, trying to appear taller, more formidable, less like someone who'd just seen her doppelgänger dressed as Santa Claus in a nightclub bathroom mirror.

"Your magic." He said it so calmly, so matter-of-factly, like he was commenting on the weather. "It spiked."

The room tilted. I gripped the counter tighter. "I don't have magic. And you both need to leave. Now."

Neither of them moved. The dark-haired one's smile faded, his expression shifting to something that looked dangerously like pity. "You're waking up."

The words shouldn't have made sense. They shouldn't have sent ice water rushing through my veins. They shouldn't have felt so catastrophically true.

The blond one pointed a finger toward the mirror behind me. "Look."

I turned, half expecting to see the Santa version of me again. Instead, the mirror was frosted over, patterns of ice spreading from the center outward, crystallizing into intricate snowflakes and spirals. It looked like something out of a winter fairy tale: beautiful, impossible, and absolutely terrifying because it hadn't been there moments ago.

"I didn't do that." My voice came out as a whisper.

"You did." The dark-haired one stepped closer, his heat filling the small space between us. "Like how you made it snow at Sinclair's."

My heart stuttered. "I didn't... who *are* you?"

"I'm Pierce." The stormy-eyed blond one remained by the door, standing guard. Against what? Who might come in? Or who might try to get out?

"Vix." He held out his hand, but I didn't move to take it. "I know this is a lot to handle, but we are trying to help you. Pierce wanted all nine of us to knock on your door, but Rudy put his hoof down about that."

My eyes widened. "Hoof?"

Pierce glared at Vix, although that wasn't saying much since his face seemed to be stuck in a scowl. "Foot. We all have big feet."

"Big feet?" I laughed, the sound high and thin with hysteria. "You expect me to believe that nine men with *big feet* have been following me to *help* me?"

Frost continued spreading across the mirror's surface, branching outward like tiny lightning bolts. The bathroom had grown cold enough that I saw my breath when I spoke.

I needed to get past these two tanks and get to safety. My mind raced through potential escape routes, calculating the odds of dodging Vix or shouldering past Pierce's immovable frame. Neither option seemed promising.

They were solid walls of muscle standing between me and the rational world where mirrors didn't frost over and strangers didn't talk about magic like it was as common as getting a coffee.

The bathroom felt claustrophobic, and the walls got closer with each panicked thought. This had gone beyond weird and into genuinely horrifying territory. My fingers twitched at my sides, ready to push, shove, or claw my way out if necessary. All I needed was one opening, one moment of distraction, and I'd bolt straight for the exit and into the comforting anonymity of the crowded club.

"You both need to back the fuck away from me." I inched to the wall, hoping to slide around until they adjusted their positions so I could slip out the door.

Vix stepped closer, hands raised in a placating gesture. "We're not trying to hurt you."

"Oh, fantastic! Two strange men corner a woman in a bathroom and promise they're not trying to hurt her. That's completely reassuring!" My fingers curled into fists as my voice rose. "What is this exactly? Some kind of cult?"

Pierce's jaw tightened. "You don't understand the danger—"

"The danger?" I cut him off, fury and fear battling for dominance. "The only danger I see is being trapped in a bathroom with two stalkers who talk about magic like it's real!"

The temperature plummeted further. The mirror made a sharp cracking sound, and both men's eyes widened. A jagged line split the frosted glass from corner to corner.

"Neve..." Vix took another step forward.

How the hell did he know my name?

I held up my hand. "Stay back! I don't know you. I don't know what game you're playing."

"This isn't a game." Pierce's voice remained steady, but his eyes kept darting to the spreading frost that now crept along the bathroom walls. "You're losing control. Let us help you."

"Help me?" I let out a sharp, disbelieving laugh. "That's what this is supposed to be?"

Vix reached out, not quite touching me. "You forgot. It's not your fault."

"Forgot what?" I was shouting now, my voice bouncing off the tiled walls. "That I'm secretly a Disney princess? That I can conjure ice out of nowhere? That I hallucinate reindeer in parks who speak to me in my mind?"

Pierce's eyebrows shot up.

The mirror cracked again, louder this time. The frost had reached the ceiling, forming intricate patterns that sparkled under the fluorescent lights. A thin layer of ice now coated the floor around my feet.

Something inside me snapped. The last thread of rationality I'd been clinging to broke apart like the mirror behind me. I lunged forward, shoving past Vix with enough force to send him stumbling into the wall.

Pierce moved to block the door, but I was faster, rage and terror lending me speed. I ducked under his outstretched arm and crashed through the bathroom door into the pulsing of the club.

The sudden heat hit me like a wall, but my breath still

fogged in front of me. I pushed through the crowd, ignoring the startled looks from dancers who shivered as I passed. Behind me, I heard Vix calling my name, but the throbbing bass quickly swallowed his voice.

I needed air. I needed space. I needed everything to make sense again.

Most of all, I needed to run.

THE DIGITAL CLOCK on Mia's microwave glowed with judgmental brightness. I'd spent three hours staring at her living room ceiling, trying to convince my racing brain that the bathroom incident had been a combination of vodka, exhaustion, and too many Christmas decorations infecting my subconscious.

Mia had accepted my faked migraine excuse with minimal questions, though I caught her concerned glances during the Uber ride back to her condo. She'd offered me tea, Advil, and even her "special" gummies before finally retreating to her bedroom with a gentle reminder that her door was open if I needed anything.

What I needed was a brain transplant. Or possibly an exorcism.

I kicked off the blanket and sat up on the pull-out sofa. The silence pressed against my eardrums with the same intensity as the nightclub speakers, but with none of the distraction. Every time I closed my eyes, I saw ice crystallizing across that mirror and those two men looking at me like I was a bomb about to detonate.

Maybe I was.

My fingers tangled in the hem of the oversized T-shirt I slept in. The condo felt too small, too warm, too... contained. Like the walls might close in if I stayed inside any longer.

I padded across the polished concrete floor, past Mia's closed door, where her gentle snores confirmed she was asleep, and straight to the sliding glass door that led to her private balcony. But even as my hand touched the cool metal handle, I knew the small concrete slab wouldn't be enough. I needed more space. More air.

The roof. Mia had mentioned that the building had a communal rooftop garden that residents rarely used.

I slipped on my shoes without socks, grabbed Mia's keycard for the shared spaces, and headed for the stairwell. Four flights later, slightly winded and wishing I had taken the elevator, I swiped the card and pushed through the heavy metal door to the rooftop.

The night air hit me like salvation. Cool but not cold, carrying the faint scent of jasmine from the planters arranged around the perimeter. Potted palm trees swayed against the backdrop of city lights, their silhouettes black against the indigo sky. I inhaled deeply, filling my lungs with something that wasn't panic for the first time since the bathroom incident.

I took three steps toward the railing when a distinct crunching sound stopped me dead.

Not alone.

My body tensed, fight-or-flight kicking in for the third time that night. I squinted into the shadows, searching for the source of the noise.

"Hello?" My voice sounded embarrassingly small.

The crunching paused briefly, then continued.

I edged toward the sound, heart hammering. As my eyes adjusted to the dimness, two massive shapes materialized near a group of planters.

Two enormous, antlered shapes.

"You have got to be fucking kidding me."

The larger of the two reindeer lifted its head, a half-eaten rose dangling from its mouth like some bizarre floral cigar. Its impossibly intelligent eyes fixed on mine with an almost human expression of guilt.

The second reindeer, slightly smaller but no less imposing, continued systematically destroying an entire row of carefully cultivated succulents.

"Okay." I pressed the heels of my palms against my eyes.

"Okay, so I'm hallucinating reindeer again. No big deal. Probably just stress-induced psychosis."

I dropped my hands and glared at the animals. "Do you have any idea how many medications I'm going to be prescribed when I tell my future therapist about you?"

The larger reindeer had the audacity to snort, like I'd told the world's lamest joke.

"Oh, I'm sorry. Is my mental breakdown inconveniencing you?" I gestured wildly at the half-destroyed garden. "You're probably eating someone's award-winning roses! I bet she's eighty-three and talks about these flowers like they're her grandchildren!"

The smaller reindeer, though 'smaller' was relative when discussing animals the size of compact cars, stopped mid-chew. He tilted his head, antlers swaying gently with the movement, and I swear he looked amused.

"This isn't happening." I paced, running my hands through my hair. "First the ice, then those men, now reindeer in Palm Springs and Los Angeles. Reindeer don't even live in California!"

The succulent destroyer took a step toward me, his movements fluid and graceful despite his massive size.

I pointed an accusatory finger at him. "Stay right there, Rudolph. I've had enough magical Christmas bullshit for one lifetime."

He stopped, but something about his relaxed and patient posture suggested he was humoring me rather than being intimidated by me.

"I don't know what's happening." My voice cracked, exhaustion and confusion finally breaking through my thin veneer of sarcasm. "People are following me, telling me I have magic. Mirrors are freezing over when I get upset. And now there are reindeer eating plants on a rooftop."

The rose thief lowered his massive head to nudge his companion, a gesture so human it sent a chill down my spine.

"You know what the worst part is?" I continued, fully committed to my rooftop therapy session with two large herbivores. "Part of me isn't even surprised. Like somewhere deep down, I've been waiting for everything to fall apart like this."

I sank onto a nearby bench, too exhausted to stand. "My whole life I've felt... wrong. Like I'm playing a part in someone else's story. And now all this weird stuff is happening, and instead of being terrified, there's this voice in my head saying, *finally.*"

The rose thief approached cautiously until he stood directly in front of me. Up close, his eyes were hazel, almost human in their expressiveness. He lowered his enormous head until we were nearly at eye level.

"If you're about to start talking telepathically to me, I will throw myself off this roof."

He blinked once, slowly, then huffed a warm breath against my face that smelled faintly of roses and something sweet I couldn't identify.

I locked eyes with the reindeer in front of me, comforted in a way that had no business making sense. A movement to my right broke our staring contest.

The second reindeer had abandoned the decimated succulents and moved onto what looked like someone's vegetable garden. His massive head lowered toward a small plot of zucchini plants, those ridiculous antlers nearly taking out a string of fairy lights.

"Oh no, absolutely not!" I jumped to my feet. "The roses were bad enough, but those zucchinis are probably someone's mental health project. Do you know how long those take to grow in this kind of environment?"

The reindeer continued his approach to the vegetables, completely ignoring my objection.

"I said no!" I lunged forward, pressing both hands against his massive shoulder to physically push him away from the garden bed.

The moment my skin made contact with his fur, electricity shot up my arms, across my chest, and straight into my brain. My vision whited out as an image flashed behind my eyes—*a snowy field, my much smaller hands reaching out to pat tiny reindeer calves that pranced around me in circles, my childish giggles echoing in the crisp air. The sensation of pure joy, of belonging, washed through me before disappearing just as quickly.*

I stumbled backward, gasping. "What the hell was that?"

The air around the reindeer began to shimmer and distort, like heat rising off asphalt in summer. His massive form blurred, contracting and reshaping until a very naked man stood where the reindeer had been.

A very naked, very attractive man with warm amber eyes and perfectly tousled dark brown hair.

My jaw dropped so fast I nearly dislocated it.

"Sorry about the zucchini," he said with an easy smile. "I've always had a weakness for garden vegetables." He made a gesture with his hand, and a pair of shorts and a tank top appeared out of thin air.

I blinked rapidly, my brain short-circuiting as it tried to process what had just happened. "You... you were..."

"A reindeer? Naked?" He stretched casually, all muscle and medium tan skin. "Sorry about flashing you. It's more comfortable to shift without clothes on."

The air behind me changed, and I spun around to find a second naked man standing where the rose thief had been. This one was taller, broader, with light beige skin, sandy blond hair, and a more serious expression.

"Dane," the second man chastised, his hazel eyes flicking to his companion as he magicked his own clothes. "We agreed to ease into this."

"She touched me!" Dane protested, gesturing wildly.

I backed away from both of them until my legs hit the bench. "Who are you people? What just happened? Why were you—" My voice cut off as connections exploded in my brain like firecrackers. "There are nine of you."

The second one nodded. "I'm Dash. That's Dane. And yes, there are nine of us."

"And you turn into reindeer." My voice was barely a whisper. "Nine reindeer."

Dane's expression brightened. "She's figuring it out!"

"My dad..." The words I wanted to say felt right but wrong, like something was stopping me from saying them.

Dash shook his head, his expression guarded. "We can't tell you directly. You have to remember on your own."

"Remember what?" Frost began forming beneath my feet, spreading outward.

"Your joy." Dane's playful demeanor softened into something gentler. "You need to find your joy again so you can return home."

I wrapped my arms around myself. "Home?"

"We can take you as far north as the magic allows. Only you can unlock the part of you that is required to go to..." He stopped for a moment, as if he couldn't find the correct word. "Jingle."

Jingle. It wasn't the first time one of them had said something about where my parents worked.

"We'll help you get to where you belong," Dane added softly.

I stared at the crystalline frost pattern expanding beneath me, feeling both terrified and oddly relieved. "And if I don't want to go?"

Dash and Dane exchanged glances.

Dane rubbed the back of his neck. "Then the damage might be permanent."

CHAPTER 7
HERD MEETING

The two-hour drive back to Palm Springs had given me plenty of time to construct elaborate theories about my apparent supernatural awakening.

My plan was simple: close all the blinds, turn off my phone, and pretend the outside world didn't exist for the next twenty-four hours. Maybe forty-eight. Or however long it took for reindeer men to stop appearing in my life.

I'd barely set my bag down when three firm knocks echoed through my living room.

"You have got to be fucking kidding me." I froze, keys still dangling from my fingertips.

The knocks came again, more insistent this time.

A normal person would ignore it. A smart person would call the police. I, however, apparently possessed neither quality because I marched to the door and yanked it open with enough force to rattle the hinges.

"What now? Is the Easter Bunny waiting to tell me I'm secretly related to—"

The words died in my throat as I stared up—because yes, *up*—at the man on my doorstep. He stood there as if he'd been casually waiting for hours, hands clasped behind his back, expression unreadable save for one arched eyebrow. He had cool ivory skin and short black hair.

But it was his eyes that made my stomach drop. Slate gray with the same unsettling intelligence I'd seen in the park. The reindeer.

"You." I gripped the door frame to steady myself.

He inclined his head slightly, a gesture both polite and somehow smug at the same time.

"Has anyone ever told you that you're absurdly tall? What are you, like six-foot-ten?" I was five-foot-nine, and he had more than a foot on me.

"Seven feet." His voice was deep, rumbling like distant thunder. "May I come in?"

I glanced behind him at my quiet suburban street, wondering what my neighbors would think if they saw me inviting Bigfoot's better-dressed cousin into my home.

"Why not?" I stepped back, waving him in with false bravado. "Make yourself at home, Comet."

He stiffened, broad shoulders going rigid as he ducked to enter my doorway. "My name is Rudy."

"Of course it is." A hysterical laugh bubbled up as I closed the door. "Rudy. As in Rudolph? Where's your glowing nose?"

His expression remained stoic, but I swore I caught a flicker of annoyance pass through those slate eyes.

He moved into my living room with surprising grace for someone whose head nearly brushed my ceiling, scanning my sparse decor with open curiosity.

I crossed my arms over my chest, trying to reclaim some sense of control. "So what, you can... track me down whenever you want?"

His massive frame made my furniture look like dollhouse accessories as he carefully lowered himself onto my couch. The poor thing creaked in protest.

"I didn't track you. I've been here before." He gestured vaguely toward my kitchen.

I followed his gaze, ice forming in my veins as realization dawned. "That was you?"

He nodded once, his expression utterly unapologetic.

"You broke into my house to bake cookies?" Frost began

creeping across my hardwood floors, spreading outward from where I stood. "What kind of twisted home invasion is that?"

Rudy's eyes tracked the spreading frost with something like satisfaction. "It wasn't breaking in, and I didn't bake here, seeing as you have no baking supplies. The others thought nostalgic food might help trigger your memories."

"The others." My nails dug crescents into my palms. "Right. Your reindeer friends who think I'm some kind of... ice creature."

"You're more than that." He studied me with unnerving intensity.

I stared at him, trying to maintain my righteous indignation, but something else tugged at me beneath the anger. It was a peculiar pull, like gravity but warmer, drawing me toward his massive frame. For one absurd moment, I imagined climbing onto his lap, burying my face against his chest, and letting him solve whatever cosmic joke my life had become.

I shook my head, backing up a step. "Look, I don't know what 'more' I'm supposed to be, but I'm just a woman with bills to pay and a spray tan addiction, not whatever magical creature you think I am."

Rudy's gaze swept over me, lingering on my face. "I see the tan didn't take."

My hand flew to my cheek reflexively. "Hey! How do you even... you know what? Never mind."

The doorbell rang, its cheerful chime completely at odds with the existential crisis unfolding in my living room. Rudy's lips quirked in what might have been the world's most microscopic smile. "That would be the others."

"The others? What do you mean the—" I didn't finish because the doorbell rang again, followed by an impatient series of knocks that sounded like someone was using my door for drum practice.

I stomped over to it and yanked it open, ready to unleash hell on the threat that awaited.

Except the threat was a wall of extra-large pizza boxes balanced in someone's arms. Behind them stood a snack food convoy of two-liter bottles of soda, bags of chips, and cookie boxes—holy Cookie Monster, so many cookie boxes.

"Special delivery!" a voice called from behind the *first* pizza tower.

The boxes shifted, revealing Dane's grinning face. Behind him stood the entire collection of men who had been appearing everywhere, crowding my entryway like this was an average potluck.

They pushed past me in a herd of masculine energy, filling my living room with their presence. Food was placed on every available surface before I could stop them.

"We figured you'd be hungry." Kip grabbed my hand, sending tingles up it, and pressed a warm cookie into my palm. "Food is always the best foundation for life-altering revelations."

"I'm partial to salty myself." Blitz ripped open a bag of chips with his teeth and dropped into my reading chair.

Vix carried in a case of energy drinks. "The sugar content in these is appalling, but apparently humans love them."

Cole silently handed me a pizza box, his blue eyes somehow making the gesture seem profound.

Pierce began arranging bottles on my coffee table. "Figured we'd need provisions for the herd meeting."

"The *what* meeting?" I clutched the cookie, watching frost creep along its edges.

"Herd meeting," Dash repeated, flopping onto my couch beside Rudy. "Nine reindeer, one North. That's a herd."

"We've got a lot to catch up on and wanted to make it comfortable for you." The man from the grocery store opened a bottle of soda and took a swig.

I ran through their names: Dash and Dane, Pierce and Vix, Cole and Kip, Donner and Blitz. Rudy. Some part of me knew with certainty I'd paired them exactly how they were supposed to be paired.

I watched the grocery store man's throat work as he swallowed. "And you're Donner."

He burped. Ugh. Men. "Excuse me, that hit harder than expected. I'm Don."

I stood rooted to the spot while nine men made themselves at home, eating food, sitting on my furniture, and acting like this impromptu magical meeting was an everyday occurrence.

The cookie in my hand smelled devastatingly good, like childhood, safety, and something just out of reach. The scent wrapped around me, warm and familiar. My shoulders dropped, just a little.

"Eat it." Rudy was watching me and waiting. I contemplated crumbling the treat in my hand in defiance, but his command and the look in his eyes told me to obey.

I examined it, my nose crinkling before I took a bite. The taste exploded on my tongue and made my eyes water with unexpected emotion. "Someone better explain why the North Pole's mascots decided to stage an intervention in my living room with cookies."

The men exchanged glances as if they'd witnessed a modern-day miracle. I tracked the silent communication passing between them. Could they speak to each other telepathically? Rudy could speak to me, so it wasn't out of the question.

I took another bite of the cookie to steady myself. "What? Why are you all looking at me like that?"

Dane bounced on his heels, practically vibrating. "You said *it*!"

"Huh? I was being sarcastic." The words felt hollow even as I spoke them, like my mouth was operating on autopilot while deeper parts of my brain stirred. "It's not like I actually believe in any of this." At least that's what I was currently telling myself.

"You're beginning to remember." Rudy looked both powerful and patient, like a mountain that had all the time in the world to wait for me to climb. And man, did I have the urge to climb him. "Your magic is reawakening even with everything stacked against it."

"Magic tied to what? Christmas spirit? Coal distribution?"

"Joy." All eyes were fixed on me as Rudy spoke. "True joy. Without it, you'll never be able to reach... Jingle."

The word "Jingle" made my chest ache, like someone had pressed on an old bruise I'd forgotten was there.

"We can't force you to remember." Kip's voice was gentle, his green eyes earnest beneath those wild red curls. He moved to stand near me, and I had the strangest urge to let him pull me into a hug. "The magic won't allow it. Some things you have to discover for yourself. We can only help you reconnect to what you've lost."

I leaned against the counter that separated the living room from the kitchen, steadying myself. "And what exactly have I lost?"

Vix snorted, crushing an empty energy drink can in one hand. "Your sense of humor is intact, at least."

Rudy's eyes seemed to glow as he spoke. "Your Christmas spirit... your joy."

My legs felt too weak to support my weight. Pierce was already moving a dining room chair for me to sit in. I gave him a grateful smile and sank into it, cookie crumbs from my shirt falling onto my lap.

The room filled with the sounds of eating as I looked around at the nine reindeer men who had crashed into my life. My brain went through everything, and either they were really messing with me, or they were under some kind of magical gag order.

I was caught between laughter and tears. These men weren't threatening me. They weren't even trying to force me to do anything. They were just... waiting. Patient and determined, like this was their job.

"How do I know this isn't some elaborate prank?" I pressed the heels of my hands against my eyes.

Cole moved with silent grace to kneel beside my chair. He took my hand, turning it palm up. "It's not. Do you feel that?"

Did he mean the weird tingle he sent up and down my arm? It radiated from where his fingertips pressed against my skin, like static electricity but warmer, more alive. The sensation skittered up to my shoulder and down into my chest, wrapping around some internal part of me.

I nodded. "What is it?"

"Connection." Cole said only the one word, but it rang true in my mind.

I could kick them all out immediately and ignore this, but that felt wrong, like I'd be ripping away a part of myself. If this wasn't a figment of my imagination, I was screwed anyway, might as well see where my delusion led me.

"What's next then? What's your grand plan for helping me find this magical joy?"

"We stay." Blitz grabbed a box of pizza and flipped it open. "Help you recover pieces of yourself, one memory and feeling at a time until we can return to Jingle."

Jingle. There it was again: Joint International Nordic Glacial Logistics and Ecology.

The artwork from the gallery flashed in my mind. My dad's face when he'd come on video chat the other day. My parents' odd behavior when I'd mentioned what was happening to me.

What I was about to say seemed absolutely absurd. "Is my dad Santa Claus?" The room tensed, nine pairs of eyes darting between each other. I reached for my phone, pulling up his contact. "I'll call and ask."

Cole's hand closed over mine, warm and surprisingly gentle considering his size. "He won't be able to confirm or deny. There are strict guidelines."

Ice formed beneath my fingertips. "Is he sick? Is something happening to him?"

"Not sick." Rudy's voice dropped lower. "Not in the traditional sense."

I pulled my hand away from Cole and stared at the melting ice in my palm, feeling something both terrifying and exhilarating unfolding inside me. "His magic is fading, isn't it? That's what the painting was about."

The silence that followed was all the confirmation I needed.

CHAPTER 8
CHRISTMAS SPIRIT
RESTORATION ACTIVITIES

I slapped at my ringing alarm three times before my hand connected with the snooze button. The morning sun sliced through the gap in my curtains as if it had a vendetta against my eyelids.

Five more minutes. Just five.

When I next opened my eyes, thirty minutes had passed. I dragged myself upright, squinting at my phone. No missed calls from work. Small miracles. After yesterday's magical reindeer intervention and impromptu "herd meeting," I'd put in for a sick day.

I probably needed a sick week.

The bathroom beckoned with promises of hot water and temporary escape from my reality. I shuffled across the room, my brain still booting up its systems.

I flipped on the light, reached for my toothbrush, and caught my reflection.

"What the actual fuckity fuck?!"

My toothbrush clattered into the sink as I leaned forward, nose practically touching the mirror. Two inches of silver roots blazed like a neon sign against my carefully maintained black hair. Two. Entire. Inches.

I grabbed a handful and held it away from my scalp to see it better. It wasn't from bad lighting or sleep deprivation. My natural color was making a very unauthorized comeback tour.

It was physically impossible to grow two inches overnight. I ran my fingers through my hair, frantically checking the length. It wasn't longer. It was... reverting. Like my body was rejecting the dye the same way it had rejected my spray tan.

I grabbed my measuring tape from my drawer and held it against the roots. Exactly two inches. Hair grew half an inch per month, max. This was four months of growth. Overnight.

"Okay, Neve. Let's review." I braced my hands on the counter. "You've got inexplicable ice powers. Your skin rejected industrial-grade spray tan. Your hair is magically un-dyeing itself. And nine men who transform into reindeer will neither confirm nor deny that your father is Santa Claus."

A broken laugh slipped free, tangled up in nerves. I threw the measuring tape back in the drawer and slammed it closed before marching toward the kitchen. Coffee. I needed coffee before I could wrap my head around any more reality-breaking revelations.

The smell of brewing coffee greeted me halfway down the hall, along with the sound of male voices and clinking dishes.

I rounded the corner to find Dane standing at my coffee maker while Dash organized a spread of pastries on my kitchen table. Both men looked up with identical expressions of innocence.

"Good morning, princess!" Dane lifted a mug in salute. His smile widened as his gaze fixed on my two-toned hair.

Dash set down a plate of Christmas-themed donuts. "The transformation is progressing nicely."

I narrowed my eyes, crossing my arms over my sleep shirt. "What did you do to my hair?"

"Nothing." Dane held out a mug of coffee toward me. "That's all you, sweetheart. Or rather, all original you, coming back out to play."

"No nicknames," I grumbled as I cautiously approached the offered coffee like it might bite. "If my hair spontaneously turns into tinsel, I'm shaving all of you bald while you sleep."

"Threats of violence already?" Dash's expression remained entirely too pleased. "And here I thought we had such a productive bonding session yesterday."

I grabbed the mug and took a sip. It was the right strength, temperature, and amount of my coffee creamer. Unnervingly perfect. "How do you know how I take my coffee?"

"Magic." Dane gave me a look so smug it might as well have been a wink.

These men were horribly frustrating, and it was precisely the wrong time to notice how their broad shoulders seemed to fill my kitchen in a way that wasn't entirely unwelcome.

Dash pulled out a chair. "We've got your whole day planned. Light Christmas spirit restoration activities to ease you back in."

"I'm sorry, you've got what?" The coffee suddenly tasted like betrayal.

I stared at the pair of them, setting my coffee down with a definitive clink. "Look, I'm not great at being handled. Not even before my life went full meltdown."

Dane leaned his hip against my kitchen counter, the morning light from the window making his amber eyes practically glow. "We could work on that." His voice dropped to a murmur that seemed to vibrate.

Something warm pooled low in my stomach. Nope. I would not become attracted to these reindeer men.

Instead, I glanced at the elaborate breakfast spread, then at the hall to my bedroom. If I moved fast enough, I could barricade myself in there for at least a few hours.

"Don't even think about it." Dash's voice held an amused warning.

I sank into the chair with a groan. "I hate Christmas." I hunched over my coffee like it could shield me from Christmas spirit intervention. "I'm guessing 'leave me alone' isn't going to work with you two?"

"Not a chance." Dane dropped a chocolate croissant onto my plate. "Look at the bright side. At least we're feeding you first."

Dash pushed a bowl of fresh berries toward me. "Consider this your official herd onboarding. Day one."

I took a reluctant bite of the croissant. The buttery layers melted on my tongue with chocolate perfection. Damn them. "I didn't agree to be onboarded."

"Yet here we are." Dash's eyes tracked over my face, lingering on my hair. "The silver hair suits you."

My hand shot up to my silver embarrassment. "I'm dyeing it back today."

Dane snorted. "Good luck with that. Your body's rejecting anything that masks your true nature. Plus, it helps with camouflage..."

I stared at my coffee, a childhood memory washing over me like an icy wave. "Camouflage..."

Six-year-old me, crouched in a snowdrift, my silver hair and pale skin making me practically invisible. The other kids called it unfair, especially when a boy wearing his mom's furry white jacket as a makeshift nibbleknot costume kept getting spotted while I remained hidden for nearly an hour.

I blinked, the kitchen coming back into focus.

"What the hell is a nibbleknot?"

"You just remembered something?" Dash leaned forward, his broad shoulders tensing with interest.

I rubbed the bridge of my nose. "I was hiding in the snow, and my hair made me invisible. There was a boy pretending to be... a nibbleknot?"

Dash exchanged a quick glance with Dane, something unspoken passing between them.

"A nibbleknot is a snow creature." Dash's voice was slow, and his tone remained careful, like he was testing the words. I knew they couldn't tell me things directly, but he at least was trying. "It's a... folklore thing among children. They're said to look like a giant knot of yarn." He looked at Dane, eyebrows arched in question.

Dane shrugged, setting down his mug. "I've never seen one. They leave blankets and cuddle people who need comfort."

"And the nibbling part? Please tell me they don't nibble on

children's toes." I shuddered at the thought of a giant furry creature making a snack of my pinky toes.

"When they eat, they nibble." Dash broke apart a blueberry muffin. "If you're curious about them, ask Rudy. He's the only one of us who's ever seen one."

My brain stuttered to a halt. "Wait. Why would Rudy have seen one?"

Dane's coffee mug froze halfway to his lips. His eyes darted to Dash with an unmistakable *oh shit* look.

Dash cleared his throat and stood abruptly. "Donut? You should try the red velvet."

"You just said they leave blankets for people who need comfort." I planted my elbows on the table, leaning forward. "What happened to Rudy?"

Dane pushed back from the table, his chair scraping loudly against the floor. "So about those Christmas spirit restoration activities! We have a whole itinerary."

"I'm not moving until you—"

A sharp knock at the front door startled us all.

"Perfect timing!" Dane practically bolted for the door, relief washing over his features.

I shot Dash a look, waiting for him to explain.

"Just some light festivities." Dash's poker face was excellent. Too excellent.

Twenty minutes later, I stared in horror at my transformed living room. The knock on the door had been from a delivery service that had set up folding tables. Every surface was covered with baking trays full of gingerbread cookies. Piping bags of frosting were arranged between sprinkle containers, candy bits, and an absurd amount of edible glitter.

I should never have left the two men unattended while I went to get ready for the day.

"What the hell happened in here?" My voice came out higher than intended.

"Christmas magic." Dane gave me a slow, dramatic blink that said, "You're welcome," as he tied an apron around his waist. *Sleigh My Name, Sleigh My Name* was written across the chest.

Dash held out an apron toward me. "You might want this. Things are about to get messy."

"I don't do messy." I took a step back, eyeing the chaos. "And I definitely don't do gingerbread."

"Today you do." Dash stepped forward, the apron still extended. "Just try. For an hour."

"Think of it as exposure therapy." Dane was already squeezing green frosting onto a cookie with concerning enthusiasm.

I snatched the apron from Dash's hand. "One hour. Then you both leave."

"Sure, princess." Dane didn't even look up as he gave his gingerbread man obscene biceps.

I tied the apron with sharp, angry movements. "And stop calling me..." My words failed me as I glanced down at the text on my chest: *Sleigh Queen*.

It felt like a tug of war was going on inside my brain, trying to decide whether or not to let me claim the nickname. It felt right, but at the same time, it made me want to kick Dash and Dane out.

"Decorate a few. That's all." Dash guided me with his hand on the small of my back to the seat between them. It pulled me away from whatever mental battle was about to pull me under.

"Fine." I reached for the white frosting, determined to get through this with minimal participation.

Dane held up his creation: a gingerbread monstrosity with a frosting six-pack and what appeared to be green sprinkle chest hair. "This is me in my peak December form."

"Horrifying." I couldn't stop the slight smile tugging at my lips.

Dash worked with methodical precision on his cookie. "I'm making you." His eyes flicked up to my face, then back down as he added two dots of blue frosting.

"That looks nothing like me."

"The scowl's not quite right yet." His finger dabbed a tiny

adjustment to the frosting mouth, his own lips curved in amusement.

Did the man want me to dump sprinkles in his eyes?

I focused on my gingerbread, intending to slap some random frosting on it and be done. But as I squeezed the piping bag, my hands seemed to move with a rhythm I didn't consciously direct. White lines swirled into intricate patterns, creating a snowflake across the cookie's surface.

My fingers hovered over the design, a strange déjà vu washing over me. I'd made this exact pattern before. Many times.

"That's beautiful." Dash's voice was soft beside me.

I stared at my work. "I don't know how I did that."

For a heartbeat, the frosting gleamed with an inner light, pulsing once beneath my fingertip. I jerked my hand back as if it had burned me.

Dane and Dash exchanged a quick glance over my head.

"What was that?" My voice came out as a whisper.

"Your connection." Dane's usual playfulness had vanished. "To the... the Jingle."

I grabbed another cookie, focusing intently as I repeated the pattern, this time adding tiny crystalline details with silver sugar. My breathing slowed. The tightness that had lived between my shoulder blades for as long as I could remember eased slightly.

"I've never decorated cookies before." The lie tasted strange on my tongue, but was it a lie if I didn't remember?

"Hmm." Dash's noncommittal hum spoke volumes.

Three cookies later, I'd relaxed into the rhythm, annoyed to find myself enjoying it. Dane's commentary on his increasingly ridiculous creations made it impossible not to laugh.

"You have to try one." Dane nudged a finished cookie toward me.

"I don't like cookies," I replied. Which was a lie, considering chocolate chip had already staged a coup in my brain.

"Try this one." Dash's eyes held a challenge as he picked up one of my creations and held it up. "Open."

The cookie hovered inches from my mouth, and the air between us hummed with something I didn't want to name. "I don't even like sweets," I muttered, yet leaned forward anyway. My lips parted, and Dash's thumb brushed against my bottom lip as he fed me the cookie. My eyes fluttered closed, both from his touch and the flavor that hit me like a physical force.

Ginger and cinnamon bloomed across my tongue, but it wasn't just the taste. It was the warmth spreading from my chest outward, rushing through my limbs.

A half-formed memory shimmered at the edge of my consciousness: *laughter echoing off high ceilings, the smell of baking everywhere, small hands covered in flour, and a deep voice telling me it was the best cookie he'd ever seen and that he'd seen billions, if not trillions.*

When I opened my eyes, Dash was watching me with an intensity that made my skin prickle with heat.

His thumb traced the corner of my mouth, catching a stray crumb. "Tell me again how you hate cookies, Neve."

I licked my lips, and his eyes tracked the movement. It would be so easy to close the distance between us and kiss him.

Wait. What?

I stood, untying my apron, which felt like it was tied too tight. "I think that's enough Christmas spirit restoration for one day."

There was only so much one woman could take, and realizing that I wanted to kiss not just Dash but also Dane and the rest of the men was too much.

CHAPTER 9
ALLERGIC TO PINE

I sank into my dining chair, dragging the plate of dinosaur-shaped chicken nuggets closer like it might be stolen if I didn't maintain constant contact. The French fries were crinkle-cut, extra crispy, and positively drowning in ketchup. They formed a comforting moat around my protein—the pinnacle of adult dining.

This was what my life had come to. Hiding in my house, eating like a toddler, and avoiding the two reindeer men who'd finally left me alone after I'd practically shoved them out the door. My lips still tingled from where Dash's thumb had brushed them.

I dunked a T-Rex head into ketchup with unnecessary force.

The doorbell rang, a jarring Christmas tune that made me drop my nugget. How had they changed the ring?

"Nope. Not tonight, Satan." I shoved another fry into my mouth. If I ignored it, whoever it was would eventually go away.

The doorbell rang again, and I groaned, pushing back from the table. If it were Dane and Dash returning with more Christmas torture, I was going to set my house on fire.

I yanked open the door, prepared to unleash my frosty wrath, and froze.

Pierce and Vix stood on my doorstep. Pierce, all rigid

71

posture and perfect hair, had his finger poised over the doorbell for another assault. Vix leaned casually against the wall, a sharp contrast to Pierce's military stance.

Both wore matching green T-shirts with *Nice-ish* emblazoned across their chests in candy-cane stripes.

My brain hit the emergency brake and skidded sideways.

"May we come in?" Pierce lowered his hand, his eyes immediately taking inventory of my house behind me.

"Are you really asking, or is that just a formality before you barge in anyway?" I stepped into their path, as if I might actually be able to stop them.

Vix's mouth quirked up at one corner. "You've got ketchup on your face."

I swiped at my cheek, feeling heat creep up my neck. "What do you want?" I stepped to the side, letting them in. They clearly weren't going to leave anyway.

Once they were inside, I double-checked that there weren't any more wayward reindeer waiting to barge in before shutting the door. Vix was already making a beeline for my kitchen.

"Your dinner looks sad," Vix commented as he took in my abandoned meal. "Are those... dinosaur nuggets?"

"They're a culinary delight." I looked between the two of them, getting a better look at their T-shirts. "Nice shirts. Did you coordinate, or was it a happy accident?"

Pierce glanced down at his chest, then at Vix's, as if just noticing they matched. "Christmas-themed clothing encourages participation in seasonal activities."

"I was being sarcastic."

"A sweater would be impractical in this climate." Pierce's eyes remained utterly serious. "You've chosen to live in a location with suboptimal winter weather."

I stared at him, waiting for the punchline. None came.

"Sadly chosen?" I waved a hand toward my kitchen window. "It's in the seventies during the day. It hardly ever rains, and there is absolutely no snow. That's not sad, that's paradise."

Vix snorted, dropping onto my couch without invitation. "It's not paradise if it smells like sunscreen instead of pine."

"What are you doing here?" I returned to my plate, grabbing a fry and biting it like it were one of their heads.

Pierce set a glossy red gift bag on my counter. "You need fresh air."

"I have windows."

"Put that on." He nodded toward the bag. "We're leaving in five minutes."

I set down my fry, spine straightening. "I'm not going anywhere. I just escaped Tweedledee and Tweedledum's Christmas cookie bonanza."

Vix leaned forward, elbows on his knees. "You can't stay in here forever, avoiding what's happening."

"Watch me."

"Five minutes." Pierce checked his watch. "Or we carry you out as is."

My gaze darted between Vix's challenging smirk and Pierce's immovable stance. They weren't bluffing.

"Fine." I snatched the bag off the counter. "But I'm lodging a formal protest."

Pierce's eyebrows rose a fraction. "Noted."

In my bedroom, I dumped the contents of the bag onto my bed. A folded T-shirt in deep crimson fell out. I held it up, groaning at the white letters that said *Very Naughty* across the chest, with *Naughty* crossed out and *Nice* written above it.

I glared at my reflection as I pulled it on. With my roots growing more obvious by the hour, I looked like a walking Christmas advertisement.

When I emerged, Vix let out a low whistle. "Now that's festive."

"I hate all of you." I grabbed my purse and phone from the counter. "Let's get this over with."

"Your enthusiasm is overwhelming." Pierce opened the door, gesturing for me to exit first.

The vehicle parked in my driveway was not what I expected.

A massive red electric pickup truck gleamed under the street-lights, its chrome accents catching the glow.

"Subtle." I climbed into the backseat, already regretting agreeing to this field trip. Where the hell were they even taking me?

Vix slid into the driver's seat while Pierce took shotgun.

"Subtlety is overrated."

"Where are we going?" I buckled my seatbelt as Vix backed out.

"East." Pierce didn't even turn around.

"That's not an answer."

"It's directionally accurate."

I slumped against the window, watching as we drove through town. "Is kidnapping part of the standard Christmas spirit restoration?"

Vix adjusted the rearview mirror, catching my eye in it. "Only for the particularly stubborn cases."

I maintained a steady stream of complaints for the entire fifteen-minute drive. The shirt was itchy. The AC was too cold. The Christmas music playing softly from the speakers was giving me hives.

Neither man seemed bothered by my griping.

I pressed my face against the window as Vix pulled into a lot illuminated by strands of multicolored lights crisscrossing overhead like a drunken spider had been tasked with decorating. The sharp, unmistakable scent of pine hit me as soon as the truck door opened, making me freeze halfway out of the vehicle.

"Welcome to Evergreen Wonderland." Vix spread his arms wide, like he was presenting me with my own personal nightmare.

"A Christmas tree lot?" I stepped out onto the gravel, my stomach tightening. "You brought me to get a Christmas tree?"

Pierce closed the passenger door. "Palm Springs has a disappointing lack of natural Christmas tree options. We would have preferred to cut one down, but this will have to do."

The lot was nearly deserted, with only a few other

customers wandering between rows of pre-cut pines. Somewhere in the distance, Michael Bublé crooned a jazzy rendition of a song that made my teeth ache. I wrapped my arms around myself, cold despite the mild evening temperature.

"Think of this as exposure therapy." Vix bumped my shoulder with his, gesturing toward the fragrant prison of holiday cheer.

I took two steps away from him. "I don't need therapy. I need immunity from holiday harassment."

Pierce's eyes tracked a young couple as they struggled with a tree, his expression calculating. "The lot closes in forty-five minutes. We have sufficient time."

"Time for what?" My voice went up an octave.

"To find your perfect tree, obviously." Vix's grin was infectious if you were the type to catch Christmas fever, which I emphatically was not.

I backed up even more, hands raised. "I'm allergic to pine."

"You are not." Pierce's eyes narrowed.

"I am! Terribly." I inhaled and then forced out a pathetic fake sneeze, followed by a cough that sounded more like I was choking. "See? Fatal. Let's go."

Vix leaned close to my ear. "Careful what you fake. Some of us see that as a challenge."

I opened my mouth for another retort when Pierce appeared on my other side. Without warning, his hand slipped into mine, warm and firm, and I nearly jumped out of my skin at the contact.

"This way." He tugged me forward, his grip leaving no room for argument.

Before I could protest or even think, Vix captured my other hand, sandwiching me between them like a very confused filling.

"What are you doing?" I tried to pull away, but they moved in unison, guiding me through the first row of trees.

"Preventing your escape." Vix squeezed my hand, his thumb brushing over my knuckles in a way that sent a completely unwelcome tingle up my arm.

Pierce's posture remained rigid as a board, but his fingers interlocked with mine with startling intimacy. "Statistical analysis shows people are sixty-nine percent less likely to run when physical contact is maintained."

"Did you make that up?" I tried to sound annoyed, but it came out more exasperated than anything as we moved deeper into the cut trees.

"I never fabricate statistics." The corner of his mouth twitched, almost imperceptibly.

The scent grew stronger as we wound through the maze of trees. I held my breath, waiting for revulsion to set in, but instead fought against a strange tugging that felt like a hook had lodged behind my sternum.

"Close your eyes." Vix's voice dropped to a whisper that tickled my ear.

"Absolutely not."

"Trust the process, North." Pierce's thumb traced a small circle on the back of my hand.

We stopped in what felt like the center of the lot, surrounded by trees of various heights, each filling the air with a crisp, wintry fragrance that felt jarringly, inexplicably familiar.

Pierce released my hand but stayed close enough that I could feel the heat coming off him. "Now find the one that calls to you."

"Trees don't talk." I wrapped my arms around my torso, annoyed to realize I already missed the warmth of their hands.

Vix chuckled, the sound low and warm in the cool evening air. "Maybe you're not listening right."

I rolled my eyes so hard I nearly gave myself a headache. "Fine. I'll play your little wintry scavenger hunt game."

A few feet away, a family with two small children giggled as they circled a modest-sized tree. The mom held up her phone, capturing their joy while the dad lifted the smaller child to touch a higher branch. Something twisted in my chest, and I turned away quickly.

"I'll just pick a tree so we can leave." I took a step forward, pretending to inspect the nearest pine with exaggerated interest.

Vix moved behind me. "That's not how this works. You don't pick the tree; it picks you."

"Technically, it's more of a resonance response than a choice." Pierce's eyes tracked my movements with unnerving focus.

I wandered a few steps deeper into the lot, their presence at my back like silent sentinels. "Let me guess, the tree will glow when I find the right one? Sing a little carol?"

My sarcasm hung in the air, unanswered. I turned to catch their reactions, but both men had stopped several paces back, watching me with identical expressions of patient anticipation.

"What?" I crossed my arms defensively.

Pierce nodded toward the rows ahead. "Continue."

With a huff, I spun back around and moved forward, determined to grab the next reasonable-looking tree and declare this mission accomplished. But something strange happened as I advanced through the rows. My steps slowed without conscious direction, and the artificial brightness from the floodlights seemed to dim around the edges of my vision.

The air grew heavier with pine, and beneath it a hint of cinnamon that couldn't possibly be there. My heart thumped harder with each step, a magnetic pull guiding me past tree after tree until I stopped abruptly in front of one nestled in the back corner of the lot.

It wasn't too spectacular, maybe seven feet tall with full, symmetrical branches. Yet something about it made my breath catch. The pull in my chest intensified, like an invisible string drawing me closer.

"This is ridiculous," I whispered, even as my hand reached out on its own accord.

My fingertips brushed the needles, and the world tilted sideways.

Snow crunched underfoot as Dad's hearty laugh echoed through the trees. The scent of pine was so sharp it made my nose tingle. My small hand was in his massive one as we trudged through white drifts.

"This one, Snowflake!" Dad's voice boomed as he pointed to a towering pine. "What do you think?"

I danced around its base, squealing in excitement. "It's perfect, Daddy! Can we decorate it tonight?"

The tree was impossibly tall in our living room, lights hanging at odd angles where I'd insisted on helping. Mom laughed as Dad lifted me to place the star.

I jerked backward, gasping as if I'd been underwater. My lungs burned, vision blurring as I stumbled.

Strong hands caught me from behind, steadying my swaying body. Pierce's chest pressed against my back, one arm wrapping around my waist with surprising gentleness.

"Breathe." His voice vibrated through me, solid and steady against the vertigo threatening to topple me.

I blinked rapidly, trying to clear my vision. "I don't... I can't..."

Pierce turned me slowly until I faced him, his storm-gray eyes searching mine with an intensity that should have been uncomfortable but somehow wasn't. His thumb brushed under my eye, coming away wet.

I hadn't even realized I was crying. "What's happening to me?"

His expression softened in a way I hadn't thought possible. One hand cupped my cheek, his thumb tracing a path along my cheekbone. "You're remembering."

"Remembering what?" I whispered, but deep down, I already knew. The memories felt like mine—were mine—yet somehow felt stolen from someone else's life. A little girl who loved Christmas. A little girl with a father who wasn't a scientist, but something more.

"I can't tell you." Pierce's eyes dropped to my lips for the briefest moment. The air between us charged with electricity, making the hairs on my arms stand up.

"What is this?" I barely heard myself speak as my eyes darted to his lips.

He was close enough that I could see flecks of blue hidden in the gray of his irises. "Let me show you."

His lips met mine with unexpected tenderness. The kiss started slow, a gentle press that rapidly deepened as his hand slid to the back of my neck. My body responded, leaning into him, fingers gripping his shirt to steady myself against a wave of heat.

His control was clear even in this, each movement deliberate yet somehow desperate. When he finally pulled back, my lips tingled with more than the physical sensation.

Another hand brushed my hair back from my face. Vix appeared at my side, his eyes warm and liquid in the Christmas lights overhead.

He didn't say a word, just looked at me like I was something he'd waited a long time for, and then leaned in, slow enough that I could have stopped him. I didn't. I met him halfway.

Vix's kiss coaxed rather than claimed, teasing and retreating until I was chasing his mouth. One hand cupped my cheek while the other traced patterns at the small of my back.

When he broke away, his usual smirk was replaced with something reverent, almost awed.

I stood frozen between them, heart knocking against my ribs like it might break free. The tastes of both men lingered on my lips, different but equally intoxicating. Something had shifted in the universe, rearranging pieces I hadn't known were out of place.

"The tree." My voice sounded far away, even to my own ears. "I want that one."

Pierce's eyebrow arched in surprise, while Vix's face split into a smile that transformed his features from merely handsome to breathtaking.

"It's a perfect tree." Vix's fingers found mine, squeezing gently.

Pierce nodded once. "Absolutely perfect."

CHAPTER 10
CURATED HOLIDAY EXPLOSION

I stood in my kitchen rereading the small white card tucked into the vase of red and white flowers I'd carried home from work. The golden lettering practically twinkled up at me: "You picked the perfect tree. Now let's make it shine."

My stomach flipped in a way that irritated me beyond reason. No signature, but who else would it be from? The reindeer men. The nine magical men who had crashed into my life with all the subtlety of a Christmas parade through a library.

I set the card down and traced the edge of a petal, memories of last night's kisses flashing through my mind like some kind of festive slideshow I couldn't shut off. Pierce's gentle touch. Vix's hungry mouth. The way I'd let both of them consume me.

The doorbell chimed a jaunty rendition of "Jingle Bell Rock," interrupting my thoughts. Yesterday, that would have made me contemplate ripping it off the wall. Today, it only made me roll my eyes. Progress, I supposed.

I opened the door to find Don and Blitz on my doorstep, each clutching sacks large enough to smuggle small children. Don's massive frame filled the doorway like a gentle giant, while Blitz bounced on his heels beside him, practically vibrating with energy.

"We come bearing decorations!" Blitz swept past me into the house before I could protest.

Don followed, ducking slightly like he might bump his head, a soft smile warming his eyes. "Hello, Neve."

"Hi." I felt unexpectedly shy as I closed the door.

My body and brain needed to get the memo that these men were off-limits. Like, priority overnight delivery, certified mail, return receipt requested, whatever it took to make the message stick. Because apparently, my self-preservation instincts had taken a holiday vacation along with my good sense.

I watched as they deposited their haul on my living room floor. They wore matching red T-shirts with *Tree Team* emblazoned across the chest in glittering gold letters. Did these guys all get together and have a shirt-making party?

Blitz opened his sack, pulled out a box labeled *Tree Magic*, and opened it with a dramatic flourish. "Prepare yourself for transformation, Neve North."

"Is the matching outfit thing going to be a regular occurrence? Because I draw the line at wearing anything with pompoms."

Don's quiet chuckle rumbled through the room. "We're honestly pretty restrained today."

"This is restrained?" I arched an eyebrow, noticing the way Don's shirt stretched across his broad shoulders. The man was built like a redwood.

"You should see our ugly sweater collection." Blitz's sharp features softened into a grin that made something warm and unwelcome curl in my belly.

"I'd rather eat coal."

"That can be arranged." Blitz dug through his bag, pulling out strings of lights that seemed to shimmer even unplugged. "We know a guy."

Don moved to the tree that Pierce and Vix had set up. He circled it thoughtfully before kneeling to examine the trunk. "A good solid tree."

I pointed at the bags they were carrying that looked very similar to Santa's sack. "Let's get on with whatever holiday explosion you've brought."

Blitz shot me a look of mock offense. "Excuse me, this is a *curated* holiday explosion."

I wandered closer, peering into Blitz's bag. "Did you rob a Christmas store?"

"Only the good parts." Blitz stepped closer. He smelled like cinnamon and pine, and I wanted to bury my face against him. "Don't worry, we'll go easy on you. First timer and all."

"I'm not a first timer." I shifted my weight and frowned. "I've decorated trees before."

Both men exchanged a look, and Blitz's fingers brushed mine as he handed me a silver ornament. The touch sent a tiny spark up my arm. "Not since you were fifteen, right?"

"How do you know that?" The ornament trembled in my fingers.

Blitz gave a half-shrug, but the casual gesture didn't match the intensity in his eyes. "Just a guess."

It wasn't a guess. His knowing look cut through me like he'd been flipping through my diary.

Shaking my head, I held up the silver ornament, and it caught the light, sending prism-like reflections dancing across my walls. Something about the way the pattern of light sparkled and refracted pulled at me, tugging a thread of memory I didn't know existed.

The great hall. Massive ceilings. A tree stretching toward the sky.

My breath caught as images flooded my mind. Not soft, warm childhood memories that had been trickling back, but something sharper. Harder.

I was fifteen, awkward and furious, standing before an enormous pine. My hands outstretched, trembling with effort as I tried to make the ornaments float onto the branches like I'd seen my father do.

"Focus, Neve. Channel your intention." A tall figure stood beside me, disapproval dripping from every perfect angle of their posture.

The ornaments shook, rose slightly, then crashed to the marble floor, shattering into a thousand glittering shards.

"Perhaps we should try again tomorrow." Their voice was crisp with annoyance.

Ice spread from beneath my feet, crackling across the polished floor.

I inhaled sharply, dropping the ornament. Don's hand shot out, catching it before it hit the ground.

"You okay?" His voice wrapped around me like a blanket.

I nodded too fast, air sticking in my lungs. "Yeah. I just got dizzy."

Don didn't press. He gave me a look that felt like it saw more than it should, then gently placed the ornament back in my hand. "This one belongs near the top."

Blitz didn't joke, didn't tease. For once, his usual sparkle dimmed slightly as he watched me. "It's coming back faster, isn't it?"

I didn't answer. I couldn't. Because, yes, something was cracking open inside me, and I didn't know what would come out once it shattered.

Instead, I turned toward the tree, lifted the ornament, and carefully placed it near the highest branch I could reach. It caught the light again, scattering fragments across the room, and for a moment, it almost felt like magic.

I turned back to the bags of decorations strewn across my living room floor, curious despite my determination to remain aloof. "So, what's the plan here?"

Blitz's face lit up as he pulled out his phone. "First, we need the proper ambiance."

He tapped the screen a few times, and my Bluetooth speaker came to life with "Have Yourself a Merry Little Christmas." The melody was jazzier than the version I knew.

"Music is non-negotiable." Don began methodically untangling a string of warm white lights, his hands moving with surprising delicacy. "These go on first."

I reached for the other end of the lights. "I'll help."

We worked in a weird, comfortable silence for a few minutes. Don led the way around the tree, his height allowing him to reach the uppermost branches while I managed the middle sections.

Blitz circled behind us, fluffing branches with theatrical

precision. "This one's a little droopy. And this one needs more... poof."

"Is 'poof' the technical term?" I handed Don the last section of lights.

Blitz tilted his head, expression tightening as he focused on a stubborn branch. "I have a PhD in Christmas Tree Aesthetics."

"From which university? North Pole State?" It was supposed to be a joke, but something told me I wasn't wrong.

Don's mouth pulled into a slow smile, and Blitz let out a bright laugh that somehow matched the music perfectly.

"Pole Tech." Blitz waved an invisible pennant flag. "Go, Snowmen!"

I snorted, not knowing if he was joking or being serious. I reached into one of the bags and pulled out a glass bird. It sent rainbow prisms dancing across my hands. Something about it felt... familiar.

Don appeared at my side, gently taking a heavy, intricately carved wooden ornament from another bag. "These go toward the bottom. For balance."

"There's a science to this," Blitz insisted, pulling out a shimmering gold ball. "Spatial distribution, color theory, and weight distribution. It's very serious business."

I hung the glass bird on a middle branch. "And here I thought all I had to do was throw stuff on until it looked pretty."

"That's for amateurs." Blitz dramatically placed his gold ornament, then stepped back to assess. "See? Already the lower left quadrant is gold heavy."

"The tree has quadrants now?" I smiled in amusement as I reached for another ornament.

"You can't just hang things willy-nilly, Neve." Blitz's feigned seriousness made Don's shoulders shake with silent laughter.

The playlist shifted to "Santa Baby," and Blitz immediately began singing along, shimmying his shoulders in a ridiculous dance that made me laugh out loud. The sound surprised me. When was the last time I'd laughed like that?

I reached up to place a snowflake, suddenly aware of how

warm I felt. My cheeks flushed, and sweat prickled at my hairline. "It's getting way too hot in here." I walked over to flip on the ceiling fan.

When I turned back, Don and Blitz were exchanging a look. Don raised his eyebrows, and Blitz gave an almost imperceptible shrug.

"What?" I planted my hands on my hips.

"Nothing." Blitz grinned. "I was wondering if you were going to accuse us of tampering with your thermostat next."

I rolled my eyes, reaching back into the bag. "Let's finish this tree before I change my mind."

We continued decorating, the tree slowly transforming into something that looked like it belonged in a magazine spread. Even I had to admit it was beautiful.

"I think the right side needs another red one." I pointed to a bare patch.

Blitz gasped dramatically. "She's getting into it, Don! Quick, document this historic moment!"

I spotted a perfect red ornament and reached for it just as Blitz's hand shot out. Our fingers tangled around the sphere.

"I saw it first!" Blitz tugged playfully.

"It's my tree!" I pulled back, laughing.

"Children, please." Don reached into the fray, but his foot caught on the edge of my area rug.

Everything happened in slow motion: Don stumbling forward, Blitz jerking backward with me still gripping the ornament, the three of us colliding.

I fell against Blitz, and he backed into the couch, taking me with him as his legs buckled. I found myself straddling him, my knees bracketing his thighs, hands braced against his chest.

He didn't move, and his eyes locked with mine. The usual playfulness was replaced with something darker and more intense. His hands came to rest lightly on my waist.

I noticed every point of contact between us: my thighs against his, his chest rising and falling beneath my palms, his fingers flexing on my waist.

Don cleared his throat from somewhere behind me.

Blitz didn't look away. Neither did I.

My body stayed perfectly still, caught in the pull of him. Panic prickled at the edges of it because I hadn't made a single move to get up. Worse, I wasn't sure I wanted to.

The heat of Blitz's body radiated through his T-shirt, warming my palms. His thumbs found the strip of skin right above the waistband of my shorts.

I should have jumped up. Should have made a joke, brushed it off, created distance. Instead, my body betrayed me by sinking a fraction lower against him.

"The ornament survived, at least." Don's deep voice rumbled close to my ear as the couch dipped, and he settled beside us.

Blitz's lips curved into a slow smile. "Neve."

Just my name. Nothing else. But the way he said it, like a question and an answer all at once, sent a shiver of anticipation through my body.

My gaze dropped to his mouth. Why did I want to know what it would feel like against mine?

"I should probably..." I started to shift, but Blitz's hands held me gently in place.

"You should probably do whatever you want to do." His eyes never left mine, an invitation without pressure.

Whatever I wanted? What a dangerous concept. Because what I wanted made absolutely no sense. I wanted to stay right where I was. I wanted to feel the solid strength of Don beside me. I wanted to lean down and press my mouth against Blitz's smiling lips and discover if he tasted like the cinnamon he smelled like.

I wanted all of it, and the force of that want terrified me.

Especially after kissing Pierce and Vix the night before.

Blitz's hand left my waist to trace a line up my arm, across my shoulder, to cup my cheek. "What do you want?"

I turned slightly, my gaze meeting Don's. His eyes were intense, pupils wide with the same hunger I saw in Blitz's. That look made something burn in my core.

Why them?

Blitz's question, along with mine, swirled in my mind, but faded beneath the louder demand of my body. I felt pulled toward them like gravity, like they were essential to my existence in a way I couldn't comprehend.

I leaned forward, closing the distance between Blitz's mouth and mine.

The moment our lips connected, a surge of heat rushed through me. Not a burning flush of embarrassment, but a deep warmth that seemed to spread from my center outward, melting the icy ball of *something* that had been building for days.

Blitz made a sound between a groan and a sigh against my mouth. His lips were soft but insistent, moving against mine with a hunger that matched the thrumming need pulsing through my veins.

One of his hands tangled at the base of my bun, angling my head to deepen the kiss. His tongue traced the seam of my lips, and I opened for him without hesitation, needing more.

Don's hand stroked down my back, following the curve of my spine. His touch ignited trails of pleasure along my skin, even through my shirt. He shifted closer, his breath warm against my neck.

"That's it." Don's lips brushed the sensitive skin right below my ear. "Take what you need from him."

My hips moved, grinding down against Blitz in search of relief from the pressure.

Blitz broke the kiss with a groan. "Fuck, Neve."

Embarrassment would've made sense. So would pulling away and pretending it never happened. But I didn't. I rolled my hips again, watching his eyes flutter closed at the sensation.

Don's teeth scraped gently against the junction where my neck met my shoulder, and I arched into the contact. "You're not ours yet, but you will be." He turned my face toward him, and his mouth claimed mine with a hunger that stole my breath.

His kiss was deep and all-consuming. His tongue swept into my mouth with confident possession, tasting me thoroughly. I moaned against his lips, my body caught between the two men in a way that felt inevitable.

Blitz's hands settled on my hips, guiding my movements as I continued to roll against him. "That's it," he breathed against my collarbone as Don released my mouth. "Show us how good it feels."

Part of me expected to feel mortified grinding desperately against a man I barely knew while another watched hungrily. Instead, I felt powerful. Wanted.

Don's mouth traveled down my neck, leaving a trail of fire wherever his lips touched. His hand splayed across my lower back, pressing me more firmly against Blitz.

Blitz shifted beneath me, adjusting his hips by the tiniest fraction, causing his cock to press against my clit through our clothes in just the right way.

"Oh, fuck," I gasped, my fingers digging into Blitz's shoulders.

The coiling tension snapped. Pleasure hit me in overwhelming waves, spreading outward from where Blitz pressed against me. My thighs trembled, my back arched, and I couldn't stop the desperate sounds escaping my throat.

Don's mouth captured mine again, swallowing my cries as I shuddered through my release. Blitz's hands tightened on my hips, holding me against him as I rode out the aftershocks.

When the intensity finally ebbed, I collapsed forward, my forehead dropping to rest against Blitz's shoulder. Reality slowly filtered back through the haze of pleasure.

What the hell had I just done?

CHAPTER 11
REINDEER ERECTILE DYSFUNCTION

I stared at the Christmas tree, fingers absently tracing the star topper in my hand. The damn thing was taunting me, waiting to be placed at the top of the perfectly decorated tree that was now a monument to my momentary lapse in judgment.

Three days had passed since I'd dry-humped Blitz while Don kissed me senseless. Three days of pretending it hadn't happened. Three days of ignoring the texts from both men, each message more concerned than the last.

What the hell was wrong with me? I'd gone from avoiding Christmas like the plague to grinding on a man named after a famous reindeer while another watched. And let's not forget I'd already kissed two others the night before.

The star glinted as I set it back in its box. I wasn't ready to finish the tree. Finishing meant accepting whatever was happening, and I wasn't there yet.

My phone buzzed.

> Kip: Meet us outside in five. Wear something comfortable!

Great. Another festive adventure with the Christmas crusaders.

I peered through my blinds to confirm my suspicions. Sure enough, the red electric truck idled in front of my house. Except this time, it had twinkling lights around the truck bed and along the doors. I wasn't sure of the legality of placing Christmas lights on vehicles, but I imagined they reined themselves in by not covering the whole thing.

At least it wasn't Blitz or Don. Or Pierce. Or Vix. At this point, I was going to need an Excel document to keep track of them all.

I grabbed my purse, locked up, and steeled myself for whatever holiday nonsense awaited me.

Kip waved enthusiastically from where he held open the truck door for me while Cole sat stoically behind the wheel, his massive frame making the steering wheel look child-sized.

I climbed into the passenger seat. "You're not wearing matching shirts. I'm almost disappointed."

Cole's mouth twitched. "Night off."

I got the distinct feeling that he was lying. "Oh really?"

Kip climbed in the back and leaned forward between the seats. "So, Neve. How's the tree?"

My face heated as I realized they knew about what I'd done with Blitz and Don. Did they know about Pierce and Vix too?

I buckled my seatbelt as the truck pulled away from the curb and sank lower in my seat. "You all must think I'm a hoe, hoe, hoe." I giggled and quickly slapped my hand over my mouth. Where the heck had that come from?

Kip patted my shoulder. "We'll forgive you for that unbelievably cringe pun."

Cole glanced over at me before he turned out of my neighborhood. "We don't think you're a hoe, as you so eloquently put it. We all feel a pull toward you in that way."

"You do?" My thighs involuntarily squeezed together at the thought of nine of them. None of it made any sense. I was usually impartial to romance and was fine without dating and sex.

Kip shifted into the middle seat and leaned forward, close enough that I caught a hint of cinnamon and pine. His eyes, bright and earnest, locked with mine. "I definitely do." His voice was soft but certain, with no trace of his usual playful banter.

There was something so disarmingly sincere about him that I had to look away, pretending to be fascinated by the Christmas lights of a passing house.

Time to change the subject. "Where are we going?"

Cole pulled onto the highway. "Holiday surprise."

"You've all been full of those lately. Almost like you're planning them to be progressively worse for me." I twisted in my seat so I could see Kip better.

Kip laughed. "Maybe we are. We're very coordinated."

"Coordinating through what, the Reindeer Telepathy Network? Do you all have group texts? Is one called 'Operation Make Neve Festive' or something?"

Kip tapped a finger to his temple. "Something like that. Our connection is deeper than phones."

I rolled my eyes. "So what, the nine of you gather in a circle, hold hooves, and beam thoughts into each other's heads? Very efficient."

Cole made an amused noise in the back of his throat. "Not exactly. Herd communication goes through the alpha."

"So there's a reindeer hierarchy? And Rudy's what, the big boss reindeer?" I was making an absolute guess since they all seemed to turn to him, and he was the biggest out of the bunch.

Kip pressed his lips together, clearly trying not to laugh. "You could say that."

My mind raced with questions. Suddenly, I remembered something from a nature documentary I'd watched during a deep Netflix hole one insomnia-filled night.

"Wait a minute. When do your antlers fall off? When I saw Rudy, Dash, and Dane, they still had theirs. Is it too early? Is it the warm temperature here?" The implications hit me like a snowball to the face as I remembered the documentary's narration about reindeer behavior. "Oh shit, it's the middle of your mating season, isn't it? Is that why I want to mount you all? You're giving off horny reindeer pheromones?"

The truck swerved slightly before Cole corrected it, his knuckles turning white on the steering wheel.

Kip's face drained of all color, his freckles standing out more than usual. He swallowed hard, his voice dropping to a whisper. "Neve, you can never talk about antlers falling off to a reindeer's face again."

I blinked, looking between them. They were both dead serious. "What? Why?"

Cole made a low, guttural noise that reminded me of thunder. "Because losing our antlers means we don't have enough magic to fly."

I couldn't help the laugh that escaped. I could get behind them shifting, but flying? That was absurd. "Seriously? Reindeer can't really fly. Plus, losing them is a natural process, isn't it?"

Cole's face was carved from stone, and Kip looked like I'd suggested we eat a baby reindeer for dinner.

"It's not a natural process for magical reindeer. It's like asking a man if he's..." Kip gestured vaguely toward his lap.

"Impotent," Cole finished bluntly.

My mouth formed a perfect O. "Oh. So, reindeer erectile dysfunction?"

Cole's jaw ticked as if he were holding back his true feelings on this topic. "Worse. It's magical dysfunction. It's very serious, Neve."

"Got it. No R.E.D. talk or asking if there are little red pills instead of blue." I held up my hands in surrender, desperate to change the subject away from anything regarding their dicks. "So why are we headed for the golf course? I'm not dressed for eighteen holes."

Cole flicked on the turn signal and steered the truck off the highway onto a side road. "We're not golfing."

A few minutes later, the truck pulled into an empty parking lot.

I groaned when I saw the sign. "An ice rink? You're joking."

"Surprise!" Kip bounced in his seat like a kid on Christmas morning, all talk of antler shedding forgotten.

"I'm wearing a tank top," I protested. "It's going to be freezing in there."

Kip reached behind Cole's seat and produced a large shopping bag. "We came prepared."

"Of course you did." I tried to peer into the bag, already dreading whatever festive monstrosities they'd brought.

Sure enough, Kip pulled out three Christmas sweaters. Mine was eye-searing red with a 3D reindeer face complete with googly eyes and a bell for a nose.

"You can't be serious." I glared at the offending sweater as I took it. The eyes on the reindeer seemed to mock me, as if they knew exactly how ridiculous I'd look. "There has to be a law against forcing someone to wear something that jingles when they walk. I have dignity. Not much, granted, but it exists. Honestly, I'd rather freeze to death."

Cole's eyes met mine as he pulled his sweater over his head. "No, you wouldn't."

Kip nodded solemnly, though his eyes danced with amusement. "Christmas sweaters are sacred traditions."

The word "tradition" hit something inside me, and I wasn't in the truck anymore.

I was sitting on a plush carpet, about six years old, giggling uncontrollably as my father strutted down a makeshift runway in our living room. He wore a sweater with a dancing snowman whose arms moved. Behind him, nine other men waited their turns, each in a more ridiculous sweater than the last.

"Next up," Mom announced in a game show host voice, "Blitzen models this year's 'Snow Much Fun' collection!"

One of the tall men spun dramatically, showing off a sweater covered in tiny fake snowballs that bounced with his movement.

"Ten out of ten!" I shouted, holding up a handmade scorecard.

I blinked back to the present, clutching the sweater to my chest.

"Neve?" Kip's voice was gentle. "You okay?"

I nodded, swallowing the lump in my throat. "Fine. Just... remembered something."

"From before?" Kip's voice lowered, his hand warm on my shoulder.

"Yeah." I pulled the hideous sweater over my head, hiding for a moment. "It was an ugly sweater contest with sweaters even worse than these. My dad was there with a bunch of his friends."

Cole's eyebrows lifted a fraction. "Your memories are returning faster now."

"They're popping up randomly. None of it makes sense." I adjusted the sweater, wincing as the bell jingled.

Kip pulled on his sweater, which had actual working Christmas lights embedded in a tree pattern. "We'll take the random pop-ups."

Tears welled up in my eyes. Why would my two very loving parents send me away and alter my memories? That seemed so cruel.

I pushed open the truck door, eager to escape the claustrophobic cab. "Let's get this over with."

Cole locked the truck and stuffed the keys into his jeans pocket. His sweater was navy blue and covered in glittery snowflakes.

"How come you get the tasteful one?" I gestured at his sweater as we walked toward the entrance.

"Seniority."

"Not fair. I should get seniority. I'm Santa's daughter; that has to be good for something." I stopped abruptly, and Kip ran into me, his arms circling my waist to stop me from face-planting.

I knew I'd already considered it, but now the thought was stronger, like it wasn't being tamped down by some subliminal force in my brain. It felt like discovering a door in a familiar wall that had always been there but was painted to match the background perfectly until this moment.

My memories weren't just missing; they'd been deliberately hidden from me. The name "Santa" echoed in my skull, too loud and too obvious to ignore.

My dad. The man in every song, every story, every childhood dream, and he was mine.

And now, standing here in this ridiculous jingling sweater with Kip's calming presence behind me, the barriers seemed to be crumbling faster than a gingerbread house in July.

My chest ached with a strange mix of awe and grief, like I'd just stumbled across the truth of who I was and realized how much of myself I'd lost without it.

"Why are my memories all over the place?" I turned, looking at both men for answers.

"It's complicated." Cole crossed his arms, appearing uncomfortable for the first time.

"It's really not. You guys can't tell me anything, but why? Is there a spell? Can you only be in the North Pole to talk about the North Pole?" I ran through all of my interactions with them and thought about how I steered myself away from anything festive. "Jingle is code for the North Pole."

Kip's eyes widened, and then the tight line of his lips broke into his usual smile. "It is, but you usually forget it pretty quickly, which is why we can't just tell you everything. The magic won't let us."

"I forget?" My brows furrowed so hard that I really hoped a permanent crease didn't form. "So I've connected myself to my dad being Santa and the North Pole already?"

"Briefly. You've been away for so long that it's hard for the magic to grant you permission to know. If we were to stay away for too long, the magic would push us away from the truth, too." Cole shrugged as if this wasn't a major piece of the puzzle he was giving me.

"So in a few minutes, I might forget all of this?"

Kip took my hand, entwining our fingers. "Yes. We think when you fight your joy, it's a snowball effect in your brain with the magic. Also, the distance from home doesn't help."

Cole's gaze was steady on mine. "You won't hold on to it yet. The magic won't let you. At least not with how long you've been away and not until you're closer to the North Pole."

"The North Pole?" I blinked, confused. "What does that have to do with anything?"

Cole sighed and looked at Kip. "This is going to be difficult if we don't take her farther north."

Kip squeezed my hand, bringing me back from the fog that had settled over my thoughts. "The ice rink? Remember? We were going to skate?"

"Right." I shook my head, feeling like I'd just woken up. What had we been talking about? Something important, something that filled me with longing, but it was gone now. "Time to embarrass myself."

Cole held the door open. "We reserved the rink."

A part of me wanted to run back to the truck, drive home, and lock myself away from all of this holiday chaos they kept dragging me into. But another part, which was growing stronger with each cookie decorated and tree trimmed, wanted to step inside.

"Fine." I marched through the door, the bell on my sweater jingling with each step. "I'm warning you both now, I have the grace of a drunk reindeer on ice."

"A drunk reindeer on the ice would win a gold medal." Kip sounded serious, but when I looked back over my shoulder, the lights on his sweater highlighted his grin.

The skating rink was predictably freezing, though not as cold as I'd expected. Maybe I was getting used to it. Or maybe the whole "frost demon" thing was working in my favor for once.

A strange sense of homecoming washed over me as I stared at the ice. The gleaming surface stretched before me, inviting in a way I couldn't quite explain.

I stood transfixed at the edge of the rink, my fingers tingling with an inexplicable anticipation, as if my body remembered something my mind had misplaced. And for once, I didn't feel like running away.

CHAPTER 12
HOT CHOCOLATE

I eyed the rental skates Cole pulled from the skate rental counter with the same enthusiasm I'd give a pair of rusty bear traps. They were white, and because everything about this situation was absurdly festive, they were trimmed with red and green laces.

"How did you manage to rent this entire place without staff?" I reluctantly sat on a bench, still feeling strangely drawn to the ice.

Cole knelt in front of me with the skates, his massive frame somehow making the bench look like dollhouse furniture. "I know people."

"You know people who just hand over keys to ice rinks?" I kicked off my shoes.

Kip dropped onto the bench beside me, his knee bumping mine. "Cole can be very convincing."

Cole pulled off my ankle socks with a frown. "These won't do." With a quick flick of the wrist, a pair of thick red and green striped socks appeared.

"Those are completely unnecessary." I tried to pull my foot away, but he took my ankle in his hand. Tingles shot up my leg, and I bit my lip.

"They're cute." Kip grabbed one from Cole and knelt at my other leg.

"I can put on my own—" My protest died as Kip grabbed my other ankle.

I was very aware of how they placed my legs on their knees as they pulled on my socks, their fingers brushing over my skin in a way that felt anything but innocent.

Kip gave me a knowing smirk as he pulled on one of my skates and laced it up. "There's nothing worse than wobbly ankles on the ice."

The overhead string lights cast everything in a warm golden glow, making everything seem sexier than it was. At least, that's what I was telling myself.

Nothing was sexy about two attractive men kneeling in front of a woman putting on her socks and skates. Nope. Nothing at all.

Cole pulled my laces. "Too tight?" His dark eyes flicked up to mine, amusement dancing in them. "You need them nice and snug, so you don't break an ankle when you inevitably wipe out."

My mouth fell open in shock. I would have expected that from Kip, but not Cole. "Your confidence in me is truly inspiring."

Kip stood, producing a pair of fuzzy red gloves from literally nowhere. One moment his hands were empty; the next, he had gloves. "For your hands." He held them out expectantly.

"Really? Are you sure they aren't for your antlers?" I held out my hands, letting him tug them into place.

The gloves fit perfectly, and that twisted something inside me. It was one thing for Kip to think about my hands being cold, but another entirely for him to get them exactly right.

I watched as Kip and Cole effortlessly slipped into their own custom black skates that had clearly seen plenty of ice time. "Did you bring your entire wardrobe to Palm Springs? Seems excessive. Where are you all staying anyway?"

Cole tightened his laces with the ease of someone who had done it a million times. "We're staying in a place outside of town."

"Nine of you in one place?" I raised an eyebrow. "That must be... cozy."

Kip grinned, standing up to test his skates. "We're used to close quarters."

I stood up, a bit wobbly, and Cole's hand immediately shot out to steady me. "Do you all live together when you're not stalking Christmas-hating women?" I gripped his arm harder than necessary, blaming it on the blades beneath my feet and not the feel of his muscles under my fingers.

Kip moved with perfect balance like he'd been born on ice. "We've lived together since we formed a herd. Makes logistics easier."

I shuffled forward, clinging to Cole like a koala to a eucalyptus tree. "And how long ago was that? For all I know, you guys could have the lifespan of vampires or something. You could be secretly three hundred years old with a taste for blood instead of cookies."

Cole let out a quiet chuckle while Kip burst into full-on laughter, his whole face lighting up.

"What? It's a legitimate question! I'm trying to figure out if I'm dealing with immortal beings or just unnaturally tall men with unexplained magical powers." I glared at them both, which only made Kip laugh harder.

"We're not vampires." Cole guided me toward the ice entrance with the patience of someone escorting a toddler. "Though Kip does have a thing for dramatic capes."

"We do age slower, but we're not that much older than you. We've been a complete herd of nine for about a decade now. Been working our way up the ranks in terms of reindeer herds, hoping to one day..." He trailed off, eyes flicking to Cole like he wasn't sure if he should continue.

Cole's expression shifted to something more serious. "The top herd gets the best job."

"Which is what exactly? Prime-time Christmas Eve flying? Special access to the cookie vault?" I took a tentative step onto the ice and immediately felt my feet trying to go in opposite directions.

Cole's arm circled my waist, pulling me against his side as my ankles betrayed me. His body was hot against mine, and I couldn't decide if I wanted to push away or burrow closer.

"Something like that," he murmured, his breath warm against my hair.

Kip skated a lazy circle around us, hands clasped behind his back. "Ready for your first lesson, Ms. North?"

I looked down at the gleaming ice beneath my skates and the strong arms keeping me upright. Whatever game these men were playing, I was already in too deep to back out now. "Ready as I'll ever be."

Kip glided backward with effortless grace, positioning himself in front of me and taking hold of my hips. "Keep your eyes on me and your knees slightly bent."

The feel of his strong hands on my hips, coupled with Cole's steady presence behind me, created a Neve sandwich I hadn't ordered but couldn't complain about.

"Like this?" I bent my knees slightly, trying to ignore how Kip's thumbs were making tiny circles against my hipbones through my jeans.

Cole's hand slid from my waist to the small of my back. "Weight centered, not too far forward or back."

"Is this what elves do in the off-season? Teach ice skating?" I wobbled slightly, and both men's grips tightened.

Kip's mouth quirked up at one corner. "We're not elves. I'm offended you can't tell the difference."

I snorted. "Sorry, I missed the class on 'Identifying Magical Christmas Creatures 101.'"

My feet found their rhythm, muscle memory awakening like someone had flipped a switch. My body remembered the glide, the balance, the sensation of floating across ice.

"Would you look at that." Cole's hand now barely touched my back.

Kip seemed surprised as I began moving more confidently. "Didn't you say you couldn't skate?"

I shifted my weight, preparing to break away from their

hold. "Apparently, it's like riding a bike. A bike I don't remember ever learning to ride."

My body hummed with a peculiar joy as I pushed forward, breaking free from their grasp and gliding across the ice with surprising control. I skated around the rink, building confidence and getting used to the new way momentum moved me forward.

"Look at you go!" Kip caught up after a while, skating backward in front of me, holding out his hands.

I took them, electricity zinging through my fingers even through my gloves. The moment our hands connected, his eyes lit up, and he yanked me forward with unexpected force.

"Whoa!" My feet scrambled to keep up as he pulled me along, building momentum with each passing second.

Kip's grin widened as we picked up speed. "Trust the ice, Neve!"

Easy for him to say when he wasn't the one being dragged across a frozen death trap. My legs wobbled beneath me but somehow kept pace as we flew around the rink.

"Ready for the handoff?" Kip's tone suggested he knew I wasn't, and before I could determine what 'handoff' meant, he spun me in a circle and released me.

I sailed across the ice, arms pinwheeling, heart lodged somewhere in my throat as momentum carried me straight toward Cole, who stood with his arms open like this was all part of some choreographed routine.

"I can't stop!" My voice came out as a panicked squeak.

Cole's expression never changed as I barreled toward him. "You don't need to."

I crashed into his chest with enough force to knock the wind out of my lungs but not enough to budge him an inch. His arms wrapped around me, steadying us both as I clung to his sweater.

"That was completely unnecessary," I mumbled against the wool.

"Was it?" Cole's voice was teasing.

The overhead speakers crackled as the music changed to a new song, and the opening notes of "Carol of the Bells" filled the rink.

I was six years old, standing on a frozen pond much larger than this rink. The northern lights danced overhead as Dad held my hands, pulling me around in circles while this exact song played from somewhere. My little legs moved instinctively, finding a rhythm in the music. His silver beard sparkled with frost, and his laughter echoed across the ice.

"That's it, Snowflake! You're a natural, like your mother!"

"Neve?" Kip's voice pulled me back, the memory slipping away like smoke.

I blinked rapidly, focusing on Cole's concerned expression as he studied my face.

"I remembered something." My voice sounded strange to my own ears. "I've skated before. With my dad."

Kip glided to a stop beside us, his hand finding my shoulder. "Everything okay?"

"Yeah, just... déjà vu." I pushed away from Cole, suddenly self-conscious about how long I'd been plastered against him. "I think I've had enough skating."

Cole nodded, his eyes never leaving my face. "We should probably head out anyway."

"Are we done with Christmas spirit activities for the day?" I attempted to sound relieved rather than disappointed as we made our way toward the exit.

Kip's freckled face broke into a wide grin. "Not quite. We've got one more stop planned."

I groaned dramatically while untying my skates, ignoring the flutter of anticipation. "Let me guess... building gingerbread houses while carolers serenade us?"

"That's a good idea." Cole knelt to help remove my skates. "You'll like this next activity more, though."

"Your track record of knowing what I'll like is questionable at best." I wiggled my toes, freed from the rental skates.

Kip left on my festive socks and helped me into my shoes. "You smiled at least seventeen times. I counted."

"I did not." I absolutely had.

Cole stood, making his and Kip's skates vanish before my eyes. "This next thing is a surprise."

"Is it really a surprise when I know it'll involve tinsel and Christmas magic?" I stood, feeling weird without my skates on.

Kip's eyes gleamed in a way that was a sure sign that mischief was brewing. What were they up to now? "Some surprises are worth the wait, Neve."

I tried to ignore the way my name sounded in his mouth. "Fine. Lead the way."

THE DRIVE from the rink passed in comfortable silence, with Kip leaning forward between Cole and me to find a Christmas station. I'd given up protesting the holiday music, especially because it seemed to help jog my memory.

I *wanted* to remember.

When I woke up from this fever dream that I was in, I was going to invest in a good therapist.

We climbed into the hills, the city lights of Palm Springs spreading out below us.

"Where exactly are we going?" I pressed my forehead against the cool window, watching the lights below.

"Somewhere quiet," was all Cole gave me, his voice a low rumble that was barely audible over the Christmas carol playing softly through the speakers.

I snorted, rolling my eyes. "That's not ominous at all. Nothing says, 'trust me' like being vague about our destination while driving into the hills at night."

"Don't worry, we're not taking you to our secret murder cabin." Kip's face split into a grin that was meant to be reassuring but somehow made me more suspicious.

"The fact that you specified 'murder cabin' rather than just 'cabin' is concerning." I crossed my arms, fighting the smile that threatened to ruin my mock suspicion.

"I can't deny that our intentions aren't entirely good." The truck slowed as Cole turned down a road and pulled into a small turnout near the edge of a cliff.

My breath caught at the sight of Palm Springs glittering below us like a carpet of diamonds.

Kip was out of the truck before I could unbuckle, practically vibrating with excitement. There was something contagious about his joy, and I smiled as I climbed out of the truck.

The desert night air immediately bit at my cheeks. The sky stretched endlessly above us, impossibly vast and scattered with more stars than I'd ever seen in the city.

Kip dropped the tailgate and shook out a blanket with a dramatic flourish before spreading it out. "Your throne awaits." He offered his hand with an exaggerated bow.

I hesitated, eyeing the makeshift seating arrangement. "Won't we freeze our asses off?" My one gripe about Palm Springs was how chilly it got at night.

Cole shut the back door of the truck, a thermos in one hand and a small silver flask and bag in the other. "That's what this is for."

The three of us sat with our legs dangling off the edge, the city lights sprawling below us as if we were sitting on the edge of the world.

Kip pushed up the sleeves of his sweater, revealing his muscular forearms. He took the thermos from Cole and unscrewed the top, releasing a cloud of fragrant steam into the night air. "Hot chocolate delivery, coming right up."

"Of course it's hot chocolate." I rolled my eyes but couldn't fight the smile tugging at my lips.

Cole pulled three Christmas-themed travel mugs from the bag he had, poured in a shot of cinnamon liquor, and handed them one by one to Kip.

I took a mug from him and inhaled the aroma. "Thanks."

He nudged my shoulder. "This is my special recipe. The secret ingredient is love."

Cole gazed out at the lights below, his profile outlined in starlight. "It's his grandmother's recipe. He makes it every year at the..."

The moment the hot chocolate touched my tongue, the world around me dissolved.

I was fourteen, steam rising around me as I stirred the heavy copper pot on the stove. The grand kitchen of the North Pole stretched endlessly in both directions, with counters dusted with flour, spices in glass jars reflecting the light, and elves bustling about with trays of sugar cookies and candy canes.

"Careful there, Miss Neve!" a man in a green apron called out as I ladled the hot liquid, filling mugs one by one on my delivery tray.

"I've got it, Figgy!" I bit my lip in concentration as I began sprinkling a special blend of spices on the hot chocolate before adding marshmallows I'd made the day before. "Dad says I make the best hot chocolate in the North Pole."

"Better than Hollyberry? She'll jinx your mittens if she hears that!"

I giggled, placing the final touch of powdered candy cane on the tops.

"Shouldn't you be practicing your magic instead of playing kitchen elf?" A man's sharp voice cut through the warmth.

My hand jerked, sending peppermint dust onto the counter. "I... I was helping."

"You're getting in the way."

Heat flashed through my veins, followed instantly by bone-deep cold. My fingers tingled, magic rising beneath my skin. It was too much, too fast.

One of the mugs shuddered, then exploded with a sharp crack, sending scalding cocoa flying right onto Figgy's arm. His yelp of pain silenced the kitchen instantly.

"I'm sorry! I didn't mean—" My voice caught as frost crept across the remaining mugs, cracking two more.

The man's voice cut like ice. "See? You can't control it. You'll never—"

My mug shook violently in my hand as reality crashed back in. The lid popped off as if it were a pot under too much pressure, the cocoa inside surging upward.

It erupted like a chocolate volcano, splashing across Kip's forearm.

I watched in horror as angry red blotches instantly appeared on his skin. My mind was simultaneously in the present and trapped in that decades-old memory. The energy inside me was spiraling out of control, and I didn't know how to stop it.

CHAPTER 13
SWEET BABY REINDEER

K ip jerked back, hot chocolate dripping from his forearm, his face contorted in pain. "Sweet baby reindeer, that's hot."

I froze, paralyzed by what had just happened and what I remembered. The mug slipped from my fingers, hitting the edge of the tailgate as it fell to the ground. Wind whipped my hair across my face with sudden fury, and the temperature seemed to plummet in seconds.

"I'm so sorry. I didn't... I can't..." My teeth started chattering, not from the cold but from something deeper, more primal. Fear. The same fear I'd felt in that kitchen memory.

Something white drifted past my peripheral vision. A snowflake. Then another. In Palm Springs. In the desert.

Cole moved with surprising speed, positioning himself directly in front of me. His massive frame shielded me from the wind that howled around us.

"Neve. Look at me." His hands, impossibly warm, cupped my face. "Focus on my voice. You're safe."

I tried to look past him at Kip, panic rising. "But he's—"

"I'm fine." Kip appeared at Cole's shoulder. The angry red mark on his arm was already fading to pink before my eyes. "See? Reindeer healing. Pretty neat party trick."

My pulse thudded, and my breath came in shallow gasps.

"The hot chocolate... I was at the North Pole. I was fourteen, and I lost control and hurt someone and—"

"Breathe." Cole's thumbs traced small circles on my cheekbones. His eyes anchored me, steady as stone. "In through your nose. Out through your mouth."

I struggled to follow his instructions, but my mind kept flashing back to that kitchen, to the elf's cry of pain, to the man's cutting words. *You can't control it.*

"You're spiraling." Cole's forehead pressed against mine. "Stay with us."

A snowflake landed on my eyelash. Another on my nose. The desert sky was spitting snow around us in a circle, as if we were inside a snow globe someone had shaken.

"I can't make it stop." My voice cracked with the admission. "I don't know how."

Cole's eyes darkened, determined. "Yes, you do."

Before I could argue, his mouth descended on mine. His lips were firm but gentle, tasting of chocolate and cinnamon whiskey. The contact sent a jolt through my system, like touching a live wire. He deepened the kiss, his tongue sweeping in with a confidence that made my knees weak.

The wind died down, and the snowflakes hung suspended in the air around us for one impossible moment before dissolving into nothing.

Cole pulled back enough to look into my eyes, his expression intense. "Better?"

I nodded, still reeling from both the kiss and the abrupt end to the weather anomaly.

"Let's make sure." Kip's voice was husky as he moved in next to Cole.

His hands tangled in my hair, angling my head as he claimed my mouth with unmistakable hunger. He tasted sweeter, the chocolate more pronounced on his tongue as it slid against mine. I melted into him, my hands fisting in his sweater to keep myself upright.

The cold that had radiated from my core moments ago

transformed into molten heat, pooling low in my belly and spreading outward until my fingertips tingled with it.

When Kip finally pulled away, his eyes glowed faintly in the darkness, his freckled face flushed with desire.

"Holy shit," I whispered, looking between the two men. "Is that how you solve all magical emergencies? Kiss the evil snow witch until she stops freaking out?"

"You're not evil." Cole's thumb danced across my bottom lip, making me forget for a moment what had even set me off.

I looked between the men who'd just kissed my impending blizzard into submission as they exchanged a look I couldn't quite interpret.

Cole's fingers brushed my cheek, drawing my attention back to him. "Do you want to talk about what you remembered?"

I shook my head, my throat tight. The memory of that kitchen, of my younger self losing control, felt like a bruise I wasn't ready to press on. "No, I just want to forget it happened."

His eyes darkened, searching mine. "Are you sure that's what you need?"

"Yes." The word came out more breathless than I intended. "Please."

Kip stepped closer, his fingers tangling with mine. "We can help with that."

Cole's hand slid from my face to the nape of my neck, his thumb pressing gently against my pulse point. "Tell us to stop, and we will."

I nodded, unable to form words as his mouth descended on mine again. This time, there was nothing gentle about it. His kiss was demanding and consuming, as if he wanted to draw out every thought from my mind and replace it with pure sensation.

Kip moved behind me, his hands finding my waist. His lips brushed the sensitive spot below my ear, making me gasp into Cole's mouth. "Is this okay?"

"More than okay." I broke away from Cole long enough to turn my head and catch Kip's mouth with mine.

Cole's hands found the hem of my jeans, unbuttoning them while Kip's fingers played with the edge of my sweater, lifting it just enough to expose a strip of skin above my waistband. The cool night air kissed my flesh, a sharp contrast to the heat building inside me.

"Too cold?" Kip's teeth grazed my earlobe.

I shook my head, arching into his touch as Cole's fingers dipped beneath my jeans, teasing along the edge of my underwear.

Cole backed me toward the tailgate, his massive frame crowding me in a way that made it hard to think. When my ass hit the metal edge, he lifted me effortlessly, setting me on the tailgate. His hands moved to my ankles, slowly removing one boot, then the other, his eyes never leaving mine.

"I've been thinking about this all night." Cole's fingers hooked into my jeans, tugging them down my legs.

Kip climbed onto the tailgate beside me, his hands finding the bottom of my sweater again. "Can I take this off?"

I lifted my arms in silent permission, but he only pushed it up, bunching the fabric above my breasts along with my bra. The night air pebbled my nipples instantly, drawing a satisfied sound from Kip.

"Fuck, look at you." His thumb brushed over one hardened peak, sending a jolt straight between my legs.

Cole finished removing my jeans and underwear in one efficient movement, leaving me bare from the waist down. I should have felt vulnerable and exposed on the tailgate, but all I felt was a heady surge of power at the naked hunger in their eyes.

"Anyone could see us," I whispered, even as I widened my knees at Cole's gentle urging. "Drones."

Kip's mouth closed over my nipple, his tongue circling the sensitive flesh. He released it with a wet pop. "We repel flying objects." His hand slid up my inner thigh, stopping short of where I wanted him.

Cole dropped to his knees between my legs, his broad shoulders pushing my thighs wider. "Tell me what you want, Neve."

I threaded my fingers through his hair, attempting to guide him where I needed him. "Your mouth. Please."

A smirk crossed his face, there and gone in an instant. "Since you asked so nicely."

At the first swipe of his tongue, I fell back onto my elbows, a strangled moan escaping. He settled in, licking and sucking with single-minded determination. Kip's mouth moved between my breasts, lavishing each with equal attention while his fingers plucked and rolled my nipples.

"The sounds you make." Kip's voice was strained as he kissed his way up to my neck.

Cole hummed against me, the vibration sending a fresh wave of pleasure coursing through my body. His tongue circled my clit before dipping lower, teasing at my entrance. When he pushed inside, I cried out, my hips bucking against his face.

"That's it." Kip's hand replaced his mouth on my breast, squeezing hard enough to walk the line between pleasure and pain. "Show us how good we make you feel."

Cole's fingers joined his tongue, one thick digit pressing inside me while his mouth focused on the bundle of nerves at my center. It pushed me toward an edge I was desperate to fall over.

"More, please," I begged, not even sure what I was asking for.

Cole seemed to understand. He added a second finger, curling them inside me to hit a spot that made stars explode behind my eyelids. My thighs began to tremble, my back arching.

Kip twisted my nipple between his fingers, sending even more heat between my legs. "You should see yourself, Neve. Spread out like a fucking feast."

Cole pulled back, his lips shiny with evidence of my arousal. "I want to feel you come on my tongue."

His mouth returned to me with renewed fervor, his fingers pumping in a rhythm that matched the pressure of his tongue. Kip leaned down, capturing my mouth in a bruising kiss that swallowed my increasingly desperate moans.

The tension built until I was a taut wire ready to snap. Cole curled his fingers once more, sucking hard on my clit, and I shattered. The orgasm ripped through me with such intensity that I nearly screamed, my body nearly levitating as pleasure crashed over me.

Cole worked me through it, easing off only when I whimpered from oversensitivity. He pressed a kiss to my inner thigh, his scruff leaving a pleasant burn on my skin. "Beautiful."

I lay there panting, staring up at the night sky, my mind blissfully empty of everything except the lingering pulses of my orgasm. Kip brushed hair from my forehead, his expression soft with wonder.

"Better?" His voice held a hint of smugness.

I nodded, my limbs feeling pleasantly heavy. "Much."

Cole rose from his knees, adjusting himself through his jeans with a grimace that told me he was far from comfortable. I reached for him, wanting to return the favor, but he caught my hand.

"Tonight was about you." He brought my palm to his lips, pressing a kiss to the center. "We have time."

Kip helped me sit up, gently pulling my sweater and bra back into place. "Cole's right. Besides, your first time with us shouldn't be on the back of a pickup truck."

Heat flooded my cheeks at the implication. "Us?"

Cole slid my underwear back up my legs, the corner of his mouth lifting in a rare full smile. "If that's what you want."

My mind filled with images so explicit my cheeks burned. "I... yes. That's definitely what I want." And I wanted it with all nine of them.

I stood on shaky legs, letting Cole button my jeans while Kip helped me back into my boots. The tenderness in their actions, after what we'd just done, made something warm unfurl in my chest. They took such good care of me.

"Thank you." I wasn't sure if I was thanking them for the mind-blowing orgasm or for helping me forget the memory that had triggered my magical meltdown.

Cole's hand cupped my cheek, his thumb tracing my lower

lip. "You never have to thank us for something we wanted as badly as you did."

I leaned into his touch, my body still humming.

Kip wrapped an arm around my waist, pressing a kiss to my temple. "Just wait."

The promise in his voice sent a fresh surge of heat to my core. I looked between them, these two men who had seen me at my most vulnerable, magically and now physically, and somehow still wanted me.

CHAPTER 14
FROZEN IN TIME

I perched on the couch, legs tucked beneath me, surveying the bizarre supernatural board meeting taking place in my living room. Empty takeout containers littered every surface, evidence of the Mexican food massacre that had just occurred. Seriously, these men ate like they were prepping for hibernation—if reindeer hibernated, which I was pretty sure they didn't.

Dane crunched into another tortilla chip, sending crumbs cascading down his shirt. "We should do something Christmassy tomorrow. Maybe caroling?"

I winced. The only thing worse than listening to Christmas music was being forced to sing it.

Don finished licking salsa off his fingers. "I think we've made excellent progress this week."

Kip grinned at me from his spot on the floor, a knowing glint in his eye that made heat rush to my cheeks. Our cliff-side activities were apparently considered "progress."

"Neve's looking less like she wants to murder candy canes on sight," Cole added, his teasing voice stirring something in me that had nothing to do with Christmas spirit.

I rolled my eyes. "I never wanted to murder candy canes. Just the people wielding them as weapons of mass cheer."

Pierce snorted from his position by the window. "An improvement."

My gaze drifted to the back of the room where Rudy stood, arms crossed, keeping his distance as usual. While the others had taken turns dragging me through their Christmas spirit boot camp, Rudy had remained conspicuously absent. I watched him as Blitz cracked a joke, and eight of them laughed. Rudy remained silent with an indifferent expression. Why did he keep himself apart? Why, when the others seemed so determined to pull me in, did he push himself away? And why did his distance bother me so much?

I stared at my fingernails, picking at the remnants of sparkly black polish I'd applied before this had all started. The color was already chipping away, which felt oddly symbolic.

"So what exactly happens next?" I glanced up, finding all of them watching me.

Dash leaned forward, elbows on his knees. "Your memories are coming at you faster now, and your magic is stronger. I think it's time to move farther north."

My stomach twisted at the word "magic." The hot chocolate explosion had been bad enough. What if next time it was worse? What if I hurt someone who didn't have superior healing?

"I'm not abandoning my life here." I gestured around my living room, at the stupid yet somehow charming Christmas decorations my house was infested with. "Palm Springs is my home."

Dash's eyebrows pulled together as he studied me. "Is working on divorces really what you want? Spending your days watching people tear apart what they once built?"

The question hit a nerve I didn't know was exposed. Before I could form a response, Vix swung his legs off the armrest where he'd been lounging. "You should quit and focus on studying for the bar. Third time's the charm, right?"

My mouth fell open. "How did you know I haven't passed?"

The room went silent as eight reindeer men found the ceiling, floor, and walls absolutely fascinating. All except Rudy, who was intently focused on me.

Heat crawled up my neck. "I've failed twice." The humiliation prickled across my skin like tiny needles. I'd told no one except Mia about the second failure. My parents didn't even know.

Blitz's fingers drummed against the coffee table. "Your magic is fighting," he muttered.

Dane slid closer on the couch, his thigh pressed warmly against mine. "You're brilliant, but law isn't your true calling."

My throat tightened. "And what exactly is my calling? Professional reindeer wrangler?"

I couldn't quite find what I really wanted to say. Even with the memories that had come back to me, the details faded quickly. I could remember skating, my dad wearing a Christmas sweater, and making hot chocolate, but all the finer details and imagery were fuzzy at best. It was as if a blackout curtain had been swapped out for one that let some light in.

I felt cornered, trapped between what my memories were hinting at and the person I'd spent over a decade becoming.

My gaze drifted to the one person who hadn't weighed in.

"What do you think, Rudy?"

The towering man didn't move from where he was leaning on a barstool at my counter, his ankles crossed. For the first time all evening, those dark eyes fixed directly on mine.

"We need to move farther north." It was direct and utterly dispassionate.

"North? Like Sacramento or San Francisco?" My voice sounded small even to my own ears because I knew he didn't mean anywhere in California.

"Farther."

"Okay, I could do Seattle." My frown deepened as Rudy shook his head. "I draw the line at snowy tundra."

Pierce rubbed his chin. "Vancouver might work. Possibly Anchorage."

I wrapped my arms around myself, already feeling the cold

seeping in. At least this time, it wasn't from wayward magic. "I have a job. A house. A life."

Kip's fingers brushed my ankle from his spot on the floor next to the couch, his touch gentle but insistent. "A life you've been sleepwalking through."

I swallowed hard. "So what, I just pack up and go? Where exactly?"

"We can vote," Cole suggested.

"Lake Tahoe might be a good choice." Dash's eyes brightened with possibility as he leaned forward. "Not too far from your life here, but with enough elevation and natural energy to help. Plus, it's beautiful."

Everyone started talking at once, excitement in their voices. My head spun with the casual way they discussed uprooting my entire existence. I pictured snow-dusted pines and glittering water, so different from my desert sanctuary, and scrunched my nose in distaste.

Rudy's voice cut through the chatter. "We're going to Klarhaven. We leave in an hour. The decision is final."

The others exchanged glances that ranged from surprise to unease.

It sounded exactly like the kind of place that would appear on one of those "World's Most Remote Locations" lists where mail arrives by dogsled once a month and everyone knows how to skin a moose. Perfect for magical reindeer men, but not for a California girl who considered a light sweater adequate winter preparation.

"Hold on." I shot to my feet, nearly knocking Dane sideways. "First of all, we're not going anywhere in an hour. Second, no one's decided anything, and third, where the actual hell is Klarhaven?"

Dash stood, his hands raised in a placating gesture. "Klarhaven is a small town up north." He turned toward the stoic giant. "Don't you think that's too much, too soon? We've only restored a fraction of her Christmas spirit. The place is... intense."

Rudy's expression didn't change, but his jaw ticked almost imperceptibly. "She needs immersion."

Pierce moved to stand beside Rudy. "With Neve's powers manifesting so unpredictably, Klarhaven might be our best option. The town has natural wards. If something goes wrong..." His eyes flicked to me. "The damage would be contained."

"Damage?" I sputtered. "What damage? Like the hot chocolate thing? I'm not an unstable nuclear reactor!"

At least I hoped I wasn't.

Blitz bounced up from his spot on the floor, excitement radiating off him like a dog about to get the zoomies. "So if we're going to Klarhaven, are we hitting Reinberg too? I miss those little maple candies they sell at The Sugar Shack. Plus, the winter festival's starting soon, right?"

"Yes, Reinberg too." Rudy's deep voice cut through the excitement. "Full immersion. We need to rip off the Band-Aid."

I crossed my arms. "Hello? I'm still here, and I haven't agreed to any of this!"

A strange choking sound drew everyone's attention to Vix, who had paled at the mention of Reinberg. His usual smirk had vanished, replaced by something almost like dread.

Don raised an eyebrow. "Problem, Vix?"

Vix slumped further into his chair, very interested in a loose thread on his shirt. "No problem. Just, you know, considerations. Maybe I should stay behind. Or wear a disguise. Or legally change my name."

Kip burst into laughter, clutching his stomach. "Oh man, they still haven't forgiven you? It's been three years!"

"What happened?" I demanded, momentarily distracted from my protest.

Vix's eyes narrowed at Kip. "It wasn't my fault. How was I supposed to know those ice sculptures weren't load-bearing?"

Cole shook his head, a smile playing at his lips. "You tried to pose on one."

Vix threw his hands up. "They looked way sturdier than they were!"

"You brought down half the display," Don added quietly.

"Minor details." Vix waved dismissively. "The point is, I might not be welcomed back with open arms."

"Or at all," Dash muttered.

My head swiveled between them as they continued discussing Vix's apparent banishment from this Reinberg place. My breathing quickened as reality sank in. They were serious. They expected me to pack up and leave with them to some winter wonderland I'd never heard of.

"Neve would love the winter market." Dane grinned, his eyes bright with memories. "There are those little star lanterns they hang between all the booths, and the ice rink in the town square is better than any indoor facility."

"Reindeer sleigh rides are a tourist favorite, but we could arrange a special one for her." Cole rubbed his hands together as if he were plotting already.

"Hot spiced wine at the Frostbite Inn." Pierce's eyes softened slightly as he licked his lips. "Definitely need to go there."

"Then there's the enormous gingerbread village Snowshoe Bakery builds every year." Kip clasped his hands under his chin, and it would have been cute if their talk about Christmas wasn't grating on my nerves.

"Don't forget the music you can hear throughout the town and the carolers in the evening." Don's voice was full of nostalgia.

"The highlight is the thirty-foot tree they light up on the first night of the festival." Blitz went to my tree, gently touching an ornament.

I felt like I was suffocating under an avalanche of Christmas cheer. Each suggestion hit me like a physical blow, my anxiety climbing with each festive image they painted. Ice rinks. Carolers. Gingerbread. Sleigh rides. Everything I'd spent years avoiding.

The temperature in the room dropped dramatically, but no one seemed to notice as they continued their enthusiastic planning of my Christmas kidnapping.

"I could probably sneak into Reinberg if I wear a hat," Vix

mused. "Oh! I could grow a beard. If it's long enough, I could even hang miniature ornaments on it."

"It's been a while since we stayed in the cabin by the lake during the winter. The stone fireplace is so cozy and perfect for decorating." Dash rubbed his hands together as if he could already feel the fire.

"Stop," I whispered, but no one heard me.

"—massive kitchen where we can bake cookies—"

"STOP!" I shouted, but my voice seemed to fade as something strange happened.

Everything slowed. The animated gestures of the men around me decelerated until they were hardly moving. Blitz's excited bouncing turned to an almost-still hover. Dane's hand, reaching for a chip, hung suspended in the air.

The sound died too, their voices stretching into long, distorted drones before fading into silence.

Only Rudy seemed different, his eyes widening slightly as he stared directly at me through the frozen tableau.

I spun in a circle, taking in the scene. This wasn't like creating snow or ice or making hot chocolate explode. This was different. This was...

I looked down at my hands, which were glowing with a soft blue light. Time. I was controlling time.

As panic began bubbling over, the frozen moment shattered. Everyone jolted back into motion, voices and movements resuming at normal speed. Several of them blinked in confusion, looking around as if they'd momentarily lost their train of thought.

"What the fuck was that?" I jumped backward and nearly tripped over the coffee table. "Did I... did you all..."

The blue glow intensified, spreading up my arms like veins of electricity. The surrounding air crackled with energy.

"Neve." Rudy took a step toward me, his expression uncharacteristically urgent. "Calm down."

"Calm down?" I shrieked, watching as frost patterns spiraled out from beneath my feet. "I stopped time! I stopped fucking time!"

Nine pairs of eyes stared at me as I backed toward the hallway, my entire body trembling. Their faces all seemed to swim together in my vision as the blue light pulsed from my skin. I could feel frost crackling under my socks with each backward movement. The air around me grew dense with cold, like I was generating my own personal winter storm.

"I can't control it!" My voice sounded strange even to my own ears, wavering and distant.

The picture frames on the wall beside me began to rattle, and I swore I could feel time wobbling around me again, stretching and contracting with my panicked breaths. This wasn't supposed to happen. Controlling weather was one thing, but time? That wasn't just dangerous; it was impossible. Even in a world of magic and shifters, some things were supposed to remain fixed.

My hands were weapons now, dangerous and unpredictable. I needed to get away from everyone before I froze them in time permanently, or worse.

They started to stand, and my anxiety shot up to new levels. "Don't come near me!"

But Rudy moved toward me anyway, closing the distance between us with purposeful strides.

I pressed myself against the wall, holding my glowing blue hands out in warning. "I said stay back! I don't know what will happen if... if..."

He seized my wrists in his hands, his grip firm but not painful. I jerked backward, trying to wrench free, terrified of what my touch might do to him.

"Let go! I'll hurt you!"

Instead of releasing me, Rudy pulled me forward, straight into his chest. His arms wrapped around me, enveloping my smaller frame completely.

My entire body went rigid with shock. In all the days since they'd arrived, Rudy had never touched me. Now he held me like he'd been doing it forever, one hand cradling the back of my head, the other splayed across my spine.

"Breathe," he commanded, his voice vibrating through his

chest and into mine. "Find where the magic is coming from and push it back."

I shook my head against him, hands trapped between us, still pulsing with that eerie blue light. "I can't."

"You can." His chin rested atop my head, warm and steady. "Close your eyes. Feel the center of it."

My panic began to ebb, replaced by the strange awareness of his heartbeat against my ear. It was slower than I would have expected, almost hypnotic in its rhythm.

I closed my eyes, focusing on that steady thump instead of my fear. Somewhere in my chest, beneath my sternum, a cold knot of energy pulsed in time with the glow of my hands.

The magic resisted when I pushed at it but then gradually receded. The blue light dimmed, the frost stopped spreading, and the crackling energy in the air dissipated until the room felt normal again.

Rudy's arms loosened slightly, but he didn't release me. His hands moved to my shoulders as he pulled back just enough to search my face, his eyes sweeping over my features with an intensity that made my breath catch.

For a moment, his gaze dropped to my mouth, and I thought he might kiss me. I *wanted* him to kiss me.

But then his expression shuttered closed again, back to that impenetrable mask. He stepped away, hands falling to his sides.

"We leave in an hour."

CHAPTER 15
FLYING REINDEER 101

"Absofuckinglutely not." I stared at the backyard full of men who had just informed me we would fly to Klarhaven. Not on a plane. Not in a helicopter. Not even strapped to a hang glider.

But on their backs. While they were reindeer.

"I'm not riding any of you." I jutted my chin out, ignoring the way Dane's eyes sparkled with amusement at my choice of words. "That is not a mode of transportation the FAA has approved."

Vix snorted. "The FAA doesn't know we exist."

"My point exactly!" I gestured wildly at the sky. "There's probably a reason magical flying reindeer aren't covered in the transportation safety guidelines!"

Don stepped forward with a bundle of clothing in his massive arms. "You'll need these."

I reluctantly accepted what turned out to be the thickest, fluffiest winter coat I'd ever touched, accompanied by snow pants, boots, gloves, and a hat with a stupid jingle bell on top. At least they were a neutral gray and not red.

"Where did all this even come from?" I ran my fingers over the impossibly soft fur lining the hood. "I don't own winter clothes."

"Magic," Blitz said, like it was the most obvious answer in the world.

"Of course." I rolled my eyes. "Because why wouldn't you be able to conjure a whole winter wardrobe out of thin air? Totally normal."

Kip nudged the boots toward me with his foot. "Better get dressed unless you want your nipples to freeze off."

I clutched the coat like a shield. "My nipples are staying exactly where they are, thank you very much."

Cole chuckled. "Put them on, Neve. It will be cold, even for someone rediscovering their ice powers."

With a dramatic sigh that would have made any teenager proud, I shrugged into the coat. It was annoyingly perfect and the right size. It was so light it barely felt like I was wearing anything, yet somehow it was incredibly warm.

"I know several good lawyers." I yanked the pants up over my jeans. "If I lose so much as a finger to frostbite, I'm suing all of you."

Pierce placed the boots in front of me. "No one's losing any body parts tonight."

I jammed my feet into the boots, which molded instantly to my feet like they'd been custom-made. "That's exactly what someone says before an arm gets cut off."

Dash held out the hat. "We won't be flying into any ice storms, and the magic will keep you warm."

My stomach lurched at the casual reminder of what was about to happen. Flying. On actual reindeer. Hundreds of feet in the air with nothing but fur and magic between me and plummeting to my death.

I tugged the hat over my ears, the bell jingling softly. "If I throw up on anyone, remember that this was your idea."

The men exchanged glances, a silent communication passing between them. Then, one by one, they stepped back, forming a loose half-circle around me in the yard.

Dane tipped his chin toward me, all casual warning. "You might want to step back a bit."

I retreated until my back hit the trunk of the lone palm tree that had survived my black thumb. From there, I watched as the most surreal transformation I'd ever witnessed unfolded.

It started with a shimmering in the air around each man, like heat waves rising from pavement. Their forms blurred, stretched, and twisted. Clothes melted away, replaced by thick fur in various shades of brown. Human features elongated into muzzles, hands and feet morphed into powerful hooves, and atop each changing head, antlers sprouted and unfurled like time-lapse photography of growing branches.

Within moments, my backyard was filled with giant reindeer. Steam rose from their nostrils in the cool air, their massive antlers gleaming in the moonlight.

"Holy shit," I whispered, frozen in place as nine sets of eyes —the same colors they'd had as humans—focused on me.

Only there weren't nine reindeer. There were eight.

Rudy still stood in human form, moving purposefully between the reindeer with my hastily packed suitcase and duffel bag. He secured them with practiced efficiency to the backs of what I somehow knew were Pierce and Cole.

One of the smaller reindeer stepped forward, kneeling gracefully in front of me. His coat was deep brown, and his eyes were unmistakably Dane's. As he lowered himself, I noticed a saddle-like contraption across his back that hadn't been there when he'd first shifted.

My legs felt like jelly as I approached. "This is insane. I am insane."

Dane snorted, nudging my hand with his muzzle.

"Fine. But if you drop me, I swear I'll come back as a ghost and haunt your reindeer ass for all eternity."

Taking a deep breath, I gripped the saddle and awkwardly swung my leg over, settling into place with all the grace of a newborn giraffe. The moment I sat, a feeling of rightness swept over me, and my brain recognized this as natural.

The saddle molded to my body like the boots had to my feet, securing me in place without feeling restrictive. My fingers found the horn and wrapped around it, the material warm beneath my touch.

A movement to my right caught my eye. Rudy was mounting the largest reindeer, which had a coat so dark brown it was almost black. Even in reindeer form, Don's quiet strength was unmistakable.

"What are you doing?" I called over to Rudy, my voice higher than normal. "Aren't you going to... you know?" I made a vague gesture at the other reindeer.

Rudy settled onto Don's back, looking far more comfortable with the whole situation than anyone had a right to. "One of us needs to communicate with you."

My brow furrowed. "But I heard you in my head when you were a reindeer in the park. You could talk to me then."

Something flickered across Rudy's face, though it was gone so quickly I might have imagined it. "It's easier to protect you this way."

Before I could question what exactly he meant by "protect," Dane rose beneath me, bringing me to a height that made me yelp and clutch the saddle horn with white knuckles.

"Wait, I'm not ready!" I looked frantically at Rudy. "What do I do? How do I steer? Is there a seatbelt on this thing?"

Rudy's lips twitched. "Just hold on. Dane knows what he's doing."

The reindeer began to move, padding to the center of my yard where there definitely wasn't enough space for eight massive reindeer to take off.

"If I die doing this," I hissed toward Rudy, "I want 'I told you so' on my tombstone."

Dane's muscles bunched beneath me, and I tightened my grip on the saddle horn so hard my knuckles ached. I don't know what I was expecting, but the reindeer floated up like balloons.

No warning. No countdown. No galloping start.

My stomach plummeted as the earth fell away, hooves still positioned as though they were standing on solid ground instead of thin air. It was like being in an elevator with no walls, except the ground dissolved beneath us as my yard shrank to dollhouse size.

"Holy shit, holy shit, holy shit," I chanted under my breath as I sent a prayer to whatever deity might be listening to not let me become a Neve pancake.

The world tilted and swayed as we rose higher, my backyard palm tree now a tiny toothpick against the sprawling grid of Palm Springs lights. The massive bodies of the reindeer were weightless against the night sky.

A thought struck me with sudden, horrifying clarity.

"What if someone sees us?" I called out, panic sharpening every syllable. "There are planes and drones and helicopters and... and telescopes! People look up!"

Rudy turned his head, his posture relaxed on Don's back. The moonlight caught his profile, calm and untroubled by our casual defiance of gravity. "They won't. Our magic bends light and hides us from human eyes."

My laugh edged toward hysteria.

I might have believed him if Dane hadn't chosen that exact moment to surge forward in a smooth, impossible leap through the air. We shot forward, the rest of the herd falling into formation around us like some kind of Christmas cavalry.

Palm Springs transformed from a recognizable grid of lights into a blurred smear of distant sparkles. My brain was confused as the world whipped by, but I could hardly feel the air move.

There was no skin-peeling, eye-watering hurricane-force wind. Just comfortable, slightly cool air and the gentle rhythmic motion of Dane's body as he practically swam through the sky.

I'd expected the saddle to chafe, for my legs to cramp, for the cold to bite through my clothes. Instead, I felt... protected.

"How fast are we going?" I shouted, despite not needing to do so. I pressed myself lower against Dane's neck, feeling exposed sitting straight up. This wasn't a casual horseback ride.

Don moved close enough that I could see Rudy's expression in the moonlight. "About five hundred miles per hour."

I blinked, waiting for the punchline.

It didn't come.

"That's not possible!" My voice cracked on the last word. "We'd be torn apart by the wind at that speed!"

A rumble vibrated through Dane's body beneath me. Was he laughing at me?

"It's possible with magic," Rudy reminded me with infuriating casualness, as though we weren't currently breaking several laws of physics. "We'll also be going through a few sky gates that will get us there faster. You'll see a slight shimmer, but there's no reason to be alarmed."

We soared over cities that flashed by too quickly to identify, desert giving way to mountains, then forests, then more mountains, higher and craggier than before. Clouds surrounded us, parting now and then to reveal glowing ribbons of highway, neat grids of towns, and dark stretches of wilderness.

I lost track of time, mesmerized by the impossible journey. My terror gradually mellowed into awe as I realized the reindeer herd moved as one, shifting and adjusting around each other with the precision of a dance. No matter how they dipped or turned, I remained perfectly balanced, as if gravity itself had been changed to keep me safely in place.

The sky gates were a little disorienting, and I quickly learned not to look down when the air shimmered in front of us. The first time we'd gone through one, a building had blinked into a mountain so fast it made my head spin.

Eventually, the snowy peaks below grew larger, and the city lights became sparser until they disappeared altogether. We gradually descended toward an endless expanse of mountains, forests, and valleys, all blanketed in snow that glowed silvery blue under the moonlight.

My breath caught at the beauty. This wasn't the manufactured winter wonderland of mall displays or holiday cards. This was winter in its purest form.

A town dotted with cabins appeared. I had absolutely no clue what time it was, but there was smoke rising from chimneys, lights coming through windows, and a few people and reindeer wandering about.

The herd dipped lower, and I saw a frozen lake glittering

like polished glass beneath us. At its edge stood a massive cabin with a steep-pitched roof and stone chimneys. Windows glowed with warm light, and even from the air, I could see a wide wraparound porch circling the entire building.

Dane's hooves touched down on the snow with impossible gentleness, the landing so smooth I barely felt the transition from air to ground. The rest of the herd landed around us, steam rising from them in the cold air.

I sat frozen in place, trying to process what had just happened.

"We're here," Rudy announced unnecessarily, hopping down from Don's back.

I stared at him, then at the enormous cabin, then at the frozen lake stretching out into the darkness.

"Welcome to Klarhaven, the gateway to Jingle." He approached Dane's side and offered his hand to help me down.

My legs wobbled as I dismounted, but surprisingly there was no soreness. The only things I felt were a lingering sense of wonder and the dawning realization that Palm Springs was thousands of miles away.

I turned in a slow circle, taking in the landscape and the cabin. "This is... it can't be real."

Even as I said it, I knew it was. The bite of cold air in my lungs, the crunch of snow beneath my boots, the weight of reality settling over me. All of it was undeniably, irrevocably real.

"It's all real," Rudy confirmed, standing beside me as the reindeer began to shimmer and transform back into men. "And so are you, Neve."

I'd never felt less real in my life.

CHAPTER 16
NOT COVERED IN THE WELCOME PACKET

I emerged from the shower in a daze, cocooned in what felt like an entire sheep's worth of fluff in towel form. My skin was flushed pink from the heat, but my brain remained as fogged as the bathroom mirror.

The last twenty-four hours kept replaying on a loop: flying across the country on reindeer-men, seeing a world blanketed in snow, and arriving at a cabin that looked like it had been plucked straight from a Christmas catalog for billionaires with a festive fetish.

I wiped a small circle in the mirror and barely recognized the woman staring back. My damp hair hung around my shoulders, the silver now twelve inches long, fading into my dyed color. The effect was like some expensive ombré I'd never have paid for at a salon but suited me in a way that made my eyes look even more intensely blue.

Every time I blinked, I half-expected to wake up in a hospital bed with a fever, hallucinating this entire thing.

Instead, I was standing in the bathroom Dash and Dane shared. It had heated floors, a shower with approximately twenty jets, and a tub that could comfortably fit three people—an observation I immediately tried to un-think.

I secured the towel more firmly around my torso, unlocked

the door connecting to Dash's room, then cracked open the door into Dane's, where I'd be sleeping.

I stepped into the bedroom, immediately stopping short at a shirtless Dane with his back to me. He stood in his closet, rifling through a collection of sweaters. The muscles in his back shifted beneath his skin as he moved hangers aside, unaware of my presence.

My mouth went dry. The towel suddenly felt very insufficient, and the room very warm despite the snow-covered landscape outside the windows.

I took a silent step backward, planning my strategic retreat into the bathroom. Maybe I could just live there. The shower was nice. I could survive on tap water and fancy hand soap.

My back collided with something solid and warm. Not a wall. A body. A very large, very firm body. Strong hands steadied me by my biceps, and I knew instantly whose they were before he even spoke. Dash.

His lips brushed against the shell of my ear, sending an entirely inappropriate shiver down my spine. "What are you doing spying?"

I froze, caught between the man behind me and the still-oblivious man in front of me. "I'm not spying," I hissed. "I'm avoiding an awkward encounter with a half-naked man while I'm in a towel."

"And yet here you are, having an awkward encounter with two half-naked men while you're in a towel." His thumb traced a small circle against my skin, and heat spread from the point of contact.

Dane turned, a dark blue sweater in hand, his eyes widening slightly before his mouth curved into that maddening grin that made my stomach do gymnastics.

Dane tilted his head, studying me. "This is a nice surprise."

I clutched the towel tighter. "This isn't what it looks like."

"It looks like you took a shower with Dash." Dane tossed the sweater onto the bed and put his hands on his hips, drawing all my attention to the V-shaped muscles leading right into his pants. "Were you planning on inviting me to your little party?"

"I was planning to spontaneously combust from embarrassment, actually." I tried to step away from Dash, but my feet refused to cooperate. "Which is going spectacularly well so far."

"You don't need to be embarrassed." Dash's voice was a low rumble against my back. "We've seen women in towels before."

"Glad to know I'm not breaking new ground in the towel-wearing department." Irrational jealousy wormed its way into my brain, and my fingers tingled. How often did these men see women in towels?

Dane took a step closer. "You aren't just any woman in a towel, though. You're ours."

I glanced between them, trapped in the most awkward and somehow thrilling moment of my adult life. Two gorgeous, shirtless men, one keeping my back warm, the other advancing with eyes that sparked with something dangerous.

"I should go find..." My voice trailed off. Find what? Dignity? Clothing? A fire extinguisher for the heat under my skin? "Why can't I think straight when you all are near me?"

"That might be a side effect." Dash's fingers traced lightly up my arm.

I raised an eyebrow. "Of what? Magical reindeer pheromones?"

Dane's laugh rumbled through the room as he took another step closer. "Something like that. We're connected to you, Neve. You're feeling it now because you're allowing yourself to."

The space between us shrank to nothing as Dane stood directly in front of me. I was officially sandwiched between them, my skin prickling with awareness.

"I'm not sure this was covered in the welcome packet." I swallowed hard, looking up at Dane.

His fingertips brushed my cheek, tucking a strand of hair behind my ear. "Some things can't be explained on paper."

Dash's hand slid around my waist. "We should give her space."

I turned in Dash's arms to face him, my back now to Dane. "I don't want space."

Dash's expression darkened, desire replacing the restraint he'd been showing so far. "The nine of us can be a lot, and we don't want to overwhelm you. It's okay if you need to take things slow."

My heart was beating so hard I could hear it in my ears. Taking on nine men was absurd. Well, eight since Rudy seemed to be the odd man out and not at all interested in me.

Dane's hands settled on my hips from behind. "What do you want?"

The heat of their bodies enveloped me, making my head swim. I'd never wanted anything more in my life. "I haven't kissed either of you yet." I didn't realize just how much it had been bothering me until the words left my lips.

Dash's gaze dropped to my mouth, and his hand came up to cradle my jaw, thumb brushing my lower lip with excruciating gentleness. "We can fix that."

When his lips finally met mine, the restraint in his kiss felt as if he was holding back an ocean. I pressed closer, silently asking for more. His control fractured, and he deepened the kiss with a groan.

Dane's lips found the sensitive spot where my neck met my shoulder, sending electricity down my spine, and my knees nearly buckled. Every time I kissed one of these men, it was like discovering a new level of desire. I reached back blindly, my fingers threading through Dane's hair, needing something to anchor me as pleasure rippled through my body.

I broke away from Dash and turned to face Dane. His playful smirk was gone, replaced by something far more intense. "Is this what you want?"

I nodded, unable to form words as Dash's hands splayed across my stomach, holding me steady.

Dane's kiss was hungry, and his tongue slipped past my lips as his hands threaded through my hair. I made an embarrassing sound as his teeth grazed my lower lip. They seemed determined to make me forget my name.

This felt like the most natural progression imaginable. It was as if my body recognized theirs before my mind could catch up.

Dash turned me back toward him, taking my lips again before he lifted me off my feet. I squeaked in surprise, my legs automatically wrapping around his waist as he carried me toward the massive bed. The towel gave up its valiant fight and slipped away, leaving me completely bare against him.

"You're beautiful." Dash's eyes trailed down my body as he laid me on the bed.

Even naked, I felt powerful with how they looked at me like I was something precious and rare.

I propped myself up on my elbows, drinking in the sight of them both. "Seems unfair I'm the only one naked."

Dane's smile turned wicked as he pushed down his sweat-pants and kicked them off, leaving me momentarily speechless. Dash followed suit, and holy fucking reindeer, they were huge.

"Is this real?" The question slipped out before I could stop it.

Dane crawled onto the bed beside me. "Let me show you how real it is." He pressed a soft kiss to my collarbone, then moved lower, tracing a path between my breasts.

Dash settled on my other side, his large hand spanning my ribcage. "Tell us what you want, Neve."

I wanted everything. All of it. Them. This burning thing building inside me that felt like it might consume me if I didn't let it out.

"I want your mouths." My skin burned everywhere their eyes traveled. "I want to feel both of you until I can't tell where I end and you begin." My chest heaved as desire pooled between my thighs, and I reached out, dragging my fingertips along Dane's forearm, then Dash's chest, electricity crackling through my veins at even the simple contact.

Dane's eyes darkened, and he cupped my pussy, his palm pressing against my clit. "This is a greedy little pussy, isn't it?"

I started to nod, but Dash leaned in to kiss me. Dane worked his hand in small circles, a finger pushing through my folds and teasing my entrance. My hips rocked into him, wanting more.

Dash broke away and moved to lie next to me, his broad shoulders against the mattress. "Come sit on my face."

My breath hitched, a shock of electricity racing from my core to my fingertips. I made a needy, desperate sound I barely recognized as my own as Dane removed his hand, leaving me aching and empty.

As I sat up and got to my knees, I caught my lower lip between my teeth, overwhelmed by the thought of straddling Dash's gorgeous face while his talented tongue explored every sensitive inch of me.

He guided me up and over him until I was straddling his face, his hands on my thighs keeping me steady. The first swipe of his tongue made me cry out, my hands flying to the headboard for support. He found every spot that drove me wild, and I knew I wouldn't last long.

Dane's hands slid up my back, steadying me as my thighs began to tremble. "You ride his face like you were made for it. Sink in deeper, let him devour that sweet pussy."

I forced my body to relax, my fingers tightening on the headboard. Dash's tongue flicked faster, his strong hands holding me in place when I tried to squirm away from the intensity. The pressure building was almost unbearable.

When his lips closed around my clit and sucked gently, I shattered, crying out loud enough that I was sure everyone in the cabin heard me.

Before I could recover, Dane was guiding me off Dash and onto my back. "I've been craving this sweet cunt since the moment I saw you."

Dane devoured me like I was the best thing he'd ever tasted, humming against my oversensitive flesh in a way that made me arch off the bed. My hands found his hair, tangling in the strands as he worked me toward another peak with devastating skill.

Dash stretched out beside me, his lips claiming mine in a deep kiss. I could taste myself on his tongue, which only turned me on more. His hand cupped my breast, thumb circling my nipple until it hardened.

With Dane between my legs and Dash tweaking my nipples, my orgasm hit me with surprising force.

Dane rose up, wiping his mouth with the back of his hand, looking immensely pleased with himself. "Good?"

I couldn't form words, so I just nodded weakly.

Dash chuckled. "I think we broke her."

Dane stretched out on my other side, his hand tracing idle patterns on my stomach. I turned toward Dash, reaching between us to wrap my hand around his length. He was hot and hard against my palm, and the groan he released when I stroked him sent liquid heat pooling between my thighs again.

"I want you inside me."

Dash didn't need to be told twice. He positioned himself between my legs, the head of his cock nudging at my entrance. Despite everything they'd already done to me to get me ready, I still felt a moment of uncertainty; he was big, and it had been a while.

"Relax, we've got you." Dash smoothed one hand up my thigh.

Dane kissed me deeply as Dash pushed forward, entering me in one slow, steady thrust. I whimpered into Dane's mouth as Dash filled me completely.

"Fuck." Dash held still once he was fully seated. "You feel incredible."

I looked up at Dash, entranced by the intensity in his eyes. When he began to move, he set a rhythm that wasn't too fast or too slow. I reached for Dane, wrapping my fingers around him. His sharp inhale was immensely satisfying.

We moved together, finding a rhythm that sent me rushing toward yet another peak. Dash's control was slipping, his thrusts becoming more urgent. I stroked Dane in time with Dash's movements, loving the sounds he made.

"I want in your mouth. Do you think you can handle that?" Dane's voice was strained as he stilled my hand.

I nodded, breathless with anticipation.

Dash reluctantly withdrew, and they rearranged us. In a flash, I was on my hands and knees, Dash behind me and Dane kneeling in front of me, his cock level with my mouth.

"Is this okay?" Dane brushed my hair back from my face, his expression serious despite his obvious arousal.

In response, I leaned forward and took him into my mouth, relishing his strangled groan. Dash positioned himself behind me, pushing back inside with a smooth thrust, and I moaned around Dane.

It was overwhelming in the best possible way. Dash gripped my hips as he took me from behind, and Dane's fingers tangled gently in my hair as I took him as deeply as I could in my mouth. I was caught in a perfect storm of sensations.

Dash reached around to circle my clit with his fingers, and I nearly came undone. I doubled my efforts on Dane, using every trick I could think of to drive him as wild as I felt.

"Neve..." Dash's voice was laced with restraint. "I'm close."

I hummed my encouragement around Dane, which made him curse colorfully. Dash's thrusts grew erratic, his fingers pressing harder against my clit. When he groaned my name and stiffened behind me, it triggered my release, pleasure washing through me as he pulsed inside me.

Dash carefully withdrew, pressing a kiss to my shoulder blade before moving aside. Dane guided me onto my back, positioning himself between my thighs.

The second he was all the way in, I knew I was done for. Dane moved with purpose, hitting spots inside me that had my toes curling. I wrapped my legs around his waist, urging him deeper.

"You're perfect," he groaned, his pace increasing. "So fucking perfect."

I was floating, heading toward something bigger than before. When it hit, it was like being struck by lightning with every nerve ending firing at once, my body arching off the bed as I cried out. He followed me over the edge seconds later, his face buried in my neck as he shuddered through his release.

After a moment, Dane rolled to the side, and Dash returned

with a warm washcloth, cleaning me with surprising tenderness before climbing into bed.

They arranged themselves on either side of me, Dane's arm draped across my waist while Dash's hand found mine, our fingers intertwining.

"Are you okay?" Dash's voice was a low rumble against my ear.

I nodded, too exhausted and content for words. I should have felt strange or at least conflicted about what had just happened. But all I felt was an overwhelming sense of rightness, like I'd found something I hadn't even known I was missing.

Dane nuzzled my hair. "Sweet dreams."

Whatever magic connected us, I was done fighting it, at least for tonight.

CHAPTER 17

HEIRESS TO A GLOBAL BREAKING-AND-ENTERING OPERATION

I was flying.

Not the claustrophobic terror of being trapped in a metal tube, but real flying—hair whipping back, adrenaline pumping, heart soaring kind of flying. A sleigh cut through the starlit sky, my small hand gripping the red side.

"Hold tight, Snowflake!"

My father's laugh boomed across the night, vibrating through the sleigh, through my chest, and all the way to my toes. His silver beard glinted with frost, and his cheeks were flushed.

The reindeer surged forward, powerful muscles rippling beneath thick fur. I felt the magic crackling between them like electric currents, saw the shimmer trailing behind us as we climbed higher than any plane could fly. Higher than logic or reason permitted.

"Look down, Neve! The entire world is waiting!"

I leaned over, clutching his arm, and there it was: a planet wrapped in darkness speckled with glittering lights, each one a home, each one waiting.

For us.

For him.

For Santa.

I gasped awake, but the dream didn't dissolve like smoke the way my memories usually did. It stayed in a high-definition replay of a moment I'd once lived. My hand flew to my mouth as I stared at the unfamiliar ceiling.

Holy. Fucking. Shit.

My dad was Santa Claus. Not "like" Santa Claus. Not "Santa-esque." Not a festive researcher with unfortunate holiday enthusiasm.

Which made me... what? Some kind of Christmas princess? The heiress to a global breaking-and-entering operation?

The bed beside me was empty, the sheets still warm where Dane and Dash had been. Had they known all along? Of course they had. Everyone had known except me.

I'd spent over a decade of my life running from something I couldn't even remember. Years thinking I was just a girl with seasonal depression and an inexplicable aversion to candy canes.

Why hadn't they told me? Why make me feel crazy for years when all they had to say was, "Hey, honey, you're kind of a big deal at the North Pole!"

The distant sound of laughter filtered through the door, along with the smell of cinnamon and the soft notes of music. I flopped back against the pillows, my chest heaving. I needed answers—real ones, not cryptic reindeer hints or more cookie-induced memory fragments.

After brushing my teeth and hair, I padded to where I'd stowed my suitcase. It was open on the floor but entirely empty. I looked around, my eyes landing on the dresser.

I marched over to it, where there was a matching set of red lace underwear and a bra, a pair of fleece-lined black leggings, a long-sleeved thermal shirt, and a cream-colored sweater with intricate snowflake patterns.

After looking in all the dresser drawers and the closet to confirm that none of my belongings were there, I snatched up the lace underwear, my eye twitching.

Had one of them picked this out? Had they all discussed my underwear preferences while I slept and conjured them with their magic? I could picture nine magical reindeer men gathered around the dining table: *Today's agenda: Neve's panties.*

I yanked on the clothes, my movements sharp with irritation. The outfit fit perfectly, and the sweater was the kind of cashmere that probably came from a magical goat that shit Skittles. The leggings hugged my curves like they'd been custom-made.

It only made me angrier.

I didn't want their perfect magical clothes. I didn't want to be part of a Christmas legacy. I wanted answers, and I wanted them without festive background music and cutesy North Pole nonsense.

The laughter downstairs grew louder and more animated. I squared my shoulders and headed for the door, my jaw set in a hard line.

I stormed down the polished wooden stairs, each step punctuating my fury. The staircase opened into a great room with a cathedral ceiling that could have housed a small herd of elephants, which, considering the size of the men currently occupying it, wasn't far off.

Eight of the nine men were spread throughout the space in a scene so sickeningly festive it belonged on the front of a Hallmark card. The open-concept kitchen gleamed with copper pots hanging from a rack and a massive island where Kip and Cole rolled out dough for cinnamon rolls. Blitz stood at the stove, stirring something that sent clouds of spiced steam into the air.

My Christmas tree from my house in Palm Springs now stood proudly in front of floor-to-ceiling windows that showcased a panoramic view of the snow outside and the still-darkened sky. Don and Pierce were wrapping garland around anything they could, while Vix hung ornaments from a giant wreath above the fireplace.

Dane and Dash occupied part of the massive dining room table, where Dash operated a sewing machine with the ease of someone who had done it a thousand times before, while Dane hand-stitched a stocking with an ornate "N" across the top.

They were making me a Christmas stocking.

My heart did fifty million things all at once, and some of my anger disappeared. The sight of Dane's careful stitching of my initial sent electricity skittering across my skin, as unwelcome as it was undeniable.

I reached the bottom of the stairs and planted myself there, arms crossed, waiting for someone to notice me. The laughter, the Christmas music playing softly from hidden speakers, the domesticity of it all grated against my raw nerves like sandpaper.

Blitz spotted me first, his smile faltering slightly at my thunderous expression. "Morning, sunshine."

All eyes swiveled to me, and their smiles dimmed as they registered my mood. My body suddenly felt tingly with unease. I didn't enjoy seeing their joy dampened by my sourness.

I scanned the room again, noting the one missing presence. "Where's Rudy?"

Dane set down his needlework. "Outside. He, uh... likes to run the perimeter in the mornings."

"Of course he does." I stepped further into the room, taking in the Christmas bomb that had exploded all over what must have been a perfectly nice living room before. "So, were any of you planning to tell me that my father is Santa Claus, or was I supposed to figure that out from the cookies and cryptic comments?"

The activity in the room stuttered to a halt. Pierce froze mid-garland hang. Kip's rolling pin stilled. Dash's foot lifted off the sewing machine pedal.

"You connected the dots." Vix's voice was soft and cautious, like I could forget it at any moment. And maybe I would, but right now it was as fresh as the snow outside.

"I had a dream, and all the other memories have become clear again." I picked up a glass ornament from a nearby box, turning it in my hand. "I've been lied to for years."

Cole wiped flour from his hands with a towel. "Your parents did what they thought was best after your magic..." His mouth slammed shut, but I couldn't tell if it was him not wanting to tell me or some magical force preventing him.

"After my magic what?" I carefully set the ornament down, though what I really wanted to do was throw it against the wall. "Meltdown? Explosion? Catastrophe? Fill in the blank for me, since apparently I'm the only one who doesn't know the story of my life."

Don stepped toward me, his expression gentle. "It's complicated, Neve."

"Then uncomplicate it. I'm tired of breadcrumbs. I deserve the whole loaf."

Dash rose from the couch, folding the half-finished stocking. "We should wait for Rudy."

"Why? Is he the designated explainer?" My voice echoed in the sudden quiet. "The alpha of information dispersal?"

I spotted movement outside the living room windows. A massive reindeer galloped with powerful strides toward a small hill that rose from the landscape like a misplaced volcano.

Rudy.

My irritation shifted targets instantly. Everyone had ambushed me with Christmas cheer, each one offering pieces of themselves to rekindle my holiday spirit.

Everyone except him.

"Where is he going?" I pointed toward the window.

Eight heads turned to follow my gaze. The massive reindeer disappeared over the crest of the hill.

Pierce moved beside me. "That's his morning routine. He'll be back inside soon for—"

"For what? More secrets? Everyone else has been trying to drown me in Christmas spirit, but your fearless leader can't be bothered to participate?"

The room fell silent. In the corner, Vix shifted uncomfortably, exchanging a look with Kip that I couldn't decipher.

I spun toward the mudroom we'd come in through the night before.

No one tried to stop me, though I heard urgent whispers. I shoved my feet into my new boots and shrugged into my jacket.

It was cold as I stepped outside, but it didn't bother me like it normally would have. Snow crunched beneath my boots as I marched across the clearing toward the hill Rudy had been running up.

As I reached the base of the hill, Rudy reappeared, but not from over the top. He trotted into view from around the side of it, his massive reindeer form covered in snow. His movements were unsteady, almost defeated.

The sight knocked the anger right out of me.

He hadn't seen me yet, and I watched as he shook snow from his coat, his powerful legs trembling slightly. He looked... vulnerable.

What had he been doing?

I took a step forward, and his head snapped up, his eyes locking onto mine. Even in reindeer form, I could read his expressions shifting from shock to shame and then indifference.

We stared at each other across the snow, steam rising from his nostrils in the frigid air. In that moment, he seemed more beast than man, wild and unpredictable and somehow achingly alone.

"What are you doing out here?" My voice came out softer than intended, my prepared tirade forgotten.

He didn't move, just watched me with those unnervingly intelligent eyes.

I took another step closer. "Everyone else is inside playing Christmas elves while you're out here doing... whatever this is." I gestured vaguely at the hill.

Rudy's gaze remained fixed on me, his massive antlers glittering in the faint light. They looked like a chandelier of ice.

"The silent treatment? Really?" I crossed my arms, fighting a shiver that had nothing to do with the cold. "That's your strategy? Blitz bakes cookies, Kip makes me skate, Don decorates, and you... what? Run up and down hills ignoring me?"

His ears flicked back, and I could have sworn a flicker of hurt crossed his reindeer features.

I closed the distance between us. Snow caked his antlers, dusting the impressive rack like powdered sugar. My hand reached up before my brain could intervene, fingers hovering beneath the lowest point of his left antler.

"You're a mess," I murmured, then brushed away the snow. My fingers trailed along the smooth curve of his antler, mesmerized by the warmth beneath the cold exterior. It felt strangely intimate, like I was crossing some unspoken boundary.

He made a deep rumbling sound, somewhere between a warning and a groan. The sound traveled up my arm, settling somewhere behind my ribs.

His eyes darkened, pupils dilating until they nearly swallowed the gray. Before I could pull away, a shimmer of magic rippled across him, and my hand was no longer touching his antler.

Fingers wrapped around my wrist, holding me suspended in the space between us. Rudy towered over me, completely naked despite the biting cold, snowflakes melting against his skin. His breaths came in ragged pulls, and his face was taut with restraint.

"Don't." His voice was rough, like he hadn't used it in days.

The cold had no effect on his bare chest. No goosebumps, no shivering, just smooth skin stretched over hard muscle. His dark hair was dusted with snow, making him look like some winter deity caught in the middle of transformation.

We stood frozen in a bubble of tension, his hand still wrapped gently around my wrist, my body painfully aware of his proximity and the power radiating from him.

"Don't what?" I whispered, my eyes falling to his lips.

"Only mates can touch antlers." His words hit me like a slap. Even naked and vulnerable in the snow, he was finding new ways to push me away.

I yanked my arm free from his grasp, stepping back so quickly I nearly stumbled. "Right. Sorry for the breach of reindeer etiquette."

My chest burned with fresh humiliation. Everyone else had welcomed me with open arms, while this man couldn't even bear my touch on his precious antlers. "Is that why you've been avoiding me? Afraid I might accidentally become your mate by petting your head?"

His expression hardened. "Neve..."

"Forget it." I turned away, blinking back the sting in my

eyes. "I get it. You didn't sign up for Santa's amnesiac daughter."

I stomped back toward the house, trying my hardest not to let my angry tears fall. Why did I care so much, anyway? I had eight other men who were clearly obsessed with me.

Behind me, I heard his heavy steps following. "Fuck, Neve, wait."

The raw desperation in his voice almost made me turn. Almost. Instead, I threw up my hand in dismissal, the universal "leave me alone" gesture.

The air crackled, and I gasped, looking over my shoulder right as a wall of ice shot up from the ground between us. I froze, staring at the translucent barrier I'd somehow conjured with nothing but a flick of my wrist.

Through the wavy distortion of the ice, I could see Rudy's blurred figure. He hadn't even flinched. Unlike me, he wasn't shocked by my impromptu ice architecture.

Yet another thing everyone knew about me that I didn't.

I turned and ran, my boots kicking up snow as I fled toward the house, leaving Rudy and my ice wall behind.

CHAPTER 18
LUMINESCENCE WINTER WONDERFROST

I stared at the sleigh, its polished wood gleaming in the pathway lights hanging overhead. It was smaller than expected and was only big enough to fit two people. One reindeer could easily pull it, and I found myself a little disappointed.

Don stood beside it, his presence doing nothing to calm the chaos brewing inside me. Blitz was already shifting, his human form melting into something massive and antlered with an ease that still made my stomach twist. Pierce and Vix lingered nearby, waiting for me to make the first move.

When they'd asked me if I wanted to get out for a while and go to Reinberg, I hadn't considered how we'd get there. Silly me.

"Do I have to?" I dug the toe of a boot into the snow. "Can't we drive? Like normal people?"

Vix grinned, throwing an arm around my shoulders and guiding me toward the sleigh. "Where's the fun in that? Besides, normal is overrated."

Normal. Right. Because nothing about this situation screamed "normal." Not the men who could shapeshift into reindeer, not the fact that my dad was apparently Santa Claus, and definitely not the way my heart raced every time one of them looked at me like I was the center of their entire world. I wasn't sure if I wanted to laugh, scream, or throw myself into the nearest snowbank and stay there until spring.

Don stepped forward, his hand brushing mine in a silent offer. His touch was grounding, like he knew exactly how off balance I felt. "It's not far. We'll take it slow."

Slow. Sure. Because watching Don shift into a massive reindeer that could probably pull a freight train was slow and relaxing. The air shimmered around him like magic always did when they shifted. By the time he settled into his reindeer form, Pierce and Vix were already circling the sleigh, their hooves kicking up tiny clouds of snow.

Blitz nudged the sleigh with his head, gesturing for me to climb in. I hesitated. "If I fall out, I'm going to make the sharpest candy cane possible and seek revenge."

Vix snorted, his breath puffing into the cold air. I shot him a glare but climbed in, sinking into the cushioned seat and pulling the thick blanket around my shoulders.

Don took the lead, magic lifting the harness and hooking him to the sleigh. I'd half expected us to lift off, but instead, we moved forward across the snow, gliding effortlessly. Don moved with a grace that shouldn't have been possible for something so large. Blitz fell in beside him, his movements more energetic, like he was barely containing his excitement. Pierce and Vix flanked us, their hooves crunching in perfect rhythm.

We passed through a clearing and into the trees bowing under the weight of the snow, their branches sparkling as if they'd been dusted with glitter. The forest was quiet except for the sound of hooves and the occasional rustle of wind through the trees. It was beautiful in a way that made my chest ache, like I was seeing something I'd been missing my entire life.

It was far too quiet, and I cleared my throat. "I'm calling my father tonight. No more secrets. I want to know everything and why I've been lied to."

Vix trotted closer to the sleigh, his eyes watching me with what looked like concern.

"Don't give me that look. He owes me an explanation. Besides, I'm still not convinced this isn't some elaborate hallucination. Maybe I hit my head at Sinclair's, and I'm in a coma dream right now."

Pierce veered close, his antlers nearly grazing the sleigh in what I took as a denial of my assessment of the situation.

"And another thing, how is this supposed to work between all of us? Do you guys... share girlfriends regularly? Is this a reindeer thing or a you thing?"

Blitz made a sound that suspiciously resembled laughter.

"That wasn't a joke," I muttered, though my cheeks warmed. "I'm curious about the logistics of dating eight magical men." It pained me not to say nine, but Rudy had made his feelings toward me very clear.

Don looked back over his shoulder and gave me a wink.

"Eyes on the road, big guy! Does this thing come with insurance? It certainly didn't come with a seatbelt." I felt along the inside of the sleigh. "We'll have to install one if you plan on flying me in this thing."

Vix made a snorting noise, and I pointed a finger at him. "You might be very confident in your sleigh-flying abilities, but I am not."

The trees thinned as we crested a hill, and the sleigh slowed as we reached the top. My breath caught in my throat.

Reinberg sprawled out before us, a picturesque winter village straight out of a storybook. Smoke curled from the chimneys of cozy cottages, and the streets were lined with twinkling lights. In the center of the village stood a massive Christmas tree, its branches adorned with glowing ornaments and topped with a glittering star. The air smelled of pine and cinnamon, and the faint sounds of laughter and music drifted toward us.

A frozen pond reflected the colors like a mirror, and tiny figures skated in graceful loops. Market stalls lined cobblestone streets, and in the distance, a magnificent clock tower rose above it all, its face glowing gold.

For a moment, all my worries and questions faded into the background, replaced by a sense of peace I hadn't felt in years. Something unfamiliar bloomed inside me, and a warmth wrapped around me like a hug, settling into my bones with quiet certainty.

I recognized it after a moment of confusion.

Joy.

The sleigh curved along a winding path until we reached an enormous barn with soaring timber beams. Lanterns hung from iron hooks, casting the cavernous space in a golden glow.

My reindeer escort slowed as the barn doors closed behind us, hooves clopping against the stone floor as we glided to a gentle stop in the center of the space. Workers stopped what they were doing, their attention drawn to the four reindeer. I clutched the blanket tighter around me, suddenly self-conscious.

A woman in a dark green cloak swept forward, her long blonde braid swinging as she moved. "Welcome back, boys!" She patted Don's flank with easy familiarity, which immediately put me on edge. "All clear to shift. No tourists."

The woman turned toward me, her bright smile freezing mid-welcome. Her eyes widened, lips parting in unmistakable recognition. It wasn't the practiced pause of someone trying to place where they'd seen me before, but something deeper, like spotting a ghost walking in broad daylight.

"Oh!" She recovered quickly, smoothing her expression into something warm but careful. "Welcome to Reinberg. I'm Astrid."

I stood from the sleigh on wobbly legs. "I'm Neve."

Her eyes flickered over my face, lingering too long on my eyes and then my hair. "Yes. You certainly are."

The reindeer shifted around me, thankfully emerging fully clothed. I wasn't mentally prepared to have other people see them naked, no matter how spectacular the view might be.

Astrid's gaze bounced between me and the men like a pinball, her expression a mixture of awe and disbelief. She took a half-step forward, then stopped herself, hands fidgeting with the clasp of her cloak. "It's really... I mean, you're actually..."

I wrapped my arms around myself. "Regular, boring Neve from Palm Springs."

The lanterns flickered, their warm light pulsing. The shadows danced along the walls as the flames brightened, casting the barn in a glow that felt almost alive. I could feel something stirring inside me, a familiar cool tingle spreading from my chest to my fingertips.

Blitz's hand slid along the small of my back. "You doing okay there, princess?"

"Don't call me that," I snapped, the nickname scraping against raw nerves.

A crackling sound drew my eyes upward. Along the massive wooden beams, frost was spreading in intricate patterns, tiny icicles forming and catching the light like crystal ornaments. The barn fell silent, the only sound the chuffing of reindeer that were apparently not shifters.

Vix whistled low. "Nice trick."

"I didn't..." But I had. The frost was receding now, melting away as quickly as it had appeared, the lanterns settling back to their normal brightness. "Sorry."

Astrid's composure snapped back into place with practiced ease. "Well! Let's not keep you standing around in a dusty old barn!" She swung a massive door open with surprising strength.

Reinberg spilled before us with twinkling lights, laughter, and music. The cobblestone streets bustled with people bundled in colorful scarves and hats, weaving between market stalls overflowing with ornaments, toys, and steaming food and drinks.

Don took my hand. "Ready?"

No. I absolutely was not ready. I was the anti-Christmas Grinch being led into the heart of Whoville.

Pierce stood on my other side, his body a wall of warmth. "We can leave anytime you want."

I took a deep breath and stepped into Reinberg. "Let's get this over with."

Everything sparkled, an assault of holiday cheer. Christmas carols floated through the air, mingling with laughter and the scent of roasting chestnuts. It was too loud, too bright, and way too festive.

"Not so bad, right?" Blitz nudged my shoulder, his eyes bright with excitement.

I shot him a look that could have frozen the sun. "It's like Christmas threw up everywhere."

Tourists clutched steaming mugs and browsed at stalls. Most people were too busy with their holiday shopping to notice us.

But as we moved deeper into the village, I noticed the shift. A woman hanging delicate glass ornaments from her stall went completely still, the bauble dangling forgotten from her fingertips as her gaze locked on me. A man scooping spiced nuts dropped his scoop with a clatter, his mouth falling open.

I tucked my chin into my scarf. "Why are they staring at me?"

Don's large hand settled protectively on my shoulder. "It's been a long time since they've seen..."

"Who? Someone who hates Christmas?"

Vix chuckled beside me, but even he was scanning the growing number of wide-eyed vendors. "Maybe they recognize your natural charm and winning personality."

I elbowed him in the ribs but pulled my coat tighter around me. The looks weren't hostile but more like people seeing a celebrity they thought was dead or a long-lost relative returning home. Their expressions held a reverence that made my skin prickle.

An older woman with silver hair stepped directly into our path, a bundle of evergreen branches clutched in her gloved hands. Her eyes widened, soft with what looked like hope. Hope for what, though?

"Excuse us," Pierce smoothly steered me around her before she could speak. "Let's head to the Frostbite Inn. It's quieter there."

I leaned closer to him, grateful for the escape. "Frostbite Inn? Seriously? Who names these places?"

We followed a winding path toward a cozy lodge nestled

behind a line of trees draped in twinkling fairy lights. The air smelled of cloves, sugar, and freshly baked bread, drawing us forward like a sensory beacon. I inhaled deeply, something loosening in my chest.

Inside, it was warm, with mismatched chairs clustered around a blazing hearth and wooden tables polished to a gleam. Garlands hung from exposed beams, and vintage ornaments caught the light from iron chandeliers. Mugs of steaming spiced wine already waited on the bar, as if they'd known we were coming.

Pierce led us toward the bar, grabbing a steaming mug and handing it to me. "This is the best hot spiced wine. Trust me."

I wrapped my fingers around the warm ceramic as I took a seat, the aroma of cinnamon and nutmeg rising with the steam. Across the room, a few people glanced our way, their curious gazes lingering a beat too long.

Vix sat down, trying to appear nonchalant as his eyes darted around the room. "So, what do you think? Better than being cooped up in the cabin?"

I took a sip of the drink, allowing myself a moment of honesty. "It's not so bad, but don't push your luck."

Pierce placed a hand on Vix's shoulder. "Don't jinx his luck because it's only a matter of time before—"

I nearly choked on my wine as the door slammed against the wall, cold air gusting through the inn. Every head turned toward the dramatic entrance of a woman in a bright purple cloak, snowflakes clinging to her wild auburn hair like tiny stars.

Her eyes scanned the room until they landed on Vix. Her expression morphed from determination to something that could only be described as vengeful delight.

"Oh shit." Vix slid down in his chair, trying to make his six-foot-something frame disappear behind Pierce. "Pretend I'm not here."

I raised an eyebrow, watching the woman brush snow from her shoulders with the flair of someone who practiced entrances in the mirror. "Friend of yours?"

"Not exactly." Vix sank lower. "It's about the ice sculpture... she's the artist."

Blitz snickered into his mug, eyes dancing with glee. "This is going to be good."

The woman stalked toward our table, her boots leaving wet prints on the wooden floor. Vix attempted to disappear completely behind Pierce, who didn't move an inch to help him.

"Some bodyguard you are," Vix muttered, eyes wide with panic.

But halfway across the room, the woman froze. Her narrowed eyes shifted from Vix to me, and her mouth fell open in shock.

I tensed, bracing for another strange reaction. Was I growing antlers? Turning blue? Had someone put a "kick me, I'm Santa's daughter" sign on my back?

Before I could check, the woman launched herself across the remaining distance and flung her arms around me, nearly knocking me off my stool. The hug was bone-crushing, her arms like steel bands around my ribs as she lifted me straight off my seat.

"Can't... breathe..." I gasped, my face mashed against her shoulder.

"Neve!" she cried, her voice thick with emotion. "It's really you!"

I stiffened in the woman's embrace, my brain desperately trying to process what was happening. My mug dangled precariously from my fingertips as she continued to squeeze me like a python with abandonment issues.

"Um," I wheezed out, "do I know you?"

The woman finally released me, holding me at arm's length with her hands gripping my shoulders. Her emerald eyes were wide and glistening with unshed tears, her face split into a grin so bright it could have powered all of Reinberg's Christmas lights.

"You don't remember me? It's Lumi! Luminescence Winter Wonderfrost?" She flipped her wild auburn hair over her shoulder, revealing the pointed tip of her ear before it disappeared again beneath her curls.

The world tilted sideways.

Lumi.

A flash of memory burst through my mind of two little girls racing down endless hallways lined with colorful packages, giggling as we slid across polished floors in fuzzy socks. Building snow forts with perfect snowballs while our parents worked. Sneaking extra candy canes from quality control.

"Your parents ran the stocking stuffer department," I whispered, my voice small and distant to my own ears.

Lumi bounced on her toes, her hands fluttering excitedly. "Yes! Mom's still there, and Dad got promoted to Small Electronics five years ago." She paused, studying my face. "Holy candy canes! You actually forgot us?"

The room started spinning a little. I groped blindly for my seat, my knees suddenly not working like they were supposed to. Don's steady hand found the small of my back, guiding me safely down onto the stool.

"I had an elf best friend," I mumbled, more to myself than anyone else. "Of course I did. Because why wouldn't I?"

Lumi's expression softened. "We thought you were never coming back. After the incident—"

"What incident?" I leaned forward, desperate for answers.

The men exchanged worried glances above my head. Pierce cleared his throat awkwardly.

Blitz slid a fresh mug of wine toward me. "I think you might need another drink."

CHAPTER 19
BLOODLINES

I stared at Lumi, my apparent childhood best friend. The wine suddenly tasted like battery acid in my mouth, but I took another sip anyway, needing something to calm me.

"Please, someone explain." My voice came out brittle, threatening to shatter with the slightest pressure.

Lumi's animated features softened. She took the stool Vix vacated, sliding onto it with a grace that seemed both familiar and alien. Her pointed ear peeked through her auburn curls again as she leaned forward, lowering her voice. "You really don't remember any of it? Your parents never told you?"

I gripped my mug tighter. "Told me what, exactly? That I'm Santa's daughter? That elves are real? That I spent my childhood in the North freaking Pole instead of in Los Angeles like I thought?"

The men around me shifted uncomfortably. Vix, apparently no longer concerned about whatever sculpture drama he'd been hiding from, studied my face with unusual intensity. "They couldn't tell her, Lumi. She's just now remembering who she is."

Lumi's brow furrowed. "The distance and time..." She then snorted. "Los Angeles is the most boring cover story ever."

"Focus, Lumi." Pierce rubbed small reassuring circles on my back.

She straightened. "Right. So, the thing is, you're... special. Even by North Pole standards."

"I'm getting that impression." I thought of all the wintry tricks I'd done so far without even trying.

"You have North Pole magic in your blood. Like, serious amounts. Not just from your father, who, yes, is Santa, but from your mother too." Lumi paused, watching me carefully. "Your mom is an elf."

The mug slipped from my fingers, but Don caught it with impossible reflexes before it could spill.

"I'm half-elf?" My words were hollow and distant. I didn't quite know how to feel about that. "Or wait, is my dad an elf too?"

Blitz rubbed my arm. "He is a chosen human who was gifted the magic of the North Pole."

Lumi looked around as if checking to make sure no one who shouldn't be listening could hear. "Your mother is one of the most powerful elves in the North Pole, and you inherited both bloodlines, plus the North Pole gifted you even more magic. It's a lot of power for one person."

I reached for one of my ears, wondering if I'd soon be growing points. "Power?"

"They were training you to control it, but when we were fifteen..." She glanced at Don, who gave an almost imperceptible nod.

"What?" It wasn't the first time someone had alluded to my lack of control. "What happened when I was fifteen?"

Lumi took a deep breath. "Your magic erupted. A complete loss of control. It was unlike anything anyone had ever seen before. Ice and snow exploded everywhere. Time kept freezing and unfreezing. Joy turned to fear and back again in waves. The main workshop was damaged, the reindeer barn nearly collapsed, and—" She swallowed hard. "Several people were hurt. No one died," she added quickly, seeing my expression.

The room tilted. I gripped the edge of the table to steady myself. "What did my parents do?"

"They made the choice to remove you from the North Pole.

To protect you." Lumi's voice was barely above a whisper, and she didn't have to say they also removed me to protect everyone else. She took my hand and squeezed.

"What caused the eruption?"

Lumi shrugged. "No one knows for sure. You were angry one moment, and then everything went sideways the next."

The implications crashed down on me like an avalanche. My throat constricted, making it hard to breathe. My whole life had been a lie, and not just a cute "your dad's Santa" lie, but a "you're a magical time bomb who almost killed people" lie.

"That's not..." I shook my head. "That can't be."

But even as I denied it, I felt something unspooling inside me, a thread of ice-cold power stretching outward. My emotions spiraled, and with them, reality itself wavered.

The clinking of glasses at the bar slowed. The crackling of the fire stretched into long, languid pops. Lumi's hair swayed in slow motion as she shifted in her seat. The sound of laughter from across the room deepened, stretching like taffy.

Time itself was bending around me.

Don's large hand settled on my arm, warm and grounding. "Breathe, Neve," he murmured, his voice somehow clear while everything else blurred.

I inhaled shakily, and the world snapped back to normal speed. Glasses clinked normally, the fire crackled at its regular pace, and conversation resumed.

Pierce stared at his hands. Blitz studied the ceiling as if it contained the secrets of the universe. Vix's expression was carefully blank. Lumi lowered her gaze to the floor.

They were giving me a moment when what they should have done was tackle me to the ground and lock me away. The kindness made my eyes burn.

But beneath that kindness, I recognized something else in the way their bodies had tensed, in how carefully they watched me from the corners of their eyes.

They were afraid.

Of me.

The realization settled into my bones with a terrible,

hollow certainty. I hadn't just been sent away from the North Pole; I had been exiled. Contained. I was the nuclear reactor they'd had to decommission, too unstable to remain operational.

My entire identity crisis seemed laughably small. I'd been angry about being lied to, but the truth was so much worse. I was a danger.

I shoved back from the bar. "I'd like to go back to the cabin now."

No one argued. No one even asked if I was okay, which I appreciated because the answer was a resounding no.

Lumi stood with me, wrapping me in another hug that felt both strange and achingly familiar. "I'll come visit tomorrow, if that's okay?"

I nodded against her shoulder, not trusting my voice. The idea that I had a friend who knew the real me was both terrifying and desperately needed.

As we pulled apart, Lumi's gaze slid to Vix, who was very interested in the pattern of the wooden floorboards. Her eyes narrowed dangerously. "And you. If you break that ice sculpture of the North Star I spent three weeks on, I will slice off an antler the next time you shift."

A surprised laugh escaped me before I could stop it. "Lumi, you know better than to threaten their antlers."

Vix's hand flew to his heart in mock offense. "I would never."

"You've done it twice already!"

"That was years ago!"

Pierce guided me toward the door with a gentle hand on my lower back. "Perhaps save the grudge match for another time?"

As we headed back to the barn, we skirted the edge of the village. The snow crunched beneath our boots, and I tried to focus on that rather than the fact that I was apparently half-elf, magically volatile, and potentially dangerous to everyone around me.

The sleigh was waiting where we left it, and I climbed aboard mechanically. The men exchanged glances before shifting into their reindeer forms. I didn't even have the energy to marvel at the transformation this time.

Pierce nudged my hand with his antlered head before moving into position. The touch almost broke me. How could they still be so gentle knowing what I was capable of?

The sleigh glided out of the barn and up the path. After a few minutes, Don veered right, leading us into a clearing in the trees. He stopped, and the men shifted back to human form.

I remained seated, staring at nothing.

Blitz approached, offering his hand. "Come on."

I stared at his outstretched palm without moving. "Why are we stopping?"

"Because you look like you're about to implode." He wiggled his fingers. "And we'd rather you didn't."

I didn't take his hand. "Shouldn't you be keeping your distance? What if I..." I swallowed hard. "What if I lose control?"

Don moved closer, his massive frame blocking the sky. "You won't."

"How can you possibly know that?" I crossed my arms. "I almost destroyed the North Pole."

Pierce stepped forward. "And yet here we are, standing before you unafraid."

"That's because you're idiots."

Vix snorted, kicking at the snow. "Well, she's got us there."

Despite everything, my mouth twitched. I pressed my lips together to stop the smile from forming and took Blitz's hand. "I was exiled for being too dangerous."

Blitz's expression softened as he pulled me to my feet. "You weren't exiled. If you were, your magic wouldn't have returned after being gone for so long, and we wouldn't have been called to you."

My eyebrows nearly shot off my forehead. "You were called to me?"

Pierce moved closer, his fingers tucking hair behind my ear. "In September, we started to feel a gentle tug that we needed to find something."

Don took my free hand. "We followed it, and it led us to you."

My throat tightened. "But... why?"

"You don't feel it?" Vix's head tilted, his eyes searching mine as he came to stand in front of me. I was now surrounded by four reindeer men who were staring at me with an intensity that made my knees wobble.

Did I feel it? The pull toward them? The inexplicable possessiveness? The bone-deep desire to make them all mine?

"I do feel something." I stepped out of their circle, overwhelmed. "Does my dad know his reindeer went on a mission to find his daughter?"

Pierce lifted his chin in defiance. "We're not the lead reindeer herd. At least not yet."

I was about to ask him to clarify the reindeer hierarchy when a snowball hit Pierce in the face with no warning. I froze, watching snow drip down his stunned face, tiny crystals clinging to his dark lashes as he blinked in disbelief.

Vix doubled over, cackling so hard he nearly collapsed. "Your face! Holy shit, your face!"

Pierce slowly wiped the slush from his cheek, his eyes narrowing dangerously as he looked between the three other men. "Who threw that?"

Don, stone-faced as ever, casually bent down and gathered a handful of snow, packing it in a way that led me to believe he was an expert at it.

"Don't you dare!" Pierce backed up, one hand raised defensively. "You know how much I hate—"

The snowball hit him square in the chest with such force he stumbled backward.

My hand flew to my mouth, stifling a surprised laugh that bubbled up unexpectedly. Something warm and forgotten flickered inside me, pushing back against the crushing weight of everything I'd learned.

Blitz scooped up a massive handful of snow. "Oh, it's on."

Chaos erupted. Snow flew in every direction as the men launched into battle with the intensity of warriors rather than grown men playing in the snow. I stood back, watching them with a mixture of disbelief and unexpected delight.

Pierce dodged a vicious throw from Vix only to slip, landing flat on his back with a muffled curse.

A laugh escaped me, and four sets of eyes turned to me.

Blitz's face split into a wicked grin. "She laughs! But not for long." He launched a snowball directly at me.

I yelped, ducking before it could hit me. "Hey! I'm not part of this!"

Vix's snowball clipped my shoulder. "You are now, princess."

I grabbed a fistful of snow, packed it tight between my gloved palms. The men had formed a loose semicircle, each armed with fresh ammunition.

I narrowed my eyes, took aim, and hurled my snowball with all my might. It hit Blitz in the face with a satisfying splat.

His expression of utter shock sent me into a fit of giggles.

"Direct hit!" I pumped my fist in the air.

"You better run." Don's voice was full of amusement.

Four snowballs flew at me simultaneously. I shrieked and darted away, heading for the edge of the clearing where trees would provide some coverage.

A snowball whizzed past my ear. Another hit my back. I scrambled behind a wide pine, frantically gathering snow.

"You can't hide forever!" Vix's voice echoed through the trees.

I peeked around the trunk and let loose. The snowball caught him in the shoulder, exploding in a puff of white.

I was already running before he could retaliate, laughing so hard my sides hurt. When was the last time I'd felt so... free?

My boot caught on something hidden beneath the snow. I tumbled forward, arms windmilling as I plunged face-first into a drift. Snow went up my nose and down the neck of my coat.

I pushed myself up, sputtering and wiping snow from my eyes. The men advanced like predators stalking prey, each with a fresh snowball.

"Not fair!" I scrambled backward like a crab. "Four against one!"

Pierce cocked his head. "Life isn't fair, North."

I raised my hands instinctively to shield myself. "Don't you dare!"

A strange tingling sensation shot up my arms. The surrounding snow shivered, then rose upward in a swirling curtain of white. It spiraled higher, curving inward, forming walls that twisted and solidified into smooth, gleaming surfaces.

Within seconds, I was sitting in the center of what looked like an elaborate snow fort, complete with elegant, spiraled walls and intricate frosted patterns etched into the surface.

I slowly lowered my hands, staring at what I'd created. "What the..."

The men stood frozen outside the small opening of my snow dome, eyes wide with identical expressions of awe.

Blitz whistled low. "Well, that's new."

I stood and ran my fingers over the nearest wall, feeling the perfect smoothness beneath my gloves. It was beautiful but strong. Soft light filtered through the translucent walls, casting everything in a soft blue glow.

I felt a flicker of wonder instead of fear. This power, whatever it was, could create beauty too.

A smile spread across my face, tentative at first, then growing into something real and genuine. "I made this."

Don stepped inside, and his eyes softened as he examined my creation. "It's magnificent."

My cheeks warmed at the simple praise.

Vix peered through one of the arched openings. "Are you going to invite us in, or did you build this fortress specifically to keep us out? Because I've got to say, that's cold. Literally."

I rolled my eyes. "Come in."

They didn't need a second invitation. Pierce ducked through first, followed by Blitz, who practically dove inside. Vix sauntered through with exaggerated casualness.

Pierce ran his hand along the curved ceiling. "How did you know how to make this?"

I shook my head, still marveling at what I'd done. "I didn't. I wanted somewhere to hide, and... this happened."

Blitz circled me, eyeing my ice creation with exaggerated suspicion. "So you conjure a magic fortress to escape us, then invite us in?" He wagged his finger. "Classic trap tactics."

I laughed, still running my fingers over the smooth wall. "I didn't even know I could—"

My words turned into a shriek as something cold and wet slid down my back. I spun around to find Blitz grinning triumphantly, empty hands raised.

"You did not just do that!"

He bounced on his toes. "Consider it payback for that face shot earlier."

I grabbed a handful of snow from the floor. "You're going to pay for that!"

The inside of my beautiful snow dome erupted into chaos. Don ducked as Vix launched a snowball at his head. Blitz created a small ammunition pile while I pelted Pierce, who retaliated by charging straight for me.

I scrambled backward. "No fair using your size advantage!"

Pierce's eyes gleamed with mischief. "All's fair in love and snowball fights."

He lunged, and I twisted away, except my boots had other ideas. My feet shot out from under me, and I grabbed Pierce's coat as I fell. We tumbled down together in a tangle of limbs, landing with a soft thud on the snowy floor.

Pierce braced himself above me, his weight pressing me gently into the snow. The laughter died in my throat as our eyes locked.

"This wasn't part of my strategy," I whispered, hyperaware of every inch where our bodies connected.

His mouth curved into a smile. "It was part of mine," he murmured right before his lips met mine.

CHAPTER 20
MAGICAL DOME

I thought my ice dome had been magical before, but the real magic was happening as Pierce's mouth moved against mine. His kiss was tentative, as though he was asking for permission. Permission I gave without hesitation, sinking my fingers into his hair and pulling him closer.

Snow melted beneath us, dampening my coat, but I couldn't have cared less. Pierce's tongue traced the seam of my lips, and I opened for him, sighing as he deepened the kiss. His weight pressed me into the ground, deliciously heavy but carefully balanced.

When he finally pulled back, his eyes had darkened. I traced the sharp line of his jaw with my fingertip.

A throat cleared somewhere above us. "As fascinating as this floor show is, some of us are getting frostbite in uncomfortable places."

I glanced up to find Vix watching us, arms crossed over his chest, one eyebrow raised in a perfect arch with heat in his eyes.

The fear that had crippled me at the inn seemed impossibly distant now, replaced by something warm and reckless. It felt... right. *I* felt right. Powerful in a way that didn't terrify me because of these men.

Pierce rolled off me, and I grabbed his sleeve. "Stay... all of you."

Blitz's usual restless energy was focused entirely on me. "What exactly are you suggesting?"

I sat up slowly, my gaze moving from Pierce to Vix to Blitz to Don.

"I'm suggesting that I'm tired of being afraid." I rose to my feet, brushing snow from my pants. "I'm tired of worrying about what I might do or who I might hurt. At least for today."

Don took a step forward. "And what would you rather do instead?"

The air crackled with tension. Four pairs of eyes fixed on me with such hunger that my breath caught.

"Something reckless." I took a step toward Don, then another.

Vix made a sound somewhere between a laugh and a groan. "You're playing with fire, princess."

"Am I?" I tilted my head, feeling strangely powerful. "Or are you playing with ice?"

A faint smile curved Don's mouth as he reached for me, his hand cupping my face with tenderness. The contrast between his gentle touch and his imposing size sent a shiver down my spine.

"Both," he murmured, before lowering his head to capture my lips.

Don kissed me with slow, thorough precision that made my knees weak. His hands spanned my waist, easily lifting me until my legs wrapped around him and we were at eye level.

When we broke apart, I was breathless and dizzy. Before I could recover, Vix was there, guiding me with his fingers on my chin.

"Fuck, yes," he growled, before claiming my mouth in a kiss that was pure fire. He was all passion and demand, his hands tangling in my hair.

When we broke apart, I was panting, my body thrumming with need. I turned my head in the other direction to find Blitz watching me.

"Blitz," I whispered, holding out my hand.

He was on me in an instant, his kiss playful but no less

174

intense, nipping at my lower lip before soothing it with his tongue. By the time he pulled away, I was trembling.

It felt too hot even with the ice walls surrounding us. A small part of me wondered if it would collapse, but I quickly banished the thought.

"This isn't exactly the most comfortable place for what I think we're all considering," Pierce observed, his voice rough.

Blitz snapped his fingers, and the floor was suddenly covered in thick, luxurious furs.

I blinked in surprise. "That's handy."

Vix helped me from Don's arms and tugged me down onto the furs, his hands already working at the zipper of my coat. "Speaking of hands, I want mine all over you... and in you."

As I sank into the soft pelts, surrounded by the heat of four powerful bodies, any lingering doubts evaporated. This felt right in a way nothing else had since my memories began returning.

"I don't know where this is going with you all, but I don't want to have to eventually choose," I confessed, watching their expressions carefully. "Between any of you or the others."

Pierce's fingers stilled. "All nine of us?"

"Eight," I corrected, thinking of Rudy as something in my heart twisted at the memory of his rejection earlier.

Blitz made a dismissive noise, his mouth busy tracing the curve of my neck. "Rudy will eventually pull his antlers out of his ass."

I ignored the comment, too distracted by Don's hands sliding beneath my coat. "Is that... allowed? All of you?"

Don's deep voice rumbled against my ear. "It's not unheard of for several members in a herd to share a mate."

"But?" I prompted, sensing hesitation.

"But never a whole herd." Pierce's eyes never left mine as he helped Vix tug my boots off. "It's unprecedented."

Vix's fingers slid up my calf, leaving trails of heat in their wake. "So is your magic. So is the pull we all feel toward you."

"We all feel it." Don's hand spanned my ribs below my breast. "That you're ours."

A flush of heat spread through me at his words. "And I'm meant to believe this is some magical connection? Not that I'm the only available woman or something?"

I couldn't quite wrap my head around this many men wanting only me. They were all attractive in every way, and it seemed too good to be true. Plus, men had needs, and I wasn't sure my pussy would survive.

Blitz snorted against my collarbone. "Trust me, if it were about availability, Vix would have—"

Vix aimed a half-hearted swat at Blitz's head. "Keep talking and I'll—"

I cut him off with a kiss, not wanting to hear the rest of that particular threat. His mouth moved hungrily against mine, his hands threading through my hair to hold me close.

When we broke apart, I found myself laughing, a sound of pure joy that bubbled up from somewhere deep. "I can't believe I'm doing this."

Pierce's fingers found the hem of my sweater, his eyes questioning. I nodded, lifting my arms as he pulled it over my head, leaving me in my bra and leggings.

"Believe it." His gaze traveled over my exposed skin with such heat I could almost feel it like a physical touch. "Red is an excellent color on you."

Around me, coats and sweaters disappeared with surprising swiftness. Soon I was surrounded by broad shoulders, muscled chests, and cocks—so many gloriously thick and large cocks.

A new flame of desire threatened to consume me entirely.

I stared at the array of naked male bodies surrounding me, my mouth going dry. While I'd spent plenty of time with these men, seeing them all gloriously nude and straining with need was a whole different situation.

I ran my fingers down Pierce's torso, tracing the firm ridges of his abdomen. "I can't believe all of you want me."

Blitz flashed a grin, kneeling beside me on the furs. "Want is an understatement."

His mouth found my neck, trailing hot kisses down to my collarbone while Don worked at removing my bra. The clasp gave way under his fingers, and it fell away, exposing my breasts.

"Beautiful." Don cupped one breast, his thumb brushing over my nipple until it hardened to a tight peak.

Vix settled between my legs, tugging at my leggings and panties in one impatient motion. He tapped my hip. "Up."

I lifted my hips, allowing him to slide the fabric down my legs. The cold air against my exposed sex made me gasp, but the heat in Vix's eyes as he stared at me quickly banished any chill.

"Fuck, look at her." Vix's hands stroked up my thighs, spreading them wider. "Already wet for us."

Pierce's mouth found mine in a demanding kiss while Blitz continued his attention on my neck and shoulders. Don's lips closed around my nipple, sucking gently while his hand teased the other breast.

Vix lowered his head between my thighs, his tongue flicking against my clit with devastating precision. The multiple points of contact had my body arching, overwhelmed by sensation.

"That's it," Pierce encouraged against my lips as I moaned. "Let us hear you."

I couldn't have held back if I tried. Every lick of Vix's tongue, every graze of teeth against my skin from Blitz, every gentle suck from Don had me climbing higher toward some precipice I couldn't quite see.

Vix slid one finger inside me, then two, curving them just right as his tongue continued its relentless assault on my clit. The pressure built impossibly high, my muscles tensing.

"She's close," Blitz observed, his voice rough with need.

"Come for us." Pierce's fingers replaced Don's on my breast, pinching my nipple hard enough to send me careening over the edge.

My orgasm rolled through me, my body arching off the furs as I cried out. Vix worked me through it, his fingers pumping slowly as I clenched around them.

When I could breathe again, I opened my eyes to find all four men watching me with hungry expressions. Their cocks stood proudly erect, intimidating in their size.

Vix wiped his mouth with the back of his hand, his grin wicked. "Wait until we're all inside you."

My eyes widened. "All of you?"

Pierce trailed his fingers down my stomach. "We can take it slow. There are many ways to pleasure you."

Blitz's eyes gleamed as he stretched out beside me. "And many places to put ourselves."

"What about..." Vix's hand slid lower, fingers grazing the cleft of my ass.

I bit my lip, heat flooding my cheeks. "I'm not ready for that. Not yet."

Vix nodded, pressing a surprisingly tender kiss to my inner thigh. "Whenever you're ready... or not. No pressure."

I glanced between them, desire building again despite my recent release. "But maybe... two of you? In my pussy?"

The collective groan that echoed through the room sent a fresh wave of arousal through me.

"Holy fuck." Blitz's cock twitched.

Don's massive hand encircled his length, stroking slowly. "Are you sure?"

I nodded, desperate to feel them inside me. "I want to try."

Pierce helped me to my knees, positioning himself on his back against the furs, his cock standing proudly.

"Come here," he beckoned, hands on my hips as I straddled him.

Don's hands replaced Pierce's, guiding me as I sank down slowly onto Pierce's length. I groaned at the stretch, my body still sensitive from my previous orgasm.

"Take your time." Pierce's face was tight with restraint.

Once I'd taken him fully, I leaned forward, bracing my hands on his chest. Behind me, Vix's fingers traced where Pierce and I were joined.

"Relax." Vix slid a finger in alongside Pierce's cock.

It was bordering on too much, but it wasn't painful. I focused on breathing, on the look of pure pleasure on Pierce's face, on the gentle kisses Blitz was pressing to my shoulder.

When Vix added a second finger, I gasped, my body shuddering. Pierce groaned beneath me, his hands flexing on my hips.

"That's it." Vix scissored his fingers gently. "Opening so beautifully for us."

After what felt like an eternity of careful preparation, Vix removed his fingers. The head of his cock pressed against me, seeking entrance alongside Pierce.

"Tell me if it's too much," Vix whispered against my ear as he began to push forward.

The stretch was intense, burning slightly. I closed my eyes, focusing on relaxing as Vix inched his way inside.

"So tight," Pierce gritted out beneath me, his body trembling with the effort of remaining still.

When Vix was finally fully inside me, I was stretched to my limit. They remained still, giving me time to adjust.

"Okay?" Don stroked my hair.

I nodded, unable to form words as pleasure began to replace the discomfort. Experimentally, I shifted my hips, drawing groans from the men.

Blitz and Don positioned themselves on either side of me, their cocks level with my face as they stroked themselves. I reached for them, wrapping my hand around Don's impressive girth while taking Blitz into my mouth.

The movement triggered Vix and Pierce to start moving, establishing a rhythm that made me moan around Blitz's cock. They moved carefully at first, then with increasing urgency as my body accepted them both.

"Look at her taking all of us." Blitz's fingers tangled in my hair.

I released him from my mouth to gasp as a deep thrust hit something perfect inside me. "Yes, right there."

Don's fingers found my clit, circling with gentle pressure that sent me spiraling toward another climax with alarming speed.

I released Blitz, turning my attention to Don's impressive length. The taste of Blitz lingered on my tongue as I wrapped my lips around Don's cock, the sheer girth of him stretching my jaw. My hand continued to work Blitz's shaft, his pre-cum making my palm slick as I stroked him.

Pierce's abs contracted as he lifted his upper body. His teeth grazed my nipple before sucking it between his lips.

"Fuck, that's hot," Blitz groaned above me, his hips jerking into my hand.

Vix's fingers pinched my other nipple, sending jolts of pleasure straight to my core. With both nipples being played with, two cocks filling me, and another stretching my lips, I couldn't stop the needy whine that escaped me.

"She's close again." Don's massive hand cupped the back of my head, not pushing but holding me steady as I took him deeper.

The pressure built inside me like a gathering storm, my body stretched and filled in ways I'd never imagined possible. Every nerve ending seemed to fire at once, my skin hypersensitive to each touch.

Pierce thrust up while Vix pushed down, hitting something deep inside that made stars explode behind my eyelids. Don's thumb brushed over my cheek in a strangely tender gesture as I hollowed my cheeks around him.

I was floating, suspended in pure sensation, my body no longer my own but a vessel for pleasure so intense it bordered on spiritual. My orgasm hit without warning, exploding through me with such force that I choked on a scream, my vision going white at the edges.

As my pussy squeezed around them, cold drops of liquid hit my face. Opening my eyes, I saw snowflakes drifting down from the ceiling.

Vix cursed, his rhythm faltering as he drove deep and stilled, pulsing inside me. Pierce followed moments later, his fingers digging into my hips as he emptied himself.

Blitz groaned, his cock swelling in my hand before he came in hot spurts across my fingers. Don, his face a mask of restrained pleasure, pushed between my lips, finding his release with a deep moan that I felt in my bones.

As we collapsed in a tangle of limbs on the furs, snow

continued to fall gently around us, dusting our heated skin with delicate crystals that melted instantly.

"Did I do that?" I watched the flakes drift lazily downward.

Blitz laughed, pressing a kiss to my shoulder. "Your magic seems to respond strongly to emotion."

I smiled, feeling strangely peaceful despite the chaos of the past weeks. "Then we should definitely do this again."

CHAPTER 21
SNOW SHARKS

We trudged through knee-deep snow toward a wide-open clearing bordered by enormous pines as the sun peeked over the horizon. It was content to hover there like an indecisive houseguest who couldn't commit to fully arriving or leaving. At this latitude in November, the pathetic glow was apparently as good as it got.

"Could we do this training thing inside? Where there's heat and coffee and better light?" I flailed my arms toward the floodlights mounted outside the cabin that seemed to struggle against the persistent semi-darkness.

Pierce adjusted his beanie. "Magic like yours needs space. Preferably outdoors, where if something goes unexpectedly, we won't destroy the cabin."

"That's super reassuring, thanks." I shoved my gloved hands deeper into my pockets and tried not to look at Rudy, who walked several paces ahead with Don, their heads bent in serious conversation.

Rudy had barely glanced at me since our confrontation yesterday, and the petty part of me was determined to match his indifference. The less petty part was busy composing elaborate, cutting speeches I'd never deliver.

My phone buzzed in my pocket. I yanked it out with embarrassing eagerness, hoping to see my parents' names on the screen. Nothing. Well, except for a low battery warning, which was splendid considering I'd just charged it. Apparently, being close to the veil led to electronic malfunctions.

I'd tried calling my parents three times since learning the truth, but each attempt went unanswered. Were they avoiding me? Did they even know I was here? Maybe they were in some remote part of the North Pole where service was spotty. Did the North Pole even have regular service? Or were they sitting around a cozy fire, staring at my name on their caller ID and debating what lie to tell me next?

Dash fell into step beside me. "You look like you're plotting murder."

"I'm processing the fact that my parents have been lying to me my entire life and now won't pick up the phone."

Kip appeared on my other side, brushing snow from his shoulders. "They sent you away to protect you."

"Yeah, well, they could have protected me *and* told me the truth. Or, I don't know, helped me control my apparently destructive magic instead of pretending it didn't exist." The snow around my boots crystallized into jagged patterns, and I couldn't tell if it was me that caused it or something else. "Someone tried, I think. I remember a man... not my dad... trying to teach me, but he was kind of an asshole about it."

We reached the center of the clearing, where Rudy and Don had stopped. The rest of the men formed a loose circle around me, and I fought the urge to shield myself from their expectant gazes.

Cole unfolded a blanket and placed it on the snow. "Sit."

"I'm not a dog." I eyed the blanket dubiously. "And won't my ass freeze?"

Vix winked. "I'll warm it up for you later."

I rolled my eyes but sat, crossing my legs and trying to ignore how the cold immediately seeped through my leggings. "So how does this work? Do I get a wand or some magic words or, oh! I want a sword!"

The men exchanged glances that did nothing for my confidence.

Don knelt beside me. "First, we need to understand your baseline. Close your eyes and focus on your breathing."

I closed my eyes, shivering slightly.

"Inhale for four counts, hold for seven, exhale for eight." Don's deep voice guided me through several rounds of breathing that seemed to be random counts he was pulling out of his ass. "Now, visualize your magic as energy flowing through your body. Where do you feel it strongest?"

I tried to focus, but all I felt was cold and a growing irritation at Rudy's silent presence somewhere to my left. "I don't feel anything except my toes freezing and one of my pussy lips going numb."

Don's patience remained unshakable. "Try again. Think of a moment when your magic activated. Like when you made the ice dome."

I recalled the exhilaration of creating the structure, the way power had surged through my fingertips. A pleasant warmth bloomed in my chest, spreading outward.

"There," I whispered, rubbing the center of my chest. "It feels like... sparklers under my skin."

Blitz clapped. "Good! Now try to direct that feeling toward your hands."

I concentrated, picturing the energy flowing down my arms. For a moment, I felt a tingling in my palms... then nothing.

"It disappeared." I opened my eyes with a frustrated huff.

Pierce squatted in front of me. "Emotion seems to be your trigger. Think of something that makes you happy."

Happy. Right. Because I had so many cheerful thoughts to choose from lately.

I closed my eyes again, searching for a joyful memory. Decorating cookies. Ice skating. The snowball fight. The magical dome and what happened inside it.

Heat flushed through me, and I heard gasps.

My eyes flew open to find a miniature blizzard swirling around me, confined to a three-foot radius.

"Holy shit." I raised my hands, watching snowflakes dance around my fingers.

Dane's eyes widened. "Try to make it bigger."

I focused on expanding the swirl, but as soon as I tried to control it, the snow collapsed into a sad little pile at my feet.

"Damn it!" Frost crackled across the blanket beneath me.

Kip brushed snow from his hair. "Don't force it. Magic responds to intention, not demand."

"What does that even mean?" I stood, shaking out my stiff legs. "This is pointless. I can't control it."

Rudy finally spoke, his deep voice cutting through my frustration. "You're not trying."

The temperature around me plummeted. "Excuse me?"

"You're wallowing in self-pity instead of focusing." His eyes met mine, indifferent as stone. "Your magic responds to your emotions, but you're letting your emotions control you instead of the other way around."

Snow began sliding across the ground toward him, forming sinister little vortexes. "You know nothing about what I'm feeling."

"Don't I?" One eyebrow rose in challenge. "Confused. Angry. Betrayed. Scared of your own power. Wondering if you'll hurt someone again."

Each word hit like a physical blow. The ground beneath us trembled slightly.

Pierce stepped between us. "We should take a break."

"No." I stepped around him, facing Rudy directly. "You think you know me so well? Fine. Tell me how I'm supposed to control something I didn't even know existed until a week ago."

"Stop fighting it." Rudy's expression softened. "Your magic isn't separate from you. It's part of you."

"A part that nearly destroyed a workshop and hurt people." My voice caught. "What if I can't control it?"

"You can." Cole's voice drew my attention. "We've all seen glimpses of it. When you're not overthinking."

Don nodded. "Like the dome. You didn't plan that, you just reacted."

"Great, so my magic works best when I'm not trying to use it. Super helpful." I kicked at the snow, watching it scatter. "And let's not forget that my dad, the actual Santa Claus, hasn't bothered to call me back. Maybe he's still afraid I'll blow up the North Pole if I come home."

The sky darkened above us, clouds gathering unnaturally fast. My hands tingled, ice crystals forming on my fingertips.

Vix whistled low. "Uh, guys, we might want to..."

A bolt of lightning cracked across the sky, followed immediately by thunder that shook the ground.

Blitz's eyes widened. "That's new."

Panic clawed at my throat. "I'm not doing that. Am I doing that?"

Another lightning bolt, closer this time. The hair on my arms stood on end beneath my jacket.

"Everyone back!" Rudy's command sent the others retreating several paces.

Everyone except him.

He moved toward me instead, his expression unreadable as the wind whipped around us, forming a miniature cyclone of snow.

"Stay back." I raised my hands, ice forming in my palms. "I don't want to hurt you."

"You won't." He stepped closer, snowflakes swirling between us.

"You don't know that!" The ice in my hands grew, jagged and dangerous. "I can't control this!"

"Then don't control it." He was close enough now that I could see the flecks of silver in his eyes. "Feel it instead."

The storm intensified, lightning illuminating Rudy's face in stark flashes. Yet he continued forward, undeterred.

"What are you doing?" My voice was barely audible over the howling wind.

"Trusting you." He reached for my ice-covered hands.

"Don't—" I tried to pull away, but his fingers closed around mine.

The moment we touched, everything stopped. The wind died. The lightning ceased. The clouds dissipated as quickly as they'd formed, leaving only the weak arctic twilight and my ragged breathing.

Rudy's hands were warm around my frozen ones, steady and strong. The ice melted between our palms, dripping onto the snow below.

"How did you do that?" I whispered, staring at our joined hands.

"I didn't." His thumb brushed over my knuckles. "You did."

For a moment, we stood like that, connected and still. Then Rudy released my hands and stepped back, his expression closing off again.

"That's enough for today." He turned away, addressing the others. "She needs rest."

I stared at my hands, still tingling from Rudy's touch. For a moment, I'd felt complete control, not by forcing my magic to obey, but by simply letting it exist alongside me.

And all it had taken was Rudy's touch.

The same Rudy who now walked away without looking back, leaving me standing alone in the snow, more confused than ever.

I KICKED AT THE SNOW, watching it spray upward in a pathetic arc before landing with a disappointing plop. It was a truly fitting metaphor for my abilities. Yesterday I'd created a freaking magical lightning storm. Today, I couldn't even make a decent snowball without it turning into something with teeth.

"Maybe try visualizing something... pleasant?" Dash suggested from a safe distance. After yesterday's incident, all nine men had developed a newfound appreciation for personal space.

"Like what? Puppies? Rainbows? My parents actually picking up their fucking phones?" I pulled my phone from my pocket and glared at it for the hundredth time. Still nothing. I was on day two of calls, texts, and increasingly unhinged voice-mails, and radio silence from the North Pole's first couple.

Pierce exchanged glances with Don. "The veil's interference makes communication spotty at best, even with Frostlink."

"Spotty would be an improvement. This is a black hole." I shoved my phone back into my pocket, where it sat like a useless brick. "And don't tell me they don't know I'm here. You guys have a weird telepathic reindeer network, right? Someone must have told Santa his daughter is having a complete magical meltdown twenty miles from his workshop."

Vix cleared his throat. "Actually, we can't exactly—"

The snow beneath him rose suddenly, twisting into a serpentine shape that lunged toward his head. He yelped and jumped backward, tripping over Dane and landing on his ass in a snowdrift.

"Sorry!" I squeezed my eyes shut, trying to unthink whatever thought had triggered snow snakes. "I didn't mean to do that."

When I opened my eyes, the snake had collapsed back into harmless powder, but three more were forming around me, slithering in sinister patterns.

Blitz whistled. "That's pretty badass. Can you make them bigger?"

"I don't know how I'm making them at all!"

As if responding to my frustration, the snakes grew, elongating into something between pythons and anacondas, their icy bodies reflecting the weak light.

Kip shuffled backward. "Can you think about something else? Literally anything else?"

I tried to focus on something harmless like vacation, palm trees, and the ocean.

Blitz's scream shattered my concentration. Where the snakes had been, now half a dozen triangular fins cut through the snow, circling us like we were chum in the water.

"Are those—"

"Snow sharks." Don watched with scientific interest as one fin changed direction and headed straight for him. He sidestepped it easily.

The fins picked up speed, creating furrows in the snow as

they raced around us. A laugh bubbled up in my throat at the absolute absurdity until one fin veered sharply, the snow rising in a wave that formed a gaping maw of icy teeth that chomped down on Blitz's calf.

"Motherfucker!" Blitz jumped, clutching his leg. The shark dissolved into powder, but Blitz's grimace remained. "That stung!"

My stomach dropped. "I'm so sorry! I didn't mean to..." My words got stuck as a lump rose in my throat. The last thing I wanted was for any of them to get hurt.

The remaining sharks froze mid-circle, then collapsed all at once. I stared at the mess I'd created, fighting back tears of frustration. "This is pointless. Everything I try turns into a disaster."

Cole approached cautiously, brushing snow from his pants. "Your magic responds to your emotions, and right now you're operating from a place of anger and frustration."

"No kidding." I caught sight of Rudy standing apart from the group, arms crossed, watching with that infuriating stoic expression. Yesterday, he'd seemed almost human, taking my hands, talking about trust. Today he was back to the silent judgment routine.

"We need to anchor you in positive emotions," Cole continued. "Joy seems to be your strongest conduit for controlling your magic."

I tore my eyes away from Rudy. "That's fantastic advice. I'll just feel joyful on command while freezing my ass off in the middle of nowhere, with no word from my parents, surrounded by men who keep telling me I'm amazing when I can't even make a decent snowball."

Cole's mouth twitched. "When you put it that way..."

"And I can't feel joy with him standing over there like some judgmental ice statue." I jabbed a finger toward Rudy. "Every time I try to do something, I can feel him watching, waiting for me to fail."

Rudy's jaw tightened, but he remained silent. Typical.

A grin spread across Kip's face, which was never a good sign when it came to him. "I think we're overthinking this. Magic lessons don't have to be so serious."

"Did you miss the part where I sent snow sharks after everyone?" I gestured to Blitz, who was still rubbing his leg.

"I didn't miss it; I thought it was awesome." Kip's eyes sparkled. "Your magic wants to play. So let's play with it instead of trying to wrangle it into submission."

Rudy finally spoke, his deep voice carrying across the snow. "This isn't a game, Kip."

"Maybe it should be." Kip winked at me. "Cole and I can work with her alone for the rest of the day. No pressure, no audience, no... intensity."

The last word was clearly aimed at Rudy, whose eyebrows drew together in disapproval. "That's not—"

"I think Kip might be onto something," Don interrupted. "Neve's magic responds best when she's relaxed and enjoying herself. Remember the dome?"

Pierce nodded. "And the snowball fight."

Heat rushed to my cheeks, and for a moment, I could have sworn tiny sparks danced across my fingertips.

Rudy's gaze flicked to my hands, then back to my face. Something unreadable passed through his eyes before he scoffed and turned away. "Fine. Do what you want."

He strode off toward the trees, shoulders rigid. The rest of the herd exchanged looks, then followed him with varying levels of reluctance.

Soon only Kip, Cole, and I remained in the clearing, the silence stretching between us until Kip clapped his hands together.

"Well, this is going to be fun."

I raised an eyebrow. "Your definition of fun needs serious recalibration."

Cole's mouth curved into a smile. "Give us a chance. I think you'll be surprised."

I smiled back. "All right, reindeer games. Show me what you've got."

CHAPTER 22
REINDEER GAMES

I crossed my arms, stomping my feet in place to get blood flowing back to my toes. Cole and Kip had vanished five minutes ago with mysterious grins and instructions to "wait right here" while they "prepared the learning environment." Which, based on previous experience, could mean anything from gathering harmless pinecones to setting up an elaborate Christmas-themed deathtrap.

Kip reappeared first, trudging through the snow, pulling three sleds on a rope behind him. "Training location secured! Follow me, Ice Princess."

I glared at the nickname but trudged after him. "If this involves sacrificing me to the winter gods, I'd like to point out that my father could technically be considered one, and he probably wouldn't appreciate it."

Cole materialized from between two pine trees. "No sacrifices today. Just hands-on joy training."

I rolled my eyes so hard I nearly strained something. "Joy training? Did you get that from a holiday self-help book?"

Kip's laughter echoed through the trees as we rounded a bend and emerged into a clearing. Unlike our previous training ground, this one featured several large snow mounds, a handful of towering pine trees, and what appeared to be the start of a crude snow track.

Cole started to untie the sleds. "Magic flows best through authentic emotion. You can't force joy, but you can create conditions where it naturally occurs."

"Like a snow obstacle course?" I eyed the clearing dubiously.

Kip's face lit up. "Exactly like that! But for our first activity, we'll make snow angels."

He flopped backward into the snow, arms and legs moving in perfect synchronicity. When he stood, brushing powder from his ass, a perfect angel impression remained; except this one had wings that curved like actual feathers and a detailed halo.

Cole nodded toward the snow. "Your turn."

"I hate to break it to you, but snow angels aren't exactly joy-inducing for most adults."

Kip clutched invisible pearls. "Blasphemy! Snow angels are timeless."

I sighed, looking between their expectant faces. "Fine. One snow angel coming right up."

I fell backward, the snow cushioning my fall. For a moment, I just lay there, staring up at the sky. Then I moved my arms and legs, feeling utterly ridiculous yet somehow lighter.

When I stood, I expected to see a misshapen snow depression, but my angel had delicate patterns radiating from where my head had been, and the wings sparkled with a bluish tint that definitely wasn't natural.

Cole's eyebrows shot up. "See? You didn't even try to use magic."

"But that's kind of the point, isn't it?" I brushed the snow from my pants. "My magic just does whatever it wants, whenever it wants."

"But there aren't any snow monsters coming after us." Kip rubbed his hands together. "Let's take things up a notch with sled races."

He grabbed a wooden sled and positioned it at the top of the largest snow mound, which sloped into a curve. "Fastest one wins. Loser has to..." He rubbed his chin.

"Build a snowman naked?" I suggested with faux innocence.

Cole choked on air while Kip's eyes widened with delight. "I was going to say the loser has to make hot chocolate for everyone, but your stakes are much better."

Cole cleared his throat and conjured a stopwatch. "Let's stick with hot chocolate for now."

I shrugged, climbing onto the sled. "Your loss."

My first run ended with me face-planting into a snowdrift after misjudging the curve. Cole's turn ended with him sliding off course and nearly taking out a small pine tree. By the time Kip went, I was laughing so hard my sides hurt, especially when he hit a hidden bump and went airborne, landing with a theatrical yelp and a flurry of snow.

"Cheater!" Kip accused when I went for my third run. "You used magic to smooth your path."

I held up my hands. "I did not! And even if I did, it would be a sign of progress, so you should congratulate me."

Cole nodded toward my hands. "Speaking of progress..."

I followed his gaze to find tiny silver-blue sparks dancing between my fingers, like miniature stars orbiting my palms. "Oh!"

The sparks faded as soon as I noticed them, but the warm hum of power still flowed through me.

Kip ran his fingers through his hair, knocking snow free. "See? Fun equals magic. Now for the real fun: a snowman decorating competition!"

I groaned. "I don't know how to make a snowman."

"We'll build them together first." Cole started to pack snow into a mound.

Thirty minutes and ten frozen fingers later, three snowmen sat lined up next to each other.

Cole gestured to the area around us, including the trees. "I've placed objects to decorate the snowmen within shouting distance. You each get two buttons for eyes, half a carrot for the nose, and you need at least six rocks or pebbles for the mouth.

There's one scarf that can only be retrieved when everything else is in place on your snowman."

I narrowed my eyes. "But you put all the items out there, so how is that fair?"

Cole rubbed the back of his neck, seeming not to have considered that issue. "You two can have a two-minute head start, and I can only walk."

I looked at his legs. "You have like nine inches on me. I think it's only fair that you can only hop like a bunny."

Kip doubled over with laughter. "Oh, this is great."

"You too." I walked backward toward the trees Cole had emerged from earlier. "And I get a one-minute head start on you."

Before they could argue, I turned and ran, my eyes scanning the snow for objects. The first thing I spotted was a red scarf hanging from the branch of a tree, and it killed me not to grab it, but rules were rules.

Thankfully, most of the objects needed were easy to spot, and soon I was filling my pockets with the required items.

Cole hopped like a deranged rabbit, his massive frame bouncing ridiculously high with each leap. Kip wasn't much better, his cheeks flushed with effort as he bounded along. Every time he hopped past a tree and nearly took out a branch with his head, I wheezed with laughter.

Soon, I was back at my snowman, placing the final pebble into its lopsided grin. It looked like it had survived a small avalanche, but technically, it met all requirements.

Kip jammed his last rock into place at the exact moment Cole did.

All three of us froze, exchanging glances that clearly communicated the same thought: That scarf is mine.

I had a split second to register their shared look before both men abandoned their rabbit personas. They took off sprinting toward the red scarf hanging from the distant pine branch, snow flying in their wake.

"Hey!" I took off after them, pumping my arms and legs with all the stamina I had left.

Cole reached the tree first, his fingers brushing the fabric as Kip crashed into him, sending them both stumbling sideways. I skidded to a halt behind them, watching as they playfully grappled, each trying to reach the scarf while blocking the other.

It dangled above them, and without thinking, I raised my hand, focused on the red fabric, and felt my fingers tingle. The scarf untangled itself from the branch and floated into my waiting palm.

Both men stopped wrestling to stare at me.

I blinked at the scarf in my hand, then at their shocked faces, and made the only reasonable decision—I ran.

"That's cheating!" Kip's indignant cry followed me as I dashed back toward our snowmen, the scarf trailing behind me like a victory banner.

Heavy footsteps crunched through the snow as they gave chase. I wove between the trees, laughing as I heard them cursing behind me. My heart pounded, not with anxiety or fear, but with genuine excitement.

I reached my snowman and triumphantly wrapped the scarf around its neck, turning as Cole and Kip stumbled to a stop, faces flushed and eyes bright.

"Victory is mine, reindeer boys!" I struck a dramatic pose beside my snowman, one hand on my hip, the other patting its scarf-adorned neck.

I barely had time to gloat before the magic took on a life of its own. The sparks weren't just dancing around my fingers anymore; they were everywhere, creating a shimmering aura around me and my snowman. It was beautiful and controlled and exactly what I'd been trying to achieve all day.

The sparks danced around me, and for once, it wasn't scary or overwhelming; it was beautiful.

Kip's eyes widened, tracking the blue lights. "Holy shit, you're doing it!"

Cole's expression softened with pride. "Joy was the key."

The magic pulsed brighter, the sensation like champagne bubbles fizzing through my bloodstream. Before I could respond, Kip rushed forward, scooping me into his arms and spinning me in a dizzying circle.

"You're a natural!" He whirled me around, my feet lifting off the ground as snowflakes swirled in our wake.

My hands gripped his shoulders for balance, and when he set me down, his face was inches from mine, eyes dancing with the reflected light of my magic. Neither of us moved for a heartbeat.

I'm not sure who closed the distance first, but suddenly Kip's mouth was on mine, his lips cold from the winter air but quickly warming against my own.

When we broke apart, Cole stood watching us, his eyes dark with intensity. The surrounding temperature shifted, and the snow beneath our feet melted, steam rising in wisps around our ankles.

Kip's fingers traced my jawline. "I think we've found an even better way to channel your joy."

Cole stepped closer, the three of us forming a triangle in the middle of the winter wonderland. He cupped the back of my neck, his thumb stroking behind my ear in a way that made me shiver.

I rose onto my toes, claiming his mouth with mine. His kiss was commanding in a way that made my knees weak.

Kip's hands found my waist, his chest pressing against my back as Cole continued to kiss me. I was sandwiched between them, surrounded by their warmth.

"Your leggings are getting wet." Kip's fingers toyed with the waistband.

Confused, I pulled back from Cole just enough to speak. My leggings were tucked into my thick socks and boots. "What?"

"Let's make sure it's not from the snow." Cole knelt and unlaced my boots. The intimacy of this massive man on his knees carefully removing my footwear caught me off guard.

As Cole set my boots aside, Kip's fingers hooked into the waistband of my leggings, slowly dragging them down my hips. "Lift your foot."

I balanced against Cole's shoulder as I raised each socked

foot, allowing Kip to pull my leggings and underwear free, exposing my lower half to the winter air. The contrast between the cold against my bare skin and the heat of their gazes made me gasp.

Cole rose to his full height, towering over me as his hands spanned my waist. "So beautiful."

Kip pressed against my back again, his hands sliding down to cup my bare ass. "Perfect."

I should have felt vulnerable, half-naked in the middle of a snowy field, but instead, I felt powerful.

Cole spun me around so my back was to him, and then he lifted me effortlessly, his forearms supporting my thighs as he spread me open. The position left me completely exposed to Kip, who stood before us with hunger darkening his eyes.

"This is definitely not in any magical training manual I've ever read." I gripped Cole's forearms, torn between embarrassment and overwhelming desire.

Cole's breath tickled my ear. "Most effective methods rarely are."

Kip's intent was clear as he stared at my exposed pussy. "Let's see how much magic we can unlock this way."

He bent forward as Cole adjusted me in his arms, tilting me enough for Kip. Kip maintained eye contact as he lowered his head between my spread thighs. The first touch of his tongue made me throw my head back against Cole's shoulder.

Kip's mouth worked magic of an entirely different kind, his tongue tracing patterns that made my toes curl. Cole's grip remained steady, his strength keeping me suspended and open as Kip feasted.

"Look at you dripping for him." Cole kissed along my neck. "I can feel your thighs already trembling."

I whimpered as Kip's tongue circled my clit, the pressure perfect enough to make my eyelids flutter.

"That's it." Cole's teeth grazed my earlobe. "Show us how good it feels. How alive your magic becomes when pleasure takes over."

Between Cole's filthy encouragement and Kip's determined

mouth, I hovered on the edge of an orgasm. My fingers dug into Cole's arms, and through half-lidded eyes, I noticed a flicker of movement near the trees.

A massive form stood partially concealed by a pine tree, unmistakable even at this distance. Rudy was watching us.

Cole followed my gaze. "Want us to stop?"

I'd been caught with my pants down and legs spread. But shame didn't stand a chance against the way Kip's mouth was working me over. "No. Let him watch."

Kip glanced over his shoulder, a wicked smile spreading across his glistening lips before he returned to his task with renewed enthusiasm.

I didn't know if reindeer had supersonic hearing, but I made sure my voice carried when I spoke. "Let him see exactly what he's missing."

Cole's grip tightened, his approval clear in the hardness pressing against my back. "That's my girl."

Kip's eyes gleamed up at me, his lips momentarily pulling away from my sensitized flesh. "You need something inside you."

My body shuddered in agreement, too far gone to form words. Through the haze of arousal, I watched as Kip's hands moved under and behind me, the sounds of a zipper and fabric rustling filling the winter air.

Cole's breath hitched. "Fuck, your hands are cold."

"Sorry, not sorry." Kip's voice was playful as he worked between us, and something hard and hot pressed against my entrance.

I inhaled sharply as Cole's cock nudged at my opening, stretching me as Kip guided him in. My head fell back against Cole's shoulder as he sank into me inch by delicious inch, his arms still supporting my weight.

"So fucking tight," Cole growled against my neck, giving me an experimental bounce that made stars explode behind my eyelids.

Kip dropped to his knees now, his attention between my legs. I whimpered as Cole began moving me up and down his cock while Kip watched. Why was that so hot, and why did I like it so much?

And then Kip's mouth was back on me, his lips closing around my clit and sucking.

My eyes were drawn instinctively to where Rudy stood partially concealed. He'd stepped further from behind the tree now, his frame no longer hidden. Even at this distance, I could see he'd freed himself from his pants, his hand working in rhythmic strokes that matched Cole's thrusts.

The sight of Rudy, hand wrapped around himself, watching us with dark, hungry eyes, made my body ache even more. His eyes locked with mine across the distance, intense and unblinking.

"Look at him watching you," Cole panted against my ear, adjusting his grip to bounce me harder on his length. "He can't look away."

Kip hummed against my clit, the vibration shooting straight through me as his tongue occasionally dipped lower, sliding alongside Cole's cock in a way that made both of us gasp. One of his hands disappeared between his own legs, working himself free as he pleasured me.

Cole's pace quickened, each thrust hitting spots inside me that made coherent thought impossible. My thighs trembled in his grip, muscles tightening as pressure built at the base of my spine.

"I'm going to—" My words cut off as Kip sucked hard on my clit.

Across the clearing, Rudy's movements became more frantic, his massive hand working faster. His jaw clenched, body tensing as he watched Cole fucking me while Kip's head bobbed between my legs.

The moment Rudy's release came, his head falling back as thick ropes of cum painted the snow at his feet, something inside me snapped. My orgasm hit with the force of an avalanche, electricity coursing through my veins as my body clamped down on Cole's cock.

"Fuck, I can feel you squeezing me," Cole groaned, his

rhythm faltering as my inner walls pulsed around him. With a few more erratic thrusts, he practically slammed me down on his cock, burying himself deep as he emptied inside me.

Kip's movements against my clit slowed, helping me ride the aftershocks before he pulled away with a groan of his own. His body tensed, hand working furiously over his length as he found his release with a strangled groan.

As my pleasure receded, reality slowly filtered back in. I'd just been thoroughly fucked outdoors while another man watched.

I glanced toward the tree line, but Rudy had already disappeared, leaving no evidence he'd been there at all. Something twisted in my chest.

It shouldn't have made me emotional, but I blinked rapidly as tears stung my eyes. He'd clearly wanted me enough to get off watching, yet he still kept his distance.

Cole gently slid me off his cock and lowered me to my feet, helping me find my balance on shaky legs.

A sudden burst of laughter broke the silence. Kip was doubled over, his shoulders shaking with mirth as he stared at something behind me.

"What's so funny?" I tugged my leggings back on, still feeling emotionally raw.

Cole zipped himself up, his eyebrows drawing together as he followed Kip's gaze. "Seriously, what is it?"

Kip pointed, barely able to speak through his laughter. "I... I came all over your snowman!"

I turned to see my poor snowman, victorious red scarf still in place, but now decorated with evidence of Kip's pleasure splattered across its snowy belly.

For a moment, I just stared, processing. Then, like a dam breaking, a giggle bubbled up from my chest, escaping in an uncontrollable flood.

"You defiled my snowman!" I wheezed, clutching my sides as the tears that had been forming broke free.

Cole's deep chuckle joined ours. "I think that counts as a disqualification. Intentional sabotage."

"Worth it." Kip wiped tears of mirth from his eyes. "Besides, I gave him quite the upgrade. He looks much happier now."

The three of us collapsed in the snow, a tangle of limbs and breathless laughter. My snowman stood witness, its pebble smile and cum-splattered stomach somehow the perfect metaphor for my new reality: messy, unexpected, and strangely perfect.

As our laughter subsided, I stared at the place where Rudy had stood. The mixture of emotions swirling inside me was too complicated to unravel.

"Are you okay?" Cole's fingers wiped away my tears that I refused to say were for Rudy. Instead, they were for my snowman.

I nodded, pulling my attention back to the two men beside me. "Yeah... Rudy is just so confusing."

Kip flopped onto his back in the snow. "That's Rudy for you. Man of few words and many broods. He's a good alpha, though. Never let him tell you otherwise."

"He'll come around." Cole's voice held a certainty I wished I could share. "Some magic takes longer to unlock."

I glanced down at my hands, surprised to find them still glowing with a soft blue light. For now, I'd focus on what I could control: my growing power and the joy these men brought me.

And if that joy didn't include a certain stubborn reindeer man, so be it.

CHAPTER 23
HOLY NUTCRACKER

I stood in Dane's closet, glaring at the explosion of festive clothing the men had gifted me. The hangers seemed to mock me with their abundance of reds, greens, and sparkly fabrics, each item more obnoxiously Christmassy than the last.

My fingers kept betraying me by drifting toward a pair of red fleece leggings with tiny silver sparkles woven into the fabric. They looked like something an elf on a bender would design after a three-day eggnog binge.

And yet.

I rubbed the fabric between my thumb and forefinger. The damn things were impossibly soft. The kind of soft that made me question my entire stance on Christmas clothing.

I yanked the leggings off the hanger and grabbed a cream sweater covered in candy canes that formed hearts with their curved tops. It was equal parts adorable and nauseating. My pride screamed in protest, but I slid into the leggings anyway. The sweater followed, settling around me in a warm hug that smelled faintly of cinnamon.

I hated how much I loved it.

When I emerged from the closet, Dane looked up from where he sat on the bed, a crochet hook moving between his fingers as he worked on a hat. His eyes widened, traveling from my sparkly leggings to the candy cane hearts hugging my torso. A low whistle escaped his lips. "Well, ho ho ho. Looks like Christmas came early this year."

I flipped him off, fighting the smile threatening to betray me. "One more Christmas pun and I'm shoving that crochet hook somewhere festive."

The bathroom door swung open in a cloud of steam as Dash emerged, a towel slung low on his hips. Water droplets clung to the defined muscles of his chest, catching the light as he moved. My mouth went dry.

"Are we ready to head into Reinberg?" His eyes landed on me, a smile tugging at his lips. "Christmas spirit looks good on you, Neve."

I tugged at the hem of my sweater. "Don't get used to it. This is purely practical."

Dane set his crocheting aside, stretching his long limbs like a satisfied cat. "Sure it is. Just like humming that Christmas song while doing the dishes last night was purely practical."

I rolled my eyes, reaching up to run my fingers through my hair. The silver strands slipped between my fingers like liquid mercury, catching the light in a way that made them almost glow. The black was completely gone.

"Oh, for fuck's sake." I examined the ends. "The universe couldn't let me keep this one little piece of myself, could it?"

Dash disappeared back into the bathroom, returning with my hairbrush. "Your hair is beautiful either way. It reminds me of starlight."

I scoffed, though the compliment warmed something deep inside me. "It's like I aged sixty years overnight."

Dane hopped off the bed, moving to stand behind me. His fingers joined mine in my hair, gently separating the strands. "This isn't gray; it's a manifestation of your magic."

Dash approached, the brush held between his fingers like an offering. "Let me braid it for you."

I blinked, surprised. "You know how to braid hair?"

A hint of a smile softened his features. "I have three sisters."

"Fine." I perched on the edge of the bed, shoulders relaxing as Dash positioned himself behind me.

There was something incredibly intimate about him doing my hair, and I quickly forgot that one of the last pieces of my previous life had disappeared overnight. I'd fought so hard against the change, but since being in Klarhaven, it felt like the missing pieces of myself were falling into place.

THIRTY MINUTES LATER, I stood frozen at the entrance to Reinberg's main square, my senses assaulted from every direction. Overhead, star-shaped lanterns hung between booths on nearly invisible silver wire, casting a warm light across the cobblestone streets. Holiday music drifted from hidden speakers, creating a gentle background to the bustling crowd.

"It's like Santa threw up all over this place." I tugged my borrowed hat lower over my ears, trying to create some barrier between me and the sensory overload.

Dash's hand found the small of my back, guiding me forward with gentle pressure. "You'll adjust. Take a deep breath."

I did so reluctantly and immediately regretted it. The air was thick with scents that made me ache with familiarity.

Dane's eyes were bright with childlike enthusiasm. "This is nothing compared to the real North Pole, but it's the closest humans get. Their joy helps feed your father's magic."

"That's not exactly a selling point for the North Pole." I crossed my arms over my candy cane sweater, trying to ignore how perfectly the festive atmosphere matched my outfit.

A group of children darted past us, their laughter ringing like bells in the crisp air. One small girl with pigtails spun in circles, arms outstretched as she tried to catch paper snowflakes falling from a nearby stall's mechanical snow machine.

Something shifted in my chest at the sight; a tiny crack in the wall I'd built against all things festive.

Dash noticed, his eyes catching mine with quiet understanding. "Come on. I know a shortcut to the best part."

We moved deeper into the market, Dane leading the way with easy charm. He exchanged cheerful greetings with vendors, stopping occasionally to chat. Like the last time I'd been in Reinberg, I didn't miss how some people froze when they spotted me, their eyes widening in silent recognition before they recovered.

"I can't decide if these people are scared of me or think I'm royalty." I hissed after the third vendor nearly dropped a tray of gingerbread.

Dane scratched the back of his neck. "Well, you *are* Santa's daughter, and most probably remember you." What he didn't say was that they probably also remembered how I'd injured people and practically destroyed the North Pole.

Dash's fingers intertwined with mine, his thumb rubbing soothing circles on my skin. "The North Pole has a hierarchy, and the Claus family sits at the top."

I was about to make a sarcastic comment when we rounded a corner, and a small wooden stall came into view. The sign above it read "Mrs. Berry's Sweet Treats" in swirling red letters, and something about it stopped me in my tracks.

The woman behind the counter was smiling with rosy cheeks, her silver hair twisted into a bun beneath a red-and-white striped hat. Steam rose from a massive copper pot beside her, and the display case held rows of brownies topped with everything from crushed candy canes to toasted marshmallows.

My feet moved forward without conscious thought, drawn by something beyond the chocolate scent hanging heavy in the air.

"Good afternoon, gentlemen." The woman's eyes twinkled as they landed on Dash and Dane, then shifted to me. For a moment, her smile faltered, a flash of recognition and surprise crossing her features before returning brighter than before. "And what a pleasure to see you again, young lady."

Again?

The world tilted slightly beneath my feet as something

stirred in the recesses of my memory, like a door long closed creaking open.

I was sixteen, standing at this very stall, but I wasn't alone. My mom was beside me, her laugh musical as she pointed to the peppermint brownies. "One of those and two hot chocolates, please."

I tugged my scarf tighter around my neck, trying to pretend I wasn't excited about the brownie we were about to share.

She dug in her ridiculous snowflake-patterned purse for her wallet. She was also wearing an over-the-top Christmas cardigan with 3D ornaments that lit up when she pressed a hidden button in the pocket. I was mortified, rolling my eyes every time a human stared too long or pointed. But Mom just laughed and sometimes pressed the button in response, making the tiny lights dance across her torso.

"We should get a peppermint brownie too," she suggested, winking at the vendor, Mrs. Berry.

"No way." I was painfully aware of how uncool it was to be there with my mom, eating Christmas desserts before Thanksgiving had even happened. "I'm not even hungry."

My stomach chose that moment to growl audibly, and both Mom and Mrs. Berry laughed.

Mrs. Berry's eyes crinkled at the corners. "Maybe an extra marshmallow for the young lady who isn't hungry."

I scowled but didn't protest when the extra marshmallow appeared, floating on my hot chocolate like a sugary island.

"You'll change your mind about the brownie," Mom said, breaking off a piece and holding it out to me. "Just like you'll change your mind about Christmas again someday."

I took the piece reluctantly, the treat smelling too good to resist.

"Never." There was more conviction than there had been last month when I begged her to stop using my nickname. Or the week before when I refused to help decorate the tree.

Something had slowly been changing since we'd moved from the North Pole to Klarhaven, then to Reinberg. My magic was no longer accessible, and I found myself wanting to be around humans more and more. The world I once knew was slowly slipping away, and I couldn't find it in myself to care.

I blinked, the stall coming back into focus as the past receded.

"Neve?" Dane's voice sounded far away. "Are you okay?"

I reached out, steadying myself against the wooden counter. "I've been here before."

Mrs. Berry's eyes softened. "Yes, dear. Many times. You and your mother loved my peppermint brownies." She reached into the display case and placed a brownie on a napkin.

My fingers trembled as I picked up the brownie, the scent of chocolate and mint rising to meet me. I took a small bite of it, and a tear slid unexpectedly down my cheek.

"I think the last time I was here was right before..." I shook my head, frustration building as I tried to grasp at wisps of a memory that dissolved upon contact. "I forgot. I forgot it all."

Mrs. Berry's eyes filled with understanding. "Some things take time to remember, dear. But they're never truly gone." She slid three steaming cups of hot chocolate across the counter. "Sometimes, the taste of something familiar can help bridge the gap."

I took a sip, letting the rich chocolate warm me from the inside out. "Thank you."

We moved away from the stall, Dash and Dane flanking me like protective bookends. Neither spoke, letting me process whatever was happening in my head. The Christmas music that had seemed so oppressive minutes ago now felt like background noise to the louder storm of half-formed memories swirling in my mind.

We drifted through the market, past stalls selling everything from hand-carved nutcrackers to homemade candy canes.

A flash of color caught my eye, drawing me toward a booth displaying handcrafted ornaments. Glass baubles hung from a miniature tree, catching the light and sending rainbow prisms dancing across the cobblestones.

There was a delicate glass ornament shaped like a snow-covered tree, tiny silver stars suspended inside as if caught in a perfect moment of winter magic. My feet stopped of their own accord, my breath catching in my throat.

The ornament seemed to call to me, drawing me forward with an invisible thread. I reached out, my fingers hovering centimeters from its surface.

It was beautiful. It was *right*. Like it had been waiting for me all along.

My fingertips brushed the cool glass, and something shifted inside me. Warmth bloomed in my chest, spreading outward through my limbs like liquid gold. The sensation wasn't uncomfortable. It was like coming home after a long journey, like finding a piece of myself I hadn't known was missing.

The air around us changed, subtly at first, with a soft golden shimmer that danced across the marketplace like sunlight on water. I thought I was imagining it until I noticed the hush that had fallen over the nearby stalls.

And then the snow began.

Not from the sky, but from nowhere at all. Perfect flakes materialized and drifted down in slow spirals. They glowed like fallen stars as they caught the light.

"I'm not doing this," I whispered, even as I felt the connection between the magic and myself, like an extension of my very being.

A small child nearby gasped in delight, jumping with hands outstretched to catch the glowing flakes. "Look, Mommy! Snow!"

All around us, people stopped to stare, faces turned upward in wonder. The ornament vendor stood frozen, mouth slightly agape as snowflakes landed on her merchandise, glittering briefly before dissolving into sparkles.

Dash's fingers entwined with mine, squeezing gently. "Actually, you *are* doing this."

Dane whistled. "Holy nutcracker. Your magic is..."

"Beautiful," Dash finished, his voice thick with emotion.

For once, I didn't argue because it *was* beautiful. This thing happening through me brought such pure joy to everyone around us. For a fleeting moment, I understood why my father dedicated his life to creating wonder.

"You!"

The sharp voice cut through the magical haze like a knife. I turned, the snow around me faltering as my joy faded.

Standing at the edge of the nutcracker stall, pointing an accusatory finger directly at me, was Mike.

Yes, *that* Mike. Nutcracker-collecting, three-Christmas-trees Mike. Palm Springs Mike, who had called me an ice demon and fled from our date like I was contagious.

His face was flushed red, not entirely from the cold, and his eyes were wide with recognition and fear.

My stomach dropped to somewhere around my ankles as our eyes locked. The magical snow stuttered, flakes freezing midair.

I stared at him, and part of me—a very loud, irritated part—wanted to conjure a snow shark and send it racing toward him. I pictured it perfectly: jaws of crystallized ice, dorsal fin cutting through the snow, Mike running and screaming about demon snow predators.

My fingers tingled with untapped power, a reminder that I could absolutely ruin his day if I wanted to. But something deeper than petty revenge stopped me. My magic wasn't meant for terrorizing nutcracker enthusiasts, no matter how satisfying it might be.

Instead, I lifted my hand and gave him my most condescending finger wave, wiggling my fingers with exaggerated cheerfulness as I called out, "Happy holidays, Mike."

Dash stepped up on my right, his presence solid and unmistakably protective. Dane mirrored him on my left, his typically playful demeanor replaced with something far more intimidating.

Mike's face drained of color faster than my spray tan had disappeared. He stumbled backward, knocking into a display of wooden ornaments that clattered to the ground. Without stopping to help, he turned and bolted, his holiday scarf trailing behind him like a surrender flag.

I watched him disappear, anxiety crawling up my throat. "Should I be worried about that? He's seen me do weird shit twice now."

Dane's shoulders relaxed as the tension dissolved. "Nah. Who's going to believe some random guy ranting about ice demons and magical snow?"

Dash's hand found the small of my back. "The townspeople here are experts at convincing human visitors that anything unusual is just a trick of the northern lights. Trust me, by tomorrow he'll have convinced himself it was all an elaborate light show."

I turned back toward the ornament stall, suddenly needing to see that glass tree again, to feel the connection that had sparked my magic. "Still. Maybe we should—"

The ornament was gone.

"Where did it go?" I moved closer to the display. "It was right here."

The vendor smiled, her eyes twinkling. "Seems someone appreciated it even more than you did, dear."

My heart sank with unexpected disappointment. "Oh."

Dash's fingers squeezed my shoulder gently. "Maybe it was meant to wake something in you, not stay with you."

"Come on," Dane looped his arm through mine. "There's a stall that sells these caramel apple things that will make you forget your own name."

We spent the next few hours wandering through the market, stopping at stalls that caught our interest. Dash helped me pick out gloves lined with the softest fur I'd ever felt.

Dane dragged us to a booth selling handcrafted wooden toys, where he had an animated twenty-minute discussion with the artisan about the proper technique for carving reindeer figurines.

As the afternoon melted into evening, the market transformed. The lanterns overhead glowed brighter against the sky, and the tempo of the music shifted to something slower, more enchanting. Families with children drifted away, replaced by couples walking arm in arm.

We found a small restaurant at the edge of the square, and over bowls of stew and crusty bread, I realized I hadn't thought about my old life all day.

The holiday music that had once felt like an assault now seemed to blend naturally with the murmur of conversation and the distant sounds of the market. The Christmas decorations no longer felt like an aggressive reminder of everything I'd lost but like pieces of a puzzle I was slowly reassembling.

As we stood to leave, I cast one last look at the twinkling market, at the joy radiating from every corner, and I didn't feel the need to shield myself from it.

CHAPTER 24
BARBARA

I changed into a pair of flannel pajama pants covered in little hot chocolate mugs and a hooded sweatshirt with a gingerbread man in the center. The festive clothes were growing on me little by little. I'd never admit it to any of the guys, but I could at least admit it to myself.

After putting on cozy socks, I padded silently down the hall as I headed toward the stairs, drawn by the sounds of laughter and the faint smell of popcorn drifting up from below. After a day of unexpected memories and magic in Reinberg, the promise of a movie night with everyone seemed nice. Normal, if you ignored the fact that they turned into reindeer.

I paused at the top of the stairs, my hand on the wooden banister. Voices floated up from the living room, low and serious, a stark contrast to the festive atmosphere I'd been expecting.

"You've been avoiding her all week." Cole's voice was more serious than I'd ever heard it, which was saying a lot since he was pretty much always serious.

My foot hovered over the first step, my body going still. I knew instantly who "her" was.

"I haven't been avoiding anyone." Rudy's voice rumbled up the stairwell, carrying that familiar note of stubborn authority that made my teeth clench. "I've been busy."

Dane's laugh held no humor. "Busy staring at the horizon from that hill for hours? Super productive, man."

A beat of silence followed, during which I held my breath.

"Why are you keeping your distance?" Dash's voice almost matched Rudy's in its superiority.

My heart climbed into my throat. I knew I should announce my presence or retreat to my room, but my feet remained rooted to the spot, my ears straining to catch every word.

"What exactly do you want me to say?" Rudy's voice sounded tired. "That I should join the rotation? Take her sledding? Bake fucking cookies?"

Something sharp twisted in my chest at his dismissive tone.

"Maybe just stop being an ass?" Kip spoke this time, his usually playful voice uncharacteristically serious. "Her magic responds differently to you since you're our alpha. We all feel it."

The wood beneath my palm grew cold, a thin layer of frost spreading from my fingertips across the banister.

"I don't think I should." Rudy's voice dropped so low I almost missed it. "What's the point?"

The room below fell silent.

I stood frozen at the top of the stairs, the silence expanding until it filled every corner of my body. What's the point? Three little words that somehow managed to both break something inside me and ignite it at the same time.

Warmth flooded my cheeks as humiliation turned quickly to anger. All this time, I thought Rudy was distant because of some deep, complicated reason. But no, he didn't think I was worth the effort.

I stepped back from the stairs, frost now coating the floor. The temperature around me plummeted, and my breath clouded in front of my face as emotions surged through me like a winter storm.

Who the fuck did he think he was? The almighty leader of the herd, too important to waste time on Santa's broken daughter? The ice beneath my feet thickened, crackling as it spread outward in jagged patterns.

My skin tingled, magic pulsing in waves that matched my racing heart. I was tired of Rudy looking at me like I was simultaneously the answer to everything and nothing worth his time.

The magic built inside me, a pressure behind my ribs that demanded release. I didn't stop it this time, didn't control the surge of power that raced through my veins. I welcomed it, letting it consume me until my vision blurred with swirling silver.

Take me away from here. Somewhere I can breathe.

The thought had barely formed before the world compressed around me, squeezing the air from my lungs. For one terrifying moment, I existed everywhere and nowhere, my body dissolving into particles of ice and starlight.

Then, with a disorienting lurch, reality snapped back into focus.

Cold bit into my feet, snow soaking through my socks and the hem of my pajama pants. I stood at the summit of a hill, the vast expanse of snow-covered landscape stretching toward mountains in the distance.

My arms wrapped around my middle, partly from the biting cold, partly to hold myself together.

This was Rudy's hill.

Why here? Of all the places my magic could have taken me, why the fuck here?

I sank to my knees in the snow, too overwhelmed to care about the cold seeping into my bones. My magic had responded to my emotions, to my need to escape, and it had brought me to the one place associated with the man who'd dismissed me entirely.

Was this a sick cosmic joke? Or was it my subconscious betraying me, revealing that even in my anger, some part of me was still drawn to him?

A tear slid down my cheek, freezing before it could fall. The wind picked up, snow swirling around me in a miniature cyclone that reflected the chaos inside me.

What was I even doing here? In this place, with these men, chasing memories of a life I wasn't sure I wanted to reclaim? My parents had let me lose my memories. My magic was unpredictable at best, dangerous at worst. And the one person who seemed to truly understand what I was going through couldn't be bothered to help me.

The cyclone of snow grew, responding to my spiraling thoughts. Ice crystals formed in the surrounding air, suspended like frozen stars.

I could leave. I could teleport myself back to Palm Springs, back to my house with its desert heat and complete lack of Christmas decorations. Back to a life where magic was something that happened in movies, not something that pulsed through my veins.

But even as the thought formed, I knew it wasn't true. I couldn't go back, not really. That life had never been mine.

Plus, my father needed me.

So where did that leave me? Kneeling in the snow on a hilltop with magic I couldn't control and a heart I couldn't protect?

I didn't belong anywhere. Not in Palm Springs, not at the North Pole, not even here with a herd of shapeshifting men who seemed determined to help me find joy while their leader kept his distance.

I was utterly alone.

The snow swirled around me, each icy crystal reflecting my isolation like tiny, frozen mirrors. I buried my face in my hands, trying to steady my breathing against the rising panic.

A strange shuffling sound pulled me from my spiraling thoughts. My head snapped up, eyes widening as I peered through the swirling snow.

Something was moving toward me.

I froze, every muscle tensing in refusal to move as the shape grew closer. It wasn't human; it was round, lumpy, and had an odd, waddling gait that made it look like a sentient pile of laundry pushing through the snow.

My magic sparked defensively at my fingertips, but instead of attacking, the creature that was roughly the size of a small car simply approached and dropped something soft and heavy around my shoulders.

"Warm." Its voice was like fabric rustling against itself, barely distinguishable from the wind.

The blanket it had placed around me was impossibly warm, even though it was covered in snow.

The creature looked like someone had gathered every lost winter scarf, mitten, and hat from the last decade and mashed them together into a lumpy, patchwork beast. Tiny antler nubs poked through the top of its head, frosted with delicate ice flowers that glowed faintly in the moonlight.

"Are you a nibbleknot?" My voice came out embarrassingly high-pitched. "Are you going to eat me?"

The creature made a sound between a snort and a chuckle, its glowing blue eyes crinkling at the corners. It grunted, shifting its bulk to sit beside me. Up close, I could see that it was wearing a complex weave of fabrics over its fur.

"Do you have a name?" I pulled the blanket tighter, surprised at how calm I felt. Was this the magic of the creature beside me, or did some part of me know it wouldn't hurt me?

The nibbleknot tilted its head, considering me. "Barbara."

I blinked. Then blinked again. "Barbara? You're a mysterious magical creature and your name is *Barbara*?"

Barbara huffed indignantly, puffing up like an offended pillow, but her form shook like she was laughing. It was either that or she was getting ready to eat me.

"I'm sorry. It's just surprising you have such a human name. It could be worse, though; your name could be Karen."

Without warning, she stood up.

"Oh no, I didn't mean to offend you!" I struggled to my feet, my legs numb.

But Barbara wasn't looking at me anymore. She waddled purposefully to the edge of the hill, then jumped, vanishing in an explosion of powdery snow that glittered like diamond dust.

I peered over the edge, trying to see where she'd landed. There was nothing there: no Barbara-shaped impression in the snow, no trail of footprints leading away. But there was a giant mound of snow at the bottom that had several large reindeer impressions.

"What the hell?" I muttered.

"They do that."

The deep voice behind me sent a jolt through my entire body. I whirled around, my blanket billowing like a cape.

Rudy stood there, a dark silhouette against the star-filled sky, watching me with his intense, unreadable eyes. He wasn't wearing a coat, just a T-shirt that clung to his muscular frame, seemingly unbothered by the cold.

My stomach dropped. Of course, he would find me trespassing on his private brooding spot.

"I was just leaving." I tightened my grip on the blanket, trying for dignity despite my snow-soaked pajama pants and sock-covered feet. "Wouldn't want to interfere with your important schedule of running up hills and jumping off, or whatever strange adrenaline shit you're into."

I tried to step past him, but he moved slightly, blocking my path without touching me.

"The nibbleknot visited you." His eyes searched mine, looking for something I couldn't name.

"Yeah. Her name's Barbara. We're best friends now. She gave me fashion advice, and we talked about our favorite reality shows." The sarcasm dripped from my voice like icicles. "Now if you'll excuse me, I need to figure out how to teleport my ass back to the cabin before I lose my toes to frostbite."

Rudy didn't move, didn't even seem to register my attempt at walking away. Instead, he studied my face with an intensity that made my skin prickle.

"They only appear when someone is worthy of comfort." His voice softened, losing some of its usual edge. "When they're truly lonely or sad."

The gentleness in his tone caught me off guard, undermining the protective wall of anger I'd been building. I swallowed hard, fighting the sudden burn of tears.

"Well, congratulations on your expert assessment. Yes, I'm

sad. Yes, I'm lonely. Don't worry, I won't bother you with any of it. What was it you said? There's no point?"

A muscle twitched in his jaw, and for a moment, something like regret flashed across his face. "You heard."

"Enough." The word came out sharper than I intended, slicing through the cold air between us. "Enough to know you'd rather avoid me than help me. Which is fine. I didn't ask to be here. I didn't ask for any of this."

The wind picked up, whipping snow around our ankles in response to my rising emotions. Rudy's gaze dropped to the swirling ice, then back to my face, his expression unreadable in the moonlight.

"That's not what I meant." His massive frame seemed to draw in on itself slightly, shoulders tensing. "You don't understand."

"Then explain it to me." I stepped closer. "Because from where I'm standing, it seems pretty clear you don't want me the way the others do."

He ran a hand down his face, looking utterly defeated. "Neve, I can't fly."

CHAPTER 25
ICICLE TITS

Rudy's confession hung in the frozen air between us, so simple yet so clearly devastating to him.

"You can't fly?" I repeated his words, trying to process their significance.

His massive frame seemed to shrink, shoulders curving inward as he looked away, his jaw clenched. "I can transform, I can run, I can lead the herd, but I can't leave the ground."

The pieces clicked together—his isolation, his distance, his reluctance to help me. It wasn't disdain. It was shame.

"That's why you come to this hill." I glanced at the edge of the hill where the nibbleknot had jumped from, seeing it differently now. This wasn't a place for him to isolate, but a futile reach toward the sky.

Rudy's eyes met mine, unguarded for once. "What kind of alpha can't do the one thing his herd is born to do? What kind of protector can't follow where the others go?"

The wind whipped around us, but the snow no longer swirled chaotically. Instead, it drifted in slow spirals, mirroring the shift in my emotions from rage to something more complicated.

"When you said, 'What's the point?' what did you mean exactly?"

"What's the point of getting close to you?" His voice cracked slightly. "What's the point of teaching you about your magic when I can't even fulfill my own purpose? The others can give you joy, carry you through the skies, and be what you need."

I took a step toward him, clutching Barbara's blanket around my shoulders. "Did it ever occur to you I don't need nine perfect reindeer? I need people who will stand beside me, flaws and all."

The faintest hint of hope flickered across his face before disappearing beneath his mask of indifference. "You don't understand what it means to be broken in our world. I'm..."

"You're what? Defective? Unworthy?" I moved closer until I stood directly in front of him, close enough to feel the unnatural heat radiating from his body. "Do you think I don't know what that feels like? I lost twelve years of my life and my identity. I've spent my entire adult existence feeling like something was missing without knowing what it was."

Something shifted in his expression, a small crack in the armor he wore so rigidly. "When my magic manifested, everyone expected greatness. I was the biggest, the strongest. The natural leader. And then..." His voice trailed off, gaze drifting toward the star-filled sky. "Everyone waited for me to soar, and I couldn't."

Without thinking, I reached out and touched his arm. His skin was warm beneath my fingertips, a stark contrast to the frigid air. "Flying isn't what makes you special."

The tension in his muscles eased slightly under my touch. "In a herd of flying reindeer?"

"In a world where everyone expects you to be one thing, your strength is in being something unexpected." I moved my hand to his chest, feeling his heart pound beneath my palm. "The others follow you because of who you are, not what you can do."

Rudy's hand came up, hesitantly covering mine. "You make it sound so simple."

"It's not. But nothing worth having ever is." A small smile tugged at my lips since I was learning that myself.

We stood there with his large hand covering mine, the

warmth of his touch spreading up my arm. The emotional honesty had cracked something open between us, but the intimate moment was quickly undermined by my body's less poetic reaction to being outside in wet pajamas.

"Well, this heart-to-heart has been lovely," I managed through chattering teeth, "but I think my tits are literally turning into icicles right now." The blanket did nothing to keep out the chill.

"You're soaked." He stepped back, his brows drawing together as he assessed my shivering form.

Before I could suggest we head back to the cabin, Rudy's frame shimmered, his outline blurring as he transformed into a reindeer. He lowered himself to the ground with a graceful dip of his knees, turning his massive head to look at me expectantly.

"What? You want me to—"

"*Get on.*"

I blinked, my mind reeling from the telepathic intrusion. "Okay, talking reindeer is still weird, no matter how many times it happens."

"*Trust me.*"

Another violent shiver racked my body, deciding for me.

"Fine, but if this is some kind of trick to dump me in a snowbank, I'm turning your antlers into icicle chandeliers." I laid the blanket across his back and awkwardly climbed onto him, clutching fistfuls of his thick fur.

This was going to be much faster to get back to the cabin since I didn't exactly know how to control teleporting.

His muscles tensed beneath me, powerful and coiled, before he launched forward with surprising speed. We tore down the hillside, and I pressed my face against his warm neck as we raced past the cabin lights glowing in the distance.

He veered sharply, plunging into the dense tree line instead of continuing toward the cabin. I squeezed my eyes shut as branches whipped past, trusting Rudy to navigate while I concentrated on not falling off. It wasn't as smooth as flying, but the magical aerodynamics created a barrier between me and the wind that would have frozen me otherwise.

Rudy finally slowed as we entered a small clearing nestled among the pines.

"Oh, wow," I breathed as I took in the steam rising from a natural pool of water.

Rudy came to a complete stop, and I slid off his back, my legs wobbling slightly as they reconnected with solid ground. The air was warm and carried the earthy scent of stone.

The surface of the steaming pool glowed, looking like scattered diamonds. The snow around the edges had melted into a perfect perimeter, creating a magical boundary between winter and warmth.

"A hot spring?" I stepped closer to the pool, feeling the heat radiating upward, already beginning to thaw my frozen limbs. "I'm surprised this place isn't packed all hours of the day and night."

Rudy shifted back to human form beside me. "No one comes here but us. Since it's within Klarhaven's boundaries, the magical properties of the veil keep humans away. This is also in our territory, and the other magical creatures know that."

"And you brought me?" I looked up at him, understanding he was extending a Christmas branch.

Oh, geez, even my comparisons were turning festive.

I stared at Rudy, momentarily forgetting the cold as his mouth curved into a smile. It wasn't the tight, controlled expression I'd seen before, but something warm and real that transformed his entire face.

He reached for the hem of my soaked sweatshirt. "You need to get out of these wet clothes."

I batted his hand away, taking a step back. "Whoa there, big guy. I can undress myself, thank you very much."

"Fine." He shrugged.

Before I could respond, Rudy began stripping down. His shirt came off first, revealing his intimidating expanse of muscle. When his hands moved to the waistband of his sweatpants, I should have looked away.

He stepped out of his pants, standing there in nothing but a pair of boxer briefs covered in a red, white, and green polka dot pattern. It was so unexpected on someone like him that I almost laughed. Until I saw the bulge underneath the pattern.

I swallowed hard. "Are those... Christmas boxers?"

He glanced down as if he'd forgotten what he was wearing. "And?"

The absurdity of this stoic mountain of a man wearing holiday underwear made something in my chest loosen, and I covered my mouth to stifle a giggle.

Rudy waded into the pool, steam curling around his torso until he was waist-deep. His boxers flew out of the water with a dramatic flourish, landing with a wet plop at my feet.

I jumped back as if they might bite. "Seriously?"

"It feels better without them."

I eyed the water suspiciously. "Are there, um, things in there? Living things? Because I've seen enough horror movies to know that naked people in mysterious bodies of water never ends well."

Rudy's eyes glinted with amusement. "The water is completely safe. The minerals have healing properties and are good for sore muscles. If you want, I can conjure you a swimsuit."

I glanced down at my wet clothes, then back at the water. "That won't be necessary."

I peeled off my hoodie and stepped out of my bottoms, leaving me in my lacy underwear. I covered my breasts with an arm as the biting air raised goosebumps across my exposed skin and hardened my nipples.

"So we're clear, these are staying on." I gestured to my underwear as I dipped one toe in the water. "No way in hell am I having a weird magical creature swim up my vagina."

Rudy laughed a full, deep laugh that echoed around the clearing. His head tipped back, eyes crinkled at the corners, and his shoulders shook with genuine mirth.

"What?" I stood there, half-naked and indignant, which only made him laugh harder.

"Nothing's going to swim up anywhere, but keep your underwear on if it makes you feel better."

I slipped into the water, moaning involuntarily as the heat enveloped my frozen limbs. "Holy shit, this feels amazing." I sank deeper, letting the heat seep into my bones. The mineral-rich pool wrapped around me like a warm hug, making my muscles loosen in ways no massage ever could.

Across from me, Rudy floated with his eyes closed, his massive frame somehow looking peaceful. I'd never seen him this relaxed before, with the permanent furrow between his brows smoothed out and his jaw slack.

The silence between us was comfortable, but questions bubbled up inside me. I watched the steam curl around his face, gathering my courage.

"Can I ask you something weird?" I traced my finger through the water, creating little swirls.

Rudy's eyes opened slowly. "You've been teleporting, freezing time, and making snow sharks. Weird has lost all meaning."

"Fair point." I chewed my bottom lip. "Why is your entire herd... attracted to me? And why am I attracted to all of you? It's not exactly normal to want to jump nine different guys."

Rudy moved through the water toward me, each ripple spreading outward like my question had disturbed something deep. When he reached me, he brushed a wet strand of silver hair behind my ear, his fingers lingering against my cheek.

"I don't know for certain, but it's not unheard of to be drawn to a mate. Your dad has also always had a special bond with his herd."

My nose wrinkled involuntarily.

Rudy's laugh echoed across the water. "No. Not like that. Though who knows? Your mother is an elf, and elves are notoriously a little more... wild."

"Sweet mother of reindeer, stop talking." I splashed water at his face.

His mouth fell open in mock outrage. "You asked!"

"And I immediately regret it." I sent another wave of water at him, this one bigger.

Rudy's eyes narrowed playfully. "You really want to start this fight?"

"Maybe I do." I lifted my chin defiantly. "What are you going to do about it, Rudolph?"

His hand sliced through the water, sending a massive splash that hit me like a tidal wave. I sputtered, wiping water from my eyes to find him grinning with smug satisfaction.

"That was a declaration of war." I lunged forward, using both arms to create the biggest splash I could manage.

Rudy ducked, most of the water sailing over his head. "You'll have to do better than that, sugarplum."

Before I could decide whether he was using a term of endearment, Rudy was advancing. I squealed and tried to swim away, my arms flailing as I moved through the water.

Strong arms wrapped around my waist, pulling me back against a wall of muscle. I could feel every hard plane of him against my back, my soaked underwear doing nothing to create a barrier between us.

"Caught you." His mouth was so close to my ear that I could practically feel his lips, and my whole body reacted before I could think.

I turned in his arms, intending to push away, but the movement pressed my bare breasts against his chest. My breath caught as tiny blue sparks danced where our skin touched.

Rudy's eyes widened, but he didn't let go.

"I have another question," I whispered, acutely aware of every place our bodies connected.

His gaze dropped to my lips, lingering there. "What?"

I swallowed hard, fighting the urge to close the distance between our mouths. "Am I going to have eight reindeer or nine?"

The question hung between us, loaded with meaning. Rudy's expression shifted, vulnerability flashing across his features before determination took its place.

Instead of answering, he cupped my cheek, his thumb

229

tracing my bottom lip. Then he leaned down and pressed his mouth to mine in a kiss so gentle it made my heart ache. His lips moved with reverence, as if he were savoring something he'd been denied access to for too long.

As his tenderness threatened to overwhelm me, he deepened the kiss. His tongue slipped past my lips, claiming me with a hunger that matched the one building inside me. His hands slid down to my waist, lifting me effortlessly until my legs wrapped around him.

I threaded my fingers through his hair, tugging slightly as our mouths moved together with increasing urgency. This wasn't like the kisses I'd shared with the others. This was Rudy pouring every unspoken word, every moment of restraint, every ounce of longing into a single, soul-shattering connection.

My body melted against his, the water lapping gently around us as we moved together. The rest of the world fell away until there was nothing but his mouth on mine, his hands on my skin, and the steam rising around us.

Something in the air shifted. At first, I thought it was the dizzying effect of Rudy's kiss, but when he pulled back slightly, his eyes focused on something to the side of us.

I followed his gaze and gasped.

The night sky had transformed. Ribbons of light unfurled across the darkness above the trees, with brilliant streams of emerald, violet, and gold weaving together like an ethereal tapestry. They pulsed and danced, creating patterns too beautiful to be random but too wild to be designed.

"Are those the Northern Lights?" I'd seen them faintly in the distance before, but this was so close I felt like I could reach out and let the colors filter through my fingers.

Rudy's arms tightened around me, his expression filled with relief. "No. It's the veil."

My eyes widened. "*The* veil?"

"Yes, the boundary between here and the North Pole." His voice was hushed, as if he were telling me a secret. "And if you can see it..." Rudy pulled me closer, his forehead resting against mine. "We can take you to the North Pole. We can take you home."

The lights intensified, stretching up into the sky, their reflection turning the hot spring into a pool of liquid magic.

Wrapped in Rudy's arms, I felt a sense of belonging so profound it brought tears to my eyes.

I belonged here. With this herd. With this man who couldn't fly but somehow made me feel like I could soar. And together we belonged in the North Pole.

CHAPTER 26
MILK AND COOKIES

I lay in bed staring at the ceiling, watching patterns of light from the veil dance across it. My mind refused to shut down despite the late hour. Tomorrow we'd cross through the veil to the North Pole, and the thought left me caught between exhilaration and terror.

Rolling onto my side, I grabbed my phone from the nightstand and checked it for the twentieth time in an hour, even though it was too late for a response.

Still nothing.

The strangest thing about this whole situation was how difficult it was to maintain my anger. Every time I tried to nurture the fury that they had let this happen to me, memories would resurface: my dad patiently teaching me to skate backward, Mom singing lullabies when I couldn't sleep, the three of us making snow angels.

How could I reconcile these warm memories with their twelve years of deception? I knew there were magical gag orders, but there had to be something they could have done, right?

I kicked off the covers and sat up, running my hands through my hair. Sleep was a lost cause. What I needed was comfort food.

Specifically, milk and cookies.

I groaned at the stereotypical craving. It was as if my brain was programmed for Christmas clichés. Soon I'd be roasting chestnuts on an open fire and letting Jack Frost nip at my nose.

Shuffling down the hallway, I took the stairs quietly, hoping to avoid waking anyone. As I reached the bottom of the stairs, a soft glow from the dining room caught my attention. I padded toward the light and paused when I saw Rudy sitting alone at the table.

He was sitting in the dark, but the glow from the veil silhouetted him against the floor-to-ceiling windows. The guys had always gathered there the most, and I'd assumed it was for the unobstructed view of nature, but now I understood. Even I was drawn to the magic of the veil, which was why I'd left the curtains open in my room.

Something hung from his fingertips, catching the light. I nearly backed away, not wanting to disturb whatever private moment he was having, when recognition hit me like a snowball to the face.

The object in his hands was the glass ornament from the market, with the snow-covered tree and tiny silver stars suspended inside. The one that had called to my magic and disappeared before I could buy it.

I must have made a sound because Rudy's head snapped up, his eyes finding mine in the dimness. His hand jerked in surprise, and the ornament slipped from his fingers.

Without thinking, I reached out with my magic, feeling it flow through me like cool water. The ornament froze mid-fall, the tiny stars inside it glittering as if celebrating my intervention.

Rudy sucked in a breath, then reached out to pluck it gently from its magical suspension. "Thanks."

I walked across the living room and into the dining room. "It was you."

He raised an eyebrow, the ornament now cradled protectively in his palm.

"You bought the ornament before I could."

His broad shoulders lifted in a half-shrug, but his eyes never left mine. "I followed you guys that day."

"Why?" I moved closer, drawn to him like a magnet.

Rudy set the ornament in a velvet-lined box. "Your magic is waking up, and I wanted to be there just in case."

I leaned my hip against the edge of the table. "Makes sense." I tucked a strand of hair behind my ear. "You and your herd have been babysitting me since you showed up in Palm Springs."

Rudy's eyes caught the light from the veil, turning them almost silver. "Not babysitting. Protecting."

"Is there a difference?"

"There most definitely is." He stood, his chair scraping softly against the floor. "I was hoping we'd be back in the North Pole by the time we did the tree lighting ceremony so you could put your ornament on it."

My heart did an annoying flutter as he held the box out to me. "Tree lighting ceremony?"

"It's a tradition on the last day of November. There's a giant tree in the central square, and everyone places an ornament on it to celebrate the coming holiday... and to get drunk before a month of working nonstop." Rudy moved into the kitchen, opening the refrigerator. "Do you want plain, chocolate, or strawberry milk?"

"Huh?" I blinked, still wrapping my head around the fact that he'd bought me the ornament to hang on the North Pole Christmas tree.

"Milk and cookies." Rudy's mouth curved into a subtle smile as he reached for a glass. "That's why you came downstairs, right?"

My jaw dropped. "How did you know that? And plain, please."

He chuckled as he pulled milk out of the refrigerator and poured a glass. "You're not as mysterious as you think." He grabbed a plate from the cabinet and moved to a cookie jar on the counter.

I watched in silence as he placed cookie after cookie onto

the plate, creating a small mountain. He carried everything back to the table and sat down. His eyes met mine, and he patted his knee.

The invitation was clear, and my heart raced as if I'd chugged three espressos.

My body was caught in a moment of indecision while my mind raced ahead to all the outcomes of this simple action. The rational part of me whispered I was far too old for sitting on someone's lap. But the other part that responded to these men in unexplained ways didn't care about rational thought.

Sighing, I lowered myself onto his lap, very aware of how solid he was beneath me.

Rudy lifted a chocolate chip cookie to my mouth, his eyes watching me with an intensity that made my stomach flip.

I parted my lips and took a bite. Whoever taught these men to bake deserved all the cold sides of pillows and the best fuzzy socks. The flavors were the perfect balance of crumb to chocolate, and I couldn't help the small sound of appreciation that escaped me.

"Good?" His voice had dropped lower and taken on a gravelly quality.

I nodded, suddenly aware of how intimate it was sitting on his lap while he fed me cookies in the middle of the night.

Rudy reached for the glass of milk, bringing it to my lips. As I took a sip, a drop escaped, trailing down my chin. Before I could react, his thumb swept across my skin, catching the droplet.

Our eyes locked as he brought his thumb to his own mouth.

I bit my lip to stop myself from whimpering and grabbed the half-eaten cookie, raising it to his lips. He took a bite, chewing slowly, his gaze never leaving mine.

My eyes landed on the crumbs at the corner of his mouth. "You have some crumbs..."

Instead of wiping them away, Rudy remained perfectly still, his eyes challenging me. My pulse thundered in my ears as I leaned forward, pressing my lips to the corner of his mouth. I meant to pull back immediately, but Rudy's hand came up to cup the back of my head, keeping me close.

The tension that had been building between us since the moment at the hot springs snapped, and I pressed my lips firmly against his. The kiss was nothing like our previous one, which had been explosive and desperate; this was slow and deep, like sinking into warm water.

Rudy's arms tightened around me, one hand splayed across my lower back while the other remained tangled in my hair. I tasted chocolate and milk on his tongue, sweetness and warmth mingling together in a way that made my magic hum beneath my skin.

The heat between us intensified with each passing second. His lips moved against mine with a deliberate pressure that made my toes curl. When I shifted on his lap, I felt him hard beneath me, and a small gasp escaped my lips.

Rudy pulled back, his eyes hooded with desire but somehow still maintaining self-control. "You haven't finished your snack." His fingers brushed across my swollen lips.

I glanced at the mountain of cookies still waiting on the plate, then back to the heat in his eyes. A boldness I hadn't known I possessed flooded through me.

"I want a different snack." I slid off his lap, lowering myself to my knees between his spread legs.

A surprised laugh rumbled through his chest. "You're talking about..."

The laugh died in his throat as my fingers found the waistband of his sweatpants. His expression shifted to something more primal as I tugged the fabric down.

When I freed him from his pants, my breath caught. His impressive length was standing at attention, a bead of pre-cum glistening at the tip. I wrapped my fingers around him, his skin hot and smooth as I stroked from base to tip.

I reached for the glass of milk with my free hand, maintaining eye contact as I took a drink of the cold liquid. A drop clung to my bottom lip, and Rudy's eyes fixated on it.

I leaned forward and took him into my mouth, the lingering

sweetness of milk mingling with his taste. His hips bucked involuntarily, pushing him deeper until he nearly hit the back of my throat. I pulled back slightly, adjusting to his size as I hollowed my cheeks.

"Fuck." The word sounded strangled, like it had been ripped out against his will.

I hummed around him, enjoying the way his hands gripped the edge of his chair, his knuckles turning white with restraint. The power I felt bringing this mountain of a man to the edge of his control was intoxicating.

I grabbed the milk again, and Rudy's eyes widened as I tilted the glass to slide his cock in.

"I told you I wanted a different snack." I reached for the plate of cookies, taking one and crushing it in my palm. He groaned as I sprinkled the cookie crumbs along his wet shaft.

"What the hell are you—" His words dissolved into a groan as I licked along his length, gathering the cookie crumbs with my tongue.

Something snapped in him then. A growl rumbled from deep in his chest as he watched me devour the improvised dessert. My arousal dampened my underwear as I took him deeper, the crumbs and milk quickly vanishing.

Just as I found a rhythm that had his thighs tensing, his fingers threaded through my hair, and he gently pulled me off him.

"Now I need a snack." He stood, towering over me, his eyes wild and predatory as he hauled me to my feet and claimed my mouth again. This kiss was demanding and desperate, his tongue sweeping into my mouth.

He pushed my T-shirt up and over my head, palming my breasts and pinching my nipples in a way that matched the urgency of his mouth. I fumbled with his shirt, desperate to feel his skin against mine. He broke the kiss long enough to grab a handful of fabric behind his neck and yank it off.

We both worked to slide my pants and underwear off, along with his sweatpants and boxers that had ended up around his knees.

I stood naked before him, illuminated by the dancing lights streaming through the windows. His eyes raked over me, drinking in every curve and hollow like a man dying of thirst. When his fingers trailed down my stomach to the apex of my thighs, I nearly collapsed.

"Please," I whispered, not even sure what I was begging for.

His touch was gentle at first, exploring my slickness with maddening restraint. When one thick finger slipped inside me, my head fell back, a moan escaping my lips. He added a second finger, stretching me, preparing me for what was to come.

Rudy dropped to his knees, his face level with my center, and my heart nearly stopped. As much as I wanted to feel his mouth on me, a more urgent need pulsed through my body.

I grabbed his shoulders, stopping him. "No."

Confusion flickered across his face.

"I need you to fuck me. Now."

Something feral flashed in his eyes, turning them nearly black. He rose to his feet in one fluid motion, spun me around, and bent me over the table. The wood was cool against my heated skin as he positioned me, lifting one of my legs to rest on the chair beside us.

The position left me exposed, my chest pressed against the table while my ass was presented to him. The head of his cock nudged at my entrance, teasing me. My fingers scrambled for purchase on the smooth surface, finding none.

"Are you sure you want me to fuck you?" His voice was strained, the last threads of his control about to snap.

"Yes."

He pushed inside, filling me inch by agonizing inch. The stretch was delicious, bordering on too much, and I bit my lip to keep from crying out. He paused when he was fully seated, allowing me time to adjust to his size.

"You okay?" His hands stroked down my back.

I nodded, unable to form words with him so deep inside me. When I pushed back against him, silently begging for movement, Rudy took the hint. He withdrew almost completely before thrusting back in, setting a rhythm that had the table creaking beneath us, which was saying a lot considering it was handcrafted and made of thick wood.

Through half-lidded eyes, I watched the veil lights dance and then blur as pleasure built within me. Each thrust pushed me closer to the edge, the angle allowing him to hit spots that made stars explode behind my eyelids.

"So fucking beautiful," he gritted out, one hand gripping my hip while the other snaked beneath me to find my clit.

The first touch of his fingers against that sensitive bundle of nerves had me keening. My inner walls clenched around him.

He pulled me upright, my back against his chest, his arm wrapped securely around my waist. The new position drove him even deeper, and I gasped at the sensation.

His other hand came up to rest gently at my throat, not squeezing but simply resting there, the weight of it oddly comforting as his hips continued their relentless pace.

"Mine," he growled into my ear, his teeth grazing the sensitive spot below my jaw.

The possessiveness in that single word pushed me closer to the precipice. His fingers returned to my clit, circling with just the right pressure as his thrusts became more erratic.

"Come for me, Neve. I need to feel you come around me."

The combination of his words, his fingers, and the fullness of him inside me shattered the last of my restraint. My orgasm hit, my body trembling so hard I thought my bones might shatter. I cried out his name, the sound echoing in the quiet room. Blue sparks danced along my skin, pulsing in time with the jolts of pleasure.

Rudy followed a moment later, his rhythm faltering as he buried himself to the hilt, his body shuddering against mine as he found his release. His arm tightened around my waist, holding me upright as my legs threatened to give out.

For several heartbeats, we remained frozen in that position, connected in the most intimate way possible, our ragged breathing the only sound in the room. The sky continued its silent dance outside the window, bathing our intertwined bodies in an otherworldly glow.

When Rudy finally slipped from my body, he turned me gently in his arms, brushing my disheveled hair from my face.

My gaze drifted to the table where our abandoned milk and cookies sat, the plate now askew from our activities. A laugh bubbled out, slightly hysterical with post-orgasmic bliss.

"What?" Rudy's eyebrows furrowed.

"I'll never look at milk and cookies the same way again."

A slow grin spread across his face, and the laughter that erupted from both of us seemed to chase away the last of my North Pole anxiety.

CHAPTER 27
MEMORY GLOBE

I felt the exact moment we passed through the veil. Not a dramatic rip in the universe like I'd expected, but a gentle ripple, like passing through a silk curtain charged with static electricity. A soft hum vibrated in my chest, and then we were through.

The North Pole unfurled beneath us like a living Christmas card.

I clung to the saddle horn on Cole's back as I stared down in awe. Festive buildings clustered together in a picturesque village, each one dusted with perfect snow that glistened under the lantern light. Cobblestone streets wound between them in graceful curves, with not a single imperfection in their paths. And rising at the center stood a castle, but not of the Disney variety. It was an elegant structure of crystal and stone that caught the light of the veil and refracted it in prismatic bursts.

Home.

Cole banked left, veering away from it. I frowned as the entire herd followed, flying toward a separate cluster of buildings on the outskirts.

"Um, where are we going?" I shouted over to Rudy, who had been stuck in his head since we'd left. "The castle's that way."

Rudy pointed in the direction we were headed, and Cole continued his descent. There was an open field beside a sprawling stable complex. The structure was beautiful, with a series of interconnected domed buildings that had light spilling from windows and doorways.

We landed, and Cole lowered his body, allowing me to slide off before stepping away. I watched in fascination as he transformed, the shift from reindeer to man still bewildering even after seeing it multiple times.

"Why aren't we landing at the castle?" I gestured toward the distant building, its turrets gleaming.

"Flight restrictions. Only Santa's sleigh team can land in the central courtyard." Rudy's hand found the small of my back. "How do you feel?"

"I don't feel like destroying anything, so that's a plus." I adjusted the straps on the backpack I'd insisted on carrying myself. It had the blanket from Barbara and the ornament tucked safely inside. Plus, a few cookies.

Okay, a lot of cookies.

Kip pulled open one of the large doors. "Are you coming? The stables are heated, and I'm freezing my balls off out here."

"Such a delicate flower." Dane smirked, already moving toward the door.

I lingered, taking it all in. The air here felt different, and it tingled against my skin. The veil and Northern Lights danced together so seamlessly I couldn't tell where one ended and the other began. It was as if they were welcoming me home.

Was this truly where I belonged? This place I couldn't even really remember?

Cole stepped closer, his tall frame blocking the wind that had picked up around us. His eyes, usually so guarded, softened as he studied my face. "Overwhelming?"

The wind abruptly stopped, and I nodded, swallowing against the tightness in my throat. "I thought I'd feel... I don't know, something more definitive when we arrived. Like a burst of recognition or my memories flooding back."

"That's not a bad thing." Blitz took my hand and tugged me forward. "Getting overwhelmed isn't good for you or your magic."

I shivered as we entered the stables, the sudden heat making my frozen cheeks tingle. The space inside was far more elaborate than I'd expected, with polished wooden beams arched overhead, stalls lined with plush bedding, and what appeared to be heated water troughs running along one wall.

"Why do you need stables if everyone shifts?" I looked around, confused at seeing reindeer in the stalls.

Don reached over a door and rubbed a reindeer between the eyes. "Most reindeer aren't shifters. These are regular reindeer; like workhorses for the North Pole."

"Regular reindeer." I blinked, taking in this information. "So there are normal animals coexisting with magical shapeshifting ones, and everyone's cool with that?"

"People ride them instead of horses here." Pierce grabbed a handful of feed and threw it into a stall. "The climate's better suited for reindeer than horses."

Dash wandered over, sighing longingly as he watched a reindeer getting some kind of hoof treatment in a corner stall. "Sometimes shifters like to spend more time in reindeer form too. I come here for spa treatments sometimes."

I stopped walking to stare at him. "Reindeer... spa treatments?"

"Don't knock it till you've tried it." Kip's smile was wicked. "I wish they did antler rubs on shifters, but that was outlawed years ago."

My magic stirred inside of me at the thought of someone putting their hands on any of their antlers, and I crossed my arms. "Good, because the only person who will be rubbing those is me."

A few groans came from the men, and a few of the reindeer in the stalls made grunting noises. With a quick glance, I could instantly tell they were shifters. Their eyes held too much intelligence, a depth no normal animal should carry.

Vix moved to stand beside me, throwing a heavy arm over my shoulders and pulling me against his side. "Kip is just pushing your buttons. Most of us just get hoof treatments. It makes them all shiny and smooth, and if I'm feeling a little wild, I'll get them painted."

My mouth dropped open. "You're telling me you come to the reindeer spa to get... pedicures?"

"Hooficures." Vix was being completely serious. "The hot mud pack for the shoulders is also incredible. Really helps with the post-flight tension."

I burst out laughing. The North Pole had reindeer spas. Of course it did. What other ridiculous things was I about to discover?

A woman with golden-colored hair looked up from where she was polishing tack, her eyes widening as they landed on me.

"By the bells," she whispered, dropping her cloth. "It's—"

"Just passing through, Marigold." Dane stepped forward. "We're headed for the castle."

She blinked rapidly, her gaze darting between each member of the herd before settling back on me. "Of course. I'll continue with the... yes."

I inched closer to Don. "Is everyone going to react like that?"

Don's hand came to rest on my shoulder, a reassuring weight. "Not everyone. Just anyone who remembers you."

"Fantastic," I muttered. "No pressure."

After a brief discussion about the best route to take to minimize people seeing me, we exited through the back of the stables and began making our way toward the castle. The men naturally fell into formation around me, with Rudy and Pierce in front, Don and Kip on my left, Cole and Blitz on my right, and Dane, Dash, and Vix bringing up the rear.

"Is this really necessary?" I glanced around at my wall of muscle and testosterone. "I feel like I'm in the witness protection program."

Kip leaned in, his lips brushing against my ear. "Think of it as a royal procession. We're your honor guard."

"Oh, well, that's much less conspicuous."

As we wound through the streets of the village, people stopped to stare. They didn't point openly or rush over, but I felt their gazes following us like physical touches against my skin.

A child tugged at her mother's sleeve, pointing at our group before being gently shushed. Vendors paused mid-transaction, their hands hovering in the air. Even the carolers on a nearby corner faltered in their melody before quickly recovering.

"They all know who I am," I whispered to no one in particular.

We rounded a corner, and the castle came into view. Now that we were on the ground, it wasn't as large as it had appeared from the air. Large doors carved from pale wood stood at the top of a wide set of stairs.

"That's it?" I gestured to the unprotected entrance. "No guards? No magical security? Anyone could walk in!"

Vix snorted. "Who exactly would storm Santa's castle?"

"I don't know. Disgruntled elves? Angry children who got coal? Rival holiday mascots?"

"Rival holiday mascots," Dash repeated, laughter in his voice. "Like the Easter Bunny staging a coup?"

"It could happen." I mumbled, feeling ridiculous but oddly disappointed. Part of me had expected more ceremony for my grand return. Perhaps guards trying to arrest me with their spears and then my dad coming to my rescue with an exuberant "ho, ho, ho."

The absurdity of my imagination made me smile through my nerves.

Rudy pushed open one of the massive doors, and we stepped into the foyer.

My breath caught in my throat.

The entrance hall was a cathedral of light and winter beauty. The floor beneath our feet was polished to a mirror shine, reflecting the soft glow from crystal chandeliers that hung like cascading icicles from a vaulted ceiling. Staircases of gleaming white marble curved up on either side, their banisters wrapped in evergreen garlands interwoven with silver ribbons and tiny bells that chimed softly in the still air.

But it was the central feature that made my heart stutter in my chest. There was a massive snow globe, easily seven feet in diameter, suspended in midair with no visible means of support. Inside, the scenes shifted and changed: children opening presents, families gathered around tables, snow falling. Each image projected outward in a shimmering light that danced across the walls.

"It's the Memory Globe." Kip took my hand. "It shows Christmas memories from around the world."

A memory pushed to the forefront of my mind. It wasn't jolting like all the memories before and didn't pull me away from the current moment. "I used to bring a beanbag down and sit and stare at this for hours."

I was so transfixed by the globe that I didn't immediately notice the figure descending one of the staircases. It wasn't until Rudy put his hand on my shoulder that I saw the movement.

And then, I couldn't breathe.

A woman glided down the steps with effortless grace, her crimson velvet cloak trailing behind her. Her silver hair, identical to what now grew on my head, was elegantly styled away from her face, revealing high cheekbones and the points of her ears.

My mother.

But not the woman I'd seen on video calls. Not the woman who had visited Palm Springs twice a year with stories of Arctic research. This woman was regal, powerful, and unmistakably magical. She was a being of winter elegance that made something stir in my blood.

She stopped mid-step when she saw me, one hand flying to her throat. "Neve."

I couldn't speak. Couldn't move. The ground beneath me tilted as past and present collided in a dizzying rush. Several pairs of arms caught me right before everything went black.

❄

I DRIFTED through a cloud of half-forgotten memories, floating in that space between sleep and waking where nothing is quite real. A gentle tug at my scalp. The crackling of a fire. The scent of peppermint.

"Hold still, little snowflake."

I was small, cross-legged on a plush rug before a roaring fireplace, watching the flames dance. Behind me, patient fingers wove through my hair, silver-white like freshly fallen snow. My mother's touch was sure and gentle as she worked, humming a melody that made my eyelids heavy.

The fire popped, sending sparks dancing upward, and I giggled as one transformed into a tiny butterfly of light before disappearing.

"Almost done."

Her voice was like bells on a winter breeze. I felt a gentle twist as she secured the braid.

"There." She moved around to face me, tucking a stray strand behind my ear. In her palm lay a silver snowflake hair clip, intricate and impossibly detailed. She fastened it at the end of my braid with reverent care. "For sweet dreams."

Her lips pressed against the crown of my head, and I leaned into her embrace, surrounded by warmth and peppermint and safety.

"Mommy, will you make the lights dance tonight?"

She smiled, and light glowed at her fingertips...

My eyes fluttered open.

This wasn't my house. This wasn't Klarhaven. The canopy bed I lay in was draped with gauzy silver fabric that caught the strange, ethereal light filtering through frosted windows. The ceiling above was painted with constellations that seemed to twinkle as I blinked.

"You're awake."

I turned my head.

My mom sat beside me, her hand warm around mine as her thumb traced small circles against my skin. Glimmera Icethorn North was her real name, but for the past decade, I had no clue.

"I fainted."

"You did." Her smile was small but reached her eyes, which

were the exact shade of blue as mine. "Quite dramatically, too. But that was mostly because of your nine reindeer."

I tried to sit up, and she immediately moved to help, arranging pillows behind me with practiced ease.

"Where are they? Where am I?" I glanced around at the unfamiliar-yet-somehow-known space.

"They're waiting in the great room, and we're in your bedroom." Her fingers lingered on the edge of a silk pillowcase embroidered with tiny snowflakes. "Though I suppose you might not remember it yet. We've kept it exactly as it was."

I let my gaze wander, taking in details that should have felt significant but weren't yet. A bookshelf filled with colorful spines. A vanity with a silver brush set. A bay window with a cushioned seat.

"I had a memory," I whispered, the words catching in my throat. "You were braiding my hair by the fire."

She released a breath that sounded like it had been held for years. "Your memories are going to return quickly now that you're back."

I swallowed hard, suddenly aware of the question I wasn't asking. Where was my father? "Why did you make me leave?"

Mom's hands twisted in her lap, her gaze falling to a loose thread on the blanket. "We never wanted you to leave. It was supposed to be temporary until you were old enough to have more control."

I stared at her, trying to reconcile the gentle woman from my memory with this stranger who had let me forget my entire life. "Temporary? It's been more than a decade."

"We thought distance from the North Pole would mute your powers enough for you to learn control at your own pace." Her fingers plucked at the thread, unraveling it slightly. "When you started rejecting holiday things, winter, anything Christmas-related, we assumed it was teenage hormones."

A bitter laugh escaped me. "Hormones? I built my entire personality around hating Christmas. I didn't even know why."

Her eyes glistened with unshed tears. "I wanted to bring you back. But..."

"But you didn't." Ice crackled across the surface of a glass of water on the bedside table. "You left me out there, thinking I was some weird human who hated Christmas."

Mom reached for my hand, and I let her take it. Her thumb resumed soothing circles against my skin. "We were advised it might take years for you to learn to use your powers, and by the time I realized you were forgetting everything, it was too late. We couldn't bring you back even if we wanted to. And we couldn't tell you anything. We failed you, and for that, I am so very sorry." A teardrop finally escaped, sliding down her cheek.

I frowned, latching onto the strange phrasing. "You were advised? By who?"

Her expression shifted, a flash of something that looked like anger crossing her features before smoothing out. "Your father's—"

The wooden door swung open, silencing her.

A tall figure filled the doorway, broad-shouldered and commanding. He took one step forward, then stopped, as if afraid to come closer. His eyes roamed my face, searching for something.

The silence stretched between us, an invisible tether pulled taut with years of secrets. When he finally spoke, his voice was rough with emotion.

"Snowflake."

CHAPTER 28
SNOWFLAKE

I blinked up at my dad. His casual red polo shirt with the Jingle logo that I'd seen hundreds of times over video calls looked ridiculously out of place in the castle.

For a moment, I almost laughed. Then my eyes fixed on his face.

He looked... tired. So tired. The silver in his beard seemed heavier than I remembered, his eyes carrying shadows I'd never noticed before. The robust, jolly man who'd always insisted on hot chocolate and bear hugs during his brief visits to Palm Springs looked hollowed out.

He crossed the room with hesitant steps, each one seeming to take effort, like he was walking through snow rather than across polished wood. The bed dipped as he lowered himself beside me.

"Snowflake," he repeated, the word hanging between us like a fragile ornament.

"Dad, you look exhausted." I wasn't about to beat around the bush. Not when so much time had been lost already.

Amusement flashed across his features. "I've just been staying up too late. Plus, too many cookies, not enough exercise."

I narrowed my eyes, refusing to let him dodge. "Your magic is fading."

Mom's hand squeezed mine, and for a beat, silence filled the space. Then he exhaled, his broad shoulders slumping forward as if relieved of a burden they'd carried for too long. "You always were too clever for your own good." He ran a hand through his silver hair. "Yes... my magic has been dwindling for years."

My throat tightened as I processed this, torn between lingering anger at everything they'd withheld from me and the unfamiliar ache of seeing his vulnerability. "How bad is it?"

He lifted his palm, and a tiny spark of red light flickered there before sputtering out. "After this Christmas, I may burn out completely."

"But you can't—" I stopped, not even sure what I was protesting. I barely understood any of this. "What happens if you... burn out?"

"I like to call it a Coal-25 situation."

I frowned. "A what?"

"You know, like Catch-22, but festive." His attempted humor fell into the growing silence between us.

I stared at him blankly.

"That's a joke, Snowflake." He sighed. "I suppose I'm not very funny anymore either."

My mom made a small sound, somewhere between a laugh and a sob. "Chris, perhaps we should wait."

"No, Glim. She deserves the truth. All of it. Joy has been fading in the world for a while now, and that impacts Christmas joy. As it fades, so does my magic. If my magic fades, then I can't deliver joy to those who need it most, which, unfortunately, will make the issue worse."

"But what about all the decorations and music and presents? Christmas is everywhere. How can joy be fading?"

"Commercialization without true spirit is like..." He searched for words. "Like a beautiful Christmas tree with no lights. The form is there, but the joy that makes it special is missing. I can only do so much. Fading joy is a year-round issue."

Ice formed along the edge of my blanket, spreading outward from where my fingers clutched the fabric. "So you're dying."

It wasn't a question.

"Not dying, exactly." He reached out, hesitating a moment before covering my hand with his. Warmth flowed from his touch, melting the ice. "Just... fading. Becoming mortal again."

"And you didn't think I should know about any of this? That I could have helped?"

My mom made a soft sound. "Neve..."

"No." I pulled my hands away from both of them. "You told me you were researchers. You let me believe I was human. Meanwhile, I'm some kind of Christmas princess with ice powers? And you're both just... fine with me finding out like this?"

Outside the frosted windows, the snow fell harder, driven by a wind that hadn't been there before.

Dad's eyes tracked the snowfall, a hint of something like pride crossing his face before sadness replaced it. "We thought we were protecting you."

"From what?"

"From yourself." His voice was gentle but unyielding. "Your magic was too strong, too wild. And then after the accident..."

Images flashed through my mind with fractured memories of blinding light, screaming, ice spreading in all directions. The feeling of being utterly out of control.

"I only remember pieces of it." I pressed my palms against my eyes, trying to force the memories into focus. "But it's like looking through frosted glass. I only know about it because of Lumi."

Dad's weight shifted on the bed. "It was my fault. I pushed you too hard with your training and wanted you to be ready too soon."

"Ready for what?"

His eyes met mine, the blue in them glowing faintly. "To take my place."

I laughed, the sound harsh and brittle. "Take your place? As Santa? That's ridiculous!"

His face remained serious. "It's not. You have enough magic to continue on with the tradition."

"I can't be..." The words evaporated on my tongue as the full weight of everything crashed down. My entire identity was unraveling—years of lies, powers I couldn't control, and now the expectation that I'd somehow save Christmas.

My chest tightened, each breath becoming more difficult than the last. The room blurred as tears welled in my eyes, spilling over before I could stop them. Ice crystals formed where they hit the blanket.

"I don't... I can't..." The sobs broke through, and magic pulsed through my veins, responding to my distress as snowflakes began swirling around the room.

For once, I didn't try to stop it. Didn't push it down or pretend it wasn't happening. I let myself break and feel everything I'd been running from: the confusion, the hurt, the anger, losing years I'd never get back.

Dad's arms wrapped around me, strong and warm and familiar. Mom pressed against my other side, her fingers stroking my hair the way she used to when I was small.

"Let it out, Snowflake," he murmured against my hair. "The storm always passes."

I don't know how long I cried, folded between them like a child. Eventually, the tears slowed, and the snow and ice around the room disappeared as if it had never been there.

I pulled back, wiping my face with the back of my hand. "I can't be Santa."

His brow furrowed. "Why not?"

I gestured at my chest with both hands. "Because I have these? Among other anatomical differences that I will not be pointing out to my father."

My mom's jaw dropped, her hand flying to cover her mouth. "Neve!"

My dad threw his head back and laughed, his eyes crinkling at the corners. It transformed his face, the exhaustion momentarily replaced with joy.

"Is that your only objection?" He leaned back, studying me with newfound amusement.

I crossed my arms. "It's a pretty significant one."

"No one actually sees me, you know." He wiped a tear of mirth from his eye. "And the few times someone has caught a glimpse over the centuries, I used a glamour."

My mom nodded, recovering from her shock. "The traditional image of Santa wasn't even created until the 1800s. Before that, the perception of gift-givers varied widely across cultures."

I squinted at him. "So, I could look like... anything?"

"More or less." He shrugged. "The magic responds to belief. Children believe in Santa Claus, so that's the form that manifests in their perception. But the actual physical form of the Yuletide Spirit is quite changeable."

The Yuletide Spirit. Fuck me, that was going to take some getting used to.

"Okay, but that's still ignoring the bigger issue." I held up my hand, where frost was still forming and melting in nervous patterns across my skin. "I can barely control this. I accidentally created snow sharks. They tried to eat Blitz."

His eyebrows shot up. "Snow sharks? That's... creative."

"It's dangerous." I dropped my hand. "What if I hurt someone? What if I mess up Christmas for everyone? What if—"

"What if you succeed?" He covered my hands with his. "What if you were always meant for this?"

I stared at our hands, his larger one nearly engulfing mine. "I don't know how."

He squeezed gently. "I suppose we have some work to do, then."

Something warm and unfamiliar stirred in my chest. Not quite hope, but maybe the possibility of it.

"Yeah," I whispered. "I guess we do."

Part of my training was how to navigate dinner with my parents and the nine men I was falling for. If I could survive an hour of torture, I would figure out the whole Santa Claus gig.

I sat between Rudy and Don at a table that stretched so long it could have hosted the entire North Pole. Crystal goblets refracted light from the chandeliers overhead, casting rainbow patterns across a tablecloth so white it practically glowed. The entire setting screamed magical North Pole royalty.

My dad sat at the head of the table, looking less like the weary man who'd confessed his fading powers and more like the jovial Santa I'd glimpsed in recovered memories. My mom, elegant in a silver gown that matched her hair, sat opposite him.

"Snowflake, you must try the frost-kissed venison." My dad gestured to a platter being carried by an elf server. "It was always your favorite."

I stared at the meat, which literally sparkled with tiny ice crystals that somehow didn't melt. "Um, isn't that a bit... cannibalistic?" I whispered to Rudy, glancing pointedly at the reindeer men surrounding me.

Rudy nearly choked on his wine. His hand found my thigh under the table and squeezed gently.

"We don't mind," Dane called from across the table, spearing a generous portion onto his plate. "Venison is delicious."

"So you've eaten... you know... deer meat while being..." I made antler gestures with my fingers.

Kip leaned forward, his eyes teasing. "Humans eat other mammals all the time. You don't see chickens getting weird about humans eating them."

My mom's unexpected laughter tinkled through the air. I stared in fascination at the woman who had masqueraded as an Arctic researcher for years. She'd transformed into someone completely different. Someone who laughed freely and whose eyes sparkled with magic when she summoned a dish from the center of the table without leaving her seat.

My dad set down his glass. "So, Cole. Tell me more about

how you all helped Neve access her magic. I understand there were some... unique methods involved."

I choked on a sip of water, remembering exactly what kind of "methods" had been employed.

Cole, bless his stoic heart, didn't even blink. "We each took different approaches based on our strengths, sir. Finding activities that sparked joy seemed most effective. Ice skating. Cookie decorating. Christmas trees."

"Snow forts." Pierce's expression was neutral despite there being nothing neutral about what happened there.

"Milk and cookies," Kip said with a straight face.

Rudy slowly turned his head in Kip's direction, and Kip's smile faltered. I bit my lip, a little turned on by Rudy's reaction and at the thought that Kip might have watched or heard.

"Tomorrow's tree-lighting ceremony will be perfect for continuing your progress." My mom beamed at me. "It's always been one of your favorite things."

I blinked rapidly, a bit disoriented. "Wait, tomorrow? What day is it?"

"November twenty-ninth." My dad's eyes crinkled with amusement.

"What?" I squeaked, pressing a hand to my forehead. "Everything's been such a blur. It's a good thing I never started celebrating Thanksgiving, or I'd be mad right now."

Rudy's hand squeezed my leg again, and my dad's gaze followed the movement before rising to meet Rudy's eyes. Something unspoken passed between them, and the atmosphere in the room shifted subtly.

"I think," my dad began, slowly setting down his fork, "it's time we discussed your intentions toward my daughter."

I groaned, dropping my head into my hands. "Dad, I'm a grown-ass woman."

"A grown woman who is powerful and has been surrounded by nine reindeer shifters who appear unusually... devoted."

"With all due respect, sir," Pierce said, his tone matter of fact, "we have every intention of being her sleigh team, but we're also her mates and intend to bond with her."

The table went silent. Even the elves serving food froze in place.

"Bond with me?" I hissed, kicking Pierce under the table, but he gave me a placid look that said he regretted nothing.

My mom set down her wine glass, her eyes widening as she looked at me. "With how they act around you, I thought you'd already completed the bonding ceremony right when you arrived."

"We immediately came here when we landed, and a bonding ceremony?" I looked from my mom to the shifty-eyed men around me. "Does it involve me rubbing their antlers and singing *Feliz Navidad* or something?"

Don coughed violently while Blitz smothered what sounded suspiciously like a laugh.

"That's not quite how it works." A small smile played at the corner of her lips. "Though the antler part isn't entirely off the mark."

My dad looked like he'd bitten into a lemon. "Glimmera, please."

My mom ignored him, leaning forward with gleaming eyes. "The bonding ritual is ancient magic. It requires absolute trust between two or more people. You would be connected by more than loyalty; your magic would intertwine with theirs."

"So I'd be, what, magically married to all nine of them?" I couldn't keep the squeak out of my voice. I had absolutely no interest in getting married.

I looked around at the nine faces watching me with expressions ranging from amusement to apprehension to something far more intense. They were serious about this.

Don moved his arm to the back of my chair, his fingers brushing my arm soothingly. "It's a bit like the whole fated-mate thing. The connection already exists between us, and the ritual simply acknowledges what's already there and magically ties us together."

"Reindeer don't bond with bites if that's what you're worried about." Vix was trying to be reassuring but failed.

My dad cleared his throat. "Perhaps this is a discussion for another time."

The look my mom shot him could have frozen fire. "Christopher."

"There's no rush." My dad tugged at his collar. "She's only just returned, and clearly they need to discuss this among themselves in private."

"A mate bond will calm her magic," my mom challenged. "When we bonded, my magic calmed substantially. Nine mate bonds would—"

"For the love of milk and cookies, can we please not talk about this?" I was pretty sure my face was red.

I wanted to reject having nine men tied to me for the rest of my life, but as dinner continued and the conversation moved on, I couldn't stop myself from wondering what it would be like.

CHAPTER 29
OF MAGIC AND REINDEER

I jolted awake, heart pounding, with absolutely no idea where I was. The ceiling above me glittered with tiny, embedded crystals, like stars frozen in ice. For one wild moment, I thought I'd manifested a bizarre snow shark aquarium in my sleep.

Then it hit me: the North Pole. Santa's castle. My home.

I sat up, running my hand over the silky sheets that practically hummed with enchantment. The room felt simultaneously foreign and achingly familiar, like a recurring dream I could never quite remember upon waking.

Something else felt different too. There was a strange tugging sensation in my chest, as if nine invisible threads were pulling me in various directions. I pressed my palm against my sternum, focusing on the feeling.

The guys. They weren't in the castle.

I knew this with absolute certainty, the same way I knew it was snowing outside without looking through the frosted windows. The awareness hummed through me like a low electrical current. In Klarhaven, I'd felt drawn to them, but here... here the pull was amplified, as if the veil had cranked our connection to eleven.

My hand drifted to the space beside me. They'd invited me

back to their house, but at least for one night I wanted to be in the castle. Plus, I had a day jam-packed with Claus business.

Holy reindeer balls, I was going to be Santa Claus.

I wondered whether they would let me change the name. Something like Mistress of the Sleigh or Maiden of the Pole.

A soft knock interrupted my thoughts.

"Come in!"

My dad opened the door and stepped inside, looking significantly less exhausted than he had yesterday. "Good morning, snowflake. Sleep well?"

I nodded, momentarily overcome by the surreal nature of this conversation. Small talk with Santa. About sleeping arrangements in his magical ice castle.

Just a normal day in the North Pole.

"I thought you might like a tour." He shifted his weight, thumbs hooked into the belt loops of completely normal jeans paired with another Jingle polo.

Thirty minutes later, I followed my dad down a long hallway attached to the castle and down a spiral staircase that opened into what could only be described as organized chaos. The central workshop sprawled before us, a massive open space bustling with more activity than Times Square on New Year's Eve.

Elves—not short caricatures but average-looking people with an ethereal quality and pointed ears—moved with purpose between workstations. Some wore practical coveralls with tool belts, while others donned more whimsical attire that shimmered with magic.

"Holy figgy pudding." I gestured wildly at the chaos before us. "This is... this is..."

"Christmas magic in action." He beamed with unmistakable pride. "This is the central hub. There are seventeen specialized workshops spread throughout the complex."

As we descended the last steps, heads turned in our direction. Conversations faltered, tools paused mid-motion, and the noise level dipped noticeably.

A tall elf with braided lime-green hair approached, his eyes widening as he recognized me. He dropped into a formal bow, right fist pressed to his heart.

"Miss Neve." His voice carried, causing a ripple effect as other elves turned to look. "The frost has returned to the mountain."

I froze, momentarily panicked by the formality and attention. Several more elves abandoned their tasks, moving toward us with expressions ranging from curiosity to outright joy.

My dad's hand settled on my shoulder. "They've been waiting for you to come home."

The weight of those words settled over me as dozens of elves bowed or waved, their faces alight with a mixture of hope and wonder that I couldn't possibly deserve.

"But I nearly destroyed everything." I looked past the elves welcoming me to find several still working or outright glaring.

Admitting I'd nearly demolished Santa's workshop felt like I'd replaced all the North Pole's cocoa with lukewarm chamomile tea.

An elf with hair striped like a candy cane stepped forward, her gaze fixed on me. "The saplings that weather the harshest winters grow the strongest roots." Her voice carried through the workshop. "You left as a frightened child, Neve North. You return a woman of magic and reindeer."

My mouth opened and closed like a malfunctioning nutcracker. What was I even supposed to say to that—thanks, I guess I'm less destructive now, or don't jinx it, I could still level this place?

"Frostwillow speaks the truth." Dad squeezed my shoulder.

A few elves nodded sagely, though I noticed others remained skeptical, whispers passing between them like currents of cold air. I couldn't blame them. Last time I'd been here, I'd apparently created the North Pole equivalent of a category-five hurricane.

The crowd parted like a shimmering sea, and my mom glided through, radiating composure. Her smile carried warmth that could melt permafrost.

"I see you've started the tour without me." My mom kissed

my dad's cheek and then looped her arm through mine. "Chris, the scheduling committee needs you for the Southern Hemisphere adjustments... again."

My dad's eyes lingered on us both with affection before he nodded and turned to address the workshop. The elves immediately resumed their activities, the momentary celebrity sighting forgotten in favor of whatever Christmas magic they were cooking up.

Mom guided me through a series of increasingly complex hallways until we emerged into an open courtyard.

"This is your training arena." She gestured to the space with a graceful sweep of her arm. "Perfect for containing... enthusiastic magic."

I narrowed my eyes. "You mean it's Neve-proof in case I go nuclear again."

"I prefer to think of it as a space where you can fully express yourself." Her lips quirked upward.

The courtyard sparkled, untouched snow covering every surface except a circular area in the center where the ground was bare stone etched with symbols I couldn't decipher.

"Let me explain something about your heritage." Mom positioned herself across from me in the circle. "Your magic is unique. My magic is precise. It shapes, whispers, and guides." She demonstrated by drawing her fingers through the air, leaving a trail of silver light that formed into a perfect snowflake. "Your father's magic is wild, abundant, and transformative."

"So, I'm basically the holiday version of a mood swing?"

Mom's laughter echoed in the space. "More like having both a scalpel and a sledgehammer at your disposal. Today we'll work on finesse."

For the next hour, my mom guided me through exercises that made me feel like a magical kindergartener. Apparently, step one was breathing on command, step two was pretending my fingers were glow sticks, and step three was making a mental Pinterest board before letting the magic loose.

I tried creating a simple ball of light, which was a beginner elf trick. Instead, I got a blinding flash that sent snow exploding upward in a fifteen-foot radius.

Next came ice shaping. My dainty little snow sculpture idea resulted in an icicle spear impaling itself six inches into the ground.

I attempted to summon a gentle flurry, but I ended up encased to my knees in rapidly forming frost.

"Shit." I struggled to free my legs, panic rising. "Mom, I can't stop it!"

"Breathe, Neve." She didn't rush to help me, instead holding my gaze steadily. "Feel the connection between your emotions and your magic. They're not separate entities; they're extensions of each other."

I closed my eyes, forcing air into my lungs. The frost crept higher, reaching my thighs.

"Remember who you are." Her voice remained calm. "The North Pole recognizes who it's gifted magic to. You belong here and are deserving of this magic."

The pressure in my chest eased slightly, and the frost stopped advancing.

"Now recall a moment of pure joy." Mom circled me slowly. "Not happiness, but joy. The kind that fills every corner of your being."

My mind flashed to the nine men who'd become my unlikely guardians, and the frost began to recede.

"Perfect." Mom's approval warmed me further. "Now reshape it. You're not destroying your magic; you're redirecting it."

I imagined the frost transforming, becoming something beautiful rather than threatening. Slowly, the ice coating my legs thinned, then reshaped itself into patterns that spiraled outward across the stone circle.

Mom clapped her hands. "Exquisite! My magic steadied after I bonded with your father. The emotional connection anchors the chaos and channels it purposefully." She winked. "The physical aspects certainly don't hurt either."

"Mom!" I slapped my hands over my ears. "I do not need to hear about you and Dad getting it on to control magic!"

"Oh please, you're nearly thirty with nine mates. I think we're past blushing about intimacy." She waved dismissively. "The point is, your connections with those men are already strengthening your control. That's how you controlled it, right? You thought of them?"

I groaned but couldn't deny she was right. Thinking of them had calmed the storm inside me almost instantly.

"Look there." Mom gestured toward the far wall of the courtyard, where a section of crystal provided a clear view of the training fields beyond.

Nine reindeer moved in perfect synchronization across the snow, their powerful bodies executing whatever maneuvers they were working on. Even from this distance, I recognized them.

A physical ache bloomed beneath my ribs, like homesickness for the people standing right in front of me. My magic surged in response, but this time it wasn't chaotic; it was a focused current flowing outward, reaching for them.

"The North Pole amplifies magical connections." Mom's voice softened. "What you're feeling is normal for mates in proximity to each other."

I walked to the wall and pressed my hand against the crystal window, watching as Rudy suddenly paused, his head lifting as if sensing something. The other reindeer followed suit, all turning toward the castle in perfect unison.

Toward me.

I traced my finger around the rim of a steaming mug, watching the miniature marshmallows slowly dissolve into the hot chocolate. The guys' kitchen was cozy, with mismatched dishes in the cabinet, a dish towel with a reindeer wearing sunglasses thrown over the oven handle, and the lingering scent of whatever ridiculously delicious thing Dane had baked earlier.

Their North Pole cabin was essentially Klarhaven 2.0, but with extras. There was a massive game room with a pool table large enough to land a small aircraft on, a movie theater with recliners that practically swallowed you whole, and stables for when shifting back to human form was too much effort.

I'd chosen to process my Christmas identity crisis in the castle, but standing in their kitchen felt more like home than any crystal-encrusted royal bedroom ever could. The thought should have terrified me, but it didn't. The castle impressed me, but this place disarmed me, sneaking past my defenses with warmth instead of splendor.

I could feel each of the guys moving through the house. There were nine distinct tugs on my soul, like someone had tied magical bungee cords between us.

"Are you going to drink that or continue your staring contest with it?" Kip leaned against the kitchen counter beside me, his eyes dancing with amusement.

I narrowed my eyes at him. "I'm strategizing the optimal whipped cream to chocolate ratio." I squirted out the fresh whipped cream that Cole had whipped up and put into a canister.

"She's nervous," Vix called from across the room, where he was adjusting the collar of his crimson jacket. "First official public appearance as Santa's daughter since her return. I'd be surprised if she weren't."

I lifted the mug to my lips, using the whipped cream mountain as a shield while I watched the guys preparing for the tree-lighting ceremony. They'd all dressed in coordinating outfits of deep greens, rich burgundies, and midnight blues that somehow looked festive without veering into tacky territory.

"It's not a coronation," I muttered into my drink.

Pierce took the mug from my hands and set it on the counter. "For the North Pole, it might as well be." He wiped a smudge of whipped cream from my upper lip with his thumb. "The first Christmas with the Claus heiress returned."

My stomach performed an elaborate gymnastics routine. "Don't call me an heiress. It's weird."

"Would you prefer ice princess?" Dane smirked from where he was helping Don with his cufflinks. "Or perhaps her royal frostiness?"

I flipped him off, earning a chorus of laughter from around the room.

Blitz approached with a garment bag draped over his arm. "Your mom sent this over."

As he held up the bag for me, I unzipped it to reveal a dress that made my breath catch. Deep red fabric with silver threading along the bodice that formed intricate snowflake patterns.

"Holy sugarplums," I whispered in awe.

Cole's warm hand settled at the small of my back. "Need help getting into it?"

My cheeks heated at the double meaning in his words. "I think I can manage clothing myself."

"Pity." Cole twisted away as I swatted at him on my way to change.

Alone in the guest bedroom, I shed my casual clothes and carefully slipped into the dress. The fabric settled against my skin, molding to my curves in a way that defied normal textile physics. When I looked in the mirror, I barely recognized myself.

My silver hair cascaded over my shoulders, catching the light with every movement. The dress made my skin glow with an inner luminescence, and my eyes shimmered like sunlight through ice.

I touched my reflection, half-expecting my fingers to pass right through it.

A soft knock on the door pulled me from my thoughts.

"Come in."

Rudy filled the doorway, his eyes widening.

"That bad, huh?" I smoothed the fabric nervously.

He crossed the room in three strides, stopping short of touching me. "You look like the North Star in human form."

I swallowed hard, caught in the intensity of his gaze. "Pretty sure that's not scientifically possible... You know what, never mind, it probably is."

His fingers brushed my cheek. "Are you ready?"

I wasn't, but I nodded anyway.

Twenty minutes later, the ten of us approached the central square, where it seemed every resident of the North Pole had gathered. The massive evergreen towered at least forty feet high, already covered in ornaments and ribbons that caught the light of the aurora dancing overhead.

Santa stood on a raised platform in front of the tree, the casual attire he'd been wearing earlier replaced by his iconic red suit. The crowd parted as we approached, whispers following in our wake.

"Is that her?"

"She's back..."

"You weren't lying about the nine of them..."

"Her magic nearly destroyed..."

My mom stood on the platform beside my dad, radiant in a gown almost identical to my own, her smile encouraging as she spotted me. As we reached the platform, my dad raised his hands, and the square fell silent.

"Citizens of the North Pole!" His voice carried effortlessly. "Tonight we gather, as we have for centuries, to honor the Spirit of Yuletide with the lighting of the Great Tree."

The crowd murmured their approval.

"This year's celebration holds special significance." His eyes found mine in the crowd. "My daughter has returned to us after twelve years in the mortal realm."

Every eye turned to me. I fought the urge to create a snow monster diversion and flee.

"Tonight, I'd like to bestow the honor of placing the final ornament to Neve." He extended his hand toward me.

The crowd erupted in cheers as my herd led me forward, forming a protective semicircle behind me.

My dad descended the steps to meet me, his eyes suspiciously bright. "I've waited for this moment longer than you know, snowflake."

I blinked rapidly, determined not to cry in front of the entire North Pole. "No pressure or anything."

He chuckled, then turned to Rudy. "The ornament, if you please."

Rudy reached into his jacket pocket and pulled out my glass ornament. It glowed faintly in his palm, pulsing in time with my heartbeat. Well, that was new.

"This is perfect." My dad nodded approvingly.

Rudy placed it in my hand, his fingers lingering against mine. The ornament warmed instantly, and the glow intensified until it illuminated our faces.

My dad led me up the platform steps and toward the massive tree. "You'll know where it belongs," he whispered.

Approaching the towering evergreen, I felt a magnetic pull toward a spot near the top, beyond normal reach. Without thinking, I raised my hand, and a gentle platform of ice formed beneath my feet, lifting me effortlessly to the perfect height.

The crowd gasped collectively.

With trembling fingers, I hung the ornament on a sturdy branch. The moment it touched the needles, magic erupted from my fingertips, traveling up the branch and spreading throughout the entire tree like wildfire.

Thousands of lights blazed to life, and the ornaments spun slowly, casting rainbow reflections across the square. Snow drifted down from nowhere and everywhere, dissolving into sparks of light when it touched anything.

The hum of the North Pole surged through me like a current, amplifying my connection to the nine men standing below. I felt their wonder, their pride, their desire, as if they were extensions of my body.

In that moment of perfect clarity, while magic flowed through my veins, I finally admitted the truth to myself.

I wanted this. I wanted them. I wanted to complete the bond that had been forming since I'd met them.

I, Neve North, wanted to be Santa Claus with nine reindeer mates.

CHAPTER 30
LIGHTS, MAGIC, REINDEER

T he snow continued to dissolve into sparks around me as my ice platform melted beneath my feet.

"Citizens of the North Pole!" My dad's voice boomed across the square. "The holiday season has officially begun! Enjoy tonight's festivities; tomorrow we begin the final countdown to Christmas Eve!"

The crowd erupted into cheers so thunderous that the sound vibrated through my chest. Some openly wept, and others jumped up and down.

My mom stepped forward, her hand slipping into my dad's. The pride radiating from her face was so bright it could have powered the tree lights all on its own. She nodded at me, a small gesture laden with a thousand unspoken words.

Cole's arm slid around my waist, anchoring me as the square transformed into a whirlwind of celebration. A band with instruments glittering with enchanted frost launched into festive music that sounded both traditional and modern.

"You're glowing," Blitz whispered into my ear.

I looked down at my hands, surprised to find they were emitting a faint silver light. "That's... new."

"And extremely hot." Vix's fingers brushed against mine on my other side.

Magical tables laden with treats appeared along the

perimeter of the square. Elves wove through the crowd with trays of steaming mugs, and the scent of cinnamon and chocolate filled the air.

Pierce snagged two glasses from a passing tray and offered one to me. "You have to try elfnog. Think eggnog, but with a kick that could make a reindeer fly without magic."

I accepted the drink, our fingers brushing in a contact that sent sparks racing up my arm. The first sip burned pleasantly down my throat before blooming into warmth that spread to my extremities.

The music shifted, and couples began spinning around a dance floor that glittered with embedded lights. My dad twirled my mom with surprising grace for a man of his stature, her silver hair fanning out as she threw her head back in laughter.

Don extended his hand to me. "May I have this dance?"

I placed my palm in his, and he pulled me into the swirling crowd.

He moved with surprising fluidity, guiding me through steps I somehow knew without being taught. It was like my body remembered that this magic, this place, and these men were written into my very cells.

"Your magic is calling to us. Can you feel it?" He spun me and pulled me into his chest again.

I could. The tug had morphed into a gravitational pull. Nine energies orbited me like I was their sun, growing stronger with each passing second.

As the song ended, Dash seamlessly cut in, his movements quicker, more playful than Don's controlled grace. Then came Pierce's smoldering intensity, Cole's gentle steadiness, Blitz's theatrical flair, Vix's dangerous edge, Kip's infectious joy, and Dane's confident lead.

The square blurred into a kaleidoscope of lights, laughter, and magic until Rudy finally stepped forward.

He stood before me, raw vulnerability in his eyes. "I need to know if this is what you want before I touch you again because once I do, I won't be able to let you go."

The noise of the celebration faded into the background as I

searched his face. The alpha who'd pushed me away and ulti-mately pulled me closer waited for my answer with barely concealed hope.

I stepped forward, eliminating the space between us. "I want this. I want all of you."

His exhale was almost violent with relief. He cupped my face between his palms, thumbs brushing my cheekbones. "Once we complete the bond, there's no going back. Nine rein-deer for eternity."

The magic surged between us, no longer content to simmer. It wanted completion.

"Take me home," I whispered.

Rudy's eyes darkened. With a nod to the others, he led me away from the square.

The tug in my chest strengthened with each step, my magic practically singing as we moved toward their cabin.

Tomorrow would bring responsibilities, training, and the reality of what it meant to be Santa's daughter. But tonight was for completing what had begun when a woman who hated Christmas met nine men who would change her life forever.

The cabin's warmth enveloped me the moment we stepped inside, but it was nothing compared to the heat of their eyes raking over me. Magic thrummed in the air like a living thing, pulsing in time with my heartbeat, or maybe it was all of our heartbeats. It was impossible to tell where mine ended and theirs began.

It had all happened so fast, yet somehow none of it seemed fast enough.

Rudy moved to the center of the living room, and I smiled. This time we weren't having a herd meeting where we discussed my loathing for everything merry and bright.

The others arranged themselves around the space, and I dropped onto Cole's lap. Kip perched next to us on the arm of the chair, while Dash leaned against the mantel, and Don stood quietly by the window. Pierce, Dane, Blitz, and Vix all sat on the sectional. All in different positions, but all with the same focus: me.

"The bonding requires each of us to seal our connection with you." Rudy's voice was low, sinking straight into my bones. "Our magic passes through you, yours through us, creating an eternal link."

My breath caught as I imagined how that would feel. "And how does this... sealing... happen?"

"It doesn't have to be sexual," Rudy clarified, his expression serious even as heat lingered in his gaze. "The intent to bond needs to be there for all parties."

I snorted. "Well, that sounds like a waste." What I didn't say was that it would waste the last few hours I'd had a butt plug in. I'd let that be a little surprise.

"Fucking hell, Neve." Dane stretched his arms out along the back of the couch, a grin splitting his face. "Rudy's not saying you can't get naked with all of us. He's saying you don't need to bone the entire herd in one night."

Kip's leg bounced as if he was holding himself back. "Even with your sped-up healing, we still want you to be able to walk tomorrow."

Laughter rippled through the room, breaking the tension that had been building. I joined in, feeling the last of my uncertainty melt away like snowflakes on warm skin.

The laughter faltered as I stood. I reached for my magic, and it responded like an eager pet. With a thought, I dissolved my dress into sparkling particles that drifted to the floor like red snow before vanishing.

"Holy shit," Blitz whispered, his eyes wide as I stood before them in nothing but icy blue lace.

"So that's how you all do it." I glanced down at my nearly naked body, oddly proud of myself. "The clothes after shifting, and all the things you've conjured."

Vix made a strangled sound. "Your first instinct was to use it to strip?"

"Are you complaining?" I cocked a hip, a newfound confidence flowing through me alongside the magic.

"Hell no." Vix's eyes had darkened to nearly black.

Nine different expressions of hunger stared back at me.

"Who goes first?" My voice came out steadier than I expected, given the molten heat pooling low in my belly.

"It forms in the order it's meant to." Rudy pushed the coffee table out of the way and conjured a fluffy fur to cover the floor along with several pillows.

"What does that mean?" I looked between them.

Don stepped away from the window and joined the others on the sectional. "It means that your magic will call to each of us, and whoever it reaches for first, that's where we begin."

I moved to the furs in the center of the room, lowering myself to my knees. The magic humming beneath my skin made every movement feel fluid and intentional.

They watched my every move, and I closed my eyes, focusing inward. If my magic was supposed to choose, I needed to let it. It sparked and reached, invisible tendrils stretching outward like vines seeking sunlight. It wrapped around three energies, pulling them toward me.

I opened my eyes to find Pierce, Dane, and Vix moving as if drawn by invisible strings. The others settled deeper into their seats, a hush of anticipation falling over them.

Pierce studied me for a moment as if assessing the situation. "May we touch you?"

I nodded, my throat suddenly too tight for words.

Vix's hands settled on my shoulders as Pierce's fingers traced the laced edge of my bra, while Dane's gaze burned hotter than any flame I'd ever felt.

"What do you feel?" Dane's lips brushed my ear, sending a cascade of tingles down my neck and across my shoulders. It made my magic pulse beneath the surface, and I leaned into it.

"Like heat under my ribs, pushing inward." Their magic pressed into me as if they were touching not just my body but something deeper.

The air in the room thickened as Pierce reached behind me, unhooking my bra. Dane slid the straps down my arms while Vix's fingers slid up the backs of my thighs, leaving goosebumps in their wake.

My nipples hardened in the cool air, drawing a rumble of

appreciation from someone on the couch. I didn't look to see who; I couldn't look away from the three men circling me like predators who'd cornered their prey.

Pierce leaned forward, capturing my mouth in a kiss that sent electricity racing through my veins. His tongue swept inside, demanding and thorough, while Dane's hands cupped my breasts, thumbs brushing over my sensitive nipples.

Vix's fingers dipped beneath the fabric of my underwear, and he discovered my little surprise. "Well, well. Seems our Christmas spirit has been very naughty indeed."

Pierce broke our kiss, eyebrow arched in question.

Vix tugged the lace down enough for the others to see the jeweled base of the plug nestled between my cheeks.

"Fuck." The word escaped Pierce in a harsh exhale.

A low whistle came from the couch.

"When did you..." Dane's question hung unfinished.

I reached back to grip Vix's hard length. "I wanted to be ready. For all of you."

Dane's eyes darkened as he lowered his head to my breast, taking a nipple between his lips. It sent liquid heat pooling between my thighs.

Vix tugged my panties down my legs, helping me lift each knee to free them completely. He moved around to my front as Pierce moved behind me.

Vix lowered himself to the fur, sliding between my spread thighs until his face hovered inches from where I ached most. "So ready and wet for us." His breath teased over my sensitive flesh, making me squirm.

Dane kissed me as Vix's tongue finally made contact, licking a broad stripe through my folds. The sensation was electric, heightened by the magic humming between us.

I arched, caught between Pierce's solid chest and Dane's mouth on mine. Vix's hands gripped my thighs, holding me open for his relentless tongue as he circled my clit before dipping lower to tease my entrance.

Dane broke our kiss, moving his lips to one of my breasts.

"Perfect." His teeth grazed my nipple before sucking it into his mouth.

I trembled, teetering on the edge of release. The magic flowed between us with golden cords binding us together, filling empty spaces I hadn't realized existed within me.

Pierce moved to my side. "I can feel you. Inside me." His voice held wonder and heat.

The bond solidified as the three of them touched me everywhere. I felt them distinctly within me now, three separate energies with unique signatures.

"I can feel you too," I gasped as Vix slid two fingers inside me while his tongue circled my clit. "All of you."

When the release came, it wasn't just physical pleasure; it was magic exploding outward, binding the four of us together in a shower of sparks that rained down around us.

I collapsed against Dane's chest as the magic settled into a warm, steady pulse within me. Three connections, solid and permanent, hummed beneath my skin.

Before I could fully recover, a shimmer rippled through the air. The remaining six men shifted forward slightly, responding to an invisible call. I felt a new pull, the magic coiling low in my belly, urging me toward the next touch, the next bond.

The night was just beginning.

CHAPTER 31
ETERNAL MAGIC

I floated in a dazed, blissful state as Pierce, Dane, and Vix retreated, their newly forged bonds pulsing inside me like three distinct heartbeats. My magic reached out again, extending across the room, seeking new connections.

Cole, Don, and Kip.

"Round two." I smiled up at them.

Cole knelt before me, brushing his fingers along my jaw. Don settled beside me, taking my hand and pressing it against his chest. The steady beat anchored me as my pulse raced in anticipation.

Kip slid in behind me. "I can't wait to see you come undone again."

Heat bloomed across my skin at his words, my magic reaching hungrily toward the three of them. Already I could feel new connections forming, different from the first three but equally as powerful.

Cole's hand slipped down to cup my breast, thumb circling my nipple until it hardened beneath his touch. "So responsive."

I arched into his hand, then gasped as Don's fingers traced a path up my inner thigh. My body was still sensitive from my first release, every touch magnified tenfold.

Don's fingers found me slick and swollen. "She's ready for us."

Kip pressed a kiss to my shoulder, then my neck, working his way up until his lips hovered beside my ear. His hand slid down my back, fingers tracing the curve of my spine before finding the jeweled base of the plug. He gave it a gentle twist, making me moan.

Cole helped me to my feet before he removed his remaining clothes. "How do you want us?"

My magic answered before I could, pulling me toward them with invisible hands. I found myself straddling Don's lap, his hard length pressed against my core while Cole moved behind me.

Kip stepped closer until his cock was level with my face.

Don's hands settled on my hips, holding me steady as Cole removed the plug. I whimpered as he eased it out, suddenly empty in a way that made me ache to be filled.

"Breathe," Cole instructed, his voice a soothing rumble against my back.

I inhaled deeply, feeling my magic pulse in response. It wanted them with an intensity that should have frightened me but instead felt unshakably right.

Don lined himself up at my entrance, the blunt head of his cock parting my folds. With excruciating slowness, he lowered me onto him, filling me inch by inch until I was seated fully in his lap.

Kip took a bottle of lube from Dane, and I heard it squirt behind me. Cole's hands spread my cheeks, a slick finger circling where the plug had been. I was already relaxed and ready from my earlier preparation, my body yielding easily as he pressed forward.

"So tight," Cole groaned, working a second finger alongside the first, scissoring them slowly. "That's our girl, open up for me."

Kip moved closer, his cock bobbing invitingly before me. I reached for him, wrapping my fingers around his length, feeling the velvet skin and rigid heat.

"You're so beautiful like this." Kip brushed my silver hair back from my face, his expression a mixture of awe and hunger.

Cole withdrew his fingers, replacing them with the head of his cock. The pressure built as he pushed forward, stretching me in a way that walked the line between pleasure and pain.

"Relax, we've got you." Don's thumbs traced soothing circles on my hips.

I leaned forward, taking Kip into my mouth as Cole sank into me fully. For a moment, we were frozen in the connection's perfection. I felt our bonds forming, weaving together with golden threads that bound us tighter than any physical joining.

Don rocked upward, and everything burst into motion.

They found a rhythm that drove me wild: Cole withdrawing as Don thrust upward, Kip sliding deeper into my mouth when the others pulled back. A perfect choreography of pleasure that left me moaning around Kip's cock.

"Her magic," Cole groaned from behind me. "It's inside me."

Don's hands flexed on my hips, his controlled façade crumbling. "I can feel it too."

Kip tangled his fingers in my hair, guiding my movements as I took him deeper. "It's like sunshine, warm and bright."

Three more bonds took root inside me, settling right where they belonged.

My orgasm hit without warning and left me trembling. Don's rhythm faltered as my walls pulsed around him.

Cole pressed his forehead between my shoulder blades, his movements growing more desperate. "Close," he growled against my skin.

Kip withdrew from my mouth, his cock slick. "I want to see your face when you come again."

I barely had time to recover before Don's thumb found my clit, circling with just the right pressure.

"Let go," Cole urged, his thrusts growing erratic. "Let us in completely."

The magic swirled around us, through us, connecting us in ways that transcended physical pleasure. I felt them in my chest, my mind, and my soul.

When I came again, it wasn't just my body that shattered.

My magic exploded outward, golden light erupting from where our bodies joined, enveloping us.

Don followed me over the edge, his release triggering Cole's. Kip came with a hoarse cry, spilling onto my breasts in pearlescent streams that transformed into glittering stardust before dissolving into my skin.

As we collapsed onto the furs together in a tangle of limbs, six solid connections hummed steadily beneath my skin.

Three more waited.

"Cookies," I mumbled once my brain finally reconnected with my mouth. "I need cookies."

Don disappeared and returned with several warm wash-cloths and a towel. "Let's get you cleaned up."

The scent of cookies wafted toward me moments later as Pierce carried a tray piled with them into the living room.

By the time I was cleaned up and had finished my snack, I felt almost human again—or whatever supernatural hybrid I was now.

I straightened in the nest of pillows and fur as three pairs of eyes locked onto me from across the room. My body should have been exhausted after two intense rounds of magical bonding, yet energy coursed through me, demanding more.

"I'm ready." My magic pulsed in agreement, reaching eagerly toward the final three men who would complete our bond.

Blitz moved like he couldn't get to me fast enough, and Dash moved just as fast, eyes dark with hunger. Rudy hung back, watching with an unreadable intensity that made my pulse trip.

I glanced at the others sprawled out in bliss. "Just so we're clear, this isn't going to happen all the time."

Kip lifted his head from Don's shoulder, a sleepy grin spreading across his face. "Liar."

Heat spread across my cheeks because he was right. This was going to happen as much as my body allowed.

Blitz stripped his shirt over his head in one fluid motion,

revealing the impressive muscles beneath. "You saved the best for last, didn't you?"

I laughed. "Clearly."

Rudy approached the furs, lowering his massive frame onto the pillows. He guided me back against his chest, positioning me between his spread legs. His skin burned hot against mine, his heartbeat a steady rhythm against my back.

I settled against him as Dash stretched out beside us, propped on one elbow. His free hand traced lazy patterns on my thigh, each touch leaving trails of heat in its wake.

Blitz remained standing, eyes roving over my body with undisguised appreciation as he removed the rest of his clothing. "I've been waiting to be inside you."

My body hummed in anticipation as he knelt between my legs, his hands sliding up my calves to my knees, gently spreading them wider.

Rudy's hands cupped my breasts from behind, thumbs brushing over my sensitive nipples. "Relax into me."

Dash leaned forward, capturing my lips in a kiss that started gentle but quickly burned hotter. His tongue slipped past my lips, exploring with strokes that matched the rhythm of his fingers now circling my clit.

Between my legs, Blitz lowered his head, replacing Dash's fingers with his mouth. The first swipe of his tongue had me arching off Rudy's chest.

"You like it when we eat your sweet pussy, don't you?" Dash trailed kisses down my neck.

"Yes," I moaned, my breaths already stuttering in my chest.

Blitz hummed and worked me with practiced skill until my thighs trembled on either side of his head.

My magic rose to meet their touches, silver-blue tendrils weaving through the surrounding air. It recognized these men as mine, reaching for the connections that would bind us together.

When Blitz finally rose, positioning himself at my entrance, I could hardly breathe through the anticipation. "Ready for me?"

I nodded, words failing me as he pushed forward, filling me in one smooth thrust that had stars bursting behind my eyelids. "Finally," he groaned, holding still as my body adjusted to him. "You feel like heaven."

Rudy's hands slid from my breasts down to my hips, helping to steady me as Blitz began to move. Dash's teeth grazed my nipple in a way that made my inner walls flutter around Blitz.

My mind swam as they worked together, responding to my body's needs. Rudy's hands anchored me to reality while Blitz and Dash pushed me toward a ledge I was eager to fall from.

The magic around us was thicker than before, golden threads mixing with my silver-blue power. The six bonds pulsed inside me, strengthening even more as the final three took shape.

"I can feel them." Blitz's rhythm faltered.

I was unable to explain how all nine of them were beginning to blend into something greater than their parts.

Rudy's lips pressed below my ear, his voice a reverent whisper. "Let go, Neve. We'll catch you."

The simple promise undid me. My release crashed over me with an intensity that bordered on painful, my body clenching around Blitz as pleasure radiated outward. Magic erupted from my skin in a blinding flash that illuminated the entire cabin.

Blitz followed me over the edge with a hoarse cry, his release triggering another surge of magic that wove into the bond. As he collapsed forward, I felt the connections snap into place.

The other men gathered around us. Pierce's fingers threaded through my hair, Vix's palm warmed my shoulder, and Cole's touch was firm on my hip. Don's fingertips traced my collarbone while Kip's hand found mine, squeezing gently. Dane and Dash each claimed a thigh, their touches grounding me as Blitz pressed his forehead to my chest.

Rudy brushed his fingers along my chin, turning my head to lock his eyes with mine.

Nine points of contact, nine men, nine reindeer—my herd.

As Rudy's lips met mine in a kiss that contained a multitude of emotions, magic roared to life around us. It spiraled upward in a column of light that seemed to pierce the ceiling, connecting earth to sky.

Heat, light, and power flooded my senses until I couldn't tell where I ended and they began. The individual threads of our connections twisted together into an unbreakable cord, binding nine souls to mine in a bond that transcended the physical.

When it finally broke, I floated in a state of perfect contentment, supported by too many hands to count. The bond had settled but continued to thrum beneath my skin, a constant reminder that I was no longer alone.

"Forever." Rudy's voice carried the weight of a vow.

"Forever," eight voices echoed, the promise resonating through the bond.

"Forever," I whispered.

They were mine now, and I was theirs for as long as magic existed in the world.

And in the North Pole, magic was eternal.

CHAPTER 32
THICK AND SPRUCEY

I wasn't sure if the pins-and-needles sensation in my left arm was from magical bonding or just Pierce's massive shoulder cutting off circulation, but either way, I needed to extract myself from the tangle of limbs before someone started drooling on me. Again.

Nine men. Nine gloriously naked men sprawled across the living room floor like we'd survived some kind of sexy apocalypse. Furs and pillows and random items of clothing created a nest that, frankly, smelled like Christmas morning and a men's locker room had a baby.

I carefully extracted my arm from beneath Pierce, who mumbled something about spiced wine in his sleep. My body felt lighter and more vibrant, like I'd been running on a half-charged battery my entire life and someone had finally plugged me in.

Holy shit, was I... *jolly*?

I waited for my usual internal groan at the holiday terminology, but it never came.

Carefully stepping over Cole's outstretched leg and dodging Kip's starfish pose, I wondered how sleeping arrangements would work. A nine-man rotation schedule? Bunk beds? I'd slept like the dead despite being sandwiched between Vix and

Dane for most of the night. Being surrounded by all of them felt right in a way nothing else ever had.

We needed a bigger bed. Like, comically large. Like, "sorry, we had to remove all the walls between bedrooms" large.

I tiptoed to the bathroom, magic pulsing under my skin. But not in the erratic, terrifying way it had been before. This felt controlled.

Turning on the hot water, I stepped into the shower. Steam filled the bathroom as I closed my eyes, feeling the bonds stirring to consciousness one by one. It wasn't mind reading exactly, more like emotional weather reports from different stations.

I closed my eyes, wiggling my fingers beneath the shower spray. They tingled with what felt like static electricity without the shock. Maybe I could try something small, like a tiny magical change to the water pressure.

I focused on the showerhead, imagining the water forming a more concentrated stream. A smile tugged at my lips as I visualized exactly what I wanted.

The showerhead sputtered, then shot a perfect arc of water across the bathroom, hitting the mirror with pinpoint accuracy.

"Ahh!" I yelped, concentrating harder. The water curved back into a normal stream, then formed into a series of floating spheres that hovered in the air.

I couldn't help but giggle. With a flick of my wrist, I sent the spheres spinning. One got away from me and splattered against the ceiling, raining back down in a pattern that suspiciously resembled a penis.

I focused again, this time on ice. A frost pattern spread across the shower door, forming intricate snowflakes that reminded me of one of my men. I was a regular Martha Stewart of magical ice decor.

I concentrated on creating a simple ice cube in my palm. Instead, I produced a perfect ice sculpture of a reindeer with an anatomically exaggerated feature.

My brain was definitely still on last night's festivities.

After finishing my shower and drying off, I stood naked in

front of the mirror. I pictured something festive, because apparently that was my brand now. My magic surged, wrapping around my body in swirls of light. When it faded, I stared at my reflection in horror and delight.

Fleece leggings hugged my legs and had printed Christmas lights that somehow twinkled. An oversized sweater proclaimed, "I LIKE THEM REAL THICK AND SPRUCEY" above an image of a massive Christmas tree.

I stepped out of the bathroom, bracing for chaos, only to find the living room transformed. Gone were the strewn pillows and tangled blankets. From the kitchen came the smell of coffee, bacon, and pancakes. My stomach growled in response.

Cole stood at the stove, flipping pancakes while Dane leaned against the counter beside him, stealing bits of bacon whenever Cole turned his back. Kip arranged berries into smiley faces on a plate of waffles, his tongue poking out in concentration.

"I'm not making your weird egg white omelets, Vix." Pierce glowered over a mixing bowl. "It's bonding day breakfast. You're eating carbs like the rest of us."

Vix, perched on the counter, kicked his bare feet against the cabinets. "My body is a temple."

"Your body was a temple of sin about six hours ago," Dash called from where he was setting the table.

I pushed experimentally at the connections between us, surprised to find I could dial it up or down at will. Useful. Even in magical relationship bliss, a girl needed mental privacy.

"She's testing the bonds." Don didn't even look up from the coffee he was pouring.

Blitz winked at me from his position by the window. "Trying to shut us out already?"

I smoothed my hands over my ridiculous sweater. "Just seeing how the volume control works."

Nine pairs of eyes swiveled toward me, taking in my festive outfit with varying degrees of amusement.

Rudy, arranging napkins with unnecessary attention to detail, froze mid-fold. "Your sweater…"

I crossed my arms over my chest defensively. "My magic dressed me."

Kip abandoned his berry art to circle me, poking at the lights on my leggings.

Cole carried a tray that held towers of pancakes and waffles. "Breakfast is ready."

We crowded around the table, a true feat of spatial engineering with ten bodies, passing plates and stealing bites from each other's food. Dane's foot hooked around my ankle under the table while Vix sulked over the stack of pancakes Pierce had placed in front of him.

"How are you feeling this morning? Feel any different?" Cole placed a few slices of bacon on my plate.

"I feel great. The bond feels like..." I searched for the right words while cutting into a waffle.

"Like coming home," Kip finished, stealing a piece of bacon off Dane's plate.

Don nodded. "The bond will settle over the next few days. Right now, it's still new, so everything feels heightened."

I took another bite of my waffle, maple syrup dripping down my chin as Dane leaned over to wipe it away with his thumb.

"Your father wants us at the training field in thirty minutes." Rudy had been quiet, and through our bond, I could sense he was on edge.

Vix jumped up, rubbing his hands together. "This is your first official sleigh training! This is huge!"

My stomach fluttered with nerves as the guys finished their breakfasts and started clearing the table. The reality was setting in: I was about to learn how to be Santa's daughter.

I HELD tight to the reins of my dad's sleigh as we glided to a gentle landing on the packed snow of the training field. If I weren't actively trying to appear composed and professional, I might have let out the kind of squeal normally reserved for winning the lottery.

"Not bad for your first official sleigh lesson." Dad patted my hand, and I loosened my death grip.

Not bad? I'd just piloted an actual sleigh through the actual sky with actual magical reindeer. The child in me—the one who apparently had been trapped inside me for twelve years—wanted to fling herself into a pile of snow and make snow angels while screaming, "I flew a sleigh!" at the top of her lungs.

Instead, I nodded with what I hoped was dignified appreciation. "Thanks. It feels natural."

"Of course it does." Dad jumped down from the sleigh with surprising agility for a man who refused to give me a straight answer about how old he actually was. "The magic is in your blood."

I climbed down after him. "It's different from riding on the backs of my—" I caught myself before saying 'men' "—reindeer."

"It's a different type of magic entirely." Dad brushed snow from his crimson coat. "Speaking of your herd, you'll be working with them and Silven for the next few hours."

My entire body went rigid at the name. "Silven?"

Dad nodded, adjusting his gloves. "My advisor. Been with me for centuries. He's been working with your herd since dawn on coordination techniques."

Something cold slithered down my spine. "Your advisor? Why haven't I met him yet?"

"You don't remember him? You used to train with him. He returned this morning from his vacation."

I glanced toward the distant field where nine dots moved in formation across the snow. My herd had been blocking their emotions all morning to help me focus on my training without distraction. At first, I'd been annoyed, but the silence had helped me connect more deeply with the sleigh magic.

"He used to train me? How so?" There were memories I still couldn't fully access, but the ones I had of training weren't positive.

Before Dad could answer, an elf came sprinting across the field, arms waving frantically.

"Emergency in the workshop, sir! The enchantment on the self-wrapping paper station has gone haywire, and it's wrapping everything, including the elves!"

Dad's expression shifted from fatherly pride to Commander of Christmas Operations in an instant. "I'll be right there." He turned to me, already backing away. "Head that way." He pointed toward the distant field where my reindeer were still moving in formation.

"But wait! I need to—"

"We'll talk later, Snowflake!" Dad called over his shoulder as he hurried away with the frantic elf. "I promise!"

I tugged my hat down firmly over my ears and started trudging toward the training field, focusing on the distant shapes of my herd. I tried reaching out through our bond again, only to hit the same emotional wall they'd put up earlier.

One moment I was slogging through ankle-deep snow, and the next—

My stomach lurched as the world blurred around me. A rush of disorientation hit me like a brain freeze, and suddenly I was standing on the training field, my boots sinking into fresh powder.

Teleporting lessons couldn't come soon enough.

Now that I was closer, I could see that my herd was hitched to a sleigh as massive as my dad's. All of my reindeer, including Rudy, were hooked to it.

A flutter of hope caught in my chest. Was Rudy flying?

"Again!" A voice sliced through the air from the other side of the reindeer, his face partially obstructed by the massive antlers everywhere.

The sleigh and eight reindeer lurched upward, wobbling precariously. My heart soared as the runners left the ground, lifting about ten feet into the air before tilting dangerously to one side. Eight sets of reindeer legs scrambled as they tried to maintain balance, but the sleigh crashed back to the snow with a sickening thud.

"Pathetic." A man strode to the front of the herd. His dark hair and eyes were almost a replica of Rudy's.

Silven, my brain supplied instantly, though I couldn't remember ever seeing him before... but that voice was very familiar.

He grabbed one of Rudy's antlers and yanked downward, forcing his head to bow. "You don't deserve these. It's a waste of perfectly good magic on a flightless beast."

The world around me tilted, colors bleeding at the edges of my vision as something unlocked in my mind.

I was fifteen, crouched behind a snowbank near the south stables; a place I wasn't supposed to be during rutting season when young reindeer were unpredictable and learning their flight magic. But curiosity had always been my downfall.

A man stood looming over a magnificent young reindeer.

"Useless creature." Silven grabbed one of his antlers. "A reindeer who can't fly? An embarrassment to Christmas itself."

"Hey!" I jumped up from my hiding spot.

Silven's hand dropped immediately, his eyes homing in on me. "Miss North, you know you aren't allowed here."

He took a step toward me, and I turned and ran. I needed to tell Dad.

The workshop wasn't far, and that's where I'd probably find him. I heard Silven behind me at first, but then he disappeared. Sighing in relief, I made it to the workshop, but as I yanked open the door, Silven was there, blocking my path.

"Miss North." His smile didn't reach his eyes. "Spying again? Your father indulges your little peculiarities far too much."

"I need to see my dad." I tried to move past him.

His hand shot out, gripping my arm.

Ice spread along my fingertips. "Let me go."

"The way I train my son is none of your concern." His voice was low and venomous.

"He's your son, and you treat him like that? You should be banished from the North Pole!"

"And you, Miss North, are an expert at parenting? Your own father lies to your face! You think he's proud of you? You're not a

Claus; you're a mistake. All that power in you is better suited for ruin than wonder."

Something inside me shattered. Magic exploded outward as I yanked free, stumbling backward through the workshop doors. Ice shot from my hands, freezing conveyor belts, destroying toy-making machines, climbing up walls—

Screams. So many screams.

Silven watched from the doorway, a satisfied gleam in his eye.

I gasped, snapping back to the present, trembling so hard my teeth chattered. Ice crawled from my boots across the snow, spreading in jagged patterns.

"It was you!" I pointed at Silven, my voice filled with rage. "You caused it!"

His head whipped toward me, eyes widening in recognition before narrowing to slits. "Miss North. What an unexpected surprise."

The air around me hummed. The snow beneath my feet swirled upward, circling my body in a miniature blizzard. "You made me think I was broken." Ice crystals formed in the air, suspended like deadly stars. "You manipulated me into losing control!"

Silven backed away, hands raised. "You're becoming too emotional. We all know what happens when you—"

There was a tremendous cracking sound as ice shot from my fingers, barely missing his head. The reindeer were bucking wildly now, bells jingling chaotically as they fought to break free from their harnesses.

Rudy lowered his massive head and charged forward, snapping the leather straps holding him to the sleigh. He galloped to my side, a saddle appearing on his back as he dipped down.

"Get on." His voice rumbled through my mind.

I scrambled onto his back as the storm of my emotions whirled around us. My other eight reindeer broke free, thundering across the snow in our direction.

Silven's face contorted with rage.

My magic surged again, and the snow before us rose,

forming a massive, hulking creature with ice for teeth. The snow monster roared, lunging toward Silven.

Silven shifted forms, transforming into a reindeer with no antlers, his coat the same color as Rudy's. He darted into the trees as my snow monster crashed into a pine, exploding in a spectacular poof of powder.

Rudy galloped across the field away from what was triggering me. Away from his father.

"Take me back!" I wanted to destroy Silven so he could never hurt my mates again. How many times had he said those words to Rudy?

The storm of my magic swirled around us, unwilling to relent.

And then Rudy's hooves left the ground.

CHAPTER 33

STOCKING FULL OF COAL

W e were flying.

Not the awkward, struggling flight of someone first taking to the sky, but a smooth, powerful lift as Rudy carried us upward, his hooves pushing against nothing but air. Behind us, the other eight rose in perfect formation. The bond between me and the others flooded with protectiveness, pride, and fierce love.

"You're flying!" I leaned forward to wrap my arms around his neck. "You're actually flying!"

His connection to me opened, and his joy was pure and unfiltered. The training field and forest—where Silven was probably pissing his reindeer pants—shrank as we soared higher and higher.

We landed on a secluded mountaintop, touching down in perfect synchronization. The storm of my magic finally quieted as the adrenaline began to fade. The ice particles that had been swirling around us like angry fireflies settled onto the snow, glittering from the aurora overhead.

Rudy's massive reindeer form shimmered beneath me, and I slid off his back just as the transformation began. Where powerful haunches had been moments before, strong human thighs emerged. I reached out to steady him as he shifted fully, catching him as he stumbled forward.

"You okay?" I held onto his biceps, searching his face. Rudy nodded, his chest heaving with exertion. Sweat beaded on his brow despite the frigid temperature, but his eyes blazed with a triumphant light I'd never seen before.

"I flew." The words came out in a breathless rush as he grabbed my hands. "Neve, I *flew*."

Eight other transformations rippled through the air around us as the rest of the herd shifted back to human form.

Dane approached first, his expression a mixture of awe and disbelief. "Holy shit, Rudy."

Kip bounded through the snow like an excited puppy. "You were majestic as fuck!"

My fingers found Rudy's, my own emotions threatening to spill over again. "What happened back there?" I swallowed hard, trying to find the right words. "Why didn't you tell me about your father?"

A shadow crossed his face. He pulled me toward a fallen log nearby, brushing snow from it before we sat. The others formed a protective circle around us, their bodies blocking the cold air.

"I didn't grow up in the North Pole." Rudy stared at our intertwined fingers. "My mother took me to Klarhaven when I was a calf."

"And your dad?"

Rudy's jaw worked for a moment before he continued. "My mom left Silven shortly after I was born. He stayed in the North Pole as Santa's lead reindeer, and she lived in Klarhaven, giving rides to human children in Reinberg." He glanced at the others, who were listening attentively. "Shortly after she left him, his antlers fell off, and he lost his ability to fly."

My eyebrows shot up.

"We didn't know that's why he lost them..." Cole crouched in front of us.

"So, he's bitter that you still have yours?" Dash moved to stand behind Rudy and placed a comforting hand on his shoulder.

"I think it's a combination of bitterness and hope that I'd fly to continue the family legacy." Rudy's thumb traced circles on the back of my hand. "When my magic fully manifested at seventeen and I moved to the North Pole, he was nice until he realized I couldn't."

The image of Silven yanking on Rudy's antler made me nauseous. "I saw him when I was fifteen and went to tell my dad, but he... well, he said some things that set me off."

"We'll kill him," Don growled, shocking all of us.

I reached over and took his hand. "No one is killing anyone, but he is definitely getting a stocking full of coal this year."

Rudy's shame leaked through our bond, a dark undercurrent beneath the triumph of his flight. His shoulders hunched forward slightly, as if he was already preparing for this joy to be stolen away.

"Hey." I squeezed his hand and waited until his eyes met mine. "You flew, Rudy. You fucking *flew*. With me. With all of us. And your father can't take that away from you."

The corner of his mouth twitched. "I always thought the bond was the missing piece." His voice dropped so low I had to lean in to hear him. "But I never believed I'd be worthy of one." He glanced around at the others, his Adam's apple bobbing as he swallowed hard. "Especially not all nine of us together."

I cupped his face between my palms, my thumbs brushing against the rough stubble of his jaw. "You aren't broken, Rudy. You never were." I held his gaze, willing him to feel the truth in my words. "I see you. I *chose* you. We all did."

Cole knelt beside us, his hand settling on Rudy's knee. "You've carried us all, even when you thought you couldn't fly."

"Alpha doesn't mean perfect." Pierce's deep voice rumbled from where he stood behind me. "It means you lead even when you're scared shitless."

Dash grinned, flicking a snowflake from Rudy's hair. "And you've been scared plenty of times."

"Remember when we found that polar bear in the stables?" Kip's eyes were bright with the memory. "You stepped in front of all of us even though your knees were knocking together."

Don nodded solemnly. "You protect us."

"Even when we're being complete assholes," Vix said.

"Which is often." Blitz elbowed Vix playfully.

Dane crouched down on Rudy's other side. "The herd chose you."

Through our bond, their emotions surged with love, loyalty, and fierce devotion, building a protective wall around Rudy that glowed like the Northern Lights.

"Besides." Kip's mischievous smile broke through the intensity of the moment. "Silven's basically the Grinch with erectile dysfunction antlers."

Rudy's laugh started as a surprised snort before growing into a full, deep belly laugh that rippled through our bond, warming me from the inside out as the others joined in.

"Erectile dysfunct-lers," Dane wheezed, doubling over.

Rudy pulled me closer in his arms, his body still shaking from laughter. His chin rested on top of my head as the others moved closer. The eight of them surrounded us, their presence solid as the mountain beneath us.

This, I realized, was what family felt like: belonging and unshakable loyalty.

"What now?" Blitz's question floated over our heads.

I snuggled deeper into Rudy's embrace, feeling his heartbeat against my cheek. "Now we go home and figure out how to deal with Silven."

"I THINK we should do a public snowballing."

"That's too kind. Let's drop him in a polar bear den."

"Sharpened candy canes are the only answer here."

"Oh! We can make him walk barefoot across shattered ornaments!"

My dad and I sat next to each other at the conference room table and exchanged looks. With eighteen reindeer in the room, the suggestions for Silven's consequences had gotten progressively more... creative.

"We aren't going to torture him," one of my dad's reindeer pinched the bridge of her nose as if this wasn't the first time an idea had spiraled out of control. "But he can't stay here, Santa."

My dad sighed, tapping the edge of his mug filled with hot chocolate.

I drummed my fingers against the polished conference table, watching these imposing magical beings go full blood-thirsty mob. It was like a corporate board meeting had merged with medieval court justice, except everyone had antlers.

"We could make him lick the candy cane forest. His tongue would stick, and he'd be there until spring thaw." A man with auburn hair punctuated his point by snapping a gingerbread cookie's head off.

A female reindeer with a tinsel-threaded braid leaned forward. "What about community service? Five thousand hours untangling Christmas lights?"

"With no magic," another added.

I caught my dad's eye, and we shared a look of amusement as the suggestions flew around us. There was something weirdly familiar about sitting beside Dad in a conference room that looked straight out of a Fortune 500 company, complete with a whiteboard where someone had actually written "Punishment Options" with a little smiley face next to it.

"So, is this what passes for criminal justice at the North Pole?" I leaned toward my dad, keeping my voice low. "Santa's sweatshop for the naughty?"

Several heads turned in my direction, a few with raised eyebrows, while others smothered laughs behind mugs of hot chocolate.

Dad ran a hand through his silver hair, not quite hiding his smile. He took another sip from his mug, and I noticed the faint tremor in his hand. The magical shimmer surrounding him had dimmed since the morning. The situation we were dealing with didn't help much with the joy needed to replenish his energy stores.

"We need to focus on practical solutions." A female reindeer with silver at her temples tapped the table. "Strip him of his advisor status and remove all authority."

"Permanent toy-testing duty." Another nodded. "Let him suffer through squeaky toys for eternity."

"The toy department doesn't deserve that punishment," Rudy muttered beside me, his jaw clenched.

Blitz gestured dramatically. "What about exile? Send him somewhere sunny. Like Florida."

Pierce shook his head. "That's crueler than the polar bear idea."

The subtle shift in my mom's posture shut everyone up. "Exile from the Pole seems most reasonable. Perhaps to Klarhaven, where he'll be close enough if needed."

"He shouldn't have power over anyone ever again. Especially not young reindeer." The memory of how Silven had treated Rudy made frost form along my fingertips.

Rudy flinched beside me, a barely perceptible movement that sent a ripple of pain through our bond. I reached under the table and found his hand, lacing my fingers through his. He squeezed, his thumb tracing small circles against my skin.

Dad nodded slowly, his brow furrowed in thought. "I'm inclined to agree with exile. But this decision can't be about vengeance." He looked around the table, making eye contact with each person. "We are Christmas. Even our justice must contain mercy."

I fought the urge to roll my eyes. "He caused me to lose control and get sent away for twelve years. He berated his own son. Where was mercy then?"

"Neve." My mom's voice was gentle but firm. "Leadership often means choosing what's fair, not what feels good. That's the burden of power."

I sank back in my chair, conflicted.

Dad pushed himself to his feet. "Neve and I will find Silven and deliver the verdict." He paused, looking at the assembled reindeer. "Exile to Klarhaven, stripped of his advisor status, with periodic review."

Rudy stood beside me, his presence solid and unwavering. "I'm coming too." His voice left no room for argument.

I looked between Rudy and my dad, warmth blooming in

my chest at Rudy's determination to face his father. The magical bond hummed with support, each of my men silently backing him.

"Are you sure?" I squeezed Rudy's hand, watching the muscle in his jaw flex.

Dad adjusted his red velvet coat with a nod. "We'll set out after dinner."

"I should be there too." Mom rose gracefully, her silver-streaked hair catching the light.

An older reindeer with snow-white hair cleared his throat. "While you're handling that unpleasant business, the rest of us should organize the annual antler competition. It's been too long since we've determined whose rack truly shines brightest."

My mouth dropped open as all of my men's faces lit up, even Rudy's. "Excuse me, a what now? Please tell me everyone is doing their own polishing."

Every face in the room turned to me with expressions ranging from scandalized to amused that I'd assume otherwise.

"It's a traditional competition," Dad explained, smoothing his beard. "Each reindeer's antlers are judged on luster, symmetry, and—"

"Girth." Blitz wiggled an eyebrow.

Heat crawled up my neck. "Sounds like it's literally a dick-measuring contest, but with antlers."

Kip snorted hot chocolate through his nose while Cole patted his back.

Don winked at me. "You can be the judge this year, princess."

"Perfect," I deadpanned. "I always dreamed my first official duty would be scoring antler porn."

And just like that, the meeting was officially over.

CHAPTER 34

NICE RACK

T he snow crunched under my boots as we approached the clearing. The stables stood behind us, their silhouettes silent witnesses to what was about to unfold. Silven waited in the center of the clearing, flanked by two stoic elves.

He looked smaller somehow. The fierce, menacing presence that I remembered had diminished, his shoulders hunched against the cold, or maybe against the weight of his actions. His gaze remained fixed on the ground as we approached.

My dad stepped forward, his imposing figure casting a long shadow across the snow. "Silven."

Silven's head lifted slightly. "Santa."

Rudy tensed beside me, his breath coming out in a controlled exhale. His emotions were churning with anger, hurt, and beneath it all, a festering wound that had never healed.

"You have served as my advisor for decades." My dad's voice held none of its usual warmth, which made me sad for him. "I trusted you with the training of our reindeer and with the safety of my daughter."

Silven's jaw clenched. "Everything I did was necessary. The North Pole needs—"

I cut in, stepping forward as ice crystals spread across my

fingers. "What the North Pole needs is support, not cruelty disguised as training."

"You know nothing of magic, girl." Silven's gaze finally landed on me, sharp and dismissive.

"You nearly destroyed us both." My voice shook with fury as sparks of blue danced around my hands. I was completely in control of it now and wouldn't be sending any snow monsters after him. "You told me I was a mistake, and you made your own son believe he was broken."

Maybe one little snow shark would be fine.

The snow beneath my feet began to shift and swirl, responding to the storm building inside me. My mom's gentle touch at my elbow calmed me.

"I did what needed to be done." Silven straightened his spine, attempting to reclaim some dignity. "Strict training builds character. Flouncing around the North Pole making snow butterflies and—"

"Enough." Dad's voice cracked like ice breaking. "Neve told me about all the things you've said to her over the years, and I'm sure it's just the tip of the iceberg."

The clearing went quiet, and Silven flinched, his eyes darting to my dad's face. There was a slight tremor in his fingers, and it gave me a tiny spark of vindictive pleasure that I wasn't entirely proud of, but I wasn't about to apologize for either.

"You once flew at the head of my sleigh." Dad's disappointment hung heavy in the air. "How could you betray that trust?"

Something flickered across Silven's face, a small fracture in his composure that surprised me. Dad's disappointment seemed to cut deeper than any threat could have.

"We've reached a decision regarding your punishment." Dad squared his shoulders, every inch the Santa Claus the world believed in. "You will be exiled to Klarhaven, stripped of all authority and status at the North Pole. You will have no contact with young reindeer and no position of influence."

Silven's face drained of color, and for a fleeting moment, I almost felt sorry for him. Almost. The same way you might feel a twinge of sympathy when someone who's been horrible gets exactly what they deserve.

But then his mask was back in place, and he looked at Rudy, sneering with bitterness before his attention turned to me.

"Your power will consume you like it did before. You aren't built to contain it, just as he..." He jerked his chin toward Rudy. "Isn't built to lead."

Rudy stepped forward, his body vibrating with tension. "If you ever come near her again, if you ever try to manipulate any member of my herd, we will make Klarhaven feel like paradise compared to what follows."

The guards moved forward, preparing to escort Silven away.

"Klarhaven's about to get its very own Grinch." I folded my arms across my chest, watching Silven's face twist with rage at my flippancy. "Hopefully, someone will knit you a heart."

The escort led Silven away, his back rigid with defiance. My mom, who had been silent throughout the whole confrontation, stepped forward.

A wave of shimmering silver magic burst from her hand, striking Silven squarely between the shoulder blades. He stumbled, gasping as his form rippled and shifted. Before our eyes, enormous antlers sprouted from his head, magnificent and gleaming in the winter light.

My jaw dropped.

Silven turned, his eyes wide with shock and something like hope.

Mom's face had transformed. The gentle, smiling woman was replaced by something ancient and fierce—a mother protecting her young.

"There is no greater punishment than getting back what you've yearned for, only to find it useless." Her voice had a steely edge that sent shivers down my spine. "Your antlers have returned, but they will never lift you from the ground the way you desire. You will never fly with another herd or lead a sleigh again. Especially not a sleigh flown by a Claus."

Silven's eyes reflected pure anguish.

"Enjoy your time in Klarhaven." Mom stepped back next to

my dad, her silver hair lifting slightly in a wind that seemed to touch only her. "Perhaps one day you'll realize how wrong you've been about leadership and strength, and about what truly matters."

The elves resumed their escort, leading a stunned Silven away. His new antlers caught the light as he disappeared into the trees, leaving nothing but hoofprints in the snow.

Dad stared at Mom with a mixture of awe and admiration. "Glim..."

"No one hurts my family." Mom smoothed down her cloak, the fierce goddess fading back into my cheerful mother before my eyes. "Now, shall we go back inside? I believe we have an antler competition to prepare for."

Rudy's hand found mine, squeezing gently as we followed my parents back toward the castle.

"Are you okay?" I whispered, feeling the tremors of emotion running through him.

His eyes met mine, stormy but clear. "For the first time in a long time... I think I might be."

❄

I sat in the center chair at the judges' table, still not believing they'd been serious about having an antler competition. The grand hall had been transformed into what I could only describe as a pageant arena, complete with a runway, spot-lights, and a panel of judges that now included me.

"And next, we have Bruce!"

A heavily muscled reindeer with a dappled coat pranced down the runway. The crowd went wild as he shook his massive rack adorned with what appeared to be an entire winter village, complete with a miniature train that chugged around the circumference of his left antler.

I leaned toward Tinsel, the elf judge to my right. "Is that an actual working model train?"

Tinsel didn't take her eyes off the spectacle. Her pencil scratched furiously across her scorecard. "Bruce is known for his mechanical innovations. Last year, he had a gondola system that carried tiny hand-carved elves between antler points."

"Of course he did." I sipped from my hot chocolate, which someone had helpfully spiked with peppermint schnapps. Three drinks in, and the absurdity had become genuinely entertaining rather than mortifying.

My dad sat in the front row next to my mom, looking more animated than I'd seen him since arriving at the North Pole. Color had returned to his cheeks, and his hearty laugh boomed across the hall as Bruce showed how the tiny inhabitants of his antler village popped out of their houses when he tilted his head a certain way.

My herd occupied the row behind Dad, having been eliminated in the first and second rounds.

"Now for our next contestant, Don!"

My mouth fell open as Don strutted onto the runway in reindeer form. His massive body gleamed under the spotlight, his coat brushed to a shine. But it was his antlers that left me speechless. He'd transformed them into a living winter wonderland that put Bruce's mechanical marvel to shame.

Each point was wrapped in thin silver wire holding tiny crystal snowflakes that caught the light, creating a constellation of stars above his head. Frozen icicles that somehow didn't melt hung strategically, and snow fell from certain points. How the hell had he managed that?

"A five on overall aesthetic impact," Tinsel whispered appreciatively beside me.

The Arctic fox shifter judge, Frost, rubbed his chin. "The snow and ice elements are a creative and ambitious touch."

"The anatomical symmetry is impeccable," added Juniper, the reindeer judge, in a tone suggesting she'd like to verify other aspects of Don's anatomy.

I shot her a look that I hoped conveyed, "Back off, he's mine." She just grinned at me.

The crowd gasped as Don lowered his head, triggering a miniature aurora borealis that rippled between his antlers in spirals of green, blue, and purple light.

I burst out laughing. Not mockingly, but with pure, unfettered joy. Don, normally so quiet and stoic, was absolutely eating up the attention. His tail wiggled with pleasure at each cheer, and when he caught my eye, he winked before executing a perfect spin that made his antler display shimmer even more dramatically.

The crowd went absolutely wild.

Across the hall, I spotted Rudy and the others stamping their feet and whistling. Even Dash, who'd been upset to be eliminated in round two for excessive wax use, cheered enthusiastically.

"Don clearly had professional help," sniffed Elmer, the fifth judge, a grumpy old elf with ice-blue glasses perched on his nose.

"Is that against the rules?" I picked up my scorecard, determined to give Don perfect marks.

"Not technically. But there's an agreement—"

"Look at Cooper," Tinsel interrupted, pointing to the final contestant waiting in the wings.

My jaw dropped for the second time that night as a massive reindeer I didn't recognize stepped onto the runway. He made even Don look small, and his antlers... good lord.

The crowd went deathly silent before erupting in thunderous applause. Cooper hadn't just decorated his antlers; he'd turned them into a full theatrical production. Lights flickered and gears turned, creating a living Santa's workshop that bustled across his rack. Tiny figurines hammered at toys, conveyor belts whirred, and reindeer took flight as each tilt of his head shifted the scene. When he reached center stage, he lowered his massive rack, and music began playing from his antlers.

Dad leapt to his feet, clapping with childlike wonder. The joy radiating from him was almost visible, a shimmering aura that seemed to strengthen with each passing moment.

"Well, I think we have our winner," Juniper murmured, scribbling perfect scores on her card.

I looked down at my scorecard, hesitating. Don's display

had been beautiful and technically impressive, but Cooper's was... transcendent.

When the final scores were tallied, Cooper won by two points. Don took second place and transformed back to human form to accept his silver antler trophy, wearing nothing but a strategically placed Santa hat.

The after-party quickly kicked into gear and sprawled across the hall, clusters of reindeer and elves celebrating with spiced cider and gingerbread cookies. I stayed in my judge's chair, enjoying the view of Don parading around with his silver antler trophy, thankfully now wearing pants.

A familiar presence settled into the chair beside me. "You did well as a judge, Snowflake." Dad's massive hand covered mine on the table. The tremor I'd noticed earlier was gone. "Though you weren't exactly subtle about your favorites."

I snorted into my drink. "I don't know what you're talking about. I was completely unbiased toward the men I'm bonded to for eternity."

Mom moved behind us, placing her hands on Dad's shoulders. Her touch seemed to immediately relax him, his posture softening under her fingers. "The antler competition always brings out the competitive spirit."

A comfortable silence fell between us, the abominable snowman in the room finally impossible to ignore. I swirled the last bit of my hot chocolate in my mug. "So... are we going to talk about Silven?"

Mom sank gracefully into the chair on my other side. "Are you all right?"

I paused, considering the question. "Yeah, I think I am. It was... satisfying seeing him face consequences."

Dad's eyes clouded with regret. "I should have seen what was happening years ago. With you. With Rudy. I didn't know the loss of his antlers affected him that deeply... he seemed overjoyed when I made him my advisor." His shoulders slumped. "I thought I was doing what was best, sending you away from the Pole. I believed the distance would keep your magic muted enough until you were ready."

Across the room, Rudy lifted Kip onto his shoulders, both of them laughing as they chased Pierce. My heart squeezed at the sight.

"I understand why you did it." The words felt true as they left my mouth. "I just wish I hadn't lost so much time. Twelve years of not knowing who I was or who you both were."

Dad nodded. "We both tried to help you, and when Silven suggested some time away, we didn't think you'd forget so quickly. There are so many who live in Klarhaven and a few in Reinberg, even."

Mom's hand covered mine. "The North Pole has its own way of working, Neve. It protects itself—and you—in ways we don't always understand. And look what it brought you." Her eyes drifted to the nine men across the room.

I followed her gaze. Dane and Vix were arguing playfully over a cookie, while Blitz attempted to balance a sprig of mistletoe on Cole's head. Dash was teaching Pierce some ridiculous dance moves that involved a lot of hip movement that was definitely *not* appropriate for a North Pole celebration. Kip and Rudy were now giving shoulder rides to young kids, and Don had put the silver antler trophy on his head like a bizarre crown.

"Everything that happened brought you here, to this moment," Mom squeezed my hand. "To them."

I watched as my men sensed my attention, nine pairs of eyes finding me across the crowded room. Nine smiles, each unique, each precious to me in ways I was still discovering.

Would I have found them if I'd stayed? If my life had followed a different path? Or was this exactly how it was always meant to unfold? The loss necessary for the finding, the forgetting essential for the remembering?

As I looked at my ridiculous, wonderful, loving herd, I couldn't imagine a timeline where they weren't mine. And that made every forgotten moment worth it.

CHAPTER 35
NAUGHTY LIST

I was still giggling about the antler competition as I walked into the cabin. The image of Don strutting down the runway with a miniature aurora borealis suspended between his antlers was going to be burned into my memory forever.

"I can't believe how seriously everyone takes that competition." I flopped onto the couch, ready for a relaxing rest of the night watching Christmas movies with my men. "Though I have to admit I'm a little disappointed I didn't get to show off my own rack."

The room went silent. Nine pairs of eyes snapped to me with an intensity that made my skin tingle. Apparently, my little joke landed with all the grace of an elf falling off the shelf.

Vix recovered first, his eyes darkening to a shade that meant trouble—the good kind. "Nobody's seeing your rack except us."

"Ever." Pierce's jaw was tight enough to crack chestnuts as he shrugged off his coat. His movements suggested he was fighting for control.

I rolled my eyes, though I couldn't quite suppress the flush warming my cheeks. "It was a joke, you possessive reindeer. It's classic North Pole humor."

There was not an ounce of amusement to be found on any

of their faces. My attempt at defusing the tension was having the opposite effect.

Kip plopped down beside me, his thigh pressing against mine. "I'd be more than willing to judge your rack in a private competition if you're feeling left out." His fingers trailed up my arm.

"Oh? What would be the criteria for first place?" I straightened in my seat, tilting my head with mock seriousness while trying to ignore the heat spreading through me at Kip's suggestion.

"Quality construction." Dash leaned against the doorframe with a smirk that could melt the North Pole's ice caps.

I laughed, playing along. "Fine. I'll show you mine if you show me yours."

The temperature in the room seemed to rise ten degrees as they exchanged glances.

Blitz's eyes gleamed as he rubbed his hands together like he'd been handed the keys to Santa's sleigh. "Sounds fair to me."

Don, still riding his second-place high, was already unbuttoning his shirt. His fingers worked each button with a deliberate slowness that made my mouth go dry.

"Wait, I wasn't actually..." My protest died on my lips as the men began to move.

They were already rearranging furniture with the efficiency of elves on December 23rd, shoving the coffee table against the wall and clearing a path through the center of the room.

Pierce dimmed the lights while Vix pointed a light toward the center of the room. The casual movie night I'd anticipated was transforming before my eyes into something altogether more... interesting.

Dane connected his phone to the speaker system, and seconds later, music started to play. Thankfully, it wasn't anything holiday-themed, which would have been a little weird considering what we were about to do.

"Should I get some dollar bills or..." I tucked a strand of hair behind my ear, trying to maintain some semblance of composure.

Rudy's eyes sparkled with a rare gleam of mischief as he rolled his shoulders in preparation. "Your undivided attention will do."

"We're taking this very seriously, so honest scoring is a must." Cole appeared with a clipboard, paper, and a pen, handing them to me. "To keep track of your unbiased scores."

I bit my lip to keep from laughing. "On a scale of one to ten? Or should I use Christmas-themed ratings? Like candy canes?"

Dane fiddled with his phone, and the music shifted to something with a deeper, more sensual beat. "Rate us however you want, sweetheart. But know that I'm aiming for nothing less than the naughty list."

With everyone on board for a little show, Blitz stepped forward first, tearing open his button-up shirt with such force that buttons pinged off the walls.

"That was my favorite shirt!" Cole's protest was drowned out by my spontaneous burst of applause.

Blitz flexed. "Worth it."

I wrote down his score. "Eight. Excessive property damage, excellent execution."

Don approached next, already shirtless. He executed a perfect body roll that ended with him on his knees in front of me, his hands sliding up my calves.

"Holy mistletoe," I whispered, my magic stirring in response. Frost patterns bloomed across the paper as I wrote his score. "Nine out of ten. Out of bounds, but much appreciated."

Pierce stepped forward next, unhooking his belt and removing it while maintaining eye contact. "Some of us prefer quality over theatrics."

The belt made a satisfying snap as he pulled it free completely, one eyebrow arched in challenge.

I swallowed hard. "Whoever said Christmas comes once a year clearly never met you guys. I give you a nine for lack of theatrics."

Kip nearly choked with laughter, while Vix was already unbuttoning his jeans, clearly impatient for his turn.

One by one, they paraded before me, each more ridiculous than the last. Cole performed a striptease, including throwing his clothes at me, which had me howling with laughter. Dash moonwalked. Kip did some kind of weird robot dance that somehow still managed to be sexy. Dane and Vix teamed up, spinning each other like they were auditioning for *Dancing with the Stars: North Pole Edition*.

By the time Rudy took his turn, I was breathless from laughing. But when he locked eyes with me, slowly removing his Henley with no frills to reveal the sculpted planes of his chest, my laughter faded into something much hungrier.

He stepped toward me, holding out his hand. "Your turn."

I looked down at my clipboard of scores that I'd stopped keeping. "I really need to catch up on my scoring."

Kip plucked the clipboard and pen from my hands. "Let's be honest here, you're a perfect ten."

I rolled my eyes but let Rudy pull me to my feet. They spread out around the room, sitting on couches and chairs or leaning against walls.

Why was I so nervous? They'd all seen me naked every which way.

I stood in the center of the room as their hungry eyes fixated on me with an intensity that made my magic spark beneath my skin.

"I don't exactly have stripping experience." I tugged at the hem of my sweater.

Don leaned forward in his seat. "Do whatever feels right."

I closed my eyes for a second, letting the rhythm sink deep under my skin. My hands drifted over my hips and up my sides before I cupped my breasts. I moved my hands back down to the hem of my sweater.

My breaths quickened as I swayed my hips, pulling my sweater over my head with a flourish. The cool air kissed my skin as I stood before them in my bra and leggings.

A chorus of appreciative groans filled the room. Pierce's eyes were locked on mine, dark and intense. Vix was practically vibrating with impatience.

I hooked my thumbs into the waistband of my leggings, sliding them slowly down my hips in a move that was half dance, half torture for everyone involved. My magic flared with my growing confidence, creating tiny glittering snowflakes that were suspended in the air around me.

"I think I should get extra points for the special effects." I kicked my leggings aside with a grin.

The answering growls told me I'd won first place.

I smiled, feeling powerful. The awkwardness that had initially gripped me melted away. These men wanted me. All of me. And I wanted them to see.

An idea sparked in my mind, and I let my magic flow. Ice crystallized in front of me, forming and reshaping until a translucent chair sat in the center of the room.

Dane whistled low. "Now that's what I call a prop."

I turned my back to them, looking over my shoulder as I reached for my bra clasp. It joined my sweater and leggings on the floor. Nine sharp inhales hit my ears at once.

I slowly turned around, and my nipples hardened from the way they all leaned forward slightly, as if drawn by an invisible force.

"This view beats any antler display I've ever seen." Dash's fingers twitched at his sides.

My heart beat wildly as I hooked my thumbs into the waistband of my underwear. For a split second, insecurity caught me off guard, but then the bond between us pulsed with reassurance and desire.

I slid the remaining fabric down, leaving me completely bare before them. I walked around the chair, trailing my finger across the back before I sat. I'd expected it to be cold, but my magic had created something that felt cool without being uncomfortable. I spread my legs wide, giving them an unobstructed view.

"Exquisite," Rudy breathed, like he had never seen me before.

Blitz adjusted his very evident erection. "Absolutely perfect."

Their praise washed over me, chasing away any lingering doubt. To know these men were turned on from just looking at me was a heady feeling. I moved my hands to my breasts, cupping their fullness, savoring how they fit perfectly in my palms. My fingers traced lazy circles around the curves before I slid my thumbs over my hardened nipples. A shiver raced down my spine as I teased myself, watching their expressions darken even more.

The way they tracked every movement of my hands made my skin tingle with awareness, and my magic responded to their collective desire by making the air shimmer around us. I pinched my nipples lightly, gasping at the sharp pleasure that shot straight between my thighs. My back arched involuntarily as I displayed myself even more on my ice throne.

Vix fisted his hands at his sides. "Fuck, that's hot."

"You look good enough to eat." Kip took a half-step forward before catching himself.

"Touch yourself," Cole said, his voice barely audible. "Let us see how you touch that glorious pussy."

Heat flooded my cheeks, but my hands moved of their own accord, trailing down my stomach, over my thighs, before finally dipping between my legs. I was already wet and aching. My fingers slid easily through my slick folds, finding the bundle of nerves that made my breath catch.

Pierce's gaze burned into me. "Yes, just like that."

"So fucking beautiful." Dane's voice was reverent.

I began to move my fingers in slow circles, my head falling back as pleasure built. The bond between us amplified everything, and I could almost feel their hands on me.

"Watch us while you touch yourself," Dash commanded.

I forced my heavy lids open, and the sight that greeted me nearly pushed me over the edge. All nine had unzipped their pants, freeing themselves, their hands working their cocks at the same pace as me.

"This is what you do to us," Don's voice was strained, his movements controlled but desperate.

"Every. Single. Day." Blitz punctuated each word with a thrust into his fist.

"Faster," I groaned, unsure if I was instructing them or myself.

They obeyed regardless, their breathing growing more ragged with each stroke. The bond between us thrummed, carrying sensations back and forth until I couldn't tell where my pleasure ended and theirs began.

I wanted more. With my free hand, I channeled my magic, cold energy swirling around my fingers. A perfectly smooth and glistening icicle formed, precisely shaped for exactly what I had in mind.

Kip's eyes widened comically. "Holy candy canes."

I trailed the icicle across my collarbone, then down between my breasts, leaving a glistening path of moisture. The cold against my heated skin sent shivers through me, my nipples hardening further.

"This might be the most North Pole thing I've ever done," I laughed breathlessly as I brought the icicle lower, circling my entrance with its cool tip.

Pierce's jaw tightened, his hand stilling momentarily. "You're killing us."

I locked eyes with Rudy as I slowly pressed the icicle inside. The delicious contrast of cold penetration and my internal heat made me gasp. My magic kept it perfectly intact, the temperature just shy of uncomfortable.

"I guess I'm finally embracing the Christmas spirit." I worked the icicle deeper, my back arching off the chair.

Dane made a strangled noise somewhere between a laugh and a groan. "That's not what that phrase means."

I fucked myself with my creation, my legs trembling as I neared my peak. My magic responded to my heightened emotions, and the ice chair beneath me glowed with soft blue light.

"We're all yours, Neve." Rudy's voice cut through the haze of pleasure. "Every part of us."

"Forever." Dane's eyes never left where the icicle disappeared inside me.

"Show us," Vix demanded, his voice rough. "Show us what it looks like when you come apart."

The raw need in their voices, the intensity of their gazes, and the bond pulsing between us was too much. I fucked myself harder, my other hand returning to work my clit.

"That's it," Pierce said through gritted teeth, his own movements growing erratic. "Let go."

A cry tore from my throat as pleasure crashed over me. Their moans joined mine, and white-hot pleasure ricocheted back and forth across the bonds until I couldn't tell where mine ended and theirs began.

My pussy clamped down on the icicle-shaped cock, and I finally let the magic holding it together go. The melting sensation made me tremble harder, my legs squeezing together.

When my pleasure finally began to retreat, I collapsed back against the chair, my chest heaving. The men looked equally wrecked, disheveled and satisfied, their eyes still fixed on me.

Cole was the first to move, tucking himself away before approaching me. He knelt beside the chair, pressing a gentle kiss to my knee. "I think we have our winner."

I laughed, breaking the intensity of the moment, and the others joined in. They fixed their clothing and moved toward me.

Dane scooped me up from the chair, cradling me against him. "First prize is a hot bath and cuddles."

"Followed by dinner." Don picked up my discarded clothes.

"And dessert." Blitz waggled his eyebrows suggestively.

I nestled against Dane's warmth, feeling utterly content.

CHAPTER 36

CHRISTMAS EVE PREGAMING

I was dragged into quality control, a sprawling room in the workshop's east wing filled with more toys than a department store on Black Friday.

"No offense, but this is ridiculous." I planted my feet as we reached the doorway, which was pointless against four determined men. "I have actual magic to practice. You know, the kind that decides whether Christmas continues to exist?"

Kip tugged my arm playfully. "This *is* actual magic practice."

"Playing with toys?" I raised an eyebrow that I hoped conveyed the full depth of my skepticism.

"Christmas Eve pregaming." Dane swept his arm toward the workshop where several elves scurried about with clipboards, measuring tools, and stopwatches.

Don simply lifted me off my feet and carried me into the room like I was a stubborn package delivery.

"Put me down, you reindeer barbarian!" I smacked his chest, which felt like hitting warm marble.

Blitz walked next to us, unfazed by me being manhandled by his herdmate. "This is where the toys are evaluated. It's literally the most important job."

Don deposited me in front of my dad, who sat cross-legged on the floor surrounded by an army of action figures arranged in an epic battle scene. His hair was mussed, his cheeks flushed pink with excitement, and he looked more like an overgrown child than Santa Claus, Bringer of Christmas Joy.

"Snowflake!" Dad beamed up at me. "Excellent timing. The galactic defenders need reinforcements against the void creatures." He held up a purple alien figurine with three eyes and articulated tentacles.

I glanced at Don, who stood quietly beside me. "I can't believe you support this."

The corner of Don's mouth twitched. "Your dad knows what he's doing."

"By playing with toys a week before the biggest delivery night of the year?"

Dad flicked his wrist, and a void creature flew through the air. "I'm absorbing joy. It's like a preflight fuel-up."

I crossed my arms. "You're a grown man playing with action figures."

"Precisely!" He made explosion noises with his mouth as he crashed two figurines together.

An elf approached with a clipboard, nodding approvingly. "Excellent destruction sounds, sir. Very realistic."

"Thank you, Pepper. I've been working on my explosion repertoire." Dad demonstrated three variations of kaboom noises, each more ridiculous than the last.

Before I could form a response, Kip grabbed my hand and pulled me toward a table covered with board games. "You're with me first. We're assessing strategy and fun factors."

"I have actual work—"

"This *is* the work," Kip insisted, opening a box labeled *Enchanted Forest Explorer*. The game board unfolded to reveal a 3D pop-up forest that actually grew tiny leaves when exposed to air.

I blinked. "Okay, that's pretty cool."

Kip grinned triumphantly. "Round one of sixteen begins now."

"Sixteen rounds?!"

An hour later, I was deeply invested in what felt like our

fourteenth game, a version of Scrabble where points were lost if you took too long on your turn.

"That's not a word!" I pointed accusingly at Kip's tiles.

"Zorlflank is absolutely a word." Kip's face remained angelically innocent. "It's what you call the left antler point when it's frosty."

"Cheater." I threw a game piece at him, which he caught easily.

Across the room, Blitz had transformed what was supposed to be a simple dollhouse review into a full theatrical production. He'd donned a tiny apron and was speaking in a high-pitched voice while manipulating a plastic mom doll.

"Harold, I told you not to bring your moose friends inside after they've been rolling in the mud!" Blitz moved the dad doll back and forth with his other hand. "But Petunia, they promised to wipe their hooves!"

A small crowd of elves had gathered, doubled over with laughter. Even Don, who'd been solving complex puzzle toys in the corner, was watching with a smile.

I stifled a laugh, but Kip caught me. "Is that joy I detect, Ms. North?"

"Shut up and play your made-up words," I muttered, but I couldn't keep the smile from my face.

After Kip thoroughly trounced me at every board game in existence, Dane led me to the electronics section. "I need to assess durability." He proceeded to fly a remote-controlled dragon directly into a wall.

"Nothing says quality control like blunt force trauma."

Dane picked up the slightly dented dragon. "We have to replicate real-world conditions." He reset the controls and aimed the dragon at a different wall.

Watching these grown men take toy testing so seriously was both ridiculous and... weirdly charming. Even Don, who approached his station with the focus of a brain surgeon, occasionally made tiny sounds of satisfaction when a puzzle piece clicked into place.

I didn't notice when Don slipped away, but he returned

with a plate of cookies and hot chocolate, sliding it my way with a warm look that sent butterflies through my stomach. "Fuel for the final round."

Blitz practically skipped over to us, still wearing the apron. "Racing time!"

The next thing I knew, I was lying on the floor, racing remote-controlled cars against Blitz, Kip, and Dane, while Don called out the play-by-play in a perfect sports announcer voice. Our cars crashed repeatedly, often spectacularly, and each collision sent me into fits of laughter that made my sides ache.

When Kip's car did a perfect flip over Dane's and landed upside down, I laughed so hard I snorted, and the feeling exploded outward from my chest.

The room filled with tiny golden sparks that drifted like fireflies.

Everyone froze, staring at the magical manifestation.

"Well done, snowflake." Dad's voice made me turn. He stood watching me, his eyes crinkling at the corners, magic radiating from him like heat from a furnace. "This is it, you know."

"What is?" I watched the sparks dance around my fingertips.

"The true heart of our magic." He knelt beside me, his own magic reaching out to mingle with mine, threads weaving together. "Joy."

THE MAIN SQUARE of the North Pole had undergone a transformation that would have made my former Christmas-hating self break out in hives.

Everywhere I looked, enchantment spilled across the space. There were booths dripping with twinkling lights that changed colors with the mood of whoever passed by, ice sculptures that moved and danced when nobody was looking directly at them, and the unmistakable scent of cinnamon, chocolate, and pine that seemed baked into the very air itself.

"You're doing that thing again." Pierce appeared at my side, his eyes fixed on my face.

I blinked up at him. "What thing?"

"That thing where you're analyzing something magical instead of experiencing it." His hand found mine, warm despite the cold. "Stop thinking so much."

Easy for him to say. My entire life had been turned upside down in the last two months. Last year at this time, I'd been drinking wine alone in my house, ignoring holiday specials and watching true-crime episodes. Now I was standing at the North Pole, silver-haired and magic-powered, preparing to help Santa deliver joy to the world tomorrow night.

Plus, you know, the whole mated-to-nine-reindeer-shifters thing.

"I'm thinking the perfect amount, thank you very much." I stuck my tongue out at him, immediately undermining any attempt at maturity.

Vix rocketed into view, his fiery energy practically visible as he skidded to a stop in front of us, sending a spray of snow over Pierce's polished boots.

"Snowball war! East field! Cole's building an ice fortress, and Dash is being all tactical about attack formations." Vix grabbed my hand. "We need you on our team because, you know..." He wiggled his fingers dramatically. "Ice powers."

Pierce brushed snow from his boots with exaggerated annoyance. "We're supposed to be savoring the cultural experience of the Winter Carnival, not engaging in childish—"

A perfectly formed snowball smacked Pierce directly in the face.

Rudy lowered his throwing arm with a satisfied smirk from twenty feet away. "Sorry. My aim's usually better than that."

"Better?" Pierce sputtered, wiping snow from his eye.

Rudy's deep voice carried easily over the carnival noise. "I was aiming for your ego. It's a much bigger target."

I burst out laughing as Pierce's face shifted from outrage to calculation.

"You have thirty seconds to prepare your defenses," Pierce

informed me, his eyes never leaving Rudy. "Then I will show our alpha what happens when he challenges someone like me."

"But I wanted to try the caramel apple bites." I looked longingly at the booth I'd been heading toward.

Pierce was already striding purposefully toward Rudy, who stood his ground with the confident stance of someone who'd just provoked a controlled avalanche.

Vix tugged my arm. "Come on! This war is starting *now*."

An hour later, I was breathless, soaked, and laughing so hard my sides hurt. The war had devolved into complete chaos, with alliances forming and breaking every few minutes. Even the village children had joined in, thrilled to battle alongside Santa's daughter and her reindeer.

Cole had built me a throne of snow from where I could unleash destruction, but Dash had eventually infiltrated our defenses by burrowing through it.

Dash held out a steaming mug to me as I brushed snow from my hair for the twentieth time.

I accepted the peace offering and took a sip, groaning at how rich it was. "Where did you get this?"

"Enchanted cocoa fountain by the music stage." Dash watched me savor the drink. "Your cheeks are pink."

"That happens when you're pelted with snowballs for an hour straight."

His gloved thumb gently brushed my cheekbone. "Joy's a good look on you, Neve."

Something fluttered in my chest that had nothing to do with the drink.

I sipped the last of the hot chocolate as Dash's fingers lingered against my cheek. His touch seemed to spread through my entire body, making me momentarily forget how soaked and freezing I actually was.

"Neve! I got you something!" Vix came toward us, carrying a plate of caramel apple pieces smothered in nuts, chocolate drizzle, and way too much edible glitter.

My eyes widened. "How did you know I wanted that?"

Vix's grin was triumphant. "You mentioned it right before

Pierce got his face rearranged by Rudy's snowball." He thrust the treat into my hands. "I got the works. The elf at the stand said it's the best one."

"You believe everything elves tell you." Pierce approached, still brushing snow from his coat. His hair remained perfectly styled despite the battle, which seemed unfair.

I took a giant bite of the apple and nearly moaned. The tartness cut through the buttery caramel in a way that made my taste buds sing.

Cole materialized at my other side, gesturing toward the village center, where a crowd was gathering. "The aurora lantern ceremony is starting. We should head over."

My stomach fluttered with nerves. Dad had mentioned this tradition, but I'd been too busy panicking about sleigh flying and present delivery lessons to really absorb the details.

"Do I need to do anything special?" I wiped caramel from my chin.

Rudy's expression softened as he watched me. "Write your wish and release your lantern when the time comes. Nothing complicated."

"Unless you count baring your soul to the cosmos as complicated," Vix chimed in, earning an elbow from Dash.

We made our way to the center of the square, where Dane, Don, Kip, and Blitz were already waiting. The entire village had gathered around a circular platform where elves distributed paper lanterns.

An elf handed me one with a small wooden stylus, the tip glowing faintly blue.

"What are you going to wish for?" Vix tried to peer over my shoulder.

Pierce pulled him back by his collar. "It's private. That's the whole point."

I stared at the blank paper, the stylus hovering uncertainly. What did I want?

I closed my eyes and let myself feel the bond connecting me to these nine impossible men. It hummed beneath my skin, warm and electric. When I opened my eyes, I knew exactly what to write.

May we always find joy together, no matter how the sleigh flies.

My dad stepped onto the platform, his presence immediately commanding attention without him saying a word. He raised his hands, and the crowd fell silent.

"Tonight, we release our hopes to the sky, where the aurora will carry them to the stars."

On his signal, the first lanterns began to rise. I held mine, waiting my turn, watching the paper glow brighter as if sensing the moment approaching.

When I finally released mine alongside my herd's, my magic surged. It swirled around the ten lanterns and sent them spiraling upward in a perfect formation that mimicked our sleigh. They glowed with silver and gold light, far brighter than the others, cutting through the night sky.

Gasps rippled through the crowd as the ten lanterns reached the aurora, merging with the cosmic light. The entire sky lit up in a display more brilliant than any I'd ever seen, with bands of color dancing and weaving together.

Warmth flooded through me, not just physical heat but something deeper, more essential.

Pure, undiluted joy.

Only when the crowd's murmurs grew louder did I notice the shimmer of magic around me. Silver-blue and gold sparks danced over my skin, visible to everyone.

Laughter bubbled up from somewhere deep inside me, spilling out into the night air. For the first time since discovering who I truly was, I was ready. Ready for Christmas Eve, ready for whatever came after, ready for this joy-filled life with my nine men.

CHAPTER 37
THE FAMILY BUSINESS

I steadied the reins, trying to look like I knew what the hell I was doing while simultaneously battling the urge to vomit from nerves. The sleigh lifted beneath me, magic thrumming through the polished wood and up my arms like electricity finding its path of least resistance.

At least I looked the part. My mom and the elves had made me a sleigh-riding ensemble straight out of a magical Vogue spread. The red velvet coat was silver-trimmed and shimmered with embedded snowflakes. White fur lined the hood and cuffs in typical Santa fashion. My red leggings were warm enough to survive the stratosphere, and my boots were charmed to never slip on ice. A belt of jingle bells cinched the coat at my waist, which seemed unnecessarily festive until I realized they rang in perfect harmony with my reindeer's harnesses. They were charmed to be silenced when entering houses.

"You've got this, Neve."

Rudy's voice in my head was steady, a warm presence against the chaos of my thoughts. The bond between us pulsed with each beat of his heart, his massive form at the front of my team, antlers gleaming with enchanted light.

I took a deep breath and straightened my spine. "Sure, no problem. Just casually flying through a portal with nine magical reindeer. Totally normal Christmas Eve activity."

The sleigh tilted upward at a steeper angle, and my stomach lurched in protest. Around me, nine energies vibrated through our bond, sending comfort and joy.

Dad's sleigh glided effortlessly beside mine, his team of reindeer cutting through the air. The silver bells on their harnesses chimed in perfect harmony with my herd's.

"Ready?" Dad's voice came through my earpiece.

I gave a jerky nod that probably screamed "absolutely not ready" in fifty different languages.

The veil shimmered ahead of us, an impossible curtain of magic that separated the North Pole from the rest of reality. Dad's sleigh slipped through first, the barrier rippling like water as he disappeared.

I mentally steeled myself and tightened my grip on the reins.

We burst through the veil, the starry night sky stretching infinitely around us. Below, the lights of a sleeping town twinkled. My first delivery would be with my dad, and then we would split up, each with our own routes.

Dad's sleigh dipped lower, and I followed, mirroring his movements. The houses grew larger, and I focused my magic along with my dad's to freeze time in the area.

Dad signaled, and both sleighs dipped lower toward a modest two-story home with a trio of inflatable snowmen in the yard. The sleighs hovered about five feet above the shingles, waiting for us.

Just as we'd practiced, I focused on teleporting into the living room. I didn't have to know what the inside looked like, just a general idea of it. My stomach swooped, and suddenly I was standing next to a couch.

There was a big dog sleeping curled up next to the fireplace, and had time not been frozen, my leg would have been within striking distance.

I blinked, trying to reorient myself.

Dad winked and gestured toward the tree. With a flourish of his hands, wrapped packages materialized, stacked perfectly beneath the lowest branches.

Right. My turn.

I concentrated on the row of stockings hanging from the fireplace mantel. I flicked my wrist, focusing my intent through the gesture, and watched with satisfaction as each stocking filled with small treasures.

The dog's frozen form caught my attention again. Its fur looked so soft.

I reached toward it, but Dad cleared his throat and shook his head, pointing to a small table where cookies and milk had been left out.

Dad picked up a sugar cookie, taking a ceremonial bite before setting it back down with a bite missing. I followed suit, grimacing as I sipped the room-temperature milk.

With another subtle gesture, Dad vanished most of the milk from the glass.

"Smart man," I mouthed.

A tingling sensation washed over me as Dad's magic enveloped us both. One moment we were standing beside the Christmas tree, and the next we were back in our sleighs.

My dad grinned at me. "You've got this, Snowflake. Remember to focus on the living room, not just inside the house. And call if you need anything at all."

"Right. Living room. Specific. Got it." I watched as he took the reins and took off, headed for the next street over.

My sleigh remained in perfect, magical suspension above the rooftop, nine magical reindeer breathing soft clouds of vapor into the frozen night.

The weight of centuries of tradition settled onto my shoulders. Just me. Alone. Delivering Christmas magic.

"That was perfect, Neve." Rudy's voice filled my mind. *"We'll be right here waiting."*

The nine bonds pulsed through me, and my racing heart settled a fraction.

"Okay," I whispered to myself. "Living room. Next house. I can do this."

I closed my eyes, focusing on the image of a cozy living room in the house next door. A bubble of magic enveloped me, and when I opened my eyes, I was staring at the back of a man in boxer shorts, frozen with a pair of nose hair trimmers. His face was contorted into what had to be the least dignified expression in human history.

"Oh, fuck me with a candy cane." I slapped a hand over my mouth.

I had clearly focused on "inside" and not "living room."

I squeezed my eyes shut again, concentrating with painful specificity on the living room of this house. The Christmas tree.

The magic swirled, and I materialized in what was, thankfully, the correct living room. An elegant tree stood in the corner.

I flicked my wrist, focusing on the wrapped presents appearing under the tree. As they materialized, my elbow knocked a glass ornament, sending it swinging precariously.

I lunged forward, grabbing for it and nearly toppled the entire tree. A glass star tree topper went flying off.

"Shit, shit, shit!"

Time might have been frozen, but physics apparently still had a sense of humor.

I cast a desperate freezing spell, halting the star's descent three inches from the hardwood floor. I returned it to its perch and backed away from the tree as if it were an armed explosive.

I needed to find the cookies, take the ceremonial bite, and get out.

On the mantel sat a plate of the most suspicious-looking oatmeal raisin cookies I'd ever seen. They were the sad, health-conscious type that were probably made with applesauce instead of butter, with raisins that looked mummified rather than plump.

I picked up the least offensive one and reluctantly took a small bite.

"Oh, sweet baby reindeer." I gagged, barely able to swallow the dry, tasteless lump. I could have magicked away the milk, but my palate was desperate for liquid, so I took a large gulp.

Unfortunately, it was almond milk, and while I had enjoyed

that before, it now tasted like liquefied cardboard with a hint of tree bark.

With the ritual complete, I concentrated on the next house.

The veil shimmered ahead, welcoming us home. We'd made millions of deliveries, and somehow I'd managed not to traumatize any children or pets.

My sleigh glided alongside Dad's as we passed through the ethereal boundary between the mortal world and the North Pole. We descended toward the castle stables, the massive wooden doors swinging open as if greeting us.

As we landed, I slumped back against the sleigh's seat, limbs feeling like they'd been replaced with jelly. Every nerve ending in my body buzzed with a mixture of exhaustion and exhilaration. I'd actually done it. I'd helped deliver Christmas.

My dad met my eyes from across the stable. "How do you feel, Snowflake?"

I let out a sound somewhere between a laugh and a groan. "Like I've been run over by nine very muscular reindeer, then peeled off the ground and stuffed into a stocking."

The stable filled with the distinctive shimmer of magic as my team transformed back into their human forms, clothing materializing as their bodies shifted. Rudy reached me first, his large hands encircling my waist as he lifted me from the sleigh with effortless strength.

"You were magnificent." His deep voice rumbled through my bones as he set me on my feet, steadying me when my knees threatened to buckle.

The others surrounded me in a circle of warmth and pride, hands reaching to touch any part of me they could.

Pierce pressed his lips to my temple. "Our Christmas queen delivered her first holiday."

"You only knocked over what? Three trees?" Vix tucked a strand of hair behind my ear.

I groaned, burying my face in my hands. "Four."

Blitz draped an arm around my shoulders. "At least you got lots of cookies."

I peered through my fingers. "Some of those things should not be considered cookies."

Dad approached our huddle, and I could see the fatigue in the slight droop of his shoulders. But his eyes still held the magic that was uniquely his. "Eating terrible cookies is a Claus rite of passage. One time, in 1985, your mother went along for the ride, and she projectile-vomited after a heinous gingerbread crime against Christmas."

"Christopher!" Mom's voice rang out as she hurried into the stables. "Must you tell that story every year?"

"Only until it stops being funny, my dear." He smiled at her, and magic shimmered between them.

Mom reached us, her hands cool against my flushed cheeks as she examined me. "You look tired but whole. No magic depletion at all."

"Just existential cookie trauma." I sighed. "Someone even left out celery, hummus, and kombucha. Who does that?"

My mom's laughter was like bells, filling the stable with its melody. "You survived your first Christmas Eve delivery. How does it feel to be part of the family business?"

The question settled over me, heavy with meaning. "It feels..." I searched for the right words. "Like coming home."

Rudy's arm tightened around my waist, his pride flowing through our bond. Dad's eyes misted slightly, and Mom squeezed my hand.

I straightened my shoulders. "Next year, any household that leaves out oatmeal raisin cookies is going straight onto the naughty list. I'm making it an official North Pole policy."

Dad threw his head back in laughter, the sound echoing off the rafters. "I've been wanting to implement that rule for centuries!"

Something settled within me. The night had been chaotic, exhausting, and completely ridiculous at times, but standing here surrounded by my herd, my parents, and the magic that flowed through all of us...

I was finally home.

REINDEER WISHES

As the lanterns spiraled toward the aurora, Neve's men watched with varying expressions of awe, pride, and wonder. Each man felt the pull of the bond, that invisible thread connecting them all to the silver-haired woman who'd changed their lives.

Rudy stood tallest among them, his broad shoulders carrying an unspoken authority against the night sky. His eyes never left Neve as she laughed, joy manifesting as literal magic around her body. After years of feeling broken because he couldn't fly, he now understood his purpose had always been to stay grounded and to be the anchor for not just her, but for the herd.

On his lantern, he'd written: *Let me be worthy of leading them all, especially her.*

Beside him, Pierce watched with careful eyes, noting every detail of the moment. For someone who'd spent years maintaining control, the chaotic whirlwind that was Neve terrified and thrilled him. As sparks danced across her skin, he felt an unfamiliar loosening in his chest. The rigid structure of his existence softened around her light.

He'd written: *May I learn to let go sometimes.*

Dash stood steady, eyes sharp, like a man who could read the horizon even when no map existed. His gaze shifted between Neve and the sky, marveling at how her magic had blossomed. The weight of protection was one he carried naturally, but with Neve, the burden felt lighter somehow.

His wish had been straightforward: *Chart a course that leads us all home.*

Dane couldn't contain his grin as he watched Neve's face light up with delight. The bond hummed between them, and he felt it like a physical touch. From the moment he'd first transformed in front of her on that rooftop garden, he'd known she was special. Now, watching her embrace her magic so fully, he felt vindicated in his immediate attraction to her chaos.

His lantern carried words that mirrored his playful heart: *More adventures, more laughter, more her.*

Vix shifted from foot to foot, unable to keep still as Neve's magic sparked to life. The fiery one of the group, he had always felt too much and too intensely. In Neve, he'd found someone whose passion matched his own, someone who didn't try to dim his light but rather added her glow to his.

He'd scrawled: *Keep burning bright enough for all of us.*

Cole stood slightly apart, observing with his typical quiet intensity. He had always been the cool, collected one and the voice of reason among chaos. Neve had melted something inside him that he hadn't realized was frozen. As she laughed beneath the dancing lights, he felt that warmth spread through the bond they all shared.

On his lantern, he'd written: *May we always feel warmth from the cold.*

Kip leaned toward Neve, eyes shining, his whole body strung tight with giddy energy as he watched the spectacle. Of all the reindeer, he had embraced the joy of their bond most easily, finding in her a kindred spirit who might roll her eyes at his antics but always ended up laughing alongside him. Seeing her joy made his heart swell with pride. He'd known all along she had it in her.

His lantern had been covered with doodles surrounding his wish: *More snowball fights, cookies, and Neve always in the middle.*

Blitz yearned to reach out and touch Neve, but he waited

patiently, not wanting to pull her out of the moment. He had always rushed from one thing to the next. She had taught him to slow down and savor moments like this one. For once, he let the moment stretch, holding it close instead of sprinting past it.

For his lantern, he'd written: *Patience to keep me in step with her.*

Don's expression remained serene as always, but his eyes betrayed the depth of his emotion. Calm had always been something that made him feel out of place, but with Neve, it became a kind of completeness. With her, his stillness wasn't a flaw; it was a foundation.

Don's lantern carried only a single word, written with quiet certainty: *Home.*

For a moment, the entire village faded away, and only the ten of them existed, bound together by something ancient and new all at once.

Magic swirled around their lanterns, arranging them just how they'd be flying through the veil on Christmas Eve. The entire sky lit up as they reached the aurora.

When the final lantern disappeared into the cosmic light, Rudy was the first to move, stepping forward to stand beside Neve as her magic continued to shimmer around them all. The others followed, forming a protective circle around their mate as villagers whispered and pointed. Not out of fear, but out of reverence. Santa's daughter had returned, and her power was magnificent.

The bond between Neve and her men pulsed with shared emotion: pride, love, desire, and beneath it all, a profound sense of rightness. Each man felt it in his own way, but the sentiment was the same. They belonged to her, and she to them, in a way that transcended ordinary understanding.

As Neve turned to face them, her eyes reflected what they all felt in their hearts. Wonder. Gratitude. Home.

Love.

And most importantly of all—joy.

※

Thank you for reading Of Magic & Reindeer!

GET digital art of Neve in her sleigh with her reindeer when you sign up for my newsletter by scanning the QR code below or visiting:

https://www.mayanicole.com/reindeerart

You're free to unsubscribe at any time.

Already subscribed? You'll still be able to get the art the same way.

ALSO BY MAYA NICOLE

Check out my website for an up to date list of books.

www.mayanicole.com

Printed in Dunstable, United Kingdom